Deadly Magic

(A Grace Holliday Cozy Mystery)

Elisabeth Crabtree

D1518458

Copyright © 2012 by Elisabeth Crabtree

All rights reserved. No part of this book may be reproduced without the written permission of the author.

First Printing, November 2012
V7/14/14

ISBN-13: 978-1475067453
ISBN-10: 1475067453

Book cover illustration by Nik Jorvik Watson.

Author's Note

This is a work of fiction. Names, characters and situations are completely fictional and a work of the author's imagination. Any resemblance to any person, living or dead is purely coincidental.

Other books by Elisabeth Crabtree

Books in the Grace Holliday Cozy Mystery Series:
Deadly Magic
Deadly Reunion
Death Takes a Holiday
Murder Games

Books in the Hatter's Cove Mystery Series:
St. Valentine's Day Cookie Massacre

Books in the Pink Flamingo Hotel Mystery Series:
Death by Pink Flamingo

Elisabeth Crabtree

Halloween
Sunday, October 31st
9:20 pm

PROLOGUE

SOMEONE WANTED HER dead. She didn't know who or why, but she knew with sickening certainty that someone wanted to kill her.

She leaned over the railing and looked at the audience below. Although, she knew that they couldn't see her, it didn't stop her from nervously scanning their faces for any sort of reaction. She repeated the incessant mantra that had been running through her mind since landing in New York a few days before. Everything will be fine. Don't worry. There's nothing to worry about.

Repeating the words again, she shook her head. Franklin was right; she was being silly. Why in the world would anyone want to kill her? She closed her eyes and counted to ten. She felt the muscles in her body relax, as she took a deep breath and opened her eyes.

Wincing at the sudden, thunderous applause that echoed through the theater, she leaned further out over the railing and looked down at the stage. To the astonishment of the crowd, Ilya, finally free from his restraints and the electrified cage, had just materialized in the middle of the stage. He threw the chains to the side of the stage, briefly glancing up as they clattered across the old wooden floor.

The magician paused for a second, surprised to see her standing on the scaffolding. She grimaced. He was probably wondering what she was doing up here so early. She shrugged her slim shoulders somewhat apologetically, remembering how he hated surprises, which she always felt was rather ironic, considering his choice of careers. Giving a slight shake of his head, he turned back to the roaring crowd, and gave them a brilliant smile.

Her heart skipped a beat. She missed this. Missed the applause. The laughter. The excitement. The way the crowd sat at the edge of their seat, trying to watch their every move. She missed the fun of it all.

Of course, not everyone was having fun, she thought ruefully, looking back out toward the audience. Squinting her eyes, she could just make out her husband, sitting in the fifth row, playing with his phone.

He's probably ready to go home, she thought in amusement. He hates parties. She smiled. Well, he's going to enjoy this one. He'll be so surprised. Just looking at him made her feel calmer. It was so good to be home. Everything was going to be fine. Taking a deep steadying breath, she reached out and checked the supports once again.

Everything will be fine, she repeated to herself.

But would it? The doubt started again. Someone had tried to kill her a few months ago, before she left for France and before she ran away. Of that, she was certain. There were far too many accidents in too short of a time to be mere coincidences.

The instant she touched down in Paris four months ago, she had felt safer. Since that moment, there had been no more strange mishaps. No more odd illnesses. Just those maddening letters, but as irritating as those letters were, they were nothing compared to the accidents. She was safe in Europe. Whomever it was that wanted to hurt her, obviously couldn't get to her there.

Fear started snaking down her spine. Reflexively, she checked the supports again, as her stomach twisted itself into knots. She shouldn't have come back. What if they tried again?

She glanced back out at the audience. If only she knew who was trying to kill her. If only she had some idea, she could protect herself. While in Europe, she had made out a possible list of suspects. To her amusement, it wasn't a very impressive list, nor was it too terribly long.

She narrowed her eyes, as a sneer crossed her face. They were out there watching the show. Her eyes focused in on them one by one. Weak-willed, pathetic, spineless, brown-nosers, every last one of them. It would be absolutely humiliating to be murdered by one of them. She told Franklin, before she left, that he should clean house. The company could function just as well with just a third of the staff. It couldn't possibly do any worse. Fire the majority of them, she said. Even Louisa. Especially Louisa, she thought bitterly. Such a hateful brat. To her surprise, he seemed to agree—at first.

She felt her jaw clench. Franklin was far too loyal and far too generous. It was no wonder that his company was circling the drain. As she shook her head, she dropped the silks and gripped the railing. It had to be someone else. It couldn't possibly be one of those incompetent fools down there. She had no doubt that each one would gladly attend her funeral, but she doubted that they had the guts to try something, at least not without fouling it up or giving up after the first failure. No. It couldn't be one of them. It had to be someone determined; someone capable of killing without mercy or remorse. Someone dangerous. Someone…

She looked down at the stage. What if…? As the blood rushed to her head, she felt her heart beating faster. No. Not Ilya. They had been friends for years. Surely, he couldn't still be mad about the boy. She felt a momentary pang of guilt before squashing it down. It turned out all right in the end. Ilya couldn't still be angry. After all, he happily agreed to let her perform with him tonight, just like old times.

Closing her eyes, she took a deep breath. Everything would be fine. Tomorrow, she would talk to Franklin about hiring a bodyguard. He would complain about the cost, but he would do it, because he loved her. He would do anything for her.

The scaffolding creaked underneath her feet as she walked over to the steps. Everything would be fine. She smiled, imagining Franklin's surprise when she appeared on stage. He would be so pleased.

Halloween
9:00 pm

CHAPTER ONE

THE DRAGON'S LAIR shook. Grace Holliday instinctively looked up at the swaying chandeliers above her head before forcing her attention back to the stage. Despite knowing that she was perfectly safe, she still gripped the sides of her armrests.

In the split second it took her to look up and back down, the previously empty stage had transformed into a veritable zoo. Four tigers, two lions, and one man now stood before the audience.

"Ladies and Gentlemen! Welcome to the Dragon's Lair!"

Grace grinned and clapped like an idiot, before remembering the incredibly handsome man sitting next to her. She quickly wiped the smile from her face and lowered her hands. Despite the fact that she had been basically stalking the man for two months straight, this was still technically a first date and she decided a little more decorum might be in order. After all, there was no reason to scare him away on the first night.

Grace slid further down in her seat and attempted to adopt a more nonchalant air. "That was interesting," she whispered, risking a glance at her date. One elegant eyebrow was arched over a deep dark hazel eye. He looked decidedly entertained. Grace feared his amusement was more at her than at the entertainer on stage.

"Having fun?" Ethan whispered back.

Torn between jumping up and down in excitement and pretending she was only mildly interested, Grace felt herself nod like a deranged bobble head. "Yeah," she said with a self-conscious shrug. "It should be an interesting night. Have you ever been to a magic show before?" she asked, only to have the woman next to her shush her.

Ethan smiled at the woman on the other side of Grace before silently shaking his head and refocusing his attention back to the stage, which now included a llama, a turkey, and three scantily clad female assistants in cages.

Grace tried not to take it personally, as she turned back toward the stage. She eagerly leaned forward in her seat. She had been excited about this night for a while now. It was her boss, Franklin Straker's, fiftieth birthday and for the last five years, he had insisted on having a lavish costume bash in celebration of his birthday, which fell on Halloween. This year's celebration, like the last two, was being held at the Dragon's Lair, a grand, Gothic styled magic theatre in the heart of New York.

Senators, lawyers, stockbrokers, actors, and news reporters were all invited and dressed as various goblins and ghouls as their station in life demanded. Anyone who was anyone, or rather, anyone that could possibly help Straker in some way, was invited to his birthday party. That usually did not include his employees, of course.

In honor of his birthday, his employees usually received the dubious honor of working late without pay. Grace wasn't sure how that happened every year, but this year was different. Two weeks ago, each employee had received formal invitations to the annual party. Of course, it seemed far more like an order than an actual invitation, but Grace didn't care. She was here and that was all that mattered.

The more pessimistic members of the office were convinced Straker had some kind of ulterior motive behind the invitation. The office pool was taking bets on the various levels of hell, which Sata…Straker was intending to put them through tonight. The pool ranged from being forced to work as servers, to being literally sawed in half. Grace had to admit it wasn't until just a few seconds before the lights dimmed and the building shook that she finally started to relax and enjoy the evening's entertainment. She had twenty on parking cars, but here she sat, happily sitting next to the man of her dreams. At least her dreams of the last two months.

Grace glanced down at her cowgirl costume and grimaced. She wished she hadn't been so frugal this year and had splurged on the harem genie outfit she had seen on the internet. At the last second, she had worried about wearing such a revealing costume to what was essentially, a work party.

She glanced back at her handsome date, dressed like a thirties gangster, complete with fedora and toy pistol. If she had known her fantasy man of the last few months would be her escort, she would have risked the potential embarrassment and had gone with the sexier genie costume. Pigtail braids and a knee-length skirt with fringe hem and matching fringe vest just did not scream sexy. Sighing softly, she played with the fringe on the hem of her skirt.

Ethan turned to look at her. Smiling, he laid his arm across the back of her seat with his fingertips just grazing her shoulder.

Grace relaxed back into her seat. Everything was perfect.

She felt a tap on her shoulder. Curious, she looked up at Ethan who, with a strange expression, was looking up and over her head. She glanced behind her and cringed. Standing directly behind her seat was an angelic Franklin Straker dressed in a white flowing robe with matching halo perched above his head—the irony of the costume was not lost on any of his employees.

He towered over her seat, his cool blue eyes boring into hers. "Find Valerie," he growled, before turning around and stumbling over the people sitting behind her. Grace sighed heavily and tried not to wince at the sound of the "owws," "shhs" and "would you move your legs" wafting from behind her.

Whispering a small apology to Ethan, Grace stood up and tried to make it down the aisle without stepping on anyone's toes. She almost made it to the end upright and with her dignity intact. Almost. A well-timed foot hooking around her ankle brought her face down in the aisle.

A cold clammy hand wrapped around her upper arm and pulled her upright. She looked up and silently swore. Grace was so focused on trying not to step on anyone, while simultaneously whispering sorry to every person she passed, that she failed to notice Allen Madison, the office menace and bane of her existence, sitting at the end of the aisle, dressed as a creepy looking blue roach with a crown perched on his slicked back blue hair. Except for the crown sitting on his head, the costume was fitting, Grace thought.

"Be careful, Grace. You wouldn't want to embarrass yourself in front of the boss," he said smugly, gripping her arm tightly.

Grace looked around at the audience, hoping that everyone's attention was focused on the stage and not on her. Except for Ethan, who was still staring at her with a sort of bemused expression, she seemed to escape notice.

"Thanks, Allen," she said, driving her heel into his foot once she was standing. "You're too kind."

Only after hearing him grunt in pain, did she finally move into the aisle and make her way to the back of the theater. Grace glanced back to the stage.

The three tigers stood on a small pedestal in the center of the stage. With each flick of the magician's hand, the tigers, one by one, did a back flip, disappearing in midair. Sighing, she placed her Stetson on her head, opened the doors, and stepped into the lobby.

Weaving her way past a small crowd surrounding a magician who was performing card tricks, Grace walked down a grand staircase, pausing every so often, hoping to catch a glimpse of Straker's personal secretary and Grace's best friend. Walking past the bar and toward the entrance, she pulled out her cell phone and quickly dialed Valerie's number.

She resisted the urge to stamp her foot when Valerie's phone went straight to voice mail. "Valerie, where are you?" Grace hissed into the phone.

"Right behind you."

Whirling around, she found herself face to face with her missing friend, dressed as a very pretty Marilyn Monroe. A platinum blonde wig covered her long brown hair.

"You're late," Grace said in a singsong voice. "You know who is asking for you."

"Asking? Since when does the old goat ask for anything?" Valerie grabbed a champagne flute from a nearby waiter and downed it in one shot. "Besides, I'm not late. I've been here since four o'clock this afternoon, desperately trying to drum up attendance. Half of our office has called in sick and the other half made up some ridiculous excuse for not coming. Sara's was by far the most inventive. She claimed that she accidentally threw her purse away when she threw her garbage out. She didn't realize what had happened until the garbage man took it away, so unfortunately, she just can't make it tonight. Personally, I think she should get points for originality. It's bad, Grace. They all know that their attendance tonight was mandatory."

"Why? Straker usually couldn't care less. I'm still surprised we were invited." Grace felt that gnawing feeling of dread return. "Why did he want us here?"

Valerie shook her head. "He didn't. It was all—" she suddenly snapped her mouth shut.

"What?"

"I can't tell you," she said reluctantly. "It's supposed to be a surprise."

"Are we going to end up parking cars?"

"No. Relax. We're just here to feed her enormous ego."

Grace was about to ask her friend to explain, when she noticed a persistent buzzing coming from the cell phone in Valerie's hand. "Are you going to get that?" Grace asked, pointing to the cell phone.

Valerie looked at the caller ID and sighed. Handing Grace her empty glass, she asked for a refill before turning on her heel and walking to an empty corner of the lobby.

Shrugging, Grace turned around and headed to the bar. She walked past a crowd of people who were milling around the small bar and froze. Her company's Vice President, Louisa Straker Burns, was standing at the far end of the bar, swaying slightly as she unsteadily brought the glass in her hand to her lips. She pulled back suddenly when some of the liquid in her glass splashed on to her costume. Sighing, she looked down at her chest before making a few ineffectual swipes at the stain spreading across her bust. With a resigned shake of her head, she finally pushed herself away from the bar and walked toward the ladies' room.

Grace breathed a sigh of relief. With any luck, she could get Valerie's drink refilled before Louisa returned. She was so focused on squeezing through a group clustered around the bar that she didn't realize Louisa had changed her mind and returned to the bar, until she heard her name called.

"Gracie," Louisa called out, one thin arm snaking out to grab Grace's arm and bring her closer. "I am so glad you are here," she slurred, throwing an arm around Grace's shoulders.

Grace cringed. Talking to Louisa was like navigating a minefield. When intoxicated, she was usually very friendly, very talkative, and downright annoying. Constantly grabbing and clutching in order to keep whomever she was speaking to from leaving, while simultaneously prying out information like a seasoned detective. When sober, she was standoffish, cold, and even more annoying with the uncanny ability to remember everything you said and did when she was drunk, but absolutely nothing she said or did.

Grace looked down at Louisa's costume which consisted of an odd mixture of Egyptian and Roman fashion elements, haphazardly thrown together, topped off with a seventeenth century powdered wig. She tried to ignore the tuffs of Louisa's shoulder length mousy brown hair poking out from underneath the wig and the sneakers on her feet. "You look nice, Louisa. Are you Cleopatra?" Grace guessed.

Louisa ignored the question. "Have you seen Daddy? Tonight's his big night." She drew Grace closer to her. "We definitely don't want to miss the show tonight. It's going to be some show," she said, with a trace of bitterness. "Were you here earlier when Daddy made his big speech?" she asked, using air quotes around big speech.

Grace recognized the trap. Louisa loved nothing more than drawing others into badmouthing her father and then reporting it all back to him. "Yes, I thought he did a wonderful job." Hiding a smile at Louisa's obvious disappointment, Grace motioned the bartender over.

"I thought he went overboard, especially with…" Louisa suddenly stopped speaking, causing Grace to turn back toward her.

Louisa was focused on something behind Grace's head. Before Grace could follow her gaze, Louisa grabbed her arm again. "Look, I was here all night, okay? You and I were together. We've been here for the last hour. Right?" she asked, digging her fingernails into Grace's skin.

Grace turned to see a red headed man in a black cape, mask, and top hat at the far end of the room, quickly striding toward them. Despite the mask, she could practically see the anger emitting from him in waves. Grace couldn't remember a time when she had seen Daniel Burns so angry. Acknowledging Grace's presence with a nod and a tight smile, he turned to his wife, wedging himself between the two women.

Seeing her chance for escape, Grace slid around Daniel and walked back into the lobby, leaving husband and wife to sort through their marital differences themselves. The last thing she wanted was to get in between Straker's daughter and her husband. She turned back just in time to see Louisa pour what was left of her drink on her husband's shirt.

Well, she thought, Straker promised everyone a night of excitement. She turned back around and scanned the crowd. Valerie was sitting on a bench near the entrance.

"Don't worry. No one knows. Look, I have to go," she said when she saw Grace approach. Grace laughed as Valerie closed the phone and pantomimed throwing it across the room. She glanced at Grace's empty hands. "Where's my drink?"

Grace quickly described the scene with Louisa. "You're more than welcome to get it yourself."

"No, thanks." Valerie shook her head. "That's it, Grace. I can't take it anymore."

"You said that last month, and the month before. What does Straker want you to do now? The show has already started."

"Wrong Straker," she said as way of explanation. "She's driving me crazy."

"Lily?" Grace guessed. "She is over three thousand miles away. How could she possibly be driving you crazy?"

Valerie rolled her eyes and grimaced. "A couple of nights ago, she called me at three o'clock in the morning. She wanted me to find some artist's phone number and address. She's planning a party and he absolutely must come." Valerie adopted a fake southern accent, "Darling, I absolutely must have him here. Darling, I absolutely must have my favorite pair of riding boots, please ship them immediately. Darling, I absolutely must go to Oktoberfest, please arrange my transportation. Oh, I decided not to go to Oktoberfest. Tourists are such a pain this time of year. I really need to go to London. Would you be a dear and take care of the arrangements? Oh, darling, I changed my mind about London, I have something else I need you to do," she mimicked. "Ugh. I can't do it, Grace. I have had it," she said, her voice rising with every word.

Grace nodded sympathetically. "Just calm down. I'm sure it won't be forever. Weren't you just telling me there's trouble in paradise? I mean look, it's his birthday, and his wife is living it up in Paris. Sounds like trouble if you ask me."

It was a well-known secret, gossiped among the office denizens in front of the water cooler that the boss' marriage was on the rocks. Recently, Lily Straker spent more time abroad than at home. Not that anyone could blame her. Franklin Straker wasn't an easy man to work for, Grace couldn't imagine what it would be like to be married to him. At the thought, an uncontrolled shiver raced down her spine.

"I am not her secretary!" Valerie said, still seething. "I am not her travel agent!"

"I know. I know," Grace responded automatically, trying to think of a way to console her friend.

"I'm quitting." At Grace's surprised look, Valerie added, "I think I'm going to move back to Texas."

"But—"

"No, I know what you are going to say. It's going to get better, but you're wrong. It's not going to get better. I can take Franklin. I know it's going to come as a complete shock to you, but she is a thousand times worse than he is."

Grace flashed back to various office meetings she had attended in the last ten years where someone was fired, spontaneously quit, or just ended up sobbing openly at the conference table. "I don't think that's possible. Lily always seems so nice."

"It's the southern accent. Trust me; the woman is not nice. In fact, her own family won't even speak to her."

In that case, maybe they're more of a match than we thought, Grace thought, tapping her finger against her lips, trying to decide whether to change her bet in the office pool. Maybe fifty on the marriage lasting over five years would be the better move.

"They're perfect for each other. He's not going to leave her no matter what she does. He loves her," she said bitterly. "I've already called my family in Texas. My brother can get a position at his company for me."

"Moving? How can you move? What about that new guy you're dating?"

Valerie sighed. "He was a bigger creep than my ex. Look, I'm sorry to be unloading on you like this. Why don't you go back to the theater? Are you here with Simon?"

"No. Simon and I are over."

"Well, that didn't take too long. What was it this time?"

"We just didn't have anything in common." At Valerie's disbelieving look, Grace added, "It was completely mutual."

"Uh huh. Why do you seem so happy then?" Valerie asked suspiciously.

"I decided to take your advice and take the bull by the horns, so to speak. Remember Mister tall, dark, and handsome across the street?" Grace didn't have to give any more detail, since both of them had spent the last few months spying on him from Valerie's office window.

Valerie nodded her head.

"I met him last night and it turns out that he doesn't live very far from me. I saw him jogging in that little park near my apartment, so I decided to take your advice."

Valerie readjusted her platinum blonde wig. "What advice was that?"

"Stop spying and go speak to him."

"And you did?"

"We ended up running at the same time and somehow bumped into each other," she said innocently.

Valerie smirked. "What a coincidence."

"Yes, it was," Grace agreed with a smile. "His name is Ethan Martin. He's an attorney and he works at Baker, Corbett, and Strand, next door to our office."

Valerie shook her head. "Grace, why in the world would you take any advice on relationships from me? You've met my ex-husband."

"You will absolutely love him, Valerie, but not too much," she said with a wink. "Like I said before, I saw him first."

"There you are," Allen said, coming up to stand next to Grace. "Mr. Straker's been looking for you. He wants to know if you've found Valerie, yet." He smiled evilly. "Luckily, I can report back that you were here chatting away and that—I—found her." Turning to Valerie, he gestured back to the theater. "Mr. Straker wants you."

"Grace already told me that, Allen." Valerie ran her eyes over his costume. A look of confusion covered her face. "What are you supposed to be?"

"It should be obvious, Valerie," he said with a sneer.

Grace tilted her head. "Yeah, you're the King of the Roaches, right?"

Allen rolled his eyes. "I'm not surprised that you don't know."

"Don't be silly, Grace. He looks more like a..." Valerie screwed her face up as she tilted it to the side. "A seventies space muppet?"

Allen shook his head. "Unbelievable. The incompetence that I have to work with," he muttered to himself, staring at the ceiling. He looked down his nose at both of them. "I'm Marty the Martian King."

Grace and Valerie exchanged confused glances, which just seemed to infuriate him even more.

"Marty the Martian King! He's world renown. He's a movie star."

"Really? Who played him?" Valerie asked.

Allen opened and closed his mouth in disbelief. "No one played him. He could clearly be seen sitting on the shelf above Clara Hart's head in the 1912 silent masterpiece *All My Horses Were Dogs*."

"Oh," they said in unison, slowly nodding their heads.

"The very first toy produced by the Straker Toy Company in 1910," he clarified. "It's the toy that launched our company. You know the one which pays both of your salaries."

"Oh! That Marty the Martian King," Grace said, nodding her head vigorously.

Valerie smiled at her. "And here I thought he was Henry the VIII."

"Well, it's easy to confuse them," Grace said. "They were so much alike."

Allen closed his eyes. "You've both worked for this company for ten years, so how could you not know who Marty the Martian King was? At least, I came prepared to represent the company. What are you two supposed to be? A cowgirl and a movie star. Neither of which have anything to do with the company."

Valerie pointed a long manicured finger at his chest. "I'll have you know that I came as Marilyn Monroe because she used to play with...," she said, glancing at Grace for help.

"Our Luna Lulu doll."

"Yes. Thank you. Our Luna Lulu doll. It was one of her favorites."

Allen's eyebrows climbed up his forehead. "That's quite impressive, considering the Luna Lulu doll didn't come out until a year after Marilyn died." Disgusted, he shook his head, before turning to Grace. "What about you? What are you supposed to be?"

"Ranger Ricky."

"Ranger Ricky was a boy doll," he said slowly, "and a dog."

"This is my interpretation of Ranger Ricky if he was a girl and human."

"Where's your badge?"

"I'm on a special super-secret assignment."

"What about your gun?"

Grace placed a hand on the hilt of her plastic toy gun. "Right here."

"Ranger Ricky came with a colt 45. That is a water pistol." He leaned over and inspected the gun. "It's not even one of ours. We have twenty different plastic guns in the toy store downstairs. Why couldn't you have used one of them?"

Grace opened her mouth to respond when she was gently pushed from behind. She took a few steps forward and turned around. A woman dressed as a vampire muttered a hurried "excuse me" as she passed by on her way to the restrooms. More and more people were milling around the lobby. "Is it intermission, already?" Grace asked in disappointment.

"It just started." Allen turned on his heel. He took a step before turning back around and adding, "Oh, by the way, I had a nice little chat with your boyfriend in there. He's really nice. He was looking for you, too. I didn't know where you were, so I found a pretty magician's assistant to help him. She was very friendly and extremely attractive. I bet they would make a nice couple. They seemed to really hit it off."

Ignoring Allen's taunt, Grace turned back to Valerie. "I better go find Ethan. I wouldn't want him to get lost around here."

Valerie looked at Grace curiously. "Why is Allen limping?"

Grace shrugged innocently as she made her way down the hall.

* * * *

Grace swore to herself silently as she closed the theater's doors. Ethan wasn't sitting where she had left him, which meant Allen might have been telling the truth. She hated it when he did that. It always threw her completely off-guard. It was just easier to believe he was always lying than to have to figure out when he was telling the truth and when he was not.

Turning, she went back into the hallway and made her way back to the lobby, straining her neck in order to catch sight of her date. Out of the corner of her eye, she caught a glimpse of a figure in a black suit and grey fedora walking past the bar, with a purple-sequined blonde in a top hat and fishnet stockings at his side.

She took two steps toward the bar when a bony hand reached out and grabbed her wrist, halting her in her tracks.

"Gracie," Louisa said, breathing heavily, "I need your help."

Grace inwardly groaned as she turned toward her company's vice president.

"Hurry and follow me," she said, dragging Grace across the lobby to a door marked EMPLOYEES ONLY.

With her hand on the doorknob, Louisa carefully looked around before opening the door. She motioned for Grace to follow, but Grace stubbornly shook her head. She knew Louisa well enough to know that if they were caught sneaking backstage, Louisa would lay the blame squarely at her feet. When Grace pointed to the sign on the door, Louisa blew out a frustrated breath. "It's okay, Grace. Daniel's planning a big surprise for Daddy and Daddy wants to know what it is."

"Then just ask Daniel."

Louisa looked dangerously close to stomping her foot. "Daniel won't tell me and Daddy wants to know. Do you want me to go back to him and tell him that you refused to help me?"

Grace quickly calculated how long she could survive on her savings before landing another job. "After you," she said with a curt nod.

CHAPTER TWO

IT WAS EERIE backstage. At least, that's where Grace assumed she was, as she weaved her way past several large boxes of magical equipment. Louisa had abandoned her five minutes into their little excursion into the bowels of the Dragon's Lair. As soon as they had come to a door marked STAGE, Louisa had stopped and ordered Grace to stand by the door and wait for Daniel or the *surprise* to walk past, before she turned and stumbled down the hallway, muttering something about Daniel and whores.

Waiting for what seemed like an eternity, but was more than likely no longer than thirty seconds, Grace decided to head back to the lobby, before she was caught hanging around backstage. She lost her way when she ducked behind a row of costumes to avoid a group of stagehands moving equipment toward the back of the stage. That was ten minutes ago.

She paused and frowned unhappily at the scene in front of her. It was like a maze. Every time she turned a corner, thinking she was coming to the end, she would find another row of costumes or huge boxes blocking her way.

She cocked her head to the side. She could just make out voices coming from her left, behind several long racks of costumes.

Unable to get around the racks or to move the costumes to the side, Grace bowed her head in resignation. After spending ten minutes trying to navigate through a maze of horrors, Grace decided she had no pride left. All she wanted was to get out without somehow landing on stage. With a sigh, she dropped to her knees and crawled through the rack of clothes. Moving a red cape out of the way, she rolled out into what appeared to be another hallway. To her delight, an exit door was only a few feet away.

"Stop!"

Grace's heart sank. If she ended up being thrown out of Straker's birthday party for trespassing backstage, Allen would have a field day. Obviously, something no one wanted. Grimacing, she reluctantly turned around to see . . . no one. The hallway was completely empty.

Shrugging, she reached for the exit door handle.

"You shouldn't be here."

Grace looked around. Other than a ventriloquist dummy lying on the floor a few feet away between two doors, the hallway was empty. She looked down at the dummy. It's cold, dead eyes stared back at her. Grace raised an eyebrow. Surely not, she thought, in amusement.

She opened her mouth to say something when she heard what sounded like a slap and a woman softly sobbing.

Not the dummy, she thought, as she walked down the hallway searching for the source of the sobbing. She approached the door to the right of the dummy.

"Please, it's over between us ... I did what you wanted ...You're hurting me!"

Grace grabbed the doorknob.

Locked.

She reached up and pounded on the door. Whatever was happening, she hoped she could stop it from going any further. She was hitting the door so loudly that she didn't realize someone had come up behind her until she felt a tap on her shoulder.

Turning around, she found herself face to face with a pretty blonde in a purple-sequined waistcoat, fishnet stockings, and bow tie.

"Hello," the magician's assistant said with a smile. "I'm sorry, but you can't be back here."

Pointing to the door, Grace quickly explained what she had heard.

Concerned, the blonde reached into her pocket and pulled out a key. Opening the door, she stepped into the room and looked around. She looked back at Grace with a concerned expression. "There's no one here."

Grace walked into a lavish dressing room, and if Grace had to guess, just by the way it was decorated, it was Ilya Dragovich's own dressing room. On every wall hung performance pictures of the magician in question, intermixed with vintage posters of famous magicians, and several dangerous looking swords and daggers. "I'm positive there was someone here," Grace said. "Is there any other way out of this room?"

"Wait here," the assistant said with a sigh. She passed the small settee in the center of the room and walked over to a large, red dressing screen in the corner of the room. No sooner had she disappeared behind the screen than Grace heard the tell-tale sound of a door opening and shutting. A few seconds later the young woman returned.

"Well, no one's here now and you can't be here, so let me get you back to your seat," she said, motioning for Grace to proceed her out of the room.

Sighing, Grace walked out and headed to the exit.

"Oh, not that way," the young woman said while locking the door. "That will take you back out into the alley." She smiled. "Trust me, you don't want to go that way. I accidently got locked out one day. Scary and it was in complete daylight, too. Besides, it's storming outside. Just follow me and I'll take you back to the lobby."

Doing as she was told, Grace followed the magician's assistant back down the center aisle.

"What were you doing back here anyway?" the assistant asked.

Grace decided to be honest. "I have no idea."

The blonde looked at her in confusion, but didn't comment. "Papa would be furious if he found out anyone was back here, so we'll just sneak you back out. Try not to look at anything."

Easier said than done. "Who's your dad?"

"Oh, I'm sorry. I should have introduced myself. I'm Belle Dragovich. Ilya Dragovich's daughter," she said, holding out her hand.

Grace shook the other woman's hand. "I had no idea he had children."

Belle smiled ruefully. "We're one of his greatest secrets. He was always worried about kidnapping and such when we were kids." Belle opened a door and led her down a darken hallway to another door marked STAGE. "He's finally loosened up some."

Grace froze. "Wait, I don't want to go on stage."

"Don't worry. This is a side door." Belle quickly stepped aside, as the door suddenly swung inward and Lily Straker walked through, wearing a pink robe.

Surprised, Grace said, "Mrs. Straker, I didn't know you were back in town."

"Glenda!"

Close enough, Grace thought in amusement. "I thought you were still in Europe."

"I came back for Franklin's birthday. It's supposed to be a surprise," Lily Straker stammered. "You shouldn't be back here."

Belle reached for Grace's hand. "I was just taking her back to her seat."

"You better, before your father finds out that you have another guest back here."

"Another guest?" Belle asked. "What are you talking about?"

"Michael is here."

"Of course, he's here," Belle said in annoyance. "He works for you, doesn't he?"

"No. I mean he's backstage." Lily frowned. "You know how your father feels about him."

"I didn't invite him back here," Belle said sharply, as the door opened again and Ilya Dragovich walked into the hallway.

Grace immediately recognized him from his poster hanging in the hallway. She knew he was handsome, but he was even more striking up close with dark brown, almost black, penetrating eyes, strong features, and a full head of silky black hair. She took an involuntary step back as he looked down at her, his attractive face set in a scowl. "Belle," he said warningly.

"She got lost. I was just taking her back to her seat," Belle said, backing away from her father and dragging Grace with her.

The magician smiled at Grace. "I'm sorry, Miss . . .?"

"Holliday, *Grace* Holliday," she said, glancing at Lily who was nervously looking around.

"I'm sorry, Ms. Holliday, no one is allowed back here," he said, apologetically with a slight Russian accent.

"Oh, leave her alone, Ilya," Lily snapped. "She's not a spy. She works for my husband, and Belle was just going to take her back to her seat."

"Well, that is going to have to wait now," he said rather testily. "We're moving some equipment." Turning to Grace, he smiled charmingly. "If you don't mind, my daughter is going to escort you back to one of the dressing rooms to wait. When we have everything in place, you will be returned to your seat."

Grace sighed. "I really should get back to my date."

Lily waved her hand dismissively. "I'm sure it won't hurt him to wait. He probably won't even notice you're gone."

Belle looked at Grace with a small, apologetic smile. "It won't take long. I promise."

Nodding her assent, Grace followed the two women back to the dressing rooms.

"We'll just stay in my father's dressing room for a few minutes and then I'll take you to your seat," Belle said, as she unlocked the door.

"Are you sure you want to bring her in your father's dressing room," Lily warned.

Grace caught Belle rolling her eyes. "She's already seen his room."

Lily made a disbelieving sound.

"It's fine," Belle said impatiently, as she pushed open the door. "There's nothing in here she can't see."

Before Belle could enter, Lily reached out and gripped her arm. She stared down at the younger woman. "I'm sure there are better places to take her."

Belle raised her chin. "I've been working for my father for three years now. I think I know what I can and can't do."

Lily reluctantly dropped her hand. Shrugging, she pushed the door open and walked inside. "Oh! Ilya's redecorated. Very nice."

Lily picked up a vase sitting on the small coffee table in the center of the room. "Very pretty. I see your hand at work here, Belle. You should really think about going into interior design work. I think you have an eye for it." Lily sat the vase down and walked to the bookcase.

"I like what I'm doing," Belle said irritably.

Lily didn't respond. Instead, she walked to the bookcase. Running her hand over book spines, she muttered, "He'd never read these in a million years."

Belle threw Grace an apologetic look. "Sorry. We'll make it up to you, *Grace*," she said brightly. "Right?"

Nodding her head, Grace followed Belle into the room and sat down on the settee.

"It won't take them long to get everything in place. I guess we could have blindfolded you, but…" Belle suddenly stopped speaking and looked down.

Grace followed her gaze. A pendant in the shape of a golden dragon was lying on the floor.

"But we wouldn't want to mess up your hair and makeup." Belle reached down and picked the object off the floor. She held the pendant in her hand and sighed.

"What do you have there?" Lily asked.

Belle wordlessly walked around the settee and handed the pendant to the older woman.

Lily turned the object over in her hand. "Well, how did that get there?"

Belle shrugged, as she sat down on the chair next to Grace. "I don't know. Kind of strange, especially since you haven't been in here since I redecorated."

Lily didn't respond. She sat next to Grace, still holding the pendant in her hand. Looking at it curiously, she wordlessly shook her head.

"It's very pretty," Grace said, attempting to fill the awkward silence that was developing.

Lily smiled. "Thank you, Glenda."

Belle mouthed, "Sorry," at Grace before saying, "my father gave that to her when she retired."

"Yes, it's one of a kind." Lily proudly handed it to Grace to admire.

Grace gingerly picked up the solid gold pendant. A bright green stone sat in the place of the dragon's eye. Handing it back to Lily, she asked, "Is that an emerald?"

"Yes. My birthstone." Shrugging, Lily stood up and thrust the pendant into her robe pocket. She looked down at her robe. Patting the other pocket, she asked, "Have you seen my phone, Belle? I can't seem to find it."

Belle pulled at the sequined bow tie at her neck, revealing a long red scar. "I think Tabitha has it. She said something about finding a phone in the dressing room."

Lily blew out a breath and shook her head. "When she comes off the stage, do me a favor and grab it from her, please. I don't want her to lose it."

"She's not going to lose it, Lily."

"Please, Belle, just do as I ask without complaining, for once." Walking over to the dressing table, she shrugged off her robe, revealing a purple sequined waistcoat, bow tie, and leotard. She threw the robe over the dressing screen and sat down at the table.

"Oh! You're going to be in the show?" Grace asked excitedly.

"Don't tell anyone," Lily ordered. "Franklin still thinks I'm in Europe. I want him to be surprised." She peered into the mirror and frowned at her reflection. "Although, I'm surprised he doesn't already know. That secretary of his," she said with a touch of irritation. "I wouldn't be surprised if she hasn't already given it away." She opened up the end table drawer. Picking up a bottle of lotion, she began slathering it on her arms. "I know that lush of a daughter of his found out somehow." She looked at Grace as if noticing her for the first time. "Oh well, Franklin will be happy to see me. He's been begging me to come home for the last three months."

Opening her mouth to ask how she enjoyed her trip, Grace suddenly let out a squeal when she felt something wet and cold touch her ankle.

Belle looked at her in alarm. They both bent over and looked under the settee as a large white rabbit hopped out. He ran around the side of the settee.

"Abry!" Belle said, as she jumped up and raced after the bunny. Finally capturing the errant bunny, she cuddled him to her chest, as he squirmed. "There you are. I have been looking for you all day."

Grace walked over to the bunny. "Oh, he's so cute. Can I pet him?"

"Sure." Belle pushed the bunny into her arms. "His name is Abry, which is short for abracadabra. Please, don't let him go. He's such a pain to catch when he gets loose."

"Of course," Grace said, desperately trying to keep the squiggling rabbit in her arms.

"Since when does Ilya use a rabbit in his act?" Lily asked, touching up her make-up.

"He doesn't. He's not a performing rabbit, he's a pet. I'm just rabbit sitting for my brother." Belle reached down and nuzzled the bunny's face with her own.

"Has your father tracked him down, yet?"

Turning to Lily, Belle said, "Yes, but don't bring it up to Papa. He's not too happy right now."

"Why? What did he do this time?"

Belle looked embarrassed. "He's . . . in jail."

"Why am I not surprised?" Lily asked sarcastically.

Still holding the squirming rabbit, Grace sank down onto the settee. The sound of hammering just outside the door surprised her into loosening her grip on the bunny. Seizing on her momentary lapse in concentration, he immediately jumped to the floor and raced around the settee. Not wanting him to get lost, Grace clumsily chased after him.

"It's not his fault," Belle said defensively. "I'm not sure what happened, but apparently he tried to put on a show and the building accidentally caught on fire. No one got hurt," she said quickly. "It was an accident. He tried to contain it, but the owners dragged him away and let the place burn down. Papa said the investigator he hired, told him that the owners encouraged the fire act, and then set the place up to burn on purpose. They were trying to collect the fire insurance. It was really their fault that it burnt to the ground."

"So, why is he in jail?" Lily asked. She moved her feet out of the way as Abry hopped past her and disappeared behind the dressing screen.

"Well, by the time the investigator gave the police his findings, and they had decided to let him go, he escaped."

Lily groaned.

Grace carefully walked up to the wooden screen. She peered over the top. Abry was hiding under a clothes laden chair. She could just see his little white tail poking out from underneath a pair of jeans. Finally cornering the bunny, Grace quietly tiptoed around the screen, carefully reached over and picked him up, only to have him squirm out of her arms again and hop under the dressing room table. Abry glared at her balefully from behind Lily's feet.

"So, they charged him with escape," Belle said. "They caught him, but then he escaped again, which brought more charges. Anyway, they have him under lock and key, and Papa said he is leaving him there. You know his temper. Papa told him not to leave, but…"

Angrily, Lily slammed the hair brush in her hand down on the table. "They're just alike. Bull headed. He can't seriously leave his only son to rot in jail."

Lily's anger scared the bunny into hopping out of his hiding place. Grace bent forward as Abry raced straight toward her. Just as her fingers grazed soft fur, her Stetson fell to the floor, scaring the poor rabbit into changing directions, and hopping as fast as his large bunny feet could towards the settee.

"He's not rotting in jail," Belle said patiently. "I spoke to him last week. He sounded fine."

"Absolutely ridiculous." Lily picked up the hairbrush again and pointed it at Belle. "Don't worry, I'll have a talk with Ilya."

Picking up her hat and securely fastening it to her head, Grace got on her hands and knees and reached underneath the settee. Her hand brushed against a small piece of satin laying near the front. Curious, she dragged the cloth out and looked down. She quickly tossed it back on the floor when she realized she was holding small, pink, satin panties in her hand. "Bleeck," she muttered disgustedly. Giving up on catching the rabbit, she wiped her hands on her cowgirl skirt and stood up.

Still angry, Lily paced the length of the room. "I can't believe Ilya would do that. No. I'm going to have a talk with him as soon as the show is over. There's no reason—"

"No. Please don't," Belle begged. "Everything will work out. Just stay out of it, Lily."

Trying to ignore what appeared to be nothing more than family drama, Grace walked over to admire the pictures on the wall. There were thirty or forty pictures of past performances lined up in a nice grouping. The vast majority of them were black and white photos of Ilya Dragovich on stage performing. A couple of Belle. A few others of people she didn't recognize. In the center was a large color picture of Dragovich on the stage with four women in different colored costumes, suspended in midair over his head. "Lily, is that you?" Grace asked, pointing to the woman in the red sequin costume, directly over Ilya's head.

Momentarily stopping her frantic pacing, Lily walked over to Grace and looked at the picture she was pointing to. "Yes, that's me. That was taken about twelve years ago. Right before I retired."

Belle walked up behind them. She pointed toward the woman at the far end of the photo, wearing a purple costume, similar to the ones Lily and Belle were now wearing. "That's my mother."

Grace felt Lily stiffen. "Yes, there's Juliet."

"That was her last performance," Belle said sadly.

"No, Belle, this was taken a month before, while we were in Italy." Moving to another picture, Lily tapped the frame and smiled. "Now, this is a good one of me."

The picture featured Lily, suspended upside down, and holding onto a silken scarf. Lily smiled. "I was a bit of an acrobat in my younger days."

Hearing the door open, all three women turned around. Ilya was standing in the doorway. "Belle, I just saw Michael."

"Papa, I didn't invite him," Belle whined.

"He was hanging around the costume room, so I had security throw him out."

Belle groaned. "What do you want me to do about it? He's not here to see me."

Shaking her head, Lily grabbed her robe off the screen. "How are all of these people getting back here, anyway? Your security used to be better than this, Ilya."

Instead of answering, Ilya turned his attention to Grace. Smiling, he presented his hands for inspection. Turning them over, he showed her that they were empty. "Thank you so much for your cooperation. I hope you will join us again," he said seductively, while two tickets magically appeared in one hand, and a red rose appeared in the other.

Happily, Grace took the tickets and rose.

Taking her elbow, Ilya steered her to the door. "My daughter will walk you to your seat now."

Lily stepped in front of her and reached for the door.

"Where are you going?" Ilya grabbed her wrist and pulled it away from the door. "I need to speak to you."

Prying his fingers away from her wrist, Lily said icily. "I'm going to get into place."

"You have plenty of time. The second intermission just started. I need…"

"It's getting awfully crowded here, Ilya. I don't want to be seen. I told you, I want Franklin to be surprised."

"Stay in here. No one will see you back here."

"I want to check the supports."

"I thought you already did that."

Lily frowned. "I want to check them again."

"Tabitha can…"

"Tabitha is a silly, irresponsible, nitwit, who can barely tie her own shoes." She tilted her head to the side as she looked at him thoughtfully. "Why don't you want me to check the supports?"

"Why are you acting like this?" Realizing Grace and Belle were still standing behind them; he lowered his voice and moved to the side. "I'm not trying to stop you, Lily. I just want five minutes of your time."

"Later, after the show." Her voice softened as she reached up to pat his face. "I have a few things I want to say to you, too." Lily turned the doorknob and walked out into the hallway.

There were a few seconds of awkward silence before Belle stepped in front of Grace and motioned her to follow. Nodding, Grace walked through the door. As she did, she noticed one of the other dressing room doors open slightly. Daniel Burns stood on the other side, facing away from her. Next to him stood another magician's assistant. Catching Grace in the hallway, the girl's eyes widened before she quickly shut the door.

CHAPTER THREE

IGNORING THE DIRTY looks she was receiving from her co-workers, Grace carefully made her way down the aisle toward her seat. She was relieved to see that Ethan hadn't abandoned her in her absence. He threw her a confused glance as she sat down.

Taking off her hat and placing it on her lap, she smiled and mouthed "sorry" to him. Disappointed that he didn't return her smile, she turned around and looked for Valerie. She found her seated a row away to the right, sitting next to Straker, rhythmically nodding her head at whatever Straker was whispering into her ear. Poor Val, Grace thought with amusement. She also noticed, somewhat irritated, that Louisa was back in her seat, sound asleep. She glanced back at Ethan. Leaning over, she whispered, "What did I miss?"

"A few levitation tricks, some comedian, a couple of card tricks. You know, the usual."

"Dragovich hasn't performed yet, has he?"

"Um, yeah, he was pretty amazing, actually. The best part was when he hypnotized the guy at the end of our row dressed like..." His eyebrows drew down in thought. "A blueberry with a crown."

Grace looked down the end of the aisle. "Allen?"

Nodding, Ethan grinned. "Dragovich put him under. It was pretty funny. He had him hopping around the stage, saying the most ridiculous things. I wish I knew how to hypnotize people. He did it quickly, too. One second, Allen was saying he couldn't be hypnotized and the next, he was completely under Dragovich's control. It was incredible."

"Oh, I wish I had been here to see that." Grace looked around the audience wondering if anyone was videotaping the show. She would pay anything to get a copy of Allen hopping around the stage.

She looked up toward the ceiling, as a white mist appeared over the audiences' heads and floated toward the stage. She watched mystified as the mist formed into the shape of a man and began walking around the stage. It was just the barest of an image, but Grace easily recognized Ilya Dragovich's form. He appeared translucent. She could see right through his body to the red velvet curtains hanging in the background. He walked toward the edge of the stage, eventually solidifying to rapturous applause.

Happy that she hadn't missed the entire show, Grace felt that silly grin return.

"Once upon a time," the magician began in a melodious voice, "there was a very beautiful young maiden who lived in an enchanted land. And like many beautiful young maidens, who live in enchanted lands, she had her share of suitors. Mere mortal men lined the countryside in the hopes of just catching a glimpse of her. Her fame spread across the countryside, eventually reaching a very famous and powerful magician, who upon hearing of our maiden's famed beauty, set out to see her for himself. He came to her little enchanted village and so great was her beauty and charm, he was immediately captivated. That night, he asked her guardian permission to lodge in his castle in the hopes of romance. Permission was granted, but with one caveat. The magician must entertain the family. So, entertain he did, in the hopes of winning the hand of the fair maiden. Now legend has it the maiden was not impressed. She refused every offer of marriage. She heartlessly returned every gift. Naturally, left with no recourse, the magician turned her guardian into a stag and imprisoned the fair maiden in a crystal chest. I'm sure everyone here would have done the same."

The audience's laughter turned to gasps when a sparkling crystal chest appeared over their heads and floated to the stage. Reaching out an elegant hand, he magically brought the chest down until it was hovering just a few inches off the floor.

"Now the Grimm brothers in their retelling of this fairy tale would have you believe that the hero of the piece, the poor magician, was defeated by the fickle lady's guardian and then her heart was won by a mere tailor." With the flick of his wrist, the chest rose up six feet and swiveled around before gently floating back down and hovered a foot from the stage. "I'm sure as everyone has already guessed, that is not actually what happened. It was the cruel and wicked guardian who locked away our maiden and the wonderfully understanding, kind-hearted magician who released her. Our maiden was dramatically transformed by her captivity and once released, she happily accepted the magician's proposal."

Grace watched as one of the assistants left the stage and walked up the center aisle. As the magician's assistant approached, Grace realized she was the same girl she saw with Daniel Burns backstage a few minutes before.

"But to reenact our tale, I need a beautiful maiden," Ilya continued. "Who should play the part of the beautiful maiden?"

Several female hands went up in the audience, which was just as well with Grace. As excited as Grace was about coming to the Dragon's Lair, she much preferred to be an observer rather than a participant. She also had no desire to trip over a dozen people on her way to the aisle. Unfortunately, Ethan had other ideas. He held up his hand and pointed down at Grace. To her relief, the assistant ignored all to stand by Franklin Straker's row.

Straker looked at the magician's assistant expectantly. "I ain't no beautiful maiden!"

Everyone laughed; even his employees.

Ignoring him, the assistant motioned to Valerie, who was sitting next to Straker. Valerie, who looked like she was going to be sick, shook her head.

Grace looked at her friend sympathetically, knowing her fear of enclosed spaces would prevent her from participating.

Determined, the assistant continued to hold out her hand to Valerie, who still refused to take it.

"Ah, if it isn't Marilyn Monroe. Is she our fair maiden?" Ilya asked from the stage.

Reluctantly, Valerie reached out her hand.

"Holliday!" Straker yelled out.

Grace groaned.

"Get up there!" Straker pointed to Grace. "She's your fair maiden."

Before the newly dubbed fair maiden had a chance to react, Ethan was already pushing her into a standing position and down the aisle. In her hurry to reach the aisle, Grace fumbled past her co-workers, unfortunately eliciting more than a few groans as she accidentally stomped on a few feet with her cowboy boots on the way. Allen, in a desperate attempt to get out of the way, stood up at the wrong time, causing Grace to trip over his webbed blue feet. They both tumbled to the floor. Quickly righting herself, she used Allen as a springboard and jumped to her feet. With as much dignity as she could muster, she gracefully made her way to the stage.

"Ah, if it isn't our fair maiden, better known as Calamity Jane." The magician held his hand out to Grace, who was just making it down the aisle.

Heart beating fast, hands sweating and breath coming in short, Grace took the magician's hand and allowed herself to be led to the center of the stage. Once there, she turned around and faced the crowd.

Big mistake.

There was a sudden loss of sound as the blood drained from her face. She locked her knees to keep herself from falling to the floor. She hadn't realized how many people were actually in the audience. Hundreds, she thought as a cold clammy feeling washed over her. She glanced at Belle, who was smiling at her and nodding her head encouragingly, before turning to Dragovich. A mocking smile lit up his all too handsome face. She suddenly realized that he had been speaking to her. All of the sudden, sound came back in a rush.

"What?" she asked loudly, trying to regain some semblance of control.

The audience laughed.

His smile grew wider. "What is your name?" he asked slowly.

Grace stood there for a few seconds, staring into the dark abyss of the audience, not quite comprehending the question. "I don't know."

"You don't know your name?"

"Calamity—" She stood in confusion, staring at the crowd as all those eyes stared back at her. She screwed her eyes shut. Better. Smiling, she said, "Grace Holliday."

She felt strong fingers turn her head to the side. Opening her eyes, she found herself staring up into the smiling eyes of Ilya Dragovich. "Why don't you just concentrate on me? Don't look at the crowd."

Grace breathed a sigh of relief. It was much easier staring at him than at the crowd. She noticed a small scar on his temple and briefly wondered where that came from, before moving her gaze to his lips. Oh no, what was he saying now, she thought worriedly, as she tried to reconstruct his last words. Failing, she said, "what?" as the crowd broke into laughter again.

He smiled. "I think it was better when you were looking at the crowd."

"I don't know," she repeated, which judging by the noise the crowd was making was even funnier than when she said it the first time.

The magician nodded his head sympathetically as he lightly massaged her arms. "Don't worry, this won't take long. I'm going to put you out of your misery, very soon."

"Thank you," she breathed out, relieved. That ridiculously happy grin that had been on her face earlier in the night had returned, but by now, she was beyond caring, she just wanted to get away from all of those eyes.

"Now, I have a few questions to ask you. This is very important. Have you ever heard of Amelia Dale?"

Grace wanted to say that she could barely remember her own name right now, so how could she be counted on remembering anyone else's, but that would require forming an actual sentence, which was simply beyond her abilities at the moment. She just shook her head instead.

"What I am about to do has been done before. On this very stage. On this very night in 1919, a young woman, by the name of Amelia Dale, climbed into this same chest, and died, tragically."

Grace glanced at the crystal chest hovering to her right. To her eye, it looked more like a coffin than a chest. A small pit of dread began building in her stomach as she looked at the simple three by seven foot glass box. Except for a small, clear hole in the center, most of the glass was covered with ice crystals. Just looking at it caused her body to shiver uncontrollably. She wasn't sure what was worse: the coffin or the stage. She glanced back toward the audience and felt her stomach do a little flip-flop. The stage was definitely worse, she thought automatically.

"This stage, this night, this very act is considered cursed. Other magicians are afraid to try this."

"Okay." Grace glanced over to the chest. The only thing preventing her from climbing into the chest and putting an end to her agony was the magician's strong hands gripping her arms.

"One mistake could mean the difference of life or death for you." A scarf suddenly appeared in his hands. He took her hat off and passed it to one of his assistants. Turning her around, he covered her eyes with the scarf. "You must do exactly as I say."

"Yeah, yeah, sure," she said, as her body began leaning towards the chest.

* * * *

Grace lifted the edge of her blindfold and peeked up at the glass above her head. Once hidden away from the audience, she felt calmer. She was able to think and to relax, which was odd considering she was blindfolded and locked into a glass coffin. Still, anything was better than being on that stage.

Flexing her fingers, she gripped the flashlight tightly. She ran through his instructions in her mind. It seemed pretty simple. Just lie still. Keep the blindfold on. And every time he asked if she was okay, she was to move the flashlight around. Despite her performance fright, she was excited to see what would happen next.

She didn't have to wait long. Dragovich finally called her name. Remembering his instructions, she waved the flashlight around. Suddenly, the floor beneath her began to move. She could feel herself being gently raised and then lowered. She felt as though she was being swallowed whole. The sounds of the audience and the magician faded away until there was only silence. Before she could worry about missing her cue, she heard his voice asking her if she was okay. Nothing else. Not a sound. It was eerie. She waved her flashlight once again and waited. A few seconds later she heard someone unlatching the lid to the coffin.

It's over? she thought disappointed. She wasn't sure what to expect, but it was more than a short trip and waving around a flashlight.

She wished she could see what was happening and was tempted to remove the blindfold, but she didn't. Apparently, that was one of Amelia Dale's mistakes.

"It's okay," Belle said from above her. "It's just me. I'm just going to help you out." Strong hands helped her sit up and stand. They walked a few feet on what felt like scaffolding. When they reached firmer ground, Belle turned her around and began working at the knot at the back of her head. Once the scarf was off, Grace was surprised to find herself in a staircase with Belle Dragovich standing in front of her.

"Good job, Grace."

Grace smiled. "I wish I was able to see it."

"Oh, you will, just follow me. If we hurry, you'll be in time to see Lily appear."

"Do I get to reappear?"

Belle laughed. "Of course, but later. Until then, you'll be able to watch the rest of the show from a room we have set up upstairs. We have some gifts as well. The only thing we ask is that you sign a confidentiality agreement. It's just a simple contract saying that you won't reveal anything that happened back stage."

"I don't think I could, even if I wanted to." Grace quickly followed the other woman up the stairs. As they got closer to the first floor, they could hear the gasps and applause from the audience which became even louder as they left the stairwell and walked backstage.

Suddenly, the other blonde magician's assistant ran past them, almost knocking Grace to the ground.

Belle reached out a hand to steady her. "What's wrong, Tabitha?"

Breathing heavily, Tabitha spared a glance over her shoulder. She wordlessly shook her head, as she wiped away a few stray tears.

Concerned, Belle repeated her question.

Tabitha didn't answer. She simply covered her face with her hands and ran away.

Just then, a scream echoed through the theater.

As more screams sounded throughout the building, Belle turned around and raced down a hallway with Grace closely on her heels.

Reaching the stage door, they dashed through the entry and stopped.

Lily was hanging in the center of the stage with a silken scarf wrapped around her neck.

CHAPTER FOUR

GRACE GLANCED AT Ethan, snoring softly next to her. She debated whether she should jostle him awake or let him sleep. There wasn't really anyone around who would care if he fell asleep in his seat. Except for the one lone police officer sitting on the stage watching over the crystal chest, and Grace and Ethan sitting at the end of the front row, the theater was empty.

The police had finally removed Lily's body from the stage and were now concentrating on questioning Straker, his family and several of the magicians and their employees in the back rooms. Grace had already spent thirty minutes telling the police what little she knew. She was emotionally exhausted and ready to go home, but the police insisted that she stay. She had tried to convince Ethan to go home without her, but he had steadfastly refused to leave her side. So, for the last hour they sat in silence, waiting for the police to let her go.

Ethan's elbow slipped off the arm rest. He jerked awake and looked around. Seeing Grace, he grinned sheepishly before glancing at his watch and groaning. Looking around, he asked, "Where is everyone?"

"Still being questioned."

"I don't know why," Ethan said sleepily. "It's clearly an accident."

"Are you sure?" Grace asked.

"You think she committed suicide?" He ran his hand through his short black hair. "It has to be an accident."

Grace shook her head. "I don't know. It's weird."

"This sort of thing happens all of the time. I saw this movie the other day about a magician accidentally stabbing his assistant to death in one of those magic boxes. Her husband spent the rest of the movie trying to get revenge."

Grace smiled. "That was a movie."

Ethan smiled. "Sometimes, movies mirror real life. It was really good." Stretching his arms above his head, he yawned widely. "They tell you when you could leave yet?"

"No," she said, suppressing a yawn. "I don't understand why I can't go. I told them everything I know. What could be taking so long?"

Ethan closed his eyes and leaned his head against the back of his seat. "They're probably just being thorough."

Grace looked around the nearly empty room and whispered, "Tell me what happened on the stage."

"It was awful, Grace. Be glad you were in the back and didn't see it."

"Did she die instantly?"

The police officer on the stage passed in front of them and continued to the steps on the side of the stage. Ethan lowered his voice as the cop passed near them on his way to the back of the theater. "It looked that way to me. After he put you in the chest…"

Feeling sick, Grace shuddered.

"…it rose to the ceiling. It hovered there for a while as he talked about the magician and the fair maiden again. I could see you inside the whole time, waving that flashlight whenever Dragovich called your name. When you got all the way to the top of the ceiling, he raised his hands. Then all of a sudden, there were sparks coming from the chest, the lights flickered and then the bottom fell out, the chest disappeared and…" Ethan gripped Grace's arm. "I thought it was you. She just fell straight down. At first, everyone just thought it was part of the act, but then someone screamed. Dragovich just stood there, and then the curtain suddenly closed."

"What did my boss do? Did he realize it was his wife hanging there?"

"I don't think so, at least not until someone from behind the stage ran out and asked him to go behind the curtain with her."

Grace remembered watching Straker rush to the stage. Ilya had already gotten Lily down and was preforming CPR by the time Straker arrived. The magician didn't stop until the ambulance arrived and the EMTs took over, but by then, it was too late. Lily was dead. She overheard Ilya tell Straker that Lily was supposed to slide down a silken scarf and that he didn't know what had happened. Straker looked devastated. Luckily, Valerie was there. She gently led him to a chair while they waited for the police to arrive.

Ethan sighed. "It's just such a horrible accident."

Grace looked at her watch again. She stood up. "I'm going to try to find a police officer. What more could they want from me tonight?" Just as she started to walk away, Ethan grabbed her hand and pointed to the stage.

Grace breathed a sigh of relief, as the detective that had spoken to her came onto the stage. Trailing behind him was Ilya Dragovich and a few more police officers.

Grace sat back down next to Ethan.

"I hear this is exactly how your wife died," the detective in charge said, walking to the crystal chest.

Ethan and Grace exchanged looks. Obviously, the police didn't know they were still in the audience. Making as little noise as possible, they both shrank down in their seats at the same time.

Crossing his arms in front of himself, Ilya said sharply, "No. In fact, it's nothing like how Juliet died."

The detective scratched his head. "Now that's interesting, because I was told your wife died performing a magic trick where she was suspended from the ceiling. I heard that she died right out here on this very stage."

Ilya shook his head. "Whoever told you that was lying or mistaken. My wife died in Germany, not on this stage. I didn't come to New York or to this stage until just recently."

Taking out a notepad from his breast pocket, the detective made some notes. "Uh huh." He looked up. "Go on, I'm listening."

Irritated, Ilya inclined his head. "She was not performing. If you don't believe me, you can ask the Düsseldorf police. They investigated her death at the time and ruled it an accident."

"What was the name of the police officer?"

Ilya glared at the detective.

"We'll probably want to talk to him."

"Werner Schultz."

The detective wrote the information down. "Is he still in Germany?"

"Oh, I don't know," Ilya said sarcastically, "we sort of lost touch after my wife died. Drifted apart."

The sarcasm was not lost on the detective. "Uh huh. I'm just trying to sort everything out, Mr. Dragovich. We don't want any mistakes, do we?" When Ilya didn't respond, the detective asked, "So, how many people were performing with your wife?"

"What does my wife's accident have to do with Lily?"

"We're just trying to get our facts together. The situations are so similar. It's rather curious, don't you think?"

"No," Ilya said slowly, "like I said, the situation is not the same. We were not performing. We were practicing a new illusion."

"But your wife was suspended—"

"No, she wasn't. She and one of our stage assistants were up in the rafters, setting up for the show that night, when the beam they were standing on gave way."

"Did your wife usually take part in setting up for such activities?"

Ilya hesitated. "Sometimes. It depended on the illusion. Our stage assistant was showing Juliet part of the set up."

"Didn't she already know?"

"No. Lily was actually supposed to be up there helping to set up, but she had sprained her ankle a few hours before. My wife was preparing to go in her place."

The detective looked up from his notepad. "Sprained her ankle? Gee, I didn't realize magic was so dangerous."

"She sprained her ankle running for a cab."

The detective grunted. "So, what happened to your assistant?"

"Lily?"

The detective shook his head. "The stage assistant in Germany."

"She managed to catch the next beam over. My wife was not so lucky."

"Uh huh," he said, scribbling in his notebook. "Her name? The assistant?"

Ilya sighed. "Teresa Ricardi."

"Her address?" He looked up from his notebook. "We would like to interview her as well."

"I don't know. I retired after my wife's accident to take care of my children and I haven't kept in touch."

"Retired?" The detective looked around at the stage. "It doesn't look like you retired."

"I came out of retirement a few years later."

The detective grunted. "She married?"

"Who? Teresa?"

The detective nodded.

"No, not at the time, but I heard she married one of our stage hands a few years later."

"Do you have his name? We might want to ask him a few questions."

"Possibly. I'll ask around."

"What caused the…accident?" The tone of his voice made it clear that he was putting accident in air quotes.

"It was an old stage. Termites had eaten through the beam."

"Interesting."

"Yes. Perhaps you would like to interview the termites, too?"

Amused, Grace and Ethan smiled at each other.

The detective was not so amused. "What exactly was your relationship with Mrs. Straker?"

"We were friends, nothing more."

The detective stared at Ilya. "I don't suppose you'll be willing to tell us how this trick was done. I can easily get a warrant—"

"That's not necessary. As long as you'll promise to be discreet with the information, I'll be happy to show you how it works."

Out of the corner of her eye, she noticed Ethan reach his hand up to his nose and scrunch his eyes together.

Grace glanced around. Please don't sneeze, she thought desperately.

Surprised, the detective gave Ilya a crooked smile. "That's awful nice of you, Mr. Dragovich. I thought you magicians took these sorts of things to the grave. Why are you being so forthcoming?"

"Lily was not only my former employee, but my friend. She helped me a great deal after Juliet died. I owe her quite a lot. I want to know what happened to her, too." He sighed. "It's actually quite simple. The chest is lifted up to the ceiling and behind the chest—out of view of the audience—is a small platform." Pulling back part of the curtain, Ilya pointed to the ceiling. "Lily would have been standing up at the top, waiting."

Ethan removed his hand and smiled in relief.

"Waiting for what?"

"For the chest to slide into place and my signal."

"Is that all she's doing up there?"

"No. She usually checks the silks—"

"Silks?"

"Long nylon sheets which are secured to the ceiling. Once the chest rises to the top, I hit this button." Ilya held out a small remote control. "Once I hit the button, the bottom of the chest falls out, the lights flicker on and off, and confetti and glitter rain down on the stage. At the same time, my assistant floats to the stage with the aid of the silks."

"She isn't in the chest?"

"No, she's never in the chest. She jumps off from the scaffolding."

"What does she do then?"

"She usually does a few aerial tricks while she comes down. It's actually one of the least difficult illusions I use, but the audience usually likes the story and the acrobatics."

"But that didn't happen this time?"

"No."

"Why?"

"I have no idea."

"How many people knew Mrs. Straker would be up on the scaffolding tonight?

"Myself, my daughter, and my other assistant, Tabitha. I don't know if Lily told anyone."

"I understand this was a surprise performance. Who usually does this part of the trick?"

"Tabitha."

The detective stood next to the purple silk hanging from the ceiling. Reaching for the end, he sharply tugged at the material. "Is there any way she could have accidently wrapped this around her neck?"

"No."

"You said she does some aerial acrobatics. I've seen that done before. They twist and contort their way around…"

Dragovich shook his head. "Lily has done this a thousand times. There is no way this was an accident."

"Was anyone up there with her?"

"No, she was alone."

"How do you know?"

"I could see her from the stage, sitting on the platform, waiting for her cue. There wasn't anyone else up there with her."

"Were you watching her the whole time?"

"No, but I saw her sitting there when the chest rose to the top. I didn't see anyone else."

"Was Mrs. Straker depressed?"

The magician stood there a second before crossing his arms.

"Mr. Dragovich," the detective prompted.

"No, not at all."

"You hesitated."

"Lily's been under a lot of stress lately, but I don't think she would have killed herself. Not this way."

"What sort of stress."

"I don't know. She wouldn't say."

Reaching down, the detective looked around the inside of the chest. "Why do you have a chest inside a chest here?"

"The young lady that we pulled from the audience was in the inner chest. The inner chest is lowered to the lower level, while the outer chest rises to the ceiling."

"I have several witnesses that say they could see Ms. Holliday in the chest as it was raised to the ceiling."

"Yes, of course. That's part of the illusion. I use a little trick of technology to make it seem like our guest is in the chest the entire time."

The detective sat back on his heels. "That doesn't sound very magical."

Ilya gave him a withering look. "Did you really think I levitated a two hundred pound box and a one hundred and thirty pound woman in the air with my mind?"

"One hundred and fifteen," Grace whispered to her companion.

"They're called illusions for a reason," Ilya continued.

"Uh huh. How was Mrs. Straker's relationship with her husband?"

Unable to stop himself, Ethan sneezed, causing everyone on the stage to look over to the side where they were sitting.

"Oh, Ms. Holliday," the detective said, standing up, "you're still here. Good. I have a few more questions for you, too."

Friday, December 2nd

CHAPTER FIVE

GRACE STOOD IN the center of her new office and smiled happily. An office with a view. No longer was she expected to work in a small little cubicle. She walked over to the large drafting table, set in the corner of the office and checked her supplies before moving over to the boxes lined up in a neat row by her desk.

There had been quite the turnaround at the Straker Toy Company since Lily Straker's death the month before. More so than usual. The staff was deserting the failing business, like rats off the proverbial sinking ship. One of the benefits of a high turnaround was the sudden advancement that usually followed. When the product manager that she worked under was fired two weeks ago, Grace quickly moved up into his position. As far as she was concerned, it was only fitting, since he had spent more time playing with the toys—and most of the female staff—than actually designing toys.

"Grace, is there anything else you need?" her new assistant asked.

Grace smiled, her new position at the toy company came with several new perks: a new office, better pay, more benefits, and *an assistant*. It took ten years. Ten years of hard labor in the bowels of the toy company, but she had finally made it. She looked over at the friendly older woman. "No, I can handle the rest, Ellen. Thanks."

She bent down and dug through the boxes on the floor until she found a brightly clothed doll with long wavy pink hair and big purple eyes. Her favorite design and part of the interstellar space series, which had just started taking off. It was also the doll that helped convince Straker that she deserved a promotion. Picking up the doll, she walked over to the bookshelves next to her desk. Smiling, she arranged the doll on the shelf. In a few minutes, she had ten such dolls displayed. Each had big bright eyes, pastel colored hair, and were dressed in bright colorful outfits.

Picking up another box, she rummaged around until she found some sketches of previous designs. She looked at the plain vanilla walls, wondering if Straker would let her repaint. Holding up the colorful designs, she tried to picture which color would complement her designs. She was almost sold on lilac when Valerie walked in.

"What do you think, Val? Lilac or a pastel peach?"

"I'd forget the walls right now. I just caught Allen trying to bribe your assistant."

Grace groaned. One of the cons to high turnaround was that others might take advantage of the situation as well. Grace's happiness at her sudden promotion was somewhat dampened by the fact that Allen Madison had been promoted along with her.

"Ellen told him off, didn't she?"

"Yes, but I'd keep an eye on him if I were you. He's out to get you."

"I'm not worried. What can he do? It's not like we're vying for the same job anymore."

"He can still cause trouble. The man is so sleazy, I'm surprised I haven't dated him yet."

"Don't worry, I have all the faith in the world in Ellen. She is a veritable dynamo. Anything I want, she delivers in seconds. She's so efficient." Grace pointed to her supply desk. "Look, she even organized my desk supplies by alphabet. I've messed them up dozens of times and each time I come back, they're back in order. It's amazing." She picked up a sheet of paper from her desk printer. "Look at this spreadsheet she created. I'm so lucky she's staying. I don't know what I would do without her. I don't know anything about marketing."

"Do you know anything about advertising?"

"No, why?"

"Oh, I wouldn't want to spoil the surprise. Straker has a big announcement this afternoon."

"Really? What?"

"He fired our advertising agency this morning."

Grace mulled over this bit of information. "Well, that's not exactly unexpected. He's been complaining about them for over a year now." Grace dropped the spreadsheet onto the desk. "What else?"

"Oh no, don't even waste your time. Do you think I would know? Come on, I'll walk with you to the conference room."

Grace slipped her arms into her black jacket and checked her reflection in the mirror hanging on the back of her door. She tucked her emerald green silk blouse that matched her eyes into her black pencil skirt before opening the door and following Valerie out into the hallway.

"Have you found a new roommate yet?" Valerie asked.

"No, not yet." Grace shut her door and smiled at Ellen who was busily typing away at her desk just outside Grace's office. "I'm kind of enjoying the peace and quiet." "Peace and quiet is nice, but paying your rent is even better."

"Now don't change the subject. What's Straker up to?"

"Honestly, I don't know."

"You type up the agenda."

"There isn't one for today. I promise you, I have no idea. I only found out about the advertising agency because they called to complain. Straker's been very secretive lately."

"How's he doing? Since..." Grace trailed off. It wasn't necessary to mention Lily's name. Outside of the massive amount of layoffs the company had gone through in the last month, the only other topic of conversation had been Lily's dramatic death and the coroner's ruling of suicide.

Valerie shrugged. "He's been acting very mysterious. He's planning something big."

"And you have no idea what?"

"No. To be honest, I'm rather worried about him. He's taken Lily's suicide very hard. I've been staying late the last few weeks just to make sure he's all right. I wish I knew what was going on, but he's even stopped confiding in me."

"I can't believe they think it was a suicide. She was obviously murdered."

Valerie's eyes widened. Turning to Grace, she said, "Of course, it was a suicide. She left a note."

"I wish we knew what that note actually said."

"You really think she was murdered?" Valerie whispered.

"Yes, I do."

"But the detective…"

"Think about it. Doesn't it seem somewhat strange that she would commit suicide like that? On the night of her husband's big birthday party and on the one night that she performs on stage again? In front of such a large crowd? I love a good coincidence as much as the next girl, but that's kind of pushing it."

Valerie waved her hand dismissively. "Come on, be serious. There was an investigation. They found a suicide note. If it wasn't a suicide, I'm pretty sure the police would have been all over this place by now."

"I guess so," Grace shrugged. "You're probably right. You know, I took a criminal justice class in college my sophomore year. My professor told us that there's only one reason—"

"You studied criminal justice," Straker said from behind them.

Grace and Valerie froze in surprised.

"I thought you had a degree in toy design," Straker said.

Grace, seized with a sudden panic, quickly stammered out, "No, I have a degree in business, remember?"

Straker stalked past them. "Criminal Justice, huh." He continued down the hallway toward his office, muttering, "Who gets a degree in criminal justice and comes work at a toy company?"

As soon as he disappeared around the corner, Valerie grinned. "You should never share personal details like that around here, you know that. There's no telling what he'll do with that information now."

"Do you think he heard us talking about Lily?" she asked worriedly.

"You're doomed," Valerie predicted less than helpfully.

* * * *

Grace sank into the chair closest to the door. She smiled at the rest of the design team as they entered the conference room. Straker was the last to enter. He closed the door and sat down at the end of the table.

Everyone at the table looked at him in confusion. Design meetings usually consisted of Straker, his daughter Louisa, who acted as vice president when sober; the two brand managers, his late wife, Lily, and son-in-law, Daniel; five product managers, of which Grace was now one; and a half dozen toy designers. At least once a month, they all met to discuss the current and future lines of toys that each section was working on. Today's meeting was noticeably different. They all looked from Straker to the more than half dozen empty seats in the room. The only toy designer present was Michael Talon, the Straker Magic Shoppe's toy designer. The rest were missing. Every single one of them.

Everyone's palms began sweating at once.

Straker stared at everyone at the table one by one. He didn't say a word. He just stared for a full minute. Even Louisa must have been feeling the heat. She nervously looked around the room and at her husband. The silence finally became too much for her. "Dad, I have an appointment."

"There's nowhere else you need to be." Addressing the rest of the table he said, "I'm sure all of you have noticed the changes that have been going on in our happy little family. I've decided to streamline my business. We were a little too bloated. There were far too many people doing a job one person could do easily."

It suddenly began to occur to everyone that their duties were about to be increased.

"First of all, I've eliminated several positions. Namely the designers."

They all sank into their chairs.

"We don't need them. Everyone here started out as a designer. There's no reason why you can't handle all aspects of design from start to finish." He looked around the room. In an attempt to avoid eye contact, eyes began dropping to the top of the table. The only one who didn't seem nervous was Sidney Harcourt, the Straker Magic Shoppe's project manager, sitting at the other end of the table. For some reason, the old magician seemed quite pleased.

One of the braver and more experienced product managers spoke up. "How are we going to do this?" Bianca asked. "I have three designers under me. You want me to handle all the design, research, safety inspection, and marketing all on my own, right before Christmas? How are we going to do that without help? You complained about our output at the last meeting. I have ten new designs for our newest action figure line—"

"You don't have to worry about that. Allen is taking over action figures and we're shutting down the rest of your department."

Bianca sat back, stunned.

"We're completely reorganizing the Straker Toy Company, and as a result, we're going to eliminate some toys that we used to sell. Everyone here has gotten complacent. It's time to switch things up. Only Grace has been successful with her new hippie, psychedelic alien doll line. Look at her. She doesn't have a fancy degree in toy design like Maria here, or a degree in industrial design like Bianca."

Grace tried not to notice how Maria and Bianca glared at her.

"But she's plugging along. No, she wasted four years majoring in Criminal Justice."

"Business," Grace corrected softly.

"But despite that, she created something children actually want to play with. Imagine that."

"So, what do I do here?" Bianca asked, angrily.

Straker shrugged. "I don't know. What do you do here?"

Bianca stood up. "I've worked here for over fifteen years, but that's it. I can't take it anymore. I quit." Everyone watched as she stormed out of the room, slamming the door behind her.

Grace glanced at her watch. A new record. Usually it took people a good half hour at these meetings before suddenly declaring they were quitting and stomping off.

"All right, now that it's just us, we can get down to business. Allen will keep action figures and pick up dolls, since they're basically the same thing. Those are our backbones. They've been our backbone and our biggest sellers since my great grandfather established this company in 1902."

Grace lifted her eyes off the table. Surely, he didn't say that Allen would be taking dolls. She glanced over at Allen who was smiling at her, mouthing, 'I'll need your files.'

Grace and Maria, one of the other project managers in charge of dolls, exchanged worried glances.

Shaking, Maria interrupted. "They are not the same thing. I've had dolls for over the last ten years. What am I going to do?"

"We're going to specialize in just a few types of toys. Mainly dolls, but we cannot afford to have two people working on the same type of product anymore, so I'm going to put Allen in charge of that line."

"He's only been a product manager for a month," Maria asked in disbelief. "Are you firing me?"

Straker didn't answer. Instead, he addressed Allen. "We'll have a meeting next week to discuss any new ideas you might have. Be creative. I want you to be edgy. Do something different. Something exciting."

Maria stood up. "I have given you ten years of my life."

Grace leaned back in her chair and looked at the ceiling, wondering what it would be like not to dread office meetings. By the time she was done fantasizing, Maria had left, slamming the door behind her. She looked over at Allen who was grinning from ear to ear. And then there were three, she thought ruefully. She glanced to the only other product manager left, Sidney Harcourt, who was sitting at the other end of the table.

Harcourt, every inch the older debonair magician, stroked his salt and pepper goatee. "What about my department, Franklin? Surely, you have no intention of eliminating me. The Magic Shoppe won't be able to function without an experienced magician to run it."

Straker shook his head. "I have no intention of replacing you, Sidney. The Straker Magic Shoppe, toy store and our doll lines are practically the only things keeping us afloat. You keep doing what Lily hired you to do. I'm not changing a thing."

Harcourt leaned forward. "Nothing?" He glanced at Michael Talon, otherwise known among the staff as the gloomy vampire, due to his penchant for wearing all black, all the time, from the top of his head to the tips of his toenails which peeked out of his black colored sandals. "I thought you were eliminating certain positions."

The young man in question crossed his heavily tattooed arms and glared at his supervisor. His face flushed red, but he remained quiet. Harcourt had never hidden his contempt of Michael's abilities or his shock form of magic. The older magician practiced an old school form of magic and Michael did not. It was well known through the company that the two hated each other.

"Like I said, absolutely nothing will change in the Magic Shoppe," Straker said, tapping his finger against the table. "We're going to leave it just as Lily had designed and it's going to stay that way as long as I'm in charge."

Michael thanked Straker. Leaning back into his chair, he breathed a sigh of relief.

Sidney Harcourt's frowned. "Fine. What about my promotion?"

Straker raised a bushy grey eyebrow. "What promotion?"

"Lily was the brand manager of the Magic Shoppe. What are you going to do with her position? You know, the one I've been handling since she left for Europe half a year ago."

Straker shrugged. "I've decided not to fill it just yet. Any more questions?"

Harcourt fell silent. He crossed his arms and leaned back in his chair.

Unable to stand it any longer, Grace blurted out a rather plaintive, but certainly not whiny, "What about me? If Allen's taking dolls, what do I do?"

"Don't worry," Straker said softly. "I have plans for you."

Relieved, Grace leaned back. Since she hadn't been mentioned when he was handing out job duties, she had been half-afraid she was about to be fired.

Straker smiled. "Now, that brings us to the next item on our agenda. I have a surprise for all of you. We have a new addition to our company." They watched as he stood up and opened the door. To everyone's surprise, Belle Dragovich walked through the door.

"I'm sure everyone knows Belle," Straker said. "She is Ilya Dragovich's daughter. What you may not have known is that she was also Lily's goddaughter. She will be joining our little happy family as of today."

Most of the table was too shocked to do anything, but stare. Sidney Harcourt, on the other hand, stood up. They watched as his face and hands turned purple. "I've worked here for…"

Grace leaned her head back against her chair as she tuned the rest of his speech out. She turned her mind to the task of mentally decorating her office. Perhaps a pale blue would look nice. A cotton candy type of blue. So focused was she on her fantasy that she almost missed Louisa's outburst.

"How can you do this?" Louisa's voice shook with anger as she looked from her father to Belle. Daniel quickly shushed his wife. Before she could say any more, he pulled her out of her chair and out of the room.

Straker was now standing in front of the conference table. He looked happier than he had in a month. Grace wasn't surprised. He usually was the only one happy at these meetings.

Harcourt was still standing on the other side of the table, apparently, not having quit just yet.

"How could you give her Lily's position? She's not even a magician. She's only been an assistant for a couple of years now. She knows nothing of what we do."

"That's not true," Belle countered, sliding into the seat Louisa had just vacated. "I've watched my father for years. He designed many of his illusions himself."

"And where did he get the hardware? What about the crystal chest? He didn't design that, because I did."

Straker sat down, smiling. "Enough you two," he said, laughing. "Sidney, calm down. Belle's not taking Lily's place. I already told you, I'm leaving that position open for the time being."

"Am I to compete with her?" he asked aghast.

"No, she's not going to be involved with the Magic Shoppe at all. She's going to start at the bottom and work her way up."

"I didn't want to work with you, Sidney," she said testily. "After Lily's... death, I decided that I wanted no part of magic, magicians or anything to do with them. I want to do something else with my life. When Mr. Straker heard that I had quit my father's show, he offered me a job here."

Glaring across the table at Straker, Harcourt asked, "Where is she going to work, then?"

"With Grace."

Surprised, Grace raised her hand. "And what exactly will I be doing?"

Straker frowned. "Didn't I mention?"

Grace shook her head. "No, you didn't."

"We're going to have two design branches. In addition to our doll branch, we'll tackle games. Specifically, games for teenagers. We've been stuck in the past for far too long and the future has passed us by. It's time to catch up." He looked up as Daniel re-entered the room and took his place next to Belle.

Grace eagerly sat forward. Straker had resisted video games for years now, insisting that they were nothing more than a fad that would go away with time. Grace knew he would have to give in eventually, which is why she had been taking night courses in graphic design for a couple of years now and it looked like she was finally going to get some use out of her new degree.

"We're going to do something new." Straker spread his arms wide. "Board games!"

Allen flashed a bright smile in her direction.

Grace ignored him. "Not video? Sir?"

"No," Straker said, "we're not doing video. Good old fashioned board games."

"But didn't we have a board game division that you eliminated five years ago because it was a money drain. You fired everyone on that team."

"Yes, that was a good day." Straker smiled in fond remembrance. Refocusing, he waved his hand dismissively. "But I have confidence that you'll be able to reinvent the board game landscape. It'll be great. Teenagers love board games. Remember, you need to be edgy and creative. Hey, I have an idea. Why don't you put your criminal justice degree to good use and design a mystery game. That would be fun. You like mysteries, don't you?"

Daniel looked at her sympathetically.

Straker pointed to Belle. "Belle will work with you. You can teach her the ropes."

Allen raised his hand. "What about Grace's assistant?"

"Oh," Straker said, "Grace needs an assistant."

Grace breathed a sigh of relief. At least she wasn't losing Ellen.

Allen shook his head. "But Ellen has been in the doll department for so many years."

Straker nodded. "And that's where she'll stay. Grace can get a new assistant."

Leaning back in his chair, Allen smiled at her smugly.

"Okay," Grace said reluctantly. "I'll draw up a job ad, but couldn't Ellen stay with me until we hire someone else."

"No, we don't have enough time for you to hire someone from the outside. Besides, this is a family business, Holliday. What do I always say about my employees?"

Grace looked around at the blank faces sitting around the table. Reluctantly, she repeated the last thing she had heard him say about his employees, "We're just placeholders until a super race of robots can be created."

Allen snickered, causing Straker to glare at him. Once Allen was appropriately cowed, Straker turned back and said, "My employees are like my family. I care for all of you. It hurts me when I lose a member of the family. And like any good father, I want my children to grow and advance."

Heads around the table began automatically bobbing up and down.

"We promote from within in this company," Straker continued.

"But, you fired all of the designers," Grace pointed out. "How can we promote from within?"

"Simple. Go downstairs to the toyshop and take someone from there. Belle can go with you. Since you two will be working together, you both should have a say in who gets promoted." He smiled as he looked around the table. "Well, that's it for today. Everyone get to work."

Daniel hopped to his feet and rushed out of the room. More than likely to find Louisa, Grace thought watching as the door slammed shut. Michael and Belle reached for the door handle at the same time. Grace noticed the small smile they exchanged as they fumbled with the door and walked out of the room. Only Straker, Harcourt, Allen, and Grace remained.

When the door closed behind Belle, Harcourt walked up to Straker. "I don't need any help," he said, striking the wooden floor with the end of his lion's head cane, which he used more for a prop than any actual need, with each word he spoke.

Straker sighed. "Geez, Sidney, how many times do I have to tell you? Belle isn't going to be working above, with, or under you."

"I'm not talking about her. I'm talking about the boy. He's completely incompetent and not a true magician. He doesn't study his craft. No, he goes for shock value. I'd almost prefer Belle. I might not like her father, but he at least knows what he's doing."

"Michael stays," Straker said with a hard look in his eyes.

Allen, who'd been pretending to leave, came back inside and quietly sat down next to Grace. He leaned over and whispered into her ear. "You need to tell Mr. Straker that board games are not a good idea. Ask him for some time to do some research. Do some feasibility studies. Teenagers just don't spend a lot of time with board games, anymore. He likes you, so he'll listen."

Grace glanced out of the corner of her eye, surprised that Allen was actually attempting to be helpful.

Allen stood up and left as soon as Harcourt walked out.

Seeing Grace still sitting there, Straker asked, "Do you need something, Grace?"

"About the board game …"

"I knew you would love it."

"I do. Really, I do," she lied, "but couldn't we try at least one video game. Kids just aren't playing board games like they used to."

"Nonsense, mystery games are fun. I figure you would jump at this chance to put your criminal justice degree to good use."

"It was just one class in my sophomore year. I didn't really do that well at it."

"Well, now's your chance to shine. If you have any issues, talk to Daniel."

Nodding, Grace walked out of the room. Allen was waiting for her outside. "Did you tell him what I told you to say?"

"Yeah."

"And?"

"It didn't work."

"I knew it wouldn't. Why did you waste your time?"

* * * *

Numb, Grace walked toward her office. She passed Valerie who was just emerging from her office. "So, how did it go?"

"We're heading to the future, Val. To the bright future of 1965."

"Why? What do you have to do?"

"Board games."

"Oh no, what about your interstellar doll design?"

Allen walked out of her office carrying her dolls in his arms. "Hey, look at this one," he said, holding up Major Venus Bell, a pretty doll with flowing lavender hair and green eyes. "What do you think about adding tentacles? Or gills?"

When they didn't answer, he happily walked away, calling to Ellen over his shoulder. "Just make sure to pack it all up, El. I need everything."

Valerie sympathetically patted Grace on the shoulder. "Oh, Grace, I'm so sorry. It could be worse. At least you have a job. Franklin fired Mae this morning."

"Why would he fire Daniel's secretary?"

Valerie shrugged. "She was twenty minutes late today. He never seemed to mind before."

Grace looked at her friend thoughtfully. "Have you noticed that everyone who wasn't at the magic show the night Lily died has been fired or has quit? They're all gone. Absolutely all of them."

CHAPTER SIX

GRACE CHECKED HER watch again. Twenty after nine. She looked around the almost empty restaurant, wondering what time they closed. Other than the waiters, who were sitting over in the corner staring at her, there were only a couple of elderly diners finishing their meal. She debated whether she should order something or just leave. She had already eaten several hours before, but when Ethan called her unexpectedly at eight o'clock and asked to meet her for dinner, she had immediately accepted.

Spurred into action, she tore off her cartoon kitty nightshirt, slithered into the slinkiest dress she owned, donned her eyes with the smokiest eyeliner and eye shadow in her collection, texted Valerie the good news, and called a cab. Despite a few traffic hiccups, she made it to the little Italian restaurant just a block from work, a few minutes before nine. Sitting down at a small table near the window, she quietly went over the menu while waiting. Although, Valerie and a few other co-workers had often raved of the lasagna, she had never been to this restaurant—living paycheck to paycheck often meant dining on homemade packed lunches. After she had practically memorized the menu, for want of anything else to read, she tossed it aside and stared out the window, restlessly drumming her fingers on the tabletop.

Now, here she sat, still waiting. She glanced across the street, just in time to see Louisa Burns, clad in her husband's dress shirt and a pair of purple leggings, stumble from a cab and walk toward the restaurant. With a breezy and slightly slurred, "Hi, Al," Louisa waved to the bartender and entered the ladies room.

A noise to her right caused Grace to swivel back around in her seat. Her waiter was back.

"Are you ready to order?"

Grace shook her head. She was about to admit to the shame of having been stood up when she saw Ethan walk past the window. Sighing in relief, she ordered another drink and asked the waiter to give her a few minutes. A few seconds later, an apologetic Ethan slid into the seat across from her.

He looked incredibly tired. Still handsome, but very tired.

"I'm so very sorry, Grace. I've been in court most of the day, and when I wasn't in court, I was meeting with clients."

Grace quickly assured him that she hadn't waited very long.

Seeing Ethan sitting across from Grace, the waiter zeroed in. In record time, drinks, appetizers, and dinner were ordered.

Grace looked over at Ethan, trying to decide what to say first. Where have you been is probably not a very good way to start a second date, she thought with amusement. Not if you would like a third. Although, considering that he seemed to be paying more attention to the other diners than her, coupled with the fact she hadn't heard from him in over a month and he was late to their second date, she was seriously wondering if she necessarily wanted a third date. A handsome face only goes so far. "How's work?"

"Hmm," he said to the spot just behind her head.

"Work?"

His eyes finally landed her. "Oh, work? Yes, it's fine. I'm sorry I didn't call you sooner. I still can't believe what happened. That poor woman dying like that."

Grace smiled. "I'm surprised you called."

Ethan smiled back. "Why?"

"Well, a first date that ends with a murder? How can we possibly top that? I'm afraid the rest of our dates would be dreadfully boring in comparison."

Her attempt at gallows humor fell flat.

"Murder?" he asked surprised. "I read it was a suicide."

"That's the official report."

"What makes you think otherwise?"

Grace glanced over her shoulder, suddenly aware that they weren't quite alone. The victim's stepdaughter was lurking around somewhere. Deciding it might be in poor taste to begin rattling on about a murder that might not have happened, she quickly changed the subject. She glanced around the empty dining room. "Do you think they're about to close?"

Ethan shook his head, while assuring her that the restaurant was open for another hour. "No, it's okay. I often have late night business meetings here with clients."

"Is that what this is?"

Ethan looked taken aback. "No, not at all. I'm sorry, Grace. I haven't been able to get you out of my mind since our date. You don't know how many times I've wanted to pick up the phone. It's just there was a problem with one of my firm's international clients. The day after your boss' birthday, I was on a flight to Paris. I just got back the other day. I should have called to let you know. I'm so sorry."

Grace smiled. "Oh, I wish I had known. I just left from there."

"Really?" he asked, surprised.

She nodded. "My sister lives there. My family and I decided to have Thanksgiving in Paris with her this year."

"Did you have a good time?"

"A very good time. I made out like a bandit."

He gave her a strange look.

"I did a lot of shopping," she explained. "It was nice putting all of this behind me."

The next half hour was spent eating and getting to know one another. As far as Grace was concerned, things had been going rather well at first. They talked about basic mundane things most people talk about on dates: birth places, college, hobbies, and various interests. Unfortunately, like with most of her dates, the moment she began talking about her work, the men seemed to lose all interest.

She glanced at Ethan. His head was tilted at an angle as he peered over her head. Some quicker than others, she thought, slightly amused. For some reason, men never want to hear about dolls. The only thing that really seemed to capture his attention was Lily's death, but she wasn't ready to share her theories just yet. Not with Lily's stepdaughter a few feet away.

"I've been so busy at work," Grace said.

He glanced back down at her.

"I have to come up with an idea of a board game." Ethan's eyes flitted from her to a spot just behind her head for the sixth time that night. Trying to rein in her annoyance and wondering what had captured his attention so strongly, she asked, "Is something wrong?"

"No, I'm sorry, Grace." He smiled brightly. "What were you saying?"

"I've been trying to come up with board games for teenagers."

"Oh, games. That sounds like fun." His eyes lost focus again as they travelled from her eyes to just over her head. His eyebrows drew down in a worried frown. "I love video games," he said, somewhat distractedly.

"No, not video. Board games," she said, wondering what in the world could be distracting him.

His eyes flew back to hers. "Board games? Really? For small kids?"

Grace picked up her fork and began lightly tapping it against the table. She didn't normally fidget when out on a date, but she had obviously lost his interest at some point during the meal. "No, teenagers," she said patiently.

"Ah." His voice took on a faraway tone. "Teenagers love video games."

"Ethan?"

"Hmm?"

Grace leaned over the table. "What's going on? You haven't heard a word I've said in the last five minutes."

His face flushed. "I'm sorry." Leaning in and lowering his voice to a whisper, he asked, "Do you see that woman sitting over there?"

Grace looked back to the bar. The only woman sitting at the bar was Louisa. She was just bringing a drink up to her mouth. It obviously wasn't the first of the night. An older man in a three-piece suit was sitting next to her. He was leaning into her as she was leaning away. "You two know each other?"

Looking past her shoulder, he sighed heavily. "Kind of."

"Have you and Louisa known each other long?"

His eyes refocused. "Who?"

Grace pointed to Louisa who was now resting her head on the bar. "Louisa Burns."

"Oh, I never found out her name. How do you know her?"

"She's my boss' daughter."

Shock colored his face. "Her mother—"

"No, that was her stepmother who died. How do you know her?"

"I see her here all of the time. Always alone. Usually she just has a few drinks and goes home, but there have been a few nights that she's had one too many."

"What usually happens?"

"Well, normally, Al, the bartender, calls a cab and she's driven home, but there have been a few occasions, not many, where she's caused a scene. She likes to flirt and sometimes she flirts with the wrong guy. The last time it happened, Al and I had to step in and it looks like it's going to happen again."

Turning around, Grace watched as the man next to Louisa slid off his bar stool. He wrapped one meaty hand around Louisa's arm and attempted to pull her off the stool as she shook her head.

Ethan stood, and took a few steps toward the bar, but stopped when the other man let go of Louisa's arm.

They watched as Louisa and the man exchanged a few words as he reached into his pocket and brought out a handful of bills which he tossed on top of the bar before angrily storming out of the restaurant.

Sitting back down, Ethan sighed. "I kind of feel sorry for her. I got the impression there were problems at home."

Nodding, Grace turned back around. She was about to ask if he had ever met Louisa's husband, Daniel, when she felt a cold hand slap her shoulder and a shrill voice slur, "Gracie! How are you doing, Grace? I've never seen you here before." Drink in hand, Louisa slid into the booth next to Ethan. She laid a long manicured hand on his forearm. "Hello. I've never seen you here before, either."

Ethan glanced helplessly at Grace.

"Did you see that guy over there?" Louisa pointed back to the bar. "He tried to pick me up. Like I would ever have something to do with a man like him. He's not handsome like you."

Grace leaned forward. "It's getting late, Louisa…"

Louisa shook her head, spilling her drink in the process. "No, it's never too late, Grace, never. Trust me, I know. It is never too late," she said with great solemnity. "Never." Her eyes narrowing, she looked at Grace again. "Did you see what happened today? Did you see my poor daddy? Did you see how that Jezebel weaseled her way into my company? She thinks she's so clever, but I know what she's up to." Turning to Ethan, she softly repeated, "I know what she's up to."

"I'm sorry about what happened to your stepmom," Ethan said gently.

Louisa laughed. "I'm not."

Grace and Ethan exchanged looks.

"Everyone keeps saying how they're so sorry for me. Why? I hated her. She was always interfering. She was jealous of me. I'm glad she's gone. She was even worse than Hannah."

"Hannah?" Grace asked.

Louisa nodded. "Hannah was the second Mrs. Straker—Daddy's former secretary. She was horrible. An absolute monster. She went from making coffee and running errands to the penthouse suite just like…" Louisa clumsily tried snapping her fingers. "But luckily for me, she didn't last long. Then there was Courtney, *my* friend from college. She was my maid of honor and then my step mother." She laughed. "Can you believe that?"

"I'm sorry—"

Louisa tipped back her head, resting it against the back of the booth. "But that was easy enough to fix." She leaned in conspiratorially. "Courtney was having an affair with her fitness trainer. Daddy somehow found out." She giggled again. "Then it was bye-bye, Courtney. Then there was … I don't remember. Oh, wait, yes I do. Ashley. Ashley was my daddy's secretary when he was married to Courtney. He moved Courtney out and Ashley in, practically the same day. I didn't mind Ashley. She was such a mousy little thing. Always so eager to please. Anyway, she didn't last long, because she was too nice. She divorced him after only a year of marriage. Poor little Ashley. I was actually sorry to see her go. Then he met Lily at one of his stupid birthday bashes."

She pushed her drink away and looked sadly at the table. "And now we have Lily's little mini-me, invading the office. She's going to do the same thing Lily did. My poor daddy. He never sees these women for what they are." Louisa tipped her head back and closed her eyes.

After a few seconds of silence, Ethan gently laid a hand on Louisa's forearm. "Would you like me to call a cab?"

Opening her eyes, she looked down at his hand on her arm. She roughly jerked her arm away. "I remember you. You think I've forgotten, don't you?"

Ethan looked at her in confusion.

She wagged her finger at him. "I remember you hitting on me."

He shook his head.

"Don't deny it. You're just like all of the rest. I can't go anywhere without someone trying to take me home. I am a married woman. I'm not a cheater, not like some people." She shook her head sadly. "I'm not even safe at the office."

Grace watched transfixed as the other woman's eyes closed and her head began to bob forward. She slowly leaned to the side of the booth, eventually resting her head on Ethan's shoulder.

Ethan looked at Grace helplessly, before shrugging and tapping Louisa on the shoulder.

Louisa's head snapped up. She looked from Ethan to Grace and back. "How dare you touch me!"

Grace shook her head. "Louisa, we're just—"

She angrily turned to Grace. "Don't defend him." She leaned back in her seat, breathing heavily. "Unbelievable." Louisa slid out of the booth and walked to the other side. Sliding in next to Grace, she wrapped one long bony arm around Grace's shoulders and turned to a surprised Ethan. "And right in front of your poor girlfriend. You ought to be ashamed. Come on, Grace. I'm going to take you home." Louisa grabbed Grace's hand and dragged her out of the booth. "Poor thing."

Monday, December 5th

CHAPTER SEVEN

VALERIE POUNCED THE moment Grace settled into her office the next morning. "So," she said excitedly, pulling up a chair next to Grace's desk, "how did the date go?"

"Oh..." Grace said, throwing her pencil on the desk and looking up from her newest design, "definitely better than the last one."

Valerie smiled. "Oh, good."

"Yeah, no one died this time."

Valerie's smile fell. "That bad, huh?"

Grace nodded. "I went home with Louisa."

"What? Louisa? Louisa Straker Burns?" At Grace's nod, Valerie asked, "How did that happen?"

Grace quickly recounted what happened. "She couldn't remember her address, but I was finally able to wrestle the phone away from her sometime before midnight and call Daniel."

"Oh, I'm so sorry, Grace."

"I'm starting to think it's just not meant to be."

Valerie rolled her eyes. "You give up too easily. After all, this is only your second date, and like you said, no one died this time."

"True." Grace smiled. "He is very nice. We have a lot in common, too. I've never met anyone who knows as much about twelfth century puppetry as I do."

Valerie grimaced. "I thought we agreed that you wouldn't bring that up on your dates again."

"I know, but he really is interested in it, too."

Valerie looked at her doubtfully before shrugging. "Sounds like a match made in Heaven. When are you seeing him next?"

"We didn't really have time to make plans, but he mentioned something about going to a Renaissance Fair in a couple of weeks."

Valerie made a face. "I thought we agreed you wouldn't bring that up, either?"

"I didn't. He brought it up first."

They both looked at the door as Belle Dragovich pushed the door open and shyly stuck her head in. Grace motioned for her to come in.

"I'm sorry to interrupt," she said quickly.

Grace shook her head. "It's okay. Are you ready?"

"Yep," Belle said, twirling one long blonde strand around her finger.

"Where are you two going?" Valerie asked.

Grace stood up and shrugged into her suit jacket. "Downstairs. We're going to try to find our new assistant."

"From the toy shop?" Valerie smiled. "Does Henry Bourget know?"

"Who's Henry Bourget?" Belle asked.

"He's the manager of the toy shop," Grace answered. Turning to Valerie, she said warily, "I figured I would let him know, when I went down there? Why?"

Valerie crossed her arms and leaned back in her chair, a smile playing around her lips. "I would take some ear plugs. He makes our dear leader look like a pussycat. He's been complaining for the last three months about how he's short-staffed. He's not going to be happy about this."

Grace shrugged. "None of us are happy, why should he be any different? Besides, I'll just tell him that this order is coming from Straker himself. I'm sure he's dealt with Straker before. He'll understand that there's no use arguing."

* * * *

"Absolutely not! You just march back up there and tell Straker I said no." Bourget's face turned a deep shade of red, which only served to highlight the nasty purple bruise at his temple.

"Look—" Grace began, trying not to stare at the golf ball sized injury.

"No," Henry Bourget said as he walked out of his office and pointed to the inside of the store, "you look."

Grace stood up and walked over to the door. The store was stacked high with every toy imaginable: stuffed toys, mechanical toys, electronic toys, walking toys, talking toys, toys, toys and more toys. Pretty much, what you would expect in a toy store, Grace thought. "What am I supposed to be looking for?"

"How many employees do you see out there?"

Except for the clerk at the front opening the doors for the public, the only other employee she could see was an attractive young man decorating the large Christmas tree near the entrance. "Two."

"It's right before Christmas and he expects me to run the store with basically a skeleton staff. I'm not superman. There's only me, the assistant manager, and four others." He looked toward the store. "Actually, it's more like three others." He shook his head. "Has Straker lost his mind?"

"Can't you hire more?" Belle asked softly, twisting her hair into a knot.

"No, I can't, because Straker says that we are out of money. I don't know what's going on up there," he said, pointing to the ceiling, "but we are pulling in money hand over fist down here. October was our best month in over a year. November was just as good and I'm expecting December to be even bigger, but he says we're broke. What's happening up there?"

Grace looked towards the Christmas tree. The young man decorating the tree was busy climbing a ladder that he had propped against the tree. He swiftly climbed up the rungs, one-handed, while his other arm clutched five or six teddy bears to his body. "We're downsizing," Grace said slowly, distracted by the sight of the big tree swaying back and forth.

"Yeah, I know. I heard." Henry shut the door. "None of this makes any sense. Last year, I had over thirty workers for Christmas and we weren't making nearly as much as we are now. Those little space dolls have been flying off the shelves, but the way Straker has been acting in the last couple of months, it's as if we're going bankrupt. I don't understand it."

Grace sat back down next to Belle. "I don't know what's going on, I just know that I was told to hire from within."

He held up his hands. "Frankly, I don't care. I can't spare one more employ—"

Crash.

All heads turned to the door. Henry Bourget, who was closest to the door, opened it and peeked outside. He quickly closed it and dropped his chin to his chest. Taking a deep breath, he muttered, "Excuse me," before opening the door and walking out. Grace flinched slightly as the door slammed shut behind him.

Belle caught Grace's arm before she could stand up, and walk to the door. "What are we going to do? Maybe we should call Franklin?"

Grace quickly nixed that idea. Getting Franklin Straker involved in any situation usually just made things worse, not better.

"I know, why don't we hire Michael?" Belle asked excitedly.

"He's Harcourt's assistant."

"So? Michael's not happy working for him. In fact, he absolutely despises him."

Before Grace could ask who despises whom, the door opened and Henry walked in.

"Listen, Henry, I'm sorry that you're understaffed. I'm sure Straker wouldn't mind if you hired a new employee. If not, maybe we can work out a part time arrangement—"

Henry walked around the desk and sat down. "Nonsense. You know, I was thinking about your request and Straker is absolutely right. We should hire within."

Grace was taken aback by the man's sudden turnaround. Suspicious, she narrowed her eyes. "Really? That's great," she said slowly. "You said you have four employees? Can I see their employment files?"

He shook his head, quickly. "You know, I'm so ashamed of my behavior that I'm going to give you my best employee."

"Really?" Grace asked, even more suspicious than before.

"Absolutely. I mean this is a promotion up. I think my best employee should be the one to get it." He stood up and walked to the door.

"Still, I would like to see their files."

Henry opened the door. "I've already told him the good news."

Reluctantly, Grace stood up and walked to the door. Standing outside the door was the young man she had noticed decorating the tree. He was holding a piece of tissue to a small cut over his left eye with one hand and with the other, he was pulling tinsel out of his thick, wavy blond hair.

Grace glanced toward the front entrance and the tree now lying on its side.

"He's going to be a perfect fit for upstairs," Henry said, ushering Belle out of his door and closing it quickly behind her.

* * * *

Grace stood in her office doorway and watched as her new assistant opened each one of his desk drawers, as a small trickle of worry began to prick at her mind. He seemed intelligent, but also so very young. Grace shook her head. She couldn't be much older than him, she thought to herself in amusement.

Feeling a tendril of her red-gold hair escape her French twist, she reached up and tucked it back in place. He looked up at her suddenly and smiled brightly and she felt herself smiling back at him in turn. Suddenly, inexplicably self-conscious she turned away. He was definitely handsome, she thought, as she surreptitiously watched him out of the corner of her eye. Handsome, despite the horribly ill-fitting black shirt and khaki pants that denoted him as a Straker Toy Shop employee. "How long have you worked at the toy shop?"

"Oh, only for a few weeks." Kyle swiveled around in his desk chair. "I know they said that there was a chance of advancement, but I never thought it would happen this quickly. My dad's going to be psyched. He keeps telling me that I need to find a real job. I thought it would take years," he said, waving his arm around, accidentally sweeping the phone to the floor. He bent down and retrieved the phone. "I want to thank you, Ms. Holliday for giving me a chance." He laid the receiver into the cradle backwards. "I promise, you won't regret it. So…" he said hesitantly, "what exactly am I supposed to do?"

"Basically, help Belle and me, run errands, answer the phone, and make sure our office supplies are stocked."

"Oh, okay. That sounds easy," he said, sounding relieved. He swiveled around in his chair again. "Can I decorate my desk for Christmas?"

"Sure, it's about that time anyway. I have this two foot ceramic Christmas tree that I put out on my desk each year."

"Hmm. I could buy—"

"Oh, you don't have to buy anything. Go down to the supply closet on the second or third floor. You'll probably find something there."

"Won't they mind?"

"Have you been on the second or third floor lately?" She didn't bother waiting for a response. "It's like a ghost town. I think Straker has closed the second floor off completely. After you get settled in, try there first."

"Okay." Kyle opened a desk drawer and began rummaging through it. "So, what kind of toys do you design?"

"Right now, we're designing board games, so you'll help with that, too."

"Oh," he said, smiling brightly, "I can do that. What sort of board games are you designing?"

"Well, we're still in the development stage." Which was another way of saying she still wasn't sure.

The phone, next to his elbow, let out a shrill ring. "I love board games. My family used to play them all the time when I was a kid."

Grace glanced at the ringing phone.

"My favorite was *The Adventurous Mr. Walrus*. You start on an island."

Grace stepped forward and picked up the phone.

"Oh, wait, I think that was a video game, not a board game."

"Straker Toy Company," she said into the receiver, before realizing she had it upside down.

"No, the board game I liked was the one with all the murder suspects."

Righting the phone, she quickly said the company's name again, while fantasizing about gagging the man sitting at the desk in front of her.

She smiled, pleased to hear Ethan's voice on the other end of the line, asking if she would like to meet him for lunch at his gym.

She happily agreed. Reaching around Kyle, she reached into a drawer, took out a pen and a piece of paper, and wrote down the directions to the gym. Saying good-bye, she hung up the phone, a silly grin spreading across her face.

Kyle looked at her curiously, his handsome face set in a disappointed frown. "Business meeting?"

Grace shook her head, as she dashed to her office and picked up her coat and purse. "I'll be back in an hour," she called as she walked down the hallway towards the stairs.

Distractedly digging through her purse, she bumped into Allen.

Allen looked down the hallway towards Kyle's desk. "So, I see you went down to the toy store and hired your very own boy toy." Allen shook his head reproachfully. "Shame on you."

"I did not—" Grace stopped herself. "He's not a boy toy. He comes very highly recommended."

Catching their eye, Kyle waved from his desk.

"Admit it, you or blondie hired him based on his looks alone."

"No, we did not. Not that it's any of your business, but Henry Bourget recommended him."

Allen laughed. "Whatever you say."

Just as Grace started to walk away, Allen reached out to stop her. "Hey, I want to ask you some questions."

Grace smiled. "Why? Having trouble with your designs?"

"No," he sneered. "Of course not … I just wanted to know where you disappeared to between the first and second intermissions during the magic show."

* * * *

Ethan speared a pear with his fork. "That's a rather strange question. What did you tell him?"

"I told him that I was running late and had to go," pushing the plate of fruit around on her plate with her fork.

"Good, because I wouldn't talk to him about it."

"It's no secret. I've told most of the office I was running around backstage."

"Still, if you're right and Lily was killed, it's best not to say too much. Do you think Allen might be involved in her death?"

She scoffed. "Allen? No way."

"Why?"

"I've worked with him for over five years now. Trust me, I've seen his designs, and he couldn't design a ball, much less pull off a murder committed in front of over a hundred people. Besides, he was sitting in the audience when she fell."

"I do some criminal defense work, so never underestimate the determination of a cold-blooded killer. If he wanted her dead, he would have found a way to make it happen."

Grace had to admit he was right. "Of course, that's if she was murdered." She sighed. "To tell you the truth, I don't really know for certain. I could be wrong, but the whole thing just seems so odd. Lily just didn't seem like the type to kill herself. She didn't seem depressed."

He shrugged. "Some people hide it well."

"Yeah, but strange things have been happening at work." She shook her head and smiled. Here she was with a good looking, healthy, unattached man with a good job and all she could talk about was a murder that may or may not have happened. "I'm sorry, it's probably nothing."

He looked up from his fruit salad. "What strange things?"

Grace waved her hand around. "It's nothing." She glanced around at the new facility with its floor to ceiling windows, expensive stair climbers, treadmills, and other torture equipment. Leaning over the railing, she looked through the glass to the floor below and its Olympic-sized swimming pool. "Oh, I miss swimming."

"Why don't you join?" Ethan asked. "It has everything. A heated pool; the latest equipment; outdoor and indoor track; breakfast, lunch, and dinner. I practically live here." He made a face. "I hate my apartment."

"What's wrong with your apartment?"

"Too small; too old. The only good thing is that it's so close to here." He leaned forward excitedly. "You know if you got a membership, we could meet every day before work and commute together."

She shook her head. "Too far away, besides it's a little too much out of my price range."

"I can bring a guest." He smiled. "How about Saturday and we'll make a day of it?"

Thinking of all the possibilities the weekend might hold, Grace nodded excitedly.

"Excellent." He pushed his plate away and smiled affectionately at her. "Now, what strange things have been happening at work?"

She sighed. "I didn't get a chance to tell you last night; Belle Dragovich has come to work for us."

His mouth fell open. "The magician's daughter?"

"She's Lily's goddaughter."

"And she suddenly decided she wanted to become a toy designer?"

"Yeah. It does seem a bit strange to me too. That's not all. Straker has cut down our work force to almost nothing. I have a feeling it has something to do with Lily's death."

"Do you think Straker may have killed her? The police usually suspect the husband first."

She shook her head. "You heard Louisa last night. This is the man's fifth marriage, why would he kill this one? If he had wanted her gone, he would've just divorced her like the others."

Smiling, he leaned in conspiratorially. "You want to hear my theory?"

She quickly nodded.

"It's got to be Ilya Dragovich."

"Why?"

"He had means, motive, and opportunity." He lightly rapped his knuckles on the table. "You know, I think if we put our heads together, we could figure out who killed your boss' wife."

She looked back out at the pool. "*If* she was murdered. There's a very good chance that I'm wrong. An excellent chance actually. I mean her death was ruled a suicide. They must have some proof to make them believe that. I heard she left a letter."

"Something must have made you suspicious. Maybe you saw something and didn't realize what you saw."

She shook her head.

"Did you see anything strange when you were backstage?"

"Well, Louisa's husband, Daniel Burns, was running around backstage."

"He was?"

"I saw him in a dressing room with one of the magician's assistants. I think her name was Tabitha."

"That's interesting." He leaned forward. "Anything else?"

"Belle Dragovich seemed annoyed with Lily. I don't know. Being annoying is not enough to kill someone. If it was, most of the people in rush hour would be murdered."

He smiled. "True. What about that magician? She used to work with him, correct? Did you notice anything strange between them?"

"Things did seem rather intense between them."

"How so?"

She shrugged. "I wasn't there long enough really to get a good idea, but I heard her tell him that they needed to talk."

"That sounds serious. Do you think they might have been having an affair?"

Grace debated telling him about finding the underwear and Lily's pendant in his dressing room after Lily claimed she had never been in the room before, but decided against it. In her opinion, Lily did seem genuinely confused about the whole thing. She glanced at the clock on the wall and quietly swore. She was late. Apologizing, she slid out of her seat and dashed to the door.

* * * *

"What did you do?" Valerie asked, as Grace walked past her door.

Grace turned back around and stepped into Val's office. "Nothing. Why?"

"Straker has been yelling for you for over the last hour. He wants to see you right now."

A sick feeling of dread came over her. "Why?"

"I don't know, but you better get in there. Don't forget your holy water and crucifix. It's going to be that kind of day. Oh, and cancel any plans you have for the weekend?"

"Why?"

"I don't know, but I overheard him tell Belle that you would be happy to help her Saturday. Oh, and before I forget, your new assistant blew the breaker to your office and almost burned down the building. It looks like Santa exploded over there. An electrician should be here soon. Good luck," Valerie said, opening Straker's door and pushing her forward.

CHAPTER EIGHT

"So, I HEARD you tell Valerie that you think my wife was murdered."

Grace froze. Stammering, she began apologizing profusely. "I shouldn't have said anything. I understand she left a letter. I don't know why—"

"Well, you're right. She was murdered. She didn't commit suicide." Straker pulled out a piece of paper from his desk and handed it to her. "I received this by text, less than a minute before she…" He looked to the side, blinking rapidly. Clearing his throat, he said. "Less than a minute before she fell."

Averting her eyes, Grace focused on the piece of paper in front of her.

I hate you. I despise everything about you. You've humiliated me once too often. Well, no more. You've charmed everyone around you.

Grace looked up at the man scowling at her. She quickly looked down and continued reading.

But, tonight, everyone will see the pain your cruelty can cause. Happy Birthday, darling! Hopefully, you'll be joining me soon.

"When did you receive this?" Grace asked.

"A few seconds before she fell. I know my wife and she would never have killed herself. If she hated me, she would have gone after *me*, but she wouldn't have hurt herself, never. Someone murdered her."

"But the police are convinced it was a suicide?"

"They found her phone up on the scaffolding after she died. They think she texted that note to me, wrapped the silk around her neck and jumped."

"How well do you know the other magician's assistant? Tabitha something or other."

"I've heard Lily talk about her. Why do you ask?"

Grace shrugged. "When I was backstage, Lily complained of losing her phone. Belle thought Tabitha might have picked it up."

Straker shook his head. "Belle already mentioned that to me. Tabitha said she handed it back to my wife right before she went up to the scaffolding."

"Did Belle see her hand it back?"

"No, but I don't think she killed Lily. She might have assisted in some way, perhaps, unknowingly, but I don't think she killed her."

"Why?"

"I think it's someone from this office. Someone tried to kill her before Halloween. Last May, Lily fell down an escalator. She said someone bumped into her. She wasn't hurt, so she picked herself up and came home. I didn't think much about it when she told me. A few weeks after that someone pushed her in front of a truck. Luckily, I was able to pull her back."

"Did you see who pushed her?"

"No, there were a lot of people standing around, but no one saw anything. I wrote it off as a freak accident. A couple of days after that, Lily became violently ill after having lunch with me. I figured it was just a mild case of food poisoning, but then she started getting sick whenever she ate with me. Then there was an incident with the horse."

"The horse?"

"A good friend of hers owns a stable. Lily always enjoyed riding, because she said it calmed her. The last time she went riding, her favorite horse threw her. They discovered a tack underneath his saddle."

"And she had no idea who—"

"Oh yes, she had an idea," he said angrily. "Me. She blamed me. She thought I was trying to kill her, so I could run off with my mistress."

Grace wasn't sure how to respond. She was simply surprised that he could not only find five women to marry him but a mistress, as well.

"I told her she was crazy. I didn't have a mistress, but she was convinced that I was cheating on her. I told her that, even if I were cheating, I certainly wouldn't need to kill her. I have a team of lawyers at my beck and call."

"Ah, and somehow that didn't reassure her?"

"This wasn't my first time at the rodeo, to use language you're familiar with."

"Thank you. That helps."

"We had a prenup. If I wanted her gone, I would simply have divorced her."

"Did you tell her that?"

"Of course, but she didn't believe me. She ran off to Europe to think, she said. That's when the letters started coming in."

"What letters?"

Straker reached into his desk drawer and pulled out a folder. Dumping the contents on the desk, he pushed them toward her. There were five letters in all; two on stationary and three email printouts. Grace picked the letters up and began reading.

"I'll save you some time. They all say the same thing. My wife was cheating on me with Ilya Dragovich. According to my *concerned friend*, Lily and Ilya have been having an affair for decades."

Grace threw the letters back on the desk. "Do you think they were?"

He shrugged. "It wouldn't necessarily come as a shock, but I wasn't going to do anything without speaking to her first. I ended up flying over there. Do you know how much a flight from New York to Germany costs this time of year?"

Grace shook her head.

"Anyway, I confronted her and she denied it. I didn't really expect her to admit to the affair, but then she accused me of sleeping with you."

"What? Me? What? How is that even possible?" she sputtered outraged.

"Yes, I thought it was ridiculous, too. That's when she brought out her own letters, also from a *concerned friend.*" He reached into the drawer again, pulled out another letter, and handed it to Grace.

The letter was similar in tone as to the other five, direct and to the point. Grace felt her face flush at the mention of her name.

"That's when we realized that someone was trying to tear us apart."

"When did this happen?"

"Three months ago."

"Do you know who was sending these letters? Any idea?"

"She thought it might have been Dragovich. She admitted to me that he was in love with her, but I don't think he would do something like this. It's just not his style."

"Why didn't she come home with you three months ago?"

"She was afraid that whoever was sending these letters was going to try to kill her again. I told her she was being ridiculous." To Grace's surprise, he looked ashamed.

"Did you show these letters to the police?"

"And hand them a motive for my killing her? Absolutely not. They'll say I killed her in a jealous rage or so that I could run off with my mistress. Do you know how long they questioned me? The only thing that saved me was the fact that I didn't even know she was going to be on stage that night and this note." He pointed to the suicide note. "Right now, they're confident that she committed suicide. If I show them these letters, they might start to suspect me."

"But what about those accidents with the horse and on the escalator? Surely, the police thought—"

Straker shook his head. "She didn't report them when they happened. I tried to tell them, but they just said that sometimes accidents happen."

"And you have no idea who wanted to hurt her?"

"No, but I believe that it's someone from this office."

"Why? None of the attempts on her life happened here. The first one was on the escalator, the second on the street, another at a horse farm. Surely, if it was someone at the office, she would have recognized them."

"Not necessarily. There were always a lot of people around, but that day she got sick was during Daniel's birthday party in June. The only people here were office staff."

"Did she go to the hospital that night?"

"No."

"Then you're assuming that she was poisoned, but you don't know for certain."

"No one else got sick."

"Flu?"

"That wasn't the only time she got sick and it was always when she had something to eat here."

"You still need to speak to the police."

He shook his head. "I'm not handing them a noose."

"Did it occur to you that you may have been threatened? 'Hopefully, you'll be joining me soon,'" she repeated, "That sounds like a threat to me."

He scoffed. "Who would want to kill me? Everyone loves me."

Grace resisted pointing out the multiple death threats from disgruntled employees shouted at him as they packed up their desk and left the building. "Still, even the most lovable people can pick up an enemy or two—or twenty."

"I'm not afraid. Besides, no one's tried to kill me. They went after her, not me."

Grace looked at her boss in confusion. "So, why are you telling me all of this?"

"I want you to figure out who killed her."

Grace's mouth dropped open. "You've got to be kidding?"

"No, I'm not kidding. Go out there. Ask questions. I want a daily report of your activities. I want to know who you talked to and what they said."

"Why me?"

"You've got some experience with this sort of thing."

The confusion must have registered on her face, because he quickly added, "Didn't they teach you how to investigate crimes in your criminal justice classes?"

"It was one class and no they did not."

Straker looked at her in disgust. "I'm not asking for a lot. I'm just asking you to talk to your co-workers. It's not like that isn't something out of the ordinary for you. You're always gabbing with everyone in the office when you ought to be working. Now you can add in a few extra questions."

"Such as?"

"You could ask how they felt about Lily for a start."

"And then you want me to report back?"

"That's what I'm paying you for."

"You're paying me to create toys for your business. My job description doesn't say anything about playing detective or spying on my coworkers."

His eyes narrowed. "Really? Well, I'll make sure to add it in for the next person I hire."

"But, I'm flexible," she quickly added. "I'll nose around for you, but I don't know what you expect me to find. Why don't you hire an actual detective? There must be thousands in this city."

Straker opened his desk drawer. Pulling out a handful of folders, he slammed them on the desk in front of her. "Here are ten of those so called detectives' reports."

Grace picked up the first one and began leafing through the file. She stopped when she came to her name. "What is this? I don't remember speaking to a detective."

"Remember that new intern that we hired three weeks ago and then fired a week later. He was one of them."

Well, that explained the larger than normal turnover in staff they had been experiencing lately. That, and the very large men who wandered in and out of the office delivering mail. "And?"

"Ten completely different reports, which say absolutely nothing. They don't have any idea. They don't know who sent the letters. They don't know who tried to kill her six months ago. And they don't know who killed her last month."

"They have no suspects?"

"Oh, they have suspects. All different."

"Was one of them Ilya Dragovich?"

"Yeah."

Grace pointed to the letters. "How do you know that those letters aren't legitimate?"

"That's what the others asked. I don't know for certain. I believed Lily when she said that she and Dragovich hadn't been together in years. Maybe I'm a fool, but I'm not so foolish to believe he would kill his lover in front of hundreds of people using one of his own tricks. Dragovich can be rather ruthless, but he's not stupid. No, it has to be someone else. Someone from this office."

"Then our most obvious suspects are Harcourt or Michael."

"Why them?"

"They're the only ones who work here and would have even the slightest bit of knowledge of how these illusions work."

"Not necessarily. Lily's killer might have had help. They may have paid one of Dragovich's people off. Like Tabitha, for instance. She was there that night and could have helped."

"Or Belle. Is that why Belle is here? She was there that night, too."

Straker smiled. "It's not Belle. She would never have hurt Lily. Lily was like a mother to her after her own mother died. No, I trust Belle implicitly."

Grace picked up another file. "Who were their other suspects?"

"One was convinced that you killed her."

"Me?" she asked in surprise. "Why?"

"He thought you might have sent the letter to Lily in the hopes that you could have me for yourself. He thought your being part of the act was suspicious, too."

"That's ridiculous."

"That's what I thought. You're actually the only one from the office that I believe wouldn't have killed her."

"I'm flattered, but may I ask why?"

"You're from Iowa."

Grace sat back in her chair. Before she could ask what that could possibly have to do with anything and point out that she was from Colorado, Louisa walked in.

Tuesday, December 6th

CHAPTER NINE

GRACE SAT IN her office and stared at the rain coming down in sheets past her window. She had spent all night thinking about her new job duties. She had no idea how to proceed. Lily hadn't been the friendliest of people and if she was anything like her husband, she probably had enemies lined up outside the door. Still, she couldn't see anyone from the office sitting around plotting her death.

She reached for her phone. Maybe Valerie could help. She quickly dialed her extension and asked her to come to her office.

Tearing off a large sheet of paper and throwing it in the garbage, she leaned over her design board and drew a rough sketch of the theater. Valerie had arrived by the time she finished drawing a couple of rows of seats.

Valerie stood next to her. "What are you doing?"

"Where was everyone sitting when I was doing my impression of Alice in Wonderland?"

Valerie looked at her curiously, and shrugged.

"The last time I saw Lily must have been right around the beginning of the second intermission," Grace said. "You had a good view of everyone. Do you remember where everyone was after the first intermission and before the second?"

A half-smile played around Valerie's lips. "Let's see. After you left me, I went into the theater and sat next to Straker. All of the toy shop employees were sitting in their seats." She gazed down at the crude drawing of the theater. With her index finger, she pointed out everyone's position. "Allen, Michael, and Harcourt were sitting together in your row."

"Did any of them leave?"

Valerie shook her head. "Only Allen. He ended up being called to the stage. You should have seen it, Grace. It was the funniest thing I had ever seen. I was thinking, we should get together and pay Dragovich to teach us how to hypnotize Allen. He was like a completely different person on stage."

"What did he do after he left the stage?"

"Nothing. He came back and sat down…" Valerie tilted her head to the side. "I think he left sometime after that. You know, I don't remember seeing him after you disappeared in that chest."

"What about Louisa and Daniel?"

"Louisa was sitting next to Straker. She showed up in the middle of the first intermission and fell asleep a few seconds later. Daniel showed up a few minutes after you did." Valerie grimaced and shook her head.

"What?" Grace asked, wondering about her friend's strange expression.

"She woke up after you went up on the stage. It was horrible. They sat there bickering the whole time until Straker told them to be quiet."

"What were they fighting about?"

"I don't know, but Louisa was furious. She kept asking him, where had he been? What had he been doing? If he got Straker's surprise all ready, like a good son-in-law. She just would not shut up."

"So, they weren't paying attention to my great performance. I'm shocked."

"They weren't the only ones. Harcourt was just as bad."

"Why? What did he do?"

"You know Sidney. He spent most of the night criticizing the show. He wasn't exactly quiet about it, either." She pointed to their position on the drawing. "He was sitting next to Allen in your row." She tapped at the drawing. "No, I'm certain Allen wasn't in his seat. I don't think I saw him for the rest of the night."

"What about Ethan?"

Valerie smiled. "Poor guy. He just sat there looking for you. If I thought Straker would have let me go, I would have been happy to keep him company."

Smirking, Grace wrote his name in the space provided. "Besides Allen, did you see anyone else leave after I got dragged up to the stage?"

Valerie softly shook her head. "Now that I think of it, Michael left too, but he was only gone for a few minutes. He was definitely back in his seat when Lily fell. It was so strange."

"What was?"

"His reaction. At first, we all thought it was part of the show, but when they closed the curtains, everyone in the audience started to talk at once. Several people screamed. People started to stand. Others got up and walked to the stage. Michael just sat there, staring at the floor. It was just strange. He had no reaction at all."

"That's interesting."

Valerie smirked. "I wouldn't say that. I really wasn't paying that much attention to him. I was trying to watch over Straker. Michael might have just been in shock for those few seconds I was watching him."

"Still, it was strange enough to get your attention." Grace put a question mark next to Michael's seat. "So, everyone, except Allen and I were sitting in the audience when Lily was murdered—"

"Wow, you are really taking this seriously." Valerie laughed. "Ah, I know what you're doing. You've been deputized."

Grace looked at her in surprised. "Straker told you?"

"No, I just guessed. I hate to break it to you, but you're not the first. He's already made Allen the new house detective in charge of office security."

"House detective? Allen? Well, that explains why Allen was questioning me about my whereabouts, yesterday."

"Hmm, I got the third degree, yesterday, too. I don't think I was much help." Valerie smiled. "Allen's very proud of his new title. So, what kind of title did you get?"

Grace shook her head. "Nothing."

"Well, don't feel bad. I didn't get anything either. Honestly, Grace. Everyone thinks she committed suicide. The police detectives, the private investigators Straker hired. Everyone."

Grace quickly filled her in on what she learned from Straker. "I agree with him. Someone killed her and they're going to get away with it if something isn't done."

"Well, if she was murdered, then my money's on Belle. I think she's just a little too much like Lily."

"Belle's a sweetheart," Grace protested.

"I think it's an act. I think she killed Lily, so she could have Straker."

Grace burst out laughing. "Don't be ridiculous," she spat out between big gulps of air.

Valerie smiled. "Stranger things have happened. Besides, she was acting very odd yesterday."

"What happened?"

"She disappeared for an hour while you were having lunch with Ethan. I caught her and your new assistant in the hallway closet near the elevator."

"Kyle? What were they doing?"

"They *said* they were looking for Christmas decorations."

"Maybe they were."

"In the dark?"

"Was this before or after he blew the breaker?"

"Before."

Grace had to admit that was a bit strange. "Maybe the light was broken."

"I don't think so," she said in a sing-song voice.

"But they just met yesterday morning."

Valerie shrugged. "She's a very friendly girl."

"Hmm. Belle couldn't be the killer. She was standing right next to me when Lily fell from the scaffolding. You know, Ethan suspects Ilya Dragovich."

"He's my second suspect. He and Lily have been having an affair for years, maybe they had a lover's quarrel, and he killed her."

Grace shook her head. "You can't take the letters Straker received as the absolute truth. Those letters were designed to break them apart. Don't forget that Lily received letters accusing Straker of having an affair, too and those weren't true." She shuddered. "Definitely not."

"Straker's letters may have been a lie, but hers were not. Grace, I'm telling you, she was having an affair with Ilya Dragovich and it had been going on since Straker married her. She didn't even try to hide it. I can prove it, too." She motioned for Grace to follow her out into the hallway.

They passed by Kyle who was sitting at his desk, playing with a hula dancing Santa. The multi-colored lights of over a thousand Christmas lights surrounded him, giving him an almost ethereal glow. He waved and smiled at her as she walked past.

Once they reached Valerie's office, she held up her finger to her lips and tiptoed to her filing cabinet next to her desk. Valerie thumbed through the drawers before bringing out a folder marked Lily's Expenses. Opening the folder, she showed Grace five checks, written from Lily Straker to Dragovich.

"Over fifty thousand dollars in the last year," she whispered, looking over her shoulder at Straker's office.

Picking up the last check, Grace narrowed her eyes. "Her writing is atrocious. I can't tell if that is a three or a five."

"That's not including the men's jewelry she's bought." Valerie brought out a receipt for a twenty thousand dollar watch.

"I guess this wasn't for Straker."

"He wears a cheap knock off that he got off the street. He paid five dollars for it, and brags about the thing." Valerie pushed the papers around. She handed a few more to Grace. "Look at these. Armani. Dolce & Gabbana. Hugo Boss. You see what the man wears every day. He has three suits and two of them have been here longer than we have, combined."

"How are you getting all of these receipts?"

"I have to take care of their personal bills, too. See, here is her credit card statement. Look at these purchases."

Grace glanced down at the statement, not sure what she should be looking for. Most of the purchases were at restaurants throughout Europe. "Okay."

"Now look at the dates and the places."

"All right, but what about them?"

Valerie sat down at her computer. With a couple of keystrokes, she brought up Dragovich's tour dates, but for a couple of exceptions, the dates and places matched the dates and places on Lily's credit card statement. Just in the last six months alone, Lily was in the same city at the same time as Ilya Dragovich at least fifteen times.

"Does Straker know about all of these purchases?"

Valerie looked sadly at Grace. "I don't know, but maybe. It's not like she was trying to hide her affair. She was brazen about it."

"Hello." Grace looked up to see Ethan standing at the door, with water dripping from his hair and his face. She glanced outside and saw that it was pouring. Streams of water covered the window and a flash of lightning lit up the sky.

Grace dropped the receipts down on Valerie's desk, as she returned his greeting. "What are you doing here?"

"I had some free time, so I thought I'd ask you to lunch. Are you busy?"

"No," Grace quickly reassured him, "not busy at all."

"You two seemed like you were involved in a serious conversation," he said, removing his raincoat.

Valerie picked up the folders and stuffed them back into the filing cabinet. "We were just talking about Lily Straker."

"Ah, the case." He rubbed his hands together excitedly. "Anything new?"

Grace filled him in on her new position within the company.

Ethan laughed. "So, you've been promoted to house detective."

"No, technically Allen has that title," Valerie said with a smile.

Thunder crashed overhead, as the lights dimmed and finally went out, plunging them in darkness.

Ethan walked over to the window. "The street lights are still working."

Grace joined him at the window. "The slightest little thing knocks the electricity out over here."

Craning his neck, he looked towards the buildings across the street. "No one else's is out. Don't you have a generator?"

Valerie sat down behind her desk. "Don't worry; they'll come back on soon."

Ethan looked around at the darkened office. "How long does it usually last?"

Grace shrugged. "A few minutes to a few hours. It just depends."

"Well, that means you're free for a while," Ethan said. "Why don't we all go over to my office and order lunch in?"

Valerie brought out a couple of candles and set them on top of her desk. "Our boss has a very practical outlook on electricity. As long as it's daylight and we have candles, we can still work."

Grace nodded. "If it was good enough for Abraham Lincoln, it's good enough for us," she said in a gruff imitation of Straker's voice.

"You two have to eat, so I'm sure he won't mind if you take an early lunch while the power's out," Ethan said.

"You've never met Franklin Straker, have you?" Valerie asked.

Ethan shook his head. "I can't imagine that he would care."

Grace looked over towards the window as another flash of lightning lit up the sky. Not feeling like hopping over puddles and looking like a drowned cat in the process, she said, "Let's wait until the storm lets up, anyway."

Ethan turned away from the window, reached into his pocket and brought out his cell phone. "The little sandwich shop around the corner delivers." His handsome face grimaced when his phone call failed.

"Cell phones don't really work well here," Valerie said. "You can usually get a signal downstairs."

"Sometimes in the hallway closet, too." Grace snapped her fingers and turned to Valerie. "Maybe that's what they were doing," she said, still not convinced Belle and Kyle were using the coat closet as their personal hotel room.

"Well, that's okay," Ethan said. "We can call from here. Can I use your phone?"

Valerie shook her head. "The phones are connected through the internet. When the internet goes out, so do the phones."

Grace sat in the chair next to Valerie's desk. "Occasionally, working here is like stepping through to another dimension. It's best just to sit back and take it all in stride."

Their heads glanced up at the overhead brass chandelier as the lights flickered before finally stabilizing. "Ah, see I knew it wouldn't last long," Valerie said with a smile.

Straker pushed open the connecting door between his and Valerie's offices. His gaze bounced from Valerie to Grace before finally settling on Ethan. "Who are you?"

Ethan held out his hand. "Ethan Martin."

Straker glared at him. "Do you work here?"

Ethan dropped his hand. "No. I work across the street. I was going to take Grace and Valerie out to lunch."

Straker purposely glanced at his watch. "It's 10:50."

"An early lunch?"

"What do you do for a living?"

"I'm an attorney."

"That explains it," he said gruffly. "I don't have lunch until noon, so come back then. I don't want anything fancy. The deli across the street will be fine."

"Well, I… I…" Ethan stammered.

Grace hid a smile.

"Since you're planning on taking half of my office out to lunch, I just assumed I was invited, too." Straker smiled at Ethan's shocked expression. "Twelve o'clock exactly, and don't be late," he said, slamming his office door behind him.

Still smiling, Grace pointed to the office door. "That was Franklin Straker."

* * * *

Grace laid her *History of Game Design* book on her desk and walked over to her large flip presentation board. Picking up a pen, she began writing potential character names for her board game down. She got to the third character before stopping. The only names that were coming to her were the possible suspects in Lily's murder.

Flipping over the paper, she began writing down her co-worker's names and possible motives. She was so engrossed in writing out Louisa's motives that she didn't hear Kyle walk up behind her.

"You can add gambling to your list."

Grace jumped three feet in the air. Quickly, she brought the paper down, covering her list. "I'm sorry, Kyle, did you need something?"

"I wanted to tell you that I color-coded and re-filed all of your files, like you asked me to."

"Good, thank you." Smiling, she turned around and faced him. Her breath caught in her throat. She had been so busy that she hadn't really paid much attention to him since she arrived at work that morning and found him sitting behind his desk. If it was true that clothes made the man, it was doubly so for Kyle. Gone was the oversized toy shop uniform. He now wore slim-fitting black pants and a tailored royal blue shirt that matched the color of his eyes and accentuated his broad chest. Even his hair had undertaken a transformation. It was now cut shorter and brushed back away from his face, making him seem older than he had the day before.

He looked over her head at the board behind her. "You think Lily Straker was murdered too?"

She cleared her throat. "It's just a theory—"

"Louisa has a gambling problem."

"How do you know that?"

He shrugged. "They talk about all of you in the toy store."

"They do?" Grace asked in surprise. "What do they say about me?"

"They like you, but they think you're kind of standoffish," he said with a shrug. "Jackie, the assistant manager, is convinced that you're sleeping with Mr. Straker."

"What?" she asked, her voice rising to a shrill pitch. "Where is this rumor coming from?"

Kyle waved his hand dismissively. "That's just the way Jackie is. She thinks everyone is sleeping with the boss. She was kind of suspicious of your sudden promotion after Mrs. Straker's death."

"I've been here for ten years, so I was due a promotion. Besides, Allen was promoted along with me; does Jackie think he was sleeping with the boss too?" Grace crossed her arms and turned back to her board. "We really shouldn't be paying any attention to such ridiculous rumors anyway."

"They can't stand Allen."

Grace pivoted around, pulled up her stool, and motioned for Kyle to take a seat. "What else do they say?"

"They say he's a stuck-up egomaniac with the intelligence of one of his toy muscle-man action figures and the emotional self-control of a thirteen year old girl."

"Hmm. I didn't realize how perceptive they were down at the toy store. Well, except for Jackie," she said quickly. "What else do they say about Allen?"

Kyle smiled. "They call him Caligula behind his back."

"You're kidding?" Unbidden, a vision of a debauched Roman orgy, with Allen in the center, flashed through her mind. She shuddered, quickly blocking out the image. "Never mind. I don't think I want to know anymore."

He started to rise.

"What else did they say about Louisa?"

"Oh, not much. They kind of feel sorry for Louisa. Daniel's been cheating on her for years. He was seeing Jackie on the side for a few months, but then dropped her three months ago for some new girl."

"Another girl at the toy store?"

He shook his head. "No. No one knows who, but it's not someone who works here."

"What do they think about Lily's death?"

"They think she killed herself."

Grace leaned back against her design table, a bit disappointed. "Why do they think that?"

"They said she left a note. I overheard a couple of the women say that they would have done the same if they had been married to Straker." Nervously, Kyle ran a hand through his blond hair. "The real big rumor is that the company is going down. I hope not, I really need this job."

"Henry was sort of hinting around about that."

"He thinks Louisa has gambled the profits away. Mr. Bourget went down to Atlantic City for his birthday last year and saw Louisa there. According to him, he watched her lose over twenty thousand dollars in less than an hour. When he tried to get her to go home, she accused him of hitting on her and security had to get involved."

"What about Lily? Did they have any good rumors on her?"

"They thought she was going to divorce Mr. Straker because of his affair with you. Now they just think she hung herself because of your affair."

Grace closed and opened her mouth. Finally finding her voice she declared, "I am not, have not, will not ever have an affair with Straker. Where—what—how could anyone think—"

"What are you yelling about?" Belle asked, pushing open the door and walking in.

Kyle shrugged. "I was just telling her about how her affair—"

Grace quickly interrupted. So far, that rumor was just confined to the lower floors of the company, hopefully, she could keep it from going any further. "We were just talking about our new board game."

"Oh, goodie." Pulling up a chair next to Kyle, Belle began rattling off questions.

Grace held her hands up. "We just started going over the character names."

Belle glanced at the presentation board. "Felicia Fatale, Marcus Money, Penelope Fairplay," she read. "Oh, that's so cute. Is this for the mystery game?"

Grace nodded. "Straker expressly mentioned a mystery game, so we're going to start with this one first. I was thinking though, we might use your expertise on our next game, Belle."

Belle sat up straighter. "Really? How so?"

"Well, I thought—" She closed her mouth, suddenly uncertain whether her idea of a magic game would be warmly accepted, based on Belle's declaration the day before.

"What is it?" Belle asked. "Come on, you can tell me."

Grace shook her head. "Never mind, let's just stick with the mystery for now."

"No, please tell me. What were you going to say?"

"It's not important." Grace waved her hand around. "I was just thinking we could design a trivia game and possibly a game around some type of entertainment," she hedged.

Kyle raised his hand. "What about a zombie game—"

Grace shook her head.

Kyle smiled. "Zombies are in."

"He's right," Belle said, "they're very popular nowadays."

Grace groaned. The last thing she wanted was to spend the next few months deep in zombie research. She doubted Straker would approve such a game, but he was so contrary sometimes. "I'll think about it. Do you have any other ideas?"

Kyle turned to Belle. "Hey, you're a magician, right? Why don't you do something with that?"

Belle's face lit up. "That's a great idea! I would love to do something that incorporates magic."

Grace looked back at their eager faces. Well, I guess the prohibition against magic is over, Grace thought in amusement. "That's a great idea."

Belle leaned forward. "Could we do that next?"

Grace nodded. "We can work on it at the same time, if you like."

"I have a great idea. I'm going to go to my office and write down some ideas," Belle said, jumping to her feet and walking to the door.

Kyle stood up as well and walked to the board. "Where's the detective's name?"

Grace pointed to Penelope Fairplay's name.

"Is she a private detective?"

"I thought about it, but I think I'm going to make her a police officer. Maybe," she said, picking up her pen and writing next to the character's name, "a U.S. Marshal. How does that look? Marshal Penelope Fairplay."

"Is this a girl's game?"

"No, it's for both boys and girls."

He made a face.

"What? Don't you like the name?"

"Sure, I was just thinking the detective should have a stronger name. Especially, if you're going to make her a U.S. Marshal. Marshal Penelope Fairplay just doesn't sound like a name that would strike fear into the heart of a dangerous murderer. It's just a bit too cutesy."

"It's for kids."

"It's for teenagers and there is a big difference. If you want boys to play this, you need to toughen the characters up."

"Well, I'm open to suggestions."

"How about naming her Marshal Senet Grant?"

"Senet?"

"Yeah, I've been doing some reading on board games. Senet was the name of the first board game."

"I don't think—"

The lights began flickering.

Grace looked out the window, surprised to see that the rain clouds had finally passed by.

"See, the ghost agrees with me," Kyle said with a grin.

Grace did a double take. "The ghost?"

Kyle looked around. "Didn't you know? This place is haunted."

Grace scoffed. "Who told you that?"

"Jackie. She won't even come up here anymore."

"Hmm, I think you should stop listening to Jackie. I've been here for ten years and I haven't seen anything strange."

They both looked up as the lights flickered and then shattered, causing glass, and sparks to fly over the room.

Kyle pushed her head down and shielded her from most of the sparks. When the light fixture stopped sparking, he let go of her head and looked at her, one eyebrow carefully arched.

Undaunted, she said, "Coincidence."

Wednesday, December 7th

CHAPTER TEN

"AH, THE LAND of forgotten toys." Kyle picked up a dusty baby doll. "So, this is where they all come to die." He looked around the dimly lit, dirty attic above the Straker Toy Company and made a face before pulling the string attached to the doll's back. The toy let out a plaintive, "I love you."

Grace suppressed a yawn. She had spent most of the night before tossing and turning. All she could think about were Straker's letters and Lily's supposed suicide note. She finally fell into a restless sleep somewhere around four-thirty, only to be awoken by the telephone ringing an hour later. It was just as well. Lily's death had seeped into her dreams. She could still see Dream Lily hanging over her bed, pointing an accusing finger at her. "I know you're trying to steal my husband." In her dream, Grace turned away, only to find Straker lying next to her. "This isn't my first time at a rodeo," Dream Straker said. Grace shuddered. What a horrible nightmare.

"Play with me," the doll said, as its string retracted once again.

Grace spared just a second to glance at Kyle and the doll before looking up at a row of boxes stacked on top of one another. She sighed heavily. "I can't see a thing. Did you bring that flashlight with you?"

Nodding, Kyle set the doll down on top of a box and handed her a flashlight.

She aimed the light at the top row of boxes. "I'm betting it's in one of those," she said snapping off the light and handing the flashlight back to her assistant. With Kyle's help, she pushed an old sturdy desk closer to the boxes and climbed on top. "It is kind of depressing, isn't it?"

He let go of her hand and reached for the doll again. He pulled its string. Its childlike voice abruptly slowed and deepened as the string retracted. "We'll be best friends forever and ever," it said in a suddenly creepy, deep mechanical voice.

Kyle quickly tossed the doll to the side. "Why, exactly, did you bring me to Mephistopheles' toy chest?"

She smiled down at him. "We used to sell a mystery board game in the fifties called *All the Murderers*." She shoved aside a box marked TOY CARS. "We didn't sell it for long. The Parental Committee on Un-American Activities protested. They objected to the rampant violence in the game, all because a few characters were drawn and quartered. It must be tame by today's standards." Grace handed a box down to Kyle. She suppressed a sneeze, as a cloud of dust passed by her nose. "Maybe we could revamp it a bit."

Kyle looked around at the rows of furniture and boxes. The expanse of the attic seemed to encompass the entire top floor of the building. "This is going to take forever."

Grace shoved aside another box. "No, it won't. There's actually a system up here. It's like geology. The deeper you go, the further you travel into the past." She pointed to the far end of the attic. "That would be the 1910s. That life-sized harlequin standing next to the elevator—"

"If it moves, you're on your own," he said, staring at the puppet intently.

"That's the twenties. That huge model of a bomber should be the thirties." Grace looked around at all the baby dolls lying on the desks, hanging from the rafters, and poking out of boxes. "If I'm right, we should be in the fifties. That's when our doll line took off. We just need to find a box labeled board games, discontinued or maybe murderers." She hopped off the desk and climbed onto another. Carefully making her way through the dolls, cowboys, trains, cars and model rocket ships lying around, she climbed over an old filing cabinet. "I think I see—"

"Shh."

She looked back down. Kyle was staring at the far corner of the attic. "What's wrong?"

He shook his head. "I thought I heard something."

Grace looked down at his feet. "Mice?"

He shrugged. "I wouldn't be surprised. This place is creepy. I think I'd rather—Hey, a Red Ranger Razor Rocket Launcher!" He quickly climbed over a couple of old desk chairs and a broken chandelier. Standing on his toes, he reached up for the toy which was perched on the top shelf of a metal bookcase filled with toy guns and weapons. "I haven't seen one of these in years." He jumped high in the air, his fingers just grazing the object of his affection. The metal bookcase shifted slightly as he brushed against it.

"What are you doing?" she asked worriedly.

Kyle reached over and picked up a box lying next to the desk. "Would Straker let me take the rocket launcher home?" he asked, setting the box down on the floor next to the bookcase.

"I doubt it. That was discontinued. All of them were supposed to be destroyed on the order of the Department of Health and Safety."

His head whipped around. "That's crazy. What for?"

"All sorts of things. I think the main complaints were due to the fires it started."

"But that was the best part."

Reaching above her head and using the tips of her fingers, she turned a large box around. On the side of the box was the words BOARD GAMES written in red ink. "I found it. Can you help me, Kyle . . .?" When he didn't answer, she looked over her shoulder. Kyle was carefully climbing up a makeshift pyramid of boxes. Grace watched slightly horrified as the boxes began to sway under his weight. He had just wrapped his hand around the barrel of the rocket launcher when he suddenly yelped and fell backwards toward the floor. Grace winced as boxes of toys rained down on him from above.

Worried, she hopped down from the desk. Shoving boxes aside, she kneeled down next to him. "Are you okay?"

He jumped up suddenly and immediately began pushing toys off the metal shelves. The plastic guns clattered to the floor one by one.

"What are you doing?" she asked, pulling at his arm.

He looked through the now empty metal shelves. Bending down, he threw the boxes aside until he found his flashlight. Snapping the light back on, he pointed it through the opening.

Grace looked past his shoulders. All she could see were more dolls, boxes and various other toys scattered around pieces of old furniture. "What's wrong?"

"I thought—" He snapped the light off and shrugged. "Just my imagination. Did you say you found the box?"

She nodded and led him back to the desk she had been standing on. She was just about to climb back up when the attic door flew open and Daniel Burns walked in. "What is going on up here?"

Kyle looked back at Grace with a sheepish expression. He hunched his shoulders over and slid behind her.

"We're just trying to find a box," Grace said.

Daniel looked at the boxes littering the floor. "Do you have to tear down the whole attic to find it? We could hear you from downstairs."

Grace glanced behind her shoulder at her cowering six foot one assistant. She quickly apologized and explained what they were hoping to find.

"Don't bother," Daniel said angrily, "it's not here."

Grace raised an eyebrow, wondering why Daniel seemed so angry. Allen almost set the building on fire once and Daniel barely batted an eye. "But, I found a box—"

"All those games are gone. Your predecessors tried looking for *All the Murderers* the last time Straker wanted them to come up with a mystery board game. Trust me, it's gone." He looked at her crestfallen expression and sighed. Softening his voice, he said, "Don't worry about it, Grace. It really wasn't a very good game. I'm sure you'll be able to come up with a much better design." He smiled slightly. "One that won't bring the wrath of parents everywhere down on us." He motioned for them to follow him out to the stairwell. "You have a week to come up with something. If you want, I'll go over your ideas with you before our next design meeting." He looked over his shoulder as they climbed down the steps. "You could start with some field research on the subject," he said, winking at her.

She smiled at him. "That sounds like a good idea, Daniel." She glanced over her shoulder at Kyle. "An excellent idea, in fact."

* * * *

Grace crossed her arms. "You cheated!"

"Did not!" Kyle knocked her knight off the board. "You're just bad at this game," he said with a chuckle.

Smirking, Grace grabbed his sleeve, pulled out three magic wizard cards, and held them up.

He smiled and held up his hands. "That's perfectly legal." He reached for the rules. "See, subsection M of section five C, part twenty-two says that the head troll, which is me, can use any means at his disposal once the forces of good enter the magic forest."

"It doesn't mean hoarding restoration cards."

"Any means at his disposal including, but not limited to lying, stealing—"

Grace reached for the twenty-page rulebook. "It does not say that."

He leaned back, holding the rulebook out of her reach. "I'm a troll, so what do you expect?"

Laughing, she sat back on her knees. "Fine. You win. It's a dumb game anyway. The last one was much better and far more educational."

"It was for six year olds."

Grace reached for another board game. "It was fun."

"You only say that because it was the only one you won," he said, picking up the pieces and placing them back into the box. "What's next?"

"*Dastardly Dinosaurs: A Game of Survival.*" She dumped the contents of the box on the floor. "I bet when you applied here you never realized how demanding this job is."

"It's much better than my last one."

"Oh, what did you do?"

He smiled. "Not much and my boss wasn't too happy about it." He twisted his features. "Now the job before that was interesting, for a while."

She divided the game pieces into piles. "Was it as fun as this?"

"No, not like this at all. I was in a play."

"Oh?" She looked at him in renewed interest. She had a feeling he was an actor or, at least, dabbled in it. He was certainly handsome enough to be one.

"It was an off-off-off-off-Broadway play. I got really good reviews, but it was so boring. Saying the same thing over and over and over and over and—"

She held up her hand. "Got it. So, what happened?"

"I tried to improvise, but the director and the other actors had a fit. They were being completely unreasonable. I only changed a couple of lines."

"I'm surprised. I thought most actors improvised on occasion."

"That's what I thought too, but apparently, they take a really dim view on changing Shakespeare. I thought I really added to the show." He picked up a velociraptor piece and studied it. "I mean, why should Hamlet get all the good lines?" He dropped the piece on the floor and picked up another board game. "*The Great Merlin: A Game of Magic and Wonder.* Why don't we play this one next?"

"I'm saving it for Belle. I thought she might like to play it with us."

He set the game aside. "Do you do this type of thing often?"

She shrugged. "Sometimes. When Bonnie Caster worked here, we used to have tournaments during our lunch break. I remember Lily won the last one," she said sadly. "We stopped having them when Bonnie retired."

He looked at her thoughtfully. "Do you really think Lily was murdered?"

She nodded.

He leaned forward until his face was only inches away from hers. "I could help you, you know," he said in a soft whisper. "I didn't start working here until after she died, so I'm really the only one you can trust around here. I could act as your eyes and ears. We could work on this together."

Grace looked at his eager face. He had a point. He really was the only one working for the toy company who wasn't at the magic show the night Lily died. "That sounds—"

He grinned. "I know a little something about magic and magicians. I could be very helpful."

She snapped her mouth shut, suddenly doubting herself. "Really?"

"Not much, just kid stuff, but maybe I could do some research."

"Unbelievable," Ethan said from behind her.

Grace turned her head and smiled up at Ethan, impeccably dressed in a black pinstriped suit and red silk tie, leaning against the doorframe.

"And I thought my job was difficult," Ethan said with a small shake of his head.

"Hi, Ethan," Grace said, "wanna play?"

"So, this is what you do all day?" Ethan asked with a bemused expression on his face.

"Absolutely, every day; it's awful." She pointed to the floor. "Have a seat. We could use an extra player."

Grace made the necessary introductions as she divvied up another pile of cards and tokens.

Ethan shook his head. "Sorry, I can't stay long. I just wanted to drop by and see how you were doing."

Kyle shook his head. "Horrible. We've played five games and she's only won one, and that was only because I let her win."

"You didn't let me win and you've cheated on each game."

"Did not."

"Did too," she said, yawning loudly. "I'm sorry. I didn't get any sleep last night." She looked over at Kyle and smiled. "That's probably why I lost."

Kyle held up his hand. "Don't even. You lost to a superior opponent, so just admit it."

Grace rubbed her eyes. "I admit nothing."

"Why couldn't you sleep?" Ethan asked with concern.

"Just thinking," Grace said, waving her hand dismissively.

Ethan looked over at Kyle and looked at the door. Taking the hint, Kyle slowly rose to his feet. "I'll get you a cup of coffee," he said as he left the office.

Ethan shut the door. "Did you learn any more from Straker after I left yesterday?"

Grace smiled. "Only that the deli has been short-changing him for the last year. Have you filed the complaint, yet?"

"Yeah," Ethan said with a smirk, "I'll get right on it."

"Think of the attorney's fees. There's probably a class action lawsuit there. You can take that deli for all the pastrami, ham, and turkey it has." She yawned again, suddenly very tired.

He looked down at her, his brow creasing. "You look exhausted. I hope this investigation or whatever Straker's has you doing isn't upsetting you. Maybe you should step back from it and leave it to the professionals."

She shook her head. "I'm fine, just tired. Besides, the professionals think she committed suicide. Straker and I are the only ones that really think otherwise."

He sighed heavily, before dropping into the chair in front of her desk. "Have you learned anything else since we last talked?"

"Well, I learned that Jackie from downstairs is a liar, so never believe anything she says."

He smiled. "I see you're making a lot of progress."

She ran her hand through her hair, pushing it back from her face. "None of it makes any sense and we still don't know how she was killed. Dragovich told the cops that he didn't see anyone else up there with her. How did the killer get to her if she was up there alone?"

"Dragovich could be lying." Ethan reached down and opened his briefcase. Taking out a legal pad and a pen, he crossed his leg and balanced the pad on his knee. "Why don't we sit down and think this through logically. We'll write out a timeline, starting with when you went backstage. Describe everything you saw and did, in detail. You must have seen something—"

"But I didn't."

"You must have," he insisted, "otherwise you wouldn't be so certain she was murdered."

Grace looked over at the handsome man sitting in her office, his pen poised to write down her every word. Smiling, she gazed up at him. "I have a better idea. There's a new exhibit at the history museum on fourteenth century—" The shrill ring of her desk phone interrupted her.

They looked over toward the ringing phone. Ethan reached out a hand and helped her to her feet. Hopping over the discarded board games, she picked up the phone and let out a cheery greeting.

No sound.

She repeated her greeting once again and waited. Giving up, she hung up the phone.

"Wrong number?"

Grace stared at the phone and then at Ethan. "I keep getting these weird phone calls. They don't say anything, and it doesn't happen all the time, but it seems like once a day someone calls my direct line. It happened at home this morning, too."

"It's probably nothing."

"Yeah, you're right. It's probably nothing," she said, trying to interject some confidence in her voice.

* * * *

Grace leaned against the break room refrigerator. She couldn't wait to go home and go to sleep. She reached in and pulled out a bottle of water, one for herself and one for Kyle. She was just about to exit the break room when she heard Allen yell.

"You!" Allen pointed an accusing finger at her. "It's you!"

Grace took a step back. "What?"

"You're the thief. You're the one who's been stealing the water. I bet you're the one who broke my dolls yesterday, too. I told Straker it was you, but he didn't believe me. Just admit it. You're mad because I took over your collection, aren't you?"

"Yes, Allen. In my fury, I've decided to raid the refrigerator. Have you lost your mind? Straker provides bottled water for us. Remember the snack food strike of '06. Many toys disappeared that day and were never seen again. Like that vintage set of the Mighty Man Commando Space Station. You wouldn't know anything about that, would you?"

Allen's face flushed. "I had nothing…" He raised his chin. "Prove it. Besides, that's irrelevant. You're stealing."

"We all agreed that if Straker gave us unlimited bottled water and cookies, we would stop designing toys that look like food."

"It wasn't unlimited; only one water bottle per day, not two."

"I'm getting one for my assistant."

"What about the dolls?"

"They don't drink water," she said patiently.

Grace could practically see the steam coming out of Allen's ears. "The interstellar dolls," he said, carefully enunciating each word. "Why did you break them?"

Grace's mouth fell open. She set the bottles down on the table. "What happened to my dolls?"

"Pretend all you want, but I know it was you. Just like I know you had something to do with Lily's death."

"How do you figure that, Sherlock?"

"Everyone knows you were backstage. What were you doing back there?"

"Louisa asked me to go with her."

"I doubt that. Louisa was in her seat next to Mr. Straker when the show began." Allen smiled. "You knew Lily had been in town over a week and you—"

"Wait? What do you mean over a week? As far as I know, she arrived that day."

"No, she had been staying at Dragovich's."

"How do you know that?"

"Unlike you, I make it my business to know what is going on in this company."

"That's comforting."

"Just like I know you and your, uh, *assistant* were playing around up in the attic earlier today." He shook his head in disgust. "I bet you two planned it together."

Suddenly, they heard the sound of a door slam and Louisa shouting. Grace followed Allen out into the hallway. They jumped back as Louisa threw open the door to Daniel's office. "Fix it!" she shouted over her shoulder.

Daniel leaned against the door jam. "Louisa, it's fixed. It was just a glitch. The money's in there, honey, I promise." He caught Grace's eye. Flushing, he stepped back into his office and slowly closed the door.

Grace glanced at Allen. "Well, Sherlock, you know so much, what was that about?"

Allen hesitated.

"Or don't you know?" she asked sarcastically.

"Of course, I know," he spat out.

"Well?"

"Louisa's worried about the company. She was probably going over the accounts and saw how much sabotage Daniel allowed Lily to get away with over the last year."

"Sabotage?" Grace scoffed.

"Lily was trying to destroy the company. She knew she wasn't going to get anything in the divorce because of that prenup, so she was trying to bankrupt the company before she asked for a divorce." Allen's face turned a deep purple. His hands clenched at his side. "All so that she could hurt Mr. Straker and Louisa. Louisa knew what she was up to. She warned Daniel, but he wouldn't do anything about it." He sneered at Daniel's door. "He doesn't care, but he should. This company belongs to Louisa. Her husband should be trying to protect her inheritance, but he's too busy for that."

Friday, December 9th
11:15 p.m.

CHAPTER ELEVEN

GRACE LOOKED THROUGH the peephole of her door, surprised to find Belle Dragovich standing at her door. She must have heard Grace, because the young woman suddenly smiled widely and waved.

Wearily, Grace laid her head against the door. What could she be doing here at this time of night, Grace thought, as she yawned sleepily.

"Grace, it's me," Belle said, ringing the doorbell again. "I really need to talk to you."

Sighing, Grace unlocked the door and opened it, stepping aside to let the other woman through.

To Grace's surprise, Belle stayed put. She twisted her hair around her fingers as tears filled her eyes. "I'm so sorry for coming so late, but I needed to speak to you."

Concerned, Grace quickly said, "What happened? Is everything okay?"

"No, not really." Belle pushed her blonde hair out of the face. "Things have been rather crazy tonight. My dad and I had a bad fight and I really need some help. Would you help me?"

Taken aback by Belle's tears, Grace immediately offered to help her in any way she could.

Her tears suddenly evaporating, Belle smiled before turning to the side and leaning down. "Oh, thank you so much, Grace." Belle stood up and quickly walked through the threshold carrying a rabbit cage in one hand and dragging a suitcase behind her with the other. "You are a life saver. I knew I could count on you." She dropped the suitcase on the floor and turned around in a circle. "Oh, how cute. This is so cozy. I love it. It's perfect. It's very…" She hesitated, as she stared at the crates that were acting as end tables to two folding chairs sitting in front of an old antenna television set. "It's very Spartan," she said brightly.

Still frozen by the door, Grace managed to squeak out, "Yes, that's exactly what I was going for."

Belle set the cage on the card table in the dining room. She took a moment to coo at Abry who was nibbling on a piece of rabbit food before taking off her coat and dropping it next to the cage. "So how much is my half of the rent?"

Grace slowly closed the door. "Your half?"

Belle nodded. "Yes. You need a roommate, correct?"

"Um, yeah," Grace said slowly. "How did you know that?"

"Franklin. Oh, well, Mr. Straker told me that you need a roommate."

Shocked that Straker knew that much about her life, Grace asked, "How did he know that?"

Belle shrugged. "When I told him about the argument I had with my dad, he told me about your situation. He thought this would be a perfect solution to both our problems. You get a roommate and I get a place to live."

Surprise must have been written over her face, because Belle's eyes quickly began to water again. "Oh, it's not, is it? I'm so sorry." She bent down and picked up her suitcase. "I'll leave. I shouldn't have come. I'll go back to Franklin and tell him he was wrong about you—"

Grace quickly shut the door, wondering what Straker was up to. Walking over to the distraught young woman, she assured her that it wasn't necessary to bother Straker tonight. "He's probably sleeping. I was just surprised. I figured you were living in some swanky apartment somewhere."

Belle wiped her tears away. Walking over to the folding chairs, she said softly, "I was."

Grace picked up her neglected cup of tea. After brewing another cup for Belle, she walked over to the other folding chair and sat down. "What happened?"

"Papa doesn't want me to work at the toy company. He just won't accept that I don't want to be a magician."

"So, he kicked you out?"

Belle nodded. "He's a big proponent of tough love." She shook her head. "When Lily was around, we never had to worry. She would always help out." She looked at her cup sadly, before adding, "I don't care. I don't need his money. I'm making my own now. Frank—Mr. Straker, said that if everything keeps going well, I'll be getting a big raise in a few months."

"Really?" Grace picked up her cup and took a sip. "How nice."

"Yes. Mr. Straker is so kind."

Grace choked on her tea.

"I've never met a man quite like him."

"Hmm, neither have I," Grace said, desperately trying to keep the sarcasm out of her voice.

"Can you keep a secret?"

Grace nodded.

"Franklin has asked me to marry him. That's really what my father is so angry about."

"And you've said...yes?" Grace asked hesitantly.

"Of course! Wouldn't you?"

Grace's head wobbled around between a nod and a shake, not quite sure how to answer that question.

"Please, may I stay?" Belle asked hopefully. "It would only be for a few months. Just until I get married."

Grace wanted to say no, but she needed a roommate. Desperately, she thought, glancing at the bills piling up on the kitchen counter. Realizing that it probably wouldn't be the best career move to turn the boss' future wife away, she reluctantly nodded her head. "I could use the help paying the rent, actually. There's just one problem." Grace pointed to the empty cage. "My apartment doesn't allow pets."

"Oh, that's not a problem. My brother will be taking him back soon."

"Oh, is he being releas—?" Grace's head swung back to the empty cage. "Where's Abry?"

Belle lifted a hand to point to the cage before drawing it back suddenly. Standing up, she strode to the cage, and pulled on the locked door. "I don't understand how he keeps getting out."

"He escaped?" Grace asked, glancing toward the kitchen in the hopes of catching a glimpse of the errant bunny.

"I know my father somehow taught Abry how to get out on his own, but," she said, lifting the cage up and looking underneath it, "I just don't know how he's doing it." She set the cage on the floor and opened the door. "He's a little show off. Don't worry, once he realizes no one is paying any attention, he'll climb back in and go to sleep."

Grace shook her head. "So, when will your brother be released?"

Belle looked at her in surprise. "Released?"

"Wasn't he in jail?"

"Yes. Yes, of course," she stammered. "It was all just a silly misunderstanding."

"Good. So, he's here in New York?"

"No, he's in Russia. He lives there on a little farm. It's nice. I think I have some pictures somewhere." Belle reached into her suitcase. She dug around in the suitcase for a while before sighing. "It must still be at home."

"Well, would you like the tour?" Grace stood up and led Belle toward a little hallway nestled between the kitchen bar and the living room. "It'll only take a minute, but," Grace said, pushing open a door, "this will be your room."

Belle followed her through the door into a small empty room with one lone window. "Oh, nice. It's very . . . cozy."

"I have a blow up mattress in the closet you can use for tonight."

Belle's smile grew tight. She walked back out into the living room and took an inventory of Grace's living room which mostly consisted of furniture that could be folded up and one sparsely decorated Christmas tree. "Did you just move?"

"No, I've been here for three years."

The corners of Belle's mouth quirked up. "Do you just not like furniture?"

Grace laughed. "My roommate got married two months ago and she took her furniture with her when she moved. I just haven't had a chance to redecorate."

Belle smiled brightly. "Well, I can help with that." She turned to the other door off the living room. "What's this?"

"My room." When Belle pulled her hand away, Grace quickly said, "You can see it if you like."

Belle smiled and opened the door.

Grace heard a gasp and oohs coming from the other side. Smiling, she walked into her bedroom. Belle was standing next to the open closet, holding up a dark green satin evening gown by its hanger, against her body. "This is absolutely beautiful."

"Thank you."

"It must have cost you a fortune."

"Actually, it didn't cost a thing."

Belle gasped. She laid the green dress down on Grace's bed and pulled a pink silk dress out of the closet. "Is this real silk?"

"As far as I know."

"Oh, this is absolutely beautiful," Belle said, admiring a white, woolen winter coat with its ruby red silk lining. She glanced up at Grace. "Do you think you could help me move tomorrow?"

Grace bit her lip. "Well, I have a date—"

Belle didn't let her finish. "Let's see, I have my bed and dresser." She walked out into the living room, still clutching the pink dress. "But we also need a sofa, two end tables, a couple of chairs—oh, I bet my Hepplewhite dining set would fit here perfectly," she said, turning to the dining room area.

"Are you sure you want to bring all of that? You're only going to be here a few months. You might as well wait and move it when you get married."

"Oh, it won't be any trouble. Besides, I'm not going to keep the furniture."

Grace stood up straighter. "You're not?"

"Well, I'm not going to need it when I move in with my husband."

"Won't your father miss it?"

Belle waved her hand. "He doesn't care about that sort of thing. He leaves the decorating to me and I was planning on completely revamping our apartment after I finish redecorating the dressing rooms and offices at the Dragon's Lair. It's time for a change." She walked up to the wall and looked at the battleship gray walls. "Do you like this color?"

"No, I don't," Grace said quickly. "I'm just not a very good painter."

"Michael is. I'll see if he can help us." Belle sighed sadly. "I miss Lily. She was always good at picking colors. She was good at everything."

"Yeah, she was perfect," Grace said, distracted by the possibility of free furniture. Furniture that someone else was going to be responsible for moving into her apartment. "Who were you planning on giving your furniture to?"

"No one in particular." Belle held up Grace's pink silk dress in front of herself. "I absolutely love pink."

"I bet it would look beautiful on you," Grace assured her. "You're not giving it away to friends or relatives?"

"No, most everyone I know has furniture. To be honest, it's a bit old and out of date. Do you mind if I borrow this for my date with Franklin tomorrow night?" she asked, holding out the dress to Grace.

"What are roommates for?" Grace pushed the dress back. "Share and share alike, I say. You know, it seems such a pain to move everything here and then move it out when you leave. I mean, just to turn around and give it to a perfect stranger."

"Yeah," Belle agreed. Her eyes lit up. "Hey, would you like to keep it?"

"Me?" Grace restrained herself from dancing.

"Yeah, that would be such a huge help. If you took it I wouldn't have to bother with putting an ad in the paper or trying to find someone who'd be willing to take it away."

Grace shrugged nonchalantly. "Sure, I'd be happy to take it off your hands."

"The dining room table wobbles a bit. My idiot brother broke the leg playing football in the dining room one day."

"We'll stick a book under it. It'll be fine."

"That's great. Most of the stuff is at the apartment." She snapped her fingers. "You know, one of the sofas at the Dragon's Lair would look great in here. You can pick out which one you like the best. Michael promised he would help me move and I offered to pay Kyle…" She hesitated. Blushing, she said, "I figured you probably wouldn't say no, so I already asked them if they would help me move in tomorrow. I know it's a terrible imposition but are you sure you can't reschedule your date?"

"What about Sunday?"

She shook her head. "Church and then dinner with my father. He's already mad at me and I don't want to make it any worse by cancelling. Besides, I need to make him understand that I'm a grown adult, capable of making my own decisions. I can't stay under his shadow any longer." She smiled ruefully. "Lily would have agreed." Belle turned away as her eyes suddenly filled with tears.

Grace frowned slightly as it suddenly occurred to her that she hadn't even offered her condolences to the young woman. "I'm sorry about Lily. You two must have been very close."

Belle nodded. "I loved her. She took care of us after my mother died. I don't know what we would have done without her." She smiled sadly at Grace. "You didn't see us at our best that night. Lily was just in such a bad mood. She could be a bit of a pain at times."

"Do you know why she was in such a bad mood?"

Belle shrugged. "She was just nervous. It was to be expected. It was her first performance in years." She wiped away a tear as her face darkened. "It's just so senseless. Franklin told me that you think she was murdered."

Grace nodded, wondering if he had also roped Belle into helping search for Lily's killer. "What do you think? Do you think she committed suicide?"

"No," Belle said sharply. "Not Lily. I don't care how upset she had been the last few months. She wouldn't kill herself. Someone pushed her off the scaffold that night. I don't know who killed her, but I'm going to find out. They are not going to get away with this."

"Do you have any idea who would have wanted to hurt her?"

Belle shook her head. "She could be difficult, but I just can't imagine anyone wanting to murder her."

"Who knew she would be performing that particular trick that night?"

"Just me, my father, and Tabitha."

"What about the stage hands?"

Belle shook her head. "Tabitha usually performs that illusion, so they thought it was her."

"Tabitha was the girl we ran into right before Lily died, wasn't she? Did you find out why she was crying?"

"She wouldn't tell me. I have a feeling it had something to do with her fiancé, but I haven't seen her since she quit."

"When did she quit?"

"A few days after Lily died."

Grace raised an eyebrow. "That seems rather suspicious."

Belle shook her head. "Not really, she had been planning to quit for a while. She and her fiancé were planning on eloping. She's probably in Belize like she planned. I just wish she would call me." Belle wrinkled her forehead. "She promised to keep in touch, but I'm getting kind of worried about her."

"Maybe she'll contact you soon. If she does, I'd like to talk to her." Out of the corner of her eye, Grace noticed Abry hopping out of her room. "What do you want to do about your room?"

Belle, carefully sat down on Grace's folding chair. Taking a carrot out of her purse, she softly called the bunny's name. "We'll just wait until next weekend. I can use the blow up bed until then."

Grace sighed. She really wanted to see Ethan tomorrow, but she couldn't let her new roommate sleep on a blow up bed for an entire week. Excusing herself, she called Ethan. With any luck he'd be agreeable to postponing their date.

To her surprise, he was thrilled. "That's great!"

"Okay," she said rather disappointed at his enthusiastic response. Apparently, she wasn't making as much of an impression on him as she thought.

"I'll come and help you two move."

"All right. If you want to," Grace said somewhat amused. She had never met anyone so excited at the prospect of helping someone move and said as much.

Ethan chuckled. "This is a perfect opportunity to investigate. Put your sleuthing cap on, Grace. I'll be there first thing in the morning."

Saturday, December 10th

CHAPTER TWELVE

GRACE FOLLOWED BELLE into the Straker Magic Shoppe, and past the glass topped counters, crystal gazing balls, assortment of cards, various colored velvet hoods, silk handkerchiefs, gilded bird cages, masks, ribbons, fake hands, and black cabinets and boxes, toward the back door marked STAFF ONLY. Belle briskly knocked on the door. Without waiting for an answer, she entered the room unceremoniously with a breezy, "knock, knock," thrown in for good measure.

Michael Talon stood at his workstation, pulling his long black hair away from his face and tying it into a knot at the nape of his neck. Grace was surprised to see that he added a bit of color to his normally all black attire. Instead of his usual black spider earrings, a pair of blue topaz coffins dangled from his ears. He smiled as soon as he saw Belle. To Grace, he simply nodded.

"Are you ready?" Belle asked excitedly.

He made shushing sounds as he looked over his shoulder. "Harcourt is here. He's not too happy about my leaving today."

Belle rolled her eyes. "You get a day off." She looked at him with a mixture of pity and anger. "You shouldn't let him treat you like this."

Michael shrugged one shoulder, and reached for his bag under the table. "What are we doing first?"

"I've rented a truck." Belle lifted the sheet covering Michael's workstation up high enough to peer underneath. "I figured we could go to my old apartment first and pick up my bedroom set and dining room furniture."

"Is your dad going to be there?" Michael asked.

"No, not today," she said as she dropped the sheet back down.

Michael looked between Grace and Belle. "Just the three of us?" he asked doubtfully. "I've seen your bedroom furniture, Belle. It probably weighs a ton."

"My friend Ethan," Grace said, "is going to help. He's driving the truck."

Belle sighed. "I asked our new assistant, Kyle, to help too, but he didn't show up today. So, it's just us four."

Grace couldn't help but notice that some type of silent communication passed between the two. Belle stared at the young man intently as Michael gave her a strange look before finally nodding imperceptibly.

Belle turned to open the door. "After we get that delivered, we'll head over to the Dragon's Lair and pick out a sofa and a couple of chairs."

A look of fear crossed Michael's face as he held out a hand. "Your father—"

Belle interrupted with a wave of her hand. "It's all right. Why are you so afraid of him? I already told him what we're going to do and he said that it was fine. We're just going to go in and go right out. It'll take less than thirty minutes."

"Thirty minutes?" Michael asked with a high pitched squeak.

"Well," Belle said, "I want Grace to pick out which sofa she would like to take."

To Grace's surprise, Michael began to breathe heavily. He shook his head violently. "Why don't you and Grace go to the Dragon's Lair? Pick everything out, and I'll go with Grace's friend to get your furniture. It will be quicker that way."

"Michael," Belle said annoyed, "if you would just sit down and talk to Papa—"

Michael groaned. "Belle, you don't understand."

Belle's shook her head. "I can't believe you are so frightened of him."

Harcourt threw open the door to his office. "What is going on out here? It's bad enough you're leaving me shorthanded today, but must you waste so much time nattering away?"

Michael ran his hands through his hair, loosening a few strands from the hair tie. "He's right, Belle. Maybe it would be better if I stay here."

"Good." Harcourt thumped his cane against the floor. "Get back to work."

Belle grabbed Michael by the hand. "Can I speak to you privately, please?" she asked almost plaintively. She tugged him out the doors and into the magic shop.

Unsure of what to do, Grace smiled at the old magician.

He smiled back as his sculpted left eyebrow arched above one black eye. "You're rather brave."

"How so?"

His smile turned cryptic.

Michael walked back through the doors, sans Belle.

"So, are you coming with us Michael?" Grace asked.

"Belle's going to call her father," he answered simply. "Hopefully, he'll let you pick out the furniture and have one of his stage hands to move it out front for me to pick up."

"Are you that afraid of Ilya Dragovich?" Grace asked in disbelief.

"Ha!" Harcourt thumped his cane against the floor. "And, here I thought the boy didn't have any sense at all. Of course, he's afraid. You should be, too."

Grace chuckled. "Why?"

Harcourt shrugged. "I wouldn't want to surround myself with a bunch of cold-blooded murderers."

"Oh, don't be ridiculous!" Michael snapped. Turning to Grace, and with as much bravado as he could muster, he said, "I'm not afraid. I just know when I'm not welcome."

"Really?" Harcourt asked with a disbelieving look plastered on his face. "Are you sure about that?"

Grace turned to Harcourt. "What makes you think Ilya Dragovich is a cold-blooded murderer?"

"Isn't it obvious? He killed Lily," Harcourt said matter-of-factly.

"There are a lot of people that could have killed her," Grace pointed out. "He wasn't the only magician there that night."

"Are you accusing me?" Grinning, he lifted a hand and rubbed his goatee. If Grace didn't know better, she would say he was enjoying the idea of being accused. "I was sitting in the audience. Ask Michael over here, he was right next to me."

Michael didn't say anything.

Harcourt glared at him for a few seconds before turning back to Grace. "Or that weasel, Allen. He can vouch for me. So you see, I have an alibi. Airtight, I believe it would be called. I was in the audience, surrounded by a couple hundred—easily entertained—magic fans, watching the show. I was nowhere near that scaffolding."

"Neither was Dragovich," Grace said. "He was on stage. His every move was being watched by those same magic fans."

Harcourt snorted. "That means nothing. It was him. Also, I don't have a motive. Lily and I were friends," he said still grinning. "Besides, who besides Dragovich knew Lily was going to perform that night?"

"You knew," Michael said with a small smile. "I overheard you and Louisa talking about it before the show began."

"I didn't know," Harcourt insisted. He shrugged. "I assumed she would when I heard Straker's party was going to be at the Dragon's Lair. Predictable stunt. That's the problem with Ilya. He used to be good, but now he goes for the easy illusions."

"Why would Ilya Dragovich kill her?" Grace asked. "What motive could he possibly have?"

"He didn't kill her!" Michael said harshly.

Harcourt ignored him. "I'm sure it was a crime of passion. They fought all the time. They had a big blowout a year after his wife died."

"They *did not* fight all the time," Michael countered. He turned to Grace. "You can't believe a word he says. He's just jealous."

"Were you there?" Harcourt snapped. "I was and I witnessed it with my own eyes. I witnessed one of their excruciating screaming matches during the Blackpool Magician's Convention one year. It was so unprofessional and quite embarrassing for them. It was a good year for me though." Harcourt puffed out his chest. "I won that year."

Michael dropped the bag he had been holding back on the floor and crossed his arms. "That's because Ilya Dragovich wasn't performing." Turning to Grace, he added, "He had retired the year before."

Harcourt's face flushed angrily. He turned to Michael and pointed a long bony finger in his face. "What does that have to do with anything? When I was in my prime, I could out-perform him any day of the week. I still could."

Michael's chin rose. "He won five years in a row."

Sputtering, Harcourt spat out, "He cheated five years in a row."

"He sells out every show he's involved in," Michael said.

His voice rising, Harcourt countered with, "That's because he is a sellout."

Grace held out her hands. "Gentlemen, if we could get back to the subject at hand. What happened between Lily and Dragovich?"

Michael bent down to retrieve his bag. "I'm not listening to this anymore. Ilya Dragovich had nothing to do with Lily's death. You're just a hateful, evil old man." Michael slung his bag back over his shoulder and stalked out of the room, making sure to loudly slam the door behind him.

Harcourt clucked his tongue and shook his head. "So dramatic."

"So, what happened between Dragovich and Lily in England?"

"I don't know, but I found them arguing in front of their hotel room in the middle of the night. They were trying to be quiet, but I could hear them from my room four doors away. They were both, how should I put it, rather déshabillé. I heard him tell her to stay away from his son." Harcourt shrugged. "I felt sorry for her and asked her if she would like to work with me."

"Well, whatever the problem was, it couldn't have been that serious," Grace said. "They stayed friends. He let her perform with him for Straker's birthday."

Harcourt shook his head dismissively. "That was just for that one night. He came out of retirement the year after Lily left him in England. Lily was still working with me at the time. She was all prepared to leave me and go back to being his assistant." His thin lips sneered. "But he wanted nothing to do with her. She came crawling back to me."

"She never said what the fight was about?"

"No, but it had something to do with that boy of his, Aleksis."

"How long did she work for you?" she asked while making a mental note of Belle's brother's name.

"Only for a few years. She left me high and dry during a performance in Paris one night." He shook his head, angrily. "I was about to go on stage and she ran off."

"Did she say why?"

"It had something to do with a stalker she picked up; a deranged young man who fancied himself in love with her."

Grace's tilted her head. "What was his name?"

"I don't know. Unlike Dragovich, I like to keep a strictly professional relationship with those that I work with. If their personal life doesn't affect their work, then it's none of my business. I only found out about it when she refused to perform that night."

"Was her stalker arrested?"

"I don't think so. I think he killed himself; suicide." He shrugged his shoulders. "That's not important. What's important is the fact that Ilya Dragovich is a killer, and you, young lady, have just invited his daughter to share your apartment. I doubt he's too happy about that. If I were you, I'd sleep with one eye open."

* * * *

Grace shifted in her seat nervously and looked around the empty auditorium, wishing she had gone with Belle and the others. After they left Harcourt, it was agreed that Grace would meet Belle's father at the Dragon's Lair and pick out the sofa she wanted while the others moved Belle's bedroom and dining room set into the apartment.

At first, that seemed like a great idea. Not only would she manage to avoid the heavy lifting, she could also take her time choosing which sofa would look best in her apartment. Michael was also thrilled with the plan, since it meant his contact with Ilya Dragovich would be very limited. If they planned everything right, he might be able to avoid the magician all together.

All in all it seemed like a great plan and it probably would have worked perfectly if Dragovich had been at the theater waiting for her, but according to the stage manager, the magician was running late and had requested that she wait for him in the theater. Yep, it definitely seemed like a good idea, she thought. A great idea, but that was before she realized how empty the Dragon's Lair was on a Saturday morning.

Feeling her hair stand on end, Grace looked around the theater once again. The giant, dark, empty theater, she thought as she rubbed the back of her neck. Since arriving at the Dragon's Lair, she just couldn't shake the feeling that someone was watching her.

Standing up, she walked to the stage and faced the rows of empty seats. Dragovich will be here soon, she reminded herself once again. Of course, that wasn't exactly a reassuring thought. What if Harcourt was right?

She leaned her head back and looked up to the ceiling as she thought about Lily's death. Would Ilya Dragovich really kill someone in front of his audience? In front of so many witnesses? Would he take the chance, and if he did, how did he pull it off?

She looked back toward the rows of seats. Straker said he got a text only a few minutes before she died and the police found her phone on the scaffolding after she died, so someone had to be up there. But who? "Whoever it was, texted Straker, wrapped the silk rope around Lily's neck, and then pushed her off the ledge," she said, thinking out loud.

Almost everyone was accounted for when Lily died. Harcourt, Michael, Louisa, Daniel, and Straker were all sitting in their seats. Dragovich was on the stage and Belle was walking her to the waiting room backstage.

But where was Allen and Tabitha? Grace thought back to that night. She couldn't recall seeing Allen at all after Lily's murder, but she did remember seeing Tabitha run past her and Belle, crying about something. She also remembered that the screams from the audience started just a second or two after Tabitha ran away.

Would Tabitha have had enough time to text the suicide message from Lily to Straker, push Lily off the scaffolding, and run downstairs in time to pass by them before Lily ended up in full view of the audience?

Grace hoisted herself up onto the stage. Craning her neck, she looked up toward the ceiling. It was dark, but she could just make out a scaffolding far above.

She looked around at the empty theater. It couldn't hurt to take a peek, she thought, walking to the heavy curtain and peering behind it. She noticed the stage door that she and Belle had walked through that night to see Lily's body dangling from the ceiling.

She hurried to it. As quiet as she could, she twisted the knob and went backstage, tiptoed down the corridor a few feet and then turned the corner.

If her bearings were correct, she should be just behind the stage. She looked up, but there was no sign of the scaffold. Passing some rather large boxes lying against the wall, she walked the length of the corridor. At the far end, against the wall was a ladder.

If this leads to the scaffolding above, then Tabitha is off the hook, she thought. After all, Tabitha was running toward this direction, not away from it. She wouldn't have had enough time to reach the ladder before Lily fell.

Grace reached for the rung above her head.

Snap.

She whirled around, her heart beating fast. She looked in both directions, but there was no one in sight. Holding her breath, she waited for some sound to indicate that she had been caught. When none came and no one appeared, she turned back around and quickly climbed up the ladder. Eventually, she came to small landing and another set of stairs.

Dropping to her hands and knees, she looked over the ledge to see if there was anyone following her. When she didn't see anyone, she breathed a sigh of relief before standing and walking toward the stairs.

She paused. A seven foot tall shiny black box, the type often used in magic shows to make people disappear, stood next to the stairs. Curiosity getting the better of her, Grace, very carefully and very quietly, opened the double doors and looked inside. Discovering it empty, she closed the doors, and took the first step up the stairs, cringing as they creaked and groaned with every step. She paused every few seconds to listen for any sign of movement from down below, worried that someone might hear the noise and come to investigate.

The steps eventually led to a narrow scaffold, hidden from the audience's view by a royal blue curtain, which stretched over half of the stage. She stepped on the scaffold and made her way to the center, gripping the metal railings tightly as she walked. When she came to the end, she looked over the railing at the stage below. Feeling slightly nauseous, she lifted her eyes and looked straight ahead.

Four large metal pulleys hung in front of her and attached to the railing in front of the pulleys was a hook with a thin metal wire that ran up to the ceiling. Grace reached forward and grabbed the hook. She noticed that threads of purple silk still clung to the metal wire.

Creak.

Taking a deep breath, Grace stood perfectly still.

Creak.

The scaffolding moved a little, as several more creaks could be heard from below.

Someone was coming up the stairs.

Grace looked around helplessly for a hiding place or a way to escape. Finding neither, she gripped the railing tighter, and waited.

CHAPTER THIRTEEN

WHOEVER IT WAS that was coming up the stairs was taking their own sweet time about it, Grace thought, as she waited anxiously for whoever it was to appear. With any luck, it wouldn't be Dragovich. Somehow she doubted he'd be okay with her snooping around his crystal coffin set up, despite her already knowing how the trick worked.

She held her breath as the creaks and groans became louder. Please be anyone but Dragovich, she prayed.

Grace blew out the breath she had been holding when she saw the top of a blond head appear over the steps. "Kyle!"

Startled, Kyle jumped back a little.

"What are you doing up here?" Grace whispered. "You scared me half to death."

Kyle stepped out onto the scaffolding. Taking a deep breath, he laid a hand over his heart. "Scared you? I think I'm having a heart attack. What are you doing up here?"

"I asked you first."

He carefully walked over to her. "I wanted to check out the murder scene. I mean, I figured since I was here and all." He grinned. "You too?"

She grinned back at him. "Since I was here." Her grin faltered as she looked at him. "Why are you here?"

"Belle and the others are stuck in traffic and she said to meet you here." He slid past her, accidentally knocking her forward. Gripping her shoulders, he pulled her back against his body. "Sorry about that," he said, moving her back to the center of the scaffolding. He grabbed the metal wire, examined it, and then looked over at her. "I just don't get it."

"Join the club."

Leaning forward, he reached for the rope hanging from the ceiling. It swung away slightly as the tips of his fingers brushed against it. Gripping the railing with one hand, he dropped to his haunches, stuck his head under the railing and reached for the rope.

Grace jumped forward and grabbed him by his belt. "Are you crazy?" she asked, pulling him back.

Back on the scaffold, he sat down, with his legs dangling over the stage. He looked down at the rope in his hands. "I know you think she was murdered, but I just don't see how someone could have done it without getting caught."

Grace sat down next to him. "The killer must have been up here waiting for her."

"But she would have seen them when she came up the steps. If it was someone she didn't know, surely, she would've turned around, gone downstairs, and called security."

"Then maybe it was someone she knew," Grace pointed out reasonably. "Someone she trusted. Or maybe they came up behind her."

"But how did the murderer wrap the silks around her neck? She would have put up a fight." Kyle pointed to the stage below. "Dragovich had a direct line of sight. If two people were fighting up here, he would have noticed. I just don't see how she could have been murdered."

Grace frowned. "Maybe she was killed below and the killer carried her body up here."

Kyle shook his head. He pointed to the stairs at the other end of the scaffold. "Those steps, maybe, but not the ladder below. It would have been too difficult to carry a dead body up that ladder. Not to mention too risky. They could have been seen by anyone working backstage."

She took the rope from his hand and looked at the pulleys in front of her. "I wonder—"

"Perhaps, you two would like to join me down here?" Grace cringed as Ilya Dragovich's voice rang throughout the empty theater. "If you're done, that is. I don't want to interrupt whatever it is you two are doing."

She looked past Kyle's knees. Dragovich was on the stage looking up.

Feeling slightly sick, she smiled nervously and waved, not too terribly surprised when her greeting was not returned.

* * * *

"Um, stresswoo, um stoowoo—no wait that isn't it—stausswoo—" Kyle said, his voice pitched an octave higher than his regular speaking voice.

Dragovich simply stared at Kyle and slowly shook his head.

"Wait, I've got it. Straussdoochua—"

"I think what he's trying to say is that we're so very sorry, Mr. Dragovich." Grace had been repeating the same words since coming down the ladder, but she didn't think it could hurt to say them again and again. "Very, very sorry."

Stubbornly, Kyle shook his head. "No. I'm trying to say hello. Belle's been teaching me to speak Russian. She says I'm really—" He abruptly stopped speaking when the older man picked up a rather large dragon head dagger, and began tapping it against the edge of the desk.

Grace watched as he balanced the dagger on the desk using only the tip of his finger. He dropped his finger and smiled at her as the dagger stayed in place. "What, exactly, were you two doing up there?"

Kyle and Grace exchanged looks.

"That just seems like a rather strange place for a rendezvous. Surely, there's more comfortable—"

"No." Grace quickly shook her head. "No. It's not what you're thinking," she said, awkwardly laughing. "No. He's my assistant. There's nothing going on between us. Nothing."

"Then what were you doing up there?" Dragovich repeated slowly.

Grace bit her lip before reluctantly, explaining why they both went up to the scaffolding.

"Lily committed suicide," the magician said softly.

"Are you so certain?" Grace asked.

"No," he admitted. "But very few people knew she was going to be here that night and anyone who's ever seen my act knows Tabitha usually comes down the silk after the chest rises. Only my daughter, Tabitha, and I knew she would be taking Tabitha's place in that particular illusion." He held up one finger. "And none of us had any reason to kill Lily."

"That's not exactly true." She glanced over at Kyle who was standing by a large built in bookcase in Dragovich's office.

"Really?" Dragovich asked, picking the dagger back up and turning it over in his hand. "Belle loved Lily. She was like another mother to her after my wife died."

Both of their heads turned toward the bookcase as several books fell to the floor. Kyle was using his shoulder to prop up a bookshelf which had apparently collapsed. "Sorry. It's okay. I've got it," he said as he attempted to prevent any more books from falling.

Grace looked back at Dragovich who was still staring at Kyle, softly shaking his head.

Dragovich wearily closed his eyes. Shaking his head lightly, he said, "And Tabitha's only worked for me for less than a year. She barely knows Lily."

"What about you?" Grace asked. "What was your relationship with Lily?"

Ilya dropped the knife he was playing with onto his desk. He crossed his arms and leaned back against the chair. "She was a very dear friend."

"I've heard a rumor that you two were rather close until you had a falling out at some magician's conference," Grace said.

The sound of several large books hitting the floor caused her to wince. She didn't bother turning around, as Kyle muttered a quiet, "sorry" from behind her.

Dragovich either didn't notice or didn't care. His eyes narrowed. "You've been talking to Harcourt. He loves telling that story. If you must know, Lily and I did not have a falling out." He sighed heavily before reluctantly saying, "We came to an understanding."

"Meaning?"

"Lily was my wife's best friend. She was there at our wedding and for each of my children's births. She was a major part of our life, and after Juliet died, Lily was a great help to me. She basically took charge, got us back home, and got the children enrolled in school. She took them to their recitals, games, and activities. In other words, she took care of all of us, and I was grateful. I needed her. I believed my children needed her, but..." He looked over at Kyle who was still trying to put the shelf back into place. Shaking his head, he turned his attention back to Grace. "My children became upset. They were afraid that Lily was trying to replace their mother. It wasn't true, but they were both young. Lily and I agreed that it would be best if she left. It worked out for the best. Everyone just needed some time apart. Belle, especially, started to miss her once she was gone."

Smiling slightly, Grace tilted her head. "That sounds very drama free. Nothing at all like Lily."

To Grace's surprise, Dragovich chuckled. "No, I guess you could call that the condensed version of what happened. Basically, Lily thought she knew how to raise my children better than I did and it caused some friction between us. We argued—Lily was a very passionate woman—but when it became clear that my children were becoming... confused and resentful, she stepped aside. She loved them a great deal, and they loved her. Everything worked out and Lily remained a big part of our lives until her... death."

"If everything had worked out to everyone's mutual agreement, then why didn't she join your show when you came out of retirement?"

"I asked her to, but she said she was happy with Harcourt. Now if you're done cross examining me..." he said starting to rise.

Grace walked over to the posters on the wall. "London, Paris, Vegas; you seem to be doing well for yourself."

Somewhat bemused, Dragovich leaned back in his chair. "Yes, I do quite well for myself. What are you getting at?"

Grace hesitated, not quite sure how to ask her next question. She wasn't a detective and she certainly wasn't used to questioning people about things that were none of her business. Still, Grace thought, Lily was murdered. She glanced at Kyle who was picking up a glass skull and holding it up to the light. Resisting the urge to yank it out of his hand, she turned back to Dragovich and said, "I was just curious as to why Lily gave you over fifty thousand dollars in the last year."

Dragovich looked at her strangely. "Lily didn't give me any money."

"Lily gave you three checks in July totaling fifty thousand. It doesn't appear that you need the money, so I was just curious as to why."

Dragovich stared at her for a moment, his forehead creased in a frown. He leaned forward suddenly. "When did you say this happened?" For the first time, the magician seemed confused and lost for words. Grace was just about to answer his question when his expression changed from confused to enraged.

The sound of glass breaking behind her caused her to snap her mouth shut.

Swearing in Russian, or at least, she assumed he was swearing, Dragovich slammed his hand on his desk and stood up.

Before she had a chance to react, she felt Kyle's hand slip around her waist and pull her out the door as Dragovich continued to shout at them in Russian.

They didn't stop until they were outside and standing on the sidewalk. "Well," Kyle said with a chuckle, "I think that went well, considering you practically accused the man of murder."

"Me?" she asked, shivering at the sudden change of temperature. She looked up at the gray sky and the snowflakes falling to the ground. "I was just asking questions. You were the one destroying his office."

"I didn't destroy anything... Well, that crystal skull... and the bookcase, but I don't think that's what made him mad."

Grace reached up a hand to point at Kyle's chest. "You..." A spot of red on her sleeve caught her attention.

Blood.

Blood. But she wasn't bleeding, she thought as she looked down at her hands. Remembering the crystal skull Kyle had just broken, she reached for his hands. A trickle of blood ran down one finger. She pulled a tissue out of her purse and gently dabbed at the injury, eliciting a hiss from her patient. "I don't think there's any glass in it." Pressing down, she held the tissue firmly against his finger before glancing up at his handsome face hovering just a few inches from her own. Refocusing her eyes on his hand, she asked, "Could you understand anything he was saying?"

He shook his head. "It didn't sound anything like hello, how are you, my name is Kyle, where is the restroom, or I'm an American. That's pretty much all I know at this point."

Grace smiled. "I wonder how much that crystal skull cost? Maybe, Straker won't take it out of our pay."

"You think he'll cover the cost?" he asked with a wry smile.

Grace glanced back up. She shook her head. "Probably not. I saw something similar in the Magic Shoppe today. If we both pitch in we might be able to replace it."

"I'm the one who broke the thing, so I'll take care of it," he said softly. He bent his head closer to hers. It looked as if he was about to say something when his eyes shifted up and over her head. All of a sudden, his demeanor changed. He pulled his hand from hers rather abruptly and took a quick step away from her.

Grace turned around and found Ethan standing behind them. To her surprise, he seemed rather more amused than angry or jealous. She wasn't sure whether to be happy about that or not, but before she could decide, Belle and Michael came running up.

"Why aren't you two at the loading dock?" Belle asked breathlessly. At least she assumed it was Belle, since she couldn't really see her under her stocking cap, earmuffs, two scarfs, and red pea coat.

Ethan crossed his arms. "I'm rather wondering that myself."

Kyle spoke first. "We were talking to Ilya Dragovich."

Belle turned to Grace. "Did you pick out one of the spare sofas?"

"We didn't really get to that."

Michael groaned and dropped his head back, sighing heavily.

Belle looked back and forth between Kyle and Grace. "What have you two been doing all this time?"

Kyle spoke first. "We went up—"

Grace grabbed his elbow before he could tell them about their trip to the scaffold. "We had to wait for your father to arrive and then once he did, we spoke to him for a few minutes. I guess time just got away from us."

Belle shook her head in confusion. "Didn't Papa show you the sofas?"

Kyle and Grace shook their heads.

"Okay," Belle said, still confused, "I'll take you there." She motioned for them to follow her back inside the building.

Kyle stayed rooted to the spot. "I'll wait out here."

Ethan smiled at him. "Me too."

"Me too," Michael said weakly.

Sighing heavily, Belle grabbed Michael and Kyle by their hands and dragged them into the building.

* * * *

Grace took in her newly furnished apartment and sighed in pleasure as she ran her hand over the soft blue velvet sofa. She smiled down at Abry who was sleeping on her lap.

"I can't believe how well your clothes fit." Belle stood in front of the new floor length mirror hanging in the living room and admired her reflection. She slipped Grace's hunter green Italian leather jacket over Grace's white silk dress and twirled around. "Do you think I can borrow that green silk scarf I saw on your dresser?"

Frowning, Grace looked at her dirty gray walls. "Hmm. Did you say Michael was a good painter?"

Belle nodded. "He said he can help us paint next weekend."

Grace smiled. "I have a black scarf that would look good with that outfit, too. Look in the box on the top shelf of my closet."

Ring.

Grace glanced at the phone. Reluctantly standing up, she placed the bunny on the floor, walked over to the desk, and answered the phone.

"Hello?" she asked. She waited half a beat before asking one more time. When she received no answer, she hung up the phone. "Creep," she muttered before pressing the answering machine button.

Her fingers trailed the rich mahogany finish of her new dining room table, as she walked from the dining room to the kitchen. Yawning, she opened her refrigerator as her messages began to play.

"Grace, we've had a change of plans."

Grace chuckled when Abry dashed to her side, his nose twitching. He stood on his hind feet and placed his paws against her leg, his big pink eyes looking from her to the refrigerator and back again.

"We're not having Christmas in Gatlinburg this year."

"Who's that?" Belle asked from her room.

"My twin sister, Hope," Grace called out over her shoulder. She reached into the refrigerator and pulled out a carrot stick. She smiled as the rabbit quickly grabbed the treat and hopped away.

"Mom wants to go somewhere warm, so we've decided to go to Hawaii."

"Ooh." Belle walked back into the living room, a green silk scarf tied around her throat. "Mele Kalikimaka."

"I'm going to send you some money for the baggage fees."

Grace looked up from the fridge towards the answering machine.

"Get a suitcase and start packing my clothes—"

Grace dashed over to the desk, slamming her hand on the delete button.

"Your sister sounds so nice."

Grace pressed the forward button. "Yes, she's a sweetheart."

"It's so nice that you can share clothes with your sister. I wish I had a sister. I have a brother." Belle kicked off Grace's—or in reality—Hope's heels. "It's just weird when we share clothes."

"Belle?" A soft feminine voice came over the machine. *"I hope this is your number. I've been trying to reach you on your cell phone all day, but it just keeps going to voice mail."*

Belle swore softly. She picked up her purse and pulled out her cell phone. "Battery's dead."

"Your dad gave me this number. I hope it's yours. I really need your help." The caller began crying hysterically.

Still standing by the machine, Grace asked, "Who's that?"

Belle shook her head, sadly. "Tabitha."

"I'm in a lot of trouble. Can I come by tonight? Ilya gave me your new address. I just need to talk to you for a few minutes. Could you meet me outside around eight o'clock? I'll wait across the street. Please, please, be there. Don't tell anyone I called. Not a soul, Belle. Please."

They turned to the grandfather clock.

Twenty after eight.

Belle grabbed her keys and quickly ran out of the apartment. Just as quickly, Grace crossed to the window and pulled back the drapes. Tabitha was leaning against the lamppost across the street, speaking to a man in a parked car. Suddenly, Tabitha started backing up. She held her hands out in a pleading gesture.

To Grace's surprise, Daniel Burns exited the car. He pointed to the car and made his own pleading gesture. Whatever he was saying appeared to have the desired effect on her. She suddenly launched herself into his arms. They kissed briefly, hurriedly. Pulling apart, they hopped into the car and sped away.

Ring.

Grace looked at the phone with a feeling of dread. She was starting to hate the sound of a ringing phone.

Hesitantly, she picked up the receiver and brought it to her ear.

There was no sound, just breathing.

She slammed the phone down.

Monday, December 12th

CHAPTER FOURTEEN

GRACE SWITCHED THE phone to her other ear. "No, Jeff, no zombies. I told you, it's a board game. You remember, we used to play them with Mom and Dad all the time. Yes, I know how old you are. That's why I'm calling. What do you think about a mystery game? There'll be a dead body," she cajoled. "What? No Jeff, it won't turn into a zombie. Would you just think about it? Talk it over with your friends and get back to me. Good, talk to you later." She hung up the phone and glanced up at Kyle standing in the doorway.

"What did your brother think?" Kyle asked.

Grace grimaced. "He's fifteen. It was so much easier to use him as a guinea pig five years ago."

"A zombie board game might be fun. We could make the little game pieces various body parts."

"Uh, no," Grace said slowly.

"Did he like the detective's name?"

Grace shook her head. "Hated it. Said it sounded too girly."

Kyle smiled. "See—"

"He hated yours, too."

"Oh," he said disappointed. "Did you explain that it was based on the first game?"

Nodding, she said, "He didn't care. He said it sounded dumb."

Scowling, Kyle said, "Oh, he's fifteen. What does he know?"

"He and his friends are an example of our target audience. He promised to poll his buddies and girlfriend to see what they think. We need to get an idea of what kids that age like." She shook her head as soon as he opened his mouth and added, "They have to like something besides zombies."

Kyle sighed. "You had some calls while you were talking to your brother." He glanced down at the notepad in his hand. "A Melodie Baker called. She wanted you to know that your ten-year reunion is set for next fall and that an invitation will be arriving soon."

Grace's face lit up. "Oh, that's great! I wonder if Ethan would like to go with me."

"If he's still around," he muttered.

"What was that?" she asked, despite having heard what he said.

"I didn't say anything," he said before quickly moving on to the next message in his hand. "Your sister called right after Melodie, and said don't even bother asking. She's not going to the reunion and she wanted to remind you that her closet is not a department store. You can send the clothes you swiped from her at any time now." He lifted up his hands. "Her words, not mine."

Grace crossed her arms and leaned back in her chair. "She'll get those clothes over my dead body."

Kyle stared at her.

"She knows what she did. Did you find those old designs in the attic?" she asked, quickly changing the subject. She had sent him up to the attic earlier in the morning to bring down all of the boxes from the previous board game department on the theory that even if all the copies of *All the Murderers* were missing, perhaps the designs for the board game still existed.

Kyle looked over his shoulder before shaking his head. "I found something better," he whispered. He held up his hand before turning and walking out of the room. A few seconds later he returned carrying a large plastic bag. He closed the door and walked over to her desk.

Grace leaned forward. "What did you find?"

Kyle reached into the bag and pulled out a board game. He held it up for her to see. *All the Murderers* was embossed in big red letters across the cover of the game.

Grace let out a small squeal as she reached for the game. "You found it!"

"They actually weren't hard to find. There were over twenty boxes of the game and all of them clearly labeled." He laid his hands flat against her desk and leaned forward. "I also discovered that we're not the first ones to update the game."

Still smiling, Grace waved her hand. "Yeah, I think the company tried to update it in the late nineties. It wasn't that big of a seller."

"Do you know who was put in charge of the update?"

Wondering why it was so important, Grace shook her head.

"Daniel Burns. He had to have known these games were up there. He lied to us."

She set the game on her desk. "But why lie about something so trivial," she asked bewildered.

"Got me." He frowned. "That's not all," he said, hesitantly.

"Go on," she prompted.

"Well, I think someone or something—probably someone… although you never really know—" Sighing, he sat down in the chair in front of her desk.

"What is it?" she asked, growing more curious by the second.

"You're not going to believe me."

She shook her head, quickly assured him that she would.

"I think someone's been living in the attic."

"Don't be silly," she said with a laugh.

"I'm telling you the truth. There's a mattress up there, blankets, and a little kerosene lamp." At her doubtful look, he said, "I promise you."

"Did you see anyone?"

"No, I think whoever was squatting up there is gone."

Grace reached for her phone. "I better let Straker know. He'll—"

"That's not all." His face clouded. "It might be nothing. I haven't said anything until now because I didn't want to unload this on you as soon as you came back from lunch," he said with a worried look. "I don't want to scare you."

Concerned, Grace leaned forward. "Kyle, what is it?"

"You're still getting those strange calls," Kyle said quietly. "Have they said anything yet?"

"No, but they're coming in more frequently." Kyle's jaw clenched. He drew a hand through his hair before adding, "Grace, I don't think you should investigate Lily's death by yourself. It's too dangerous to go after a killer alone. You need help."

A knock sounded at the door. A second later the door swung open and Belle stuck her head in. "There you are, Kyle. Are you ready?"

* * * *

Grace walked into Valerie's office. "Val, have you seen Daniel?"

Valerie looked up from her computer. "He's having a late lunch with Straker and Louisa. They should be back any moment. Oh, by the way, Ethan came by while you were at lunch. He said he'd call you later tonight to compare notes. I think he wants to know whether you learned anything important from Ilya Dragovich, Saturday morning."

"Not really, but I discovered something pretty interesting that night," she said, describing what she saw outside her window between Daniel and Tabitha.

"You're kidding me!" Valerie stood up and walked toward Grace. "Daniel's been fooling around with the magician's assistant?" she asked, a little too loudly for Grace's comfort.

"Shh." Grace leaned back and looked out into the hallway. Kyle was walking toward her carrying a box. He smiled at her as he passed by. Grace watched him as he continued down the hallway, wondering if he had heard Valerie's question.

Valerie put a hand to her heart, her face a mixture of pity and sorrow. "Oh, poor Louisa."

"Do you think her father knows?"

"No way. Daniel would be out the door if Straker knew." She looked at her friend suspiciously. "Why do you want to see Daniel?"

"I'm going to ask him about it. That and about the mystery game in the attic."

Valerie frowned. "What mystery game?"

Grace didn't answer. Out of the corner of her eye, she noticed Belle walking down the hallway. Belle smiled and waved as she continued down the hallway to her office.

Valerie looked from Grace to the blonde and then back. "Isn't that your jacket?"

Grace nodded.

"That looked like your skirt, too."

"Yep."

A few seconds later Belle reappeared in the hallway, carrying a box. They watched as the girl continued down the hallway until she turned a corner and disappeared from view.

"Is she styling her hair like yours, too?" Valerie asked.

"Yes, but in her defense, you have to style your hair that way in order to wear those hair clips."

A worried frown crossed Valerie's face. "You lock your bedroom door at night, I hope."

"Don't be silly. I'm not going to start worrying, until she dyes her hair red and starts answering to my name."

They fell silent as both Belle and Kyle passed by, carrying a flashlight, a rope, a camcorder, and a hacksaw.

Valerie shook her head. "Do you think someone should check on them?"

"Probably." Grace pushed herself off the wall and walked in the direction Belle and Kyle had gone. She turned the corner and walked to the conference room. Finding the room empty, she shut the door and was about to check the stairwell when she heard voices coming from her left. She looked at the closet door and sighed. After spending a few seconds debating with herself on whether she should knock or not and ultimately deciding against it, she opened the door to find Kyle sitting cross-legged on the floor while Belle stood on a box, looking at her phone.

Grace raised an eyebrow. "If Jack and Chrissy are done playing, it's time to go."

"We weren't playing," Belle said quickly, "I was checking my messages. I can't get a signal anywhere else."

Grace turned to Kyle who was just picking himself off the floor. "And you?"

Kyle jerked a thumb toward Belle. "I was waiting for her to get done. We are going to go up to the attic."

"Why?" Grace asked, with a feeling of dread coming over her.

Belle slipped her phone into her pocket. "We want to see who's hiding up there."

"Or what's hiding up there," Kyle countered

"It's not a what," Belle said in exasperation. "If you found a lamp and a mattress then it's obviously a who."

"Then where is he? He wasn't up there when I went up there this morning. So, where did he run to? And more importantly *what* did he run from?" Kyle nodded his head. "*Whoever* was squatting up there probably got scared off by *whatever* it is haunting the attic."

Belle rolled her eyes. "There is no such thing as ghosts."

"Well, that's what we're going to find out," Kyle responded icily. Turning to Grace, he said, "I really do think this place is haunted." He bent down and picked up the rope and the camcorder that was lying at his feet. Passing the camcorder to Belle, he asked, "Do you want to help us search?"

Deciding it was probably best if she supervised Kyle's little ghost hunt, Grace motioned for them to precede her to the stairwell. She reluctantly followed them up the stairs, listening with horror as Kyle recounted in excruciating detail the last ghost story he had read. When he reached the part where the poor hapless female was dragged kicking and screaming into the attic by some unseen force, Grace finally had enough. "Don't you know any happy stories?"

Belle slipped the camera strap over her head. "It sounds like the legend of Amelia Dale that Papa always tells during Halloween. The poor tragic Miss Dale, struck down by a magician's sword, doomed to haunt the Dragon's Lair forever," she intoned, shining a flashlight under her chin.

"I thought she died in the glass chest," Grace said.

Belle shrugged. "Papa likes to change it around sometimes."

"A ghost would explain some of the strange things going on here," Kyle said.

"Really?" Belle asked sarcastically. She paused on the steps and turned to Kyle. "Do you really think Lily was killed by the ghost of Amelia Dale and then came all the way over here to haunt us?"

"I said this place was haunted, not the Dragon's Lair. What, do you think the ghost called a cab? There can be more than one ghost, you know?" he asked a bit defensively.

Belle smirked. "You're right, how silly of me."

Kyle shook his head sadly. "It's probably the ghost of some poor, lonely toy worker who passed away toiling over some child's Christmas gift that they callously tossed aside a few days later."

"There's just one problem, Kyle," Grace said. "No one's ever died in this building."

When they reached the door to the attic, Grace stepped past them and turned the doorknob. "That's strange. No one ever locks this door. I'll have to go back downstairs. I don't have my keys."

"That's okay." Belle reached up to her hair and pulled out a couple of small metal picks. Grace watched in fascination as the other woman used the picks to unlock the door. Once the door was unlocked, Belle stepped back and returned the picks to her hair.

"Nice," Grace said in admiration as Belle pushed open the door to the attic. They all peered into the darkened attic. After a few seconds, Grace stepped back and waited for the other two to begin their ghost hunt. When neither of them seemed to be in any hurry, she motioned for them to go forward. When that didn't work and they remained rooted to the spot, she said, "Well, go on."

Kyle smiled. "Yeah, Belle, go on. What are you waiting for?"

Belle took out her cell phone and snapped a picture from the doorway.

"What's wrong?" Grace asked with a smile when Belle made no further movement toward the attic.

Glaring at Kyle, Belle shook her head in irritation. "It's all his fault. I was perfectly fine coming up here before he started talking about ghosts."

Kyle smirked. "I thought you said there was no such things as ghosts."

"There isn't."

"Then go on."

"You first."

"I've already been up here once today."

Sighing, Grace stepped through the doorway as they continued to bicker. She flipped on the light switch. "Okay, Kyle, where did you see the mattress?"

"Just follow me," he said, leading them down a makeshift row between desks and broken chairs on one side and old moldy boxes on the other.

They were half way through the attic when Grace heard something moving off to her right. She came to a sudden stop, causing Belle to bump into her, just as an old lamp rolled off a desk and came to rest at her feet.

She felt Belle move closer to her.

"I probably knocked into the desk without realizing it," Grace said, trying to reassure herself as much as Belle.

"Uh huh." Belle dashed around Grace and wrapped her hand around Kyle's arm. "Sure."

Grace grabbed Kyle's other arm and moved him out in front of her. "Okay, let's keep going."

Smiling, he led them down the path and made a right, beside a row of unicycles.

Belle snapped on her flashlight as they moved further away from the one light bulb hanging from the center of the attic. When they came to a dead end, she shined the light down at the floor and on to a group of old computers from the eighties.

Kyle frowned. "No, these weren't here. There was a mattress here." He looked back over his shoulder. Stepping over the monitors, he shoved a couple of boxes out of the way. "It was right here."

Grace and Belle watched as Kyle began tossing toys and boxes around, searching for the mattress, blankets and lantern he had seen earlier that morning. Thirty minutes later, he triumphantly held up a blanket he had found covering several toys from the thirties. "Here it is." He handed the blanket to Grace. "See, no dust. This is new."

Bored, Belle hopped off the desk she was sitting on. "Well, that solves that mystery."

"No, it doesn't," Kyle said. "We still don't know who was here or where they went. Hand me the camcorder. With any luck we can get whoever it is on video."

Belle slipped the camera strap over her head. "Fine, start recording, and then we'll come back tomorrow and see if anyone shows up," she said tossing the camcorder to Kyle. It landed several feet away with a clatter.

"Nice throw," Kyle said with a smirk. He walked over to the camcorder and inspected it. "It's broken."

Belle winced. "Sorry."

"Well, we can still set up the trap." He leaned down and picked up the rope he had brought with him to the attic.

Grace shook her head. "No. No traps."

Kyle's mouth fell open. "But—"

"No!" Grace dropped the blanket on the floor. "Besides, I don't think anyone's going to show now. You're the one who probably scared them off."

Belle breathed a sigh of relief. "Good," she said, walking to the elevator. "I'm getting out of here. This place gives me the willies." She looked down at the boxes stacked around the elevator door. Raising her eyebrow, she glanced back at Grace. "Why is the elevator blocked?"

"It won't rise past the fourth floor, anymore," Grace said.

Sighing, Belle turned back around and walked toward the stairwell.

Grace was just about to follow her, when she felt Kyle touch her arm.

Glancing at Belle's back, he dropped his voice to a whisper. "So, Daniel is having an affair with the magician's assistant."

Grace closed her eyes with a groan. "I was afraid you heard that."

"Do you think they killed Lily?"

"I don't know. Why would they want to kill Lily? What could they possibly gain from her death?"

He brushed past her and headed for the stairs. "I don't know? Why don't we ask him?"

CHAPTER FIFTEEN

GRACE RACED AFTER him as quick as she could, but unfortunately, he was too fast. By the time she made it down the stairs, Kyle had already located Daniel in the hallway in front of Straker's office.

"Hey, can I ask you a question?" Kyle asked, stepping in front of the other man.

Daniel looked up at him in surprise. "Of course, you're Kyle, aren't you?" He looked at the younger man curiously. "You know, you look so familiar—"

"We ran into each other downstairs at the toy store last week," Kyle said. "You were talking to Jackie."

Daniel smiled in remembrance. "Now I remember. Were you the one who waxed the store floor with car wax?"

"Yeah," Kyle admitted, self-consciously tugging on his ear.

Grace watched in sympathy as Kyle's face turned five different shades of red.

Daniel smiled. "I've been meaning to ask, how's Henry's head?"

"Better." Kyle turned to Grace. "It wasn't the whole floor, just one side. I thought it would be nice if we created a little skating rink."

Daniel reached out and clapped his hand on Kyle's shoulder. Ever the team builder, Daniel launched into a morale booster that would make any management guru proud. "That's what this company needs. People willing to test boundaries. It's so great to have you on our team. Grace has had nothing but good things to say about you."

Grace automatically nodded, despite the fact she hadn't spoken to Daniel since Kyle was hired.

Still squeezing Kyle's shoulder, Daniel said, "Now, I want you to know that even though she is your direct supervisor, my door is always open. In fact, don't even think about her or me as your supervisors. Think of us as a family. Our goal at the Straker Toy Company is to make this a happy and enjoyable place to work."

Grace stifled a yawn and resisted the urge to look at her watch.

"One where everyone is free to think and act creatively, from the product managers to the assistants—who are an integral part of this business—without fear. Now, you said you have a question. How can I help you?"

Kyle opened his mouth.

Daniel smiled. "Don't be afraid to speak your mind. Remember, this is your new home."

Kyle reflexively smiled back. "Well, I was curious…"

"Ah, curiosity! That's excellent. You've only been here for less than a week and you're already thinking creatively. I just want you to know that any ideas you have, and no idea is too dumb here at the Straker Toy Company, will be warmly accepted with an open mind."

Grace had been alternately staring at Kyle's dumbfounded expression and the floor, but something in Daniel's tone caused her to look up. Was that sarcasm she detected? Odd. Daniel was usually such a happy toy soldier in Straker's army.

"Don't be afraid to run your thoughts, concerns, or issues by me or Grace. There are no dumb ideas. What's dumb is not sharing your ideas. Any idea you have. It doesn't matter. No matter what it is, we will devote the necessary time and expense in making it a reality."

Kyle stood still, waiting for Daniel to continue. When it appeared the other man was finally silent, Kyle blew out a breath. "Well, I… I… I…" He shrugged, suddenly at a loss for words. He looked at Grace in helpless confusion.

Daniel's smile grew wider. "What's great about this company is that we don't have to answer to shareholders. We are free to experiment. Test the limits of toy design. Go places the big companies are afraid to go. Why don't you set up an appointment with Ellen? We'll sit down and have a nice chat about your future here at our company." Daniel patted Kyle's shoulder again.

Kyle stammered for a bit before indicating Grace with a curt nod, "Actually, Ms. Holliday is the one with the questions."

Daniel turned to her expectantly.

"Thanks, Kyle," she said, trying her best to keep the sarcasm out of her voice. She shook her head and turned to Daniel. "Can I speak to you? Privately?"

Daniel recognized the warning in her voice. She watched as his smile faltered. He looked at his watch and smiled apologetically. "I'm sorry, Grace, can it wait? I'm meeting Louisa—"

Grace took a deep breath. Might as well jump in. "I saw you and Tabitha Eddington outside my apartment last night."

Daniel went pale. He gripped her arm painfully, only letting go when Kyle pushed his hand away. With a harsh nod of his head, he motioned for them to follow him. He led them down to the small hallway between the bathrooms. "I don't know what you think you saw—"

Grace shook her head. "Don't bother lying to me. I saw you both kiss. How long have you and Tabitha been having an affair?"

Daniel swallowed hard. "You don't understand."

"No, I think I understand quite well. I saw you sneaking around behind the stage during the magic show with Tabitha, too." Grace guessed. She tilted her head as a sudden thought occurred to her. "Did Lily see you too?"

Kyle's eyes widened. "If she did that would give you quite the motive to kill her, wouldn't it?"

Daniel crossed his arms. "I love my wife, and frankly, it's really none of your business what I do," he said coldly.

"What were you and Tabitha doing back stage, Daniel?" Grace asked.

"What do you think?" He looked at her in surprise. "You can't seriously think we killed Lily."

"Well," Grace said, "it has crossed my mind. You two weren't very discreet. If I saw you back there, then Lily might have too. Perhaps, you were afraid that she would tell Straker."

"Yeah, if it came out you were cheating on the boss' daughter, you might lose your cushy position here," Kyle said.

Daniel laughed bitterly. "Cushy? You have to be kidding me. Do you see what I deal with on a daily basis? Between Straker's penchant of making enemies wherever he goes and my wife's penchant for drinking and gambling the profits away, we're barely surviving."

"Still…" Grace said.

"Still nothing. First of all, Straker is a businessman. Granted, he is not a very good one, but still, he is a businessman. He's ruthless, but he's not foolish. I'm the only thing keeping us afloat and he knows that. Even if Louisa divorced me, her father would never fire me. He needs me too much. Secondly, Lily is the one who introduced Tabitha to me. She practically encouraged our relationship."

"Why would she do that to her own daughter-in-law?" Grace asked aghast.

Daniel shook his head. "Revenge. Lily was convinced that Louisa was trying to sabotage her marriage to Straker, so she decided to get her back by introducing me to Tabitha."

"How was Louisa sabotaging their marriage?" Kyle asked.

When Daniel turned away, Grace answered for him, "By sending anonymous letters. Am I right?"

Daniel nodded. "I'm positive that she's the one who sent those letters from a *concerned friend* to her father, warning him of his wife's cheating ways. Making little insinuations. Trying to make Franklin paranoid. After so many stepmothers, Louisa's gotten rather good at it."

"That sounds rather cruel," Kyle said.

"Dangerous too," Grace said. "How far was Louisa willing to go to break up Lily and her father?"

"Louisa wouldn't hurt anyone," Daniel said emphatically. "Neither would I and I especially wouldn't have hurt Lily."

"What made her so special?" Kyle asked.

"Lily was a sort of ally. She actually had a good head for business. We were slowly turning this company back from the brink with the addition of the magic shop and some extra funds she brought into the company."

"Where was she getting this extra money?" Grace asked.

"Her family's rather well off." Daniel shrugged. "I think she inherited some money from an aunt or a grandmother."

"Do you have any idea who could have killed Lily?" Kyle asked.

Daniel looked uncomfortable. He shook his head while giving a half shrug.

Grace crossed her arms. "You were backstage, so you must have seen something, Daniel."

"You were back there too," he snapped as little beads of perspiration began to appear on his forehead.

"Yeah, and I saw you and Tabitha," she said. "So, what did you see?" When he didn't answer, she said, "Okay. What was Tabitha crying about that night?"

Daniel began to nervously look around. "I don't know."

Grace narrowed her eyes. "Come on, Daniel, you obviously know something. What is it?"

His eyes glanced back and forth between Kyle and Grace before finally settling on Grace. His eyes bore into hers. "I really can't say what happened to Lily. I just can't say." His eyes shifted to Kyle and then back to her.

Suddenly realizing, he didn't want to say anything with Kyle standing there, Grace said, "Fine."

Daniel smiled. "Well, if that's all—"

"No, actually I still need to talk to you about my ideas for some new board games." She turned to Kyle. "Can you go get the board game you found earlier? I want to show it to Daniel."

Kyle looked between her and Daniel. "Why don't we all go back to your office?"

"No, that's not necessary, just bring the game to Daniel's office," she said with a smile.

Reluctantly, Kyle turned around and slowly walked down the hall.

As soon as he was out of earshot, Daniel closed the distance between them. Standing as closely as possible, he whispered, "I didn't kill Lily, but I know who did."

Keeping her voice low, she whispered back, "Then go to the police."

"I can't. It's too dangerous. If I say anything, I'm a dead man."

When Allen turned around the corner, they pulled away from each other. Passing them, he nodded quickly and continued on his way.

"Daniel, the only way for you to be safe is to talk to the police."

"You don't understand. I have no proof. It could easily be turned around and blamed on me. If nothing else, I'm an accessory after the fact now." He shook his head sadly. "If it was just me, then I would go to the cops, but it's not."

"Then why are you telling me this?"

He gave her a look. "Because I like you, Grace. I don't know what my father-in-law is up to, but you're in danger. If you don't stop asking questions, you're going to end up dead like Lily. Grace…" He looked at her in concern. "That's not just speculation. That's what I was told. If you don't stop, you're next."

Grace's heart sped up. "If I'm in danger, then you need to tell me who from."

He looked over his shoulder as Michael and Sidney Harcourt turned the corner. Harcourt was berating the younger man about something. Michael looked at them curiously, as he passed by and continued down the hallway. "Look, don't trust anyone. Just keep your head down and do your job."

When he started to turn away, Grace grabbed his arm and brought him back around. "And let Lily's killer get away?"

"I promise you, Grace, that's not going to happen. I just need some time to clear some things up. Once I do, I'll go straight to the police. Just stay out of it until then."

The click clack of high heels sounded throughout the hallway. They both stepped further away from each other as Belle rounded the corner. Belle's eyes lit up when she saw Grace. "There you are, roomie. I've been looking everywhere for you. What are you doing here?"

"We're just going over the mystery board game. Daniel thinks we should rethink the whole thing."

"Right," Daniel quickly agreed. "I think you should turn it into a bloodbath."

Grace groaned. She really should have compared stories with him before saying anything.

"A bloodbath?" Belle said. "We could kill off every character and the one who survives till the end wins."

"That's a great idea!" Daniel glanced at his watch. "Well, I'm sorry, but I've got a meeting to go to."

Belle fell into place next to him. "But I thought you all were meeting in your office?"

"You ran into Kyle?" Grace asked, wondering how much Kyle had told Belle.

Belle nodded. "He thought you would want me there."

"And we do," Daniel said, "but I think we have everything worked out. You have some great ideas. I'd get started on fleshing out the designs right away."

"All of them?" Belle asked.

Grace started to shake her head, when Daniel said, "Absolutely."

Persistent, Belle asked, "Even the zombie game?"

Daniel stared at them for a few seconds before quickly agreeing. "Love zombies! What a wonderful idea, Belle!"

They really should have gotten their stories straight first, Grace thought, a bit unhappily, as she fantasized about the next few months being deep into zombie research.

"Well, things sound great. I better get going." Daniel turned away and walked down the hall to his office.

Grace turned to Belle. "Where's Kyle?"

Belle shrugged. "He was still in your office when I spoke to him."

They both walked down the hallway, Belle excitedly chattering away about her idea for the magic board game, while Grace thought back to Daniel's warning. "Belle, I forgot that I need to speak to

Valerie about something. Could you go and tell Kyle that we're not meeting with Daniel anymore?"

Grace watched as the other woman practically skipped down the hallway with a cheery, "See you soon," thrown back at her.

Opening the door to Straker's outer office, Grace found Valerie sitting at her desk, typing on the computer keyboard. She looked up as Grace entered.

"What's wrong?" Valerie asked worriedly. "You look pale."

Grace sank down in the chair next to Valerie's desk. "Daniel just told me that he knows who killed Lily and that I'm next if I don't stop asking questions."

Shocked, Valerie sat there with her mouth hanging open. Snapping her mouth shut, she said, "Then stop investigating."

"I can't do that, Val. This is where I work. Whether I like it or not, I'm stuck here and as long as I'm here, I'm going to try to find out who killed Lily. I'm not going to let someone scare me off."

"Grace," Valerie sighed, "what exactly did Daniel say?"

Still reeling, Grace related the story back. When she got to the part about Lily helping keep the business solvent, Valerie snorted. "He's lying."

"That's what he said."

"I don't care what he said. I can show you the books right now. Lily has taken money out of the company's accounts. She's never put any in."

"Why would he lie about that?"

"I don't know," Valerie shrugged. "Oh, by the way, Ethan called and left a message."

"Why didn't he call my assistant and leave a message?"

Valerie smiled. "Have you tried calling Kyle?"

Grace shook her head.

"Try it sometime. If he doesn't accidentally hang up, he leaves you on hold and then forgets about you."

"Well, the system is rather difficult to use," Grace said quickly jumping to Kyle's defense. "There's all those buttons."

Valerie looked at her.

"I have trouble with it myself. Kyle's new, but I'm sure he'll figure it out soon enough."

Valerie leaned back in her chair. Her lips began to curve up. "What?"

She shook her head. "Nothing. I've just noticed that you tend to get rather defensive when anyone criticizes your new assistant."

"Oh, I do not," Grace said quickly.

Valerie laughed.

Grace shook her head. "Whatever. What did Ethan want?"

"He's coming by to take you to lunch at," Valerie checked the clock on the computer, "well, in just about ten minutes."

"Good, I'm starving. You want to come with us?"

Valerie nodded. "I wonder what he'll say about Daniel's warning."

"Let's not tell Ethan about what Daniel said just yet."

"Are you worried he'll get upset?" Valerie smiled. "He seems to care about you a great deal."

"I just think we should be careful about what we say right now. The whole 'you're in danger, Grace' thing has kind of upset me."

"I know. Me too." Valerie leaned over the desk. "You know, I think he's falling in love with you, Grace. I've seen the way he looks at you. His face just lights up whenever you're around. I don't think he'd be happy hearing that you're next on the killer's hit list."

Grace stood up. "Which is why we shouldn't say anything, yet."

"All right, I won't tell, but you're going to have to tell him eventually."

"Eventually," she agreed as she walked out the door and down the hallway.

Grace opened the door to her office, surprised to find Kyle and Belle kneeling on the floor, surrounded by scraps of her latest designs. Everywhere she looked, were bits and pieces of paper.

Normally, Grace would have been upset, but considering she felt like ripping up the designs and starting anew many times the day before, she couldn't really muster up the anger necessary to yell at them. Besides, hearing that you were next to be killed, tended to put things into perspective, she thought as she quietly closed the door behind her.

She stepped around Kyle and sat down at her desk. They watched her from their position on the floor, waiting for her to say something. She folded her hands on the desk. "I take it that you two would like to start over."

Belle and Kyle looked at each other for a moment before rapidly speaking at once.

Grace held up her hands. "Wait, one at a time."

Kyle nodded at Belle, who nodded back.

Belle shook her head. "You found it, you tell her."

Kyle got to his feet. Nervously, he ran his hand through his hair, pointing to the papers scattered on the floor. "I didn't do this."

"Who did?" Grace asked.

"I don't know. I came down here to pick up the game just like you asked me to do and I found them like this."

Grace looked at Belle, "Why didn't you tell me what had happened when we met in the hallway?"

She raised herself to her knees. "I had no idea."

"No," Kyle said, "we ran into each other outside the door. She never came inside until just a few minutes ago."

Standing up, Grace walked around the desk and kneeled down. She picked up a few scraps and tossed them into the waste basket next to the desk. "What a mess. Why would someone destroy my designs? They weren't that bad."

"That's not all they did." Kyle stood up and walked over to the flip board. "I think you should take a look at this. Someone has edited your list."

Grace stood up and walked over to the board. "Edited?" she asked, looking over the board. She didn't notice it at first. It wasn't large or written in a bright color. It was actually very unremarkable, but quite frightening just the same. At the top of the page, where Grace had written *Who killed Lily Straker?*, there was one small change. Lily's name had been crossed out and underneath her name someone had written *Grace Holliday.*

She looked at Kyle and then down at his ink stained hands.

"I swear, I didn't do this."

Belle touched Grace on the shoulder. "Grace, I think you should be worried."

* * * *

Grace picked up the phone and dialed Straker office number. She needed to speak to her boss. If anyone could get the truth out of Daniel it was Franklin Straker, she thought as she waited for him to pick up the phone. As soon as he answered, she quickly explained what had happened to her office.

"Sounds like corporate espionage. Clearly our competitors are getting worried," Straker said.

"I very much doubt our competitors care one bit about what we do. It was a message from Lily's killer."

"Don't be ridiculous. Why would Lily's killer care about your game designs?"

"I'm sure they don't. It was a message for me to stop asking questions," she said, describing how Lily's name was crossed off and her's written in.

"Excellent! That's perfect."

"Perfect?"

"Absolutely, you must be making the killer nervous."

"Good, because he's making me nervous. I think we should call the police."

"No. They're not going to do anything about a couple of torn pieces of paper. Look, you just keep doing whatever you're doing and keep me informed."

"There's more. I spoke to Daniel. He knows who killed..." She paused at the sound of a click. "Hello? Hello? . . . I cannot believe he just hung up on me."

Grace sighed as she replaced the phone receiver back in its cradle. She glanced behind her shoulder. Belle was hovering behind her. "Where's Kyle?"

"I ... I think he went to get something to drink."

Grace looked at Belle's worried face. "Everything's going to be fine, Belle."

"But someone wrote your name—"

"Just someone's idea of a sick joke."

"I think you should take it seriously."

"I am." Grace turned the corner and walked down the hall towards Straker's office. "Trust me, I am."

Belle followed close behind. Just as they reached Straker's office, Valerie ran out in a rush, almost knocking into them.

"Have you two seen Daniel?" Valerie asked in a panic.

"What's wrong?" Grace asked.

"Louisa's been hurt. She's being rushed to the hospital," Valerie said quickly.

Belle gasped. "Where's Franklin?"

"He just left down the back stairs," Valerie said, dashing down the hall.

Grace and Belle followed her towards Daniel's office. They ran into Kyle who was coming from the opposite direction. One look at their face must have clued him in that something was wrong. He immediately stopped and turned around.

Belle quickly filled him in on what they knew, as Valerie knocked and entered Daniel's office, quietly closing the door behind her.

"Do you have any idea what happened?" Kyle asked.

Grace shook her head. "It must be bad, because I've never seen Valerie so upset before."

Belle twirled her hair around her fingers. "How awful."

"Do you want me to go with you to the hospital?" Grace asked.

Belle stopped twisting her hair. "Me? Why would I need to go?"

"Well, your fiancé's daughter is in the hospital. I think he would want you there." Grace said patiently.

Belle looked at her blankly for a moment before saying, "Right. Yes, of course. I mean, no, you don't have to come. I'll be fine."

Kyle interrupted. "Actually, I think someone should go with you."

Belle looked ready to protest, but then suddenly agreed. "Yeah, you're right. Grace, would you mind?"

Grace shook her head. "Not at all."

"I think I left my jacket in the conference room," Belle said. "I'll go get it."

"I'll wait for you here," Grace said. She leaned up against the wall as Belle dashed down the hall towards the conference room.

Daniel threw open his office door. "How bad is she?" he asked, as he pulled on his winter coat.

"I don't know," Valerie said. "They wouldn't say."

Grace backed out of the way as Daniel moved down the hallway and toward the elevator doors. She watched as he turned the corner and walked out of her sight. Valerie followed. She leaned up against the wall near the conference room. "Straker is already on his way, Daniel. He said he'd meet you at the hospital." She glanced at Grace and gave her a pained look.

"What is taking the elevator so long?" Daniel asked.

Suddenly, Grace heard the ding announcing the arrival of the elevator. A few seconds later she heard Ethan's voice. "Oh, I'm sorry. Excuse me."

A few seconds after that she heard Allen. "Oops," he said, "would you watch where you're going?"

"I'm sorry. I need to get past," Daniel said, his voice sounding strained.

"Hi, Val." Ethan greeted.

Grace watched as Val half-heartedly waved.

"Oh, hey, Daniel," Allen said, "I really need to talk to you—"

"Excuse me," Ethan said again.

"Not now, Allen," Daniel said gruffly.

"But I really wanted to talk to you about my new designs. I think you're really going to like—" Allen said.

"I said not now!" Daniel shouted.

"Can I just get past—" Ethan said, sounding irritated.

A few seconds later, Allen passed down the hallway, his face flushed.

Grace took a step towards the elevator, wondering what was going on over there. "Maybe, I should go with Daniel. Why don't you take Belle—"

Kyle's hand wrapped around her upper arm and pulled her back. She looked up at him in surprise.

"I don't think that's a good idea, Grace," he said.

Before Grace could respond, the elevator alarm sounded. She looked back towards the hall. Valerie was still leaning against the wall. Only now, her eyes were opened wide and her hand was covering her mouth. She dropped her hand and screamed as she slowly slid down the wall.

CHAPTER SIXTEEN

ETHAN REACHED VALERIE first and gently laid her down on the floor.

Grace knelt down next to them. "Is she okay?"

"I think so." He lifted her wrist and checked her pulse. He slowly blew out his breath in a relieved gush. "I think she just fainted." He gently patted Valerie's face and called her name until her eyelids began to flutter.

Grace closed her eyes and took a deep breath, as she silently sent a prayer of thanks.

"What happened?" Valerie asked weakly.

Instead of answering, Grace looked up at Belle, who was just emerging from the conference room, sans jacket and then at Kyle. "Can one of you go get her some water?"

Belle started to turn away, but to Grace's surprise, Kyle yanked her back and shook his head.

Irritated, Ethan snapped at them, "Never mind. Just get out of the way." He easily lifted Valerie up into his arms and carried her into her office where he gently laid her down on the couch.

Grace laid her hand on Ethan's arm. "What happened?"

"I have no idea. She just screamed and passed out." He looked utterly bewildered. "Stay with Valerie. I'll get some water." He glared at Kyle who was hovering by the door, effectively blocking his way out. "Do you mind?"

Kyle slowly backed up and let the other man through.

Valerie lifted a hand to her head. "I can't believe I just fainted."

Grace knelt by the couch. "Are you okay?" she asked worriedly. "Do you want me to call for an ambulance?"

"No, I think I'm okay." Valerie sat up slowly. "I'm sorry, I don't know what happened. I just got dizzy all of a sudden."

"You didn't get dizzy," Kyle said a bit too forcefully. "You were scared. You saw something."

Valerie shook her head slowly. "I skipped breakfast, and I think my blood sugar just dropped."

Grace didn't particularly like how Kyle had said it, but she had to agree with him. Valerie saw something that terrified her and now she was making excuses. "What did you see, Val?"

Valerie let out a small, embarrassed laugh. "Nothing. I'm just tired." Unsteadily, Valerie rose to her feet. "I'm just going to freshen up a bit." Grace followed her into Straker's office, not too subtlety closing the door on Belle and Kyle. Once behind closed doors, Grace sank down into the chair in front of Straker's desk.

Opening the door to his private bathroom, Valerie splashed some water on her face. When she came out, she had lost that sickly pale look and was beginning to get some color in her cheeks. She sat down next to Grace.

"What happened?" Grace asked in concern.

"Grace, you're never going to believe me." Valerie pushed her bangs out of her face and rubbed a hand across her eyes. "No one is."

"Just start from the beginning."

Valerie laughed softly. "Oh, it's just so ridiculous. When Daniel gets back, we'll ask him what he saw."

"What is it, Val? What made you faint?"

Valerie's face turned red. "I can't believe I'm saying this, but… I think I saw a ghost."

"Grace," Ethan called as he opened the door. Grace noticed Kyle and Belle standing behind him, peering over his shoulder. "I need to talk to you."

She glanced at Valerie.

"It's okay," Valerie said with a small smile. "I'm starting to feel better."

Nodding, Grace walked over to Ethan.

Ethan opened his mouth to say something when Belle suddenly grabbed the water bottle from his hand and carried it to Valerie who set it down on the desk in front of her without opening it.

"Hey," Michael Talon said from the doorway, "Is everyone okay?" At Grace's nod, he looked over at Kyle. "Where's Belle?"

"She's in Straker's office," Kyle said.

Michael came further into the room. He awkwardly cradled one arm, as he craned his neck to see past Grace.

Grace was about to ask what was wrong with his arm when Ethan gently took her elbow. He leaned forward and said in hushed tones, "I think something may be wrong."

Kyle who had moved to stand next to Grace, raised an eyebrow. "What?"

Ethan straightened. In clipped tones, he said, "The elevator's stuck between two floors."

Michael finally stopped trying to catch a glimpse of Belle and focused on Grace. "They're trying to force open the doors now."

Rubbing a circle with his hand on her back, Ethan said gently, "I'm going to see if I can help."

Grace took his arm. "I'll go with you."

Kyle gently pushed Michael out of the way and went to her other side. "Me too."

Ethan looked at him for a second before softly shaking his head. "Great. The more the merrier."

* * * *

Grace leaned against the wall. Rolling her shoulders, she tried to work the kink that was beginning to form out of her back. She looked to her right and then her left and sighed. Kyle stood on one side while Ethan stood on the other. For some reason, that neither man seemed willing to explain, they had so far refused to speak to one another and had directed all comments and questions to her or rather, through her. She was starting to get a headache.

"Can you see what's going on now?" Kyle asked her.

Grace didn't bother pointing out that at five foot five she was at a slight disadvantage compared to his six foot one frame. Instead, she passed the question over to Ethan who was standing closer to the elevator doors and had a slightly better view than she had.

"They're still working on the doors," Ethan said craning his neck to see past the rescue workers.

"Why isn't Daniel saying anything?" Grace asked as a small pit of dread began to form in her stomach. There had been no communication with Daniel since the elevator doors closed over an hour ago. Absolutely nothing since he pushed the elevator alarm. He hadn't screamed for help. He hadn't made an emergency call. Nothing. "What is going on?"

She glanced back and forth between the two men who each shrugged. Sighing, she motioned for Kyle to follow her down the hall. Once they were away from everyone else, she pivoted around and confronted him. "What did you mean that I could get hurt?"

"What?"

"Right before Valerie fainted, you grabbed my arm, and said, that I could get hurt."

His clear blue eyes clouded. "I just meant that you shouldn't go anywhere alone. Someone threatened you today, remember? We need to stick together."

Sounds reasonable, she thought. She looked past his body at the crowd gathered at the elevator. "Come on, let's go back. Surely, it can't take much longer."

Grace walked back down the hallway. She stood next to Ethan, who smiled at her and wrapped his arm around her shoulders. He kissed her gently on the forehead.

Kyle looked away. "I'm going to see if I can get any closer." Grace watched as he weaved his way past their coworkers who were standing on their tiptoes looking over the emergency crew's shoulders.

With his arm still wrapped around her shoulder, Ethan led her down the hallway. "I've wanted to talk to you since Saturday. I found something in Belle's apartment when I was helping her move that you should see." He reached into his pocket and handed her a ripped up picture of a young Belle, maybe, thirteen or fourteen years old. Her head was leaning on a blond-haired, blue-eyed Michael Talon's shoulder and standing behind the two teenagers was a woman. Someone had cut the picture in two, cutting the woman's head off, leaving only her shoulders and the gold dragon pendant with an emerald green eye that was fastened to her coat visible. "I wonder who the woman was standing behind Belle?"

Grace handed the picture back. "Lily Straker."

Ethan's eyebrows rose. "How can you tell?"

"That's her pendant and the boy next to Belle is Michael Talon."

Ethan peered down at the picture. "He looks familiar."

"He should. He sitting against the wall," she said pointing to Michael.

Ethan looked from the picture to Michael and back again. "Some transformation."

Just then, someone shouted for everyone to move back.

Ethan stood on his tiptoes. "I think they may have gotten the doors open. I'll be right back. I'm going to go see what's going on," he said, as he walked back toward the elevators.

She looked across the hallway at Michael, who sat on the floor, unsuccessfully trying to make his sleeves longer. Her eyes traveled to the floor and to the small drops of red that had splattered near his hand. She pushed herself off the wall and weaved her way around the other onlookers until she was next to Michael. She slid down next to him and asked him if he was okay.

"Yeah, sure, why do you ask?"

Grace pointed to the black bandana wrapped around his wrist. "Did you cut yourself?"

"Oh," he said, pushing his black hair back away from his face, "I was working on a disappearing sword trick and accidentally nicked myself."

"Is it bad?" she asked, reaching for his wrist.

Michael smiled. "I don't think I'll need stiches."

She dropped her hand. "Where's Belle? I thought she was sitting over here with you?"

He tugged his sleeve back down. "She went to the hospital to be with Mr. Straker."

"I'm surprised you didn't go with her."

He shook his head. "She doesn't want me." He paused. Blushing, he added, "I mean, she didn't want me to go with her."

"I'm surprised. You two seem rather close. How long have you both known each other?"

"Not long enough." He stood up suddenly. "I better get back down to the magic shop. Harcourt will probably dock my pay if I stay here any longer." He started to turn away but stopped as the sounds of several people gasping reached their ears. They looked back toward the elevator in time for Ethan and Kyle to turn the corner and walk back toward her.

She looked at Ethan's grim face and asked, "What's going on?"

Ethan shook his head. "It's not good."

"Daniel's not moving," Kyle said. "I think he's dead."

Grace gasped. "How?"

"Someone stabbed him in the back," Ethan said.

"Are you sure?" Michael asked.

"Positive. I saw the dagger myself when the doors opened," Ethan said.

"What kind of dagger?" Grace asked.

Ethan shrugged. "I don't know. I think it had a dragon's head."

* * * *

Grace sat in Straker's office waiting for him to appear. The police had left with Daniel's body hours ago, but were still questioning everyone that was at work that afternoon. They had been tight-lipped. So far, she had learned nothing more than the fact that Daniel was dead.

The door opened and Grace turned around. Straker was standing in the doorway and she could just make out Kyle and Valerie sitting on the couch behind him. Straker softly closed the door.

"What are you doing in here?" he asked gruffly. "Shouldn't you be out there questioning the witnesses?"

"The police are doing that. How's Louisa?"

He grunted. Sitting down behind his desk, he leaned back in his chair. "Fine, she's at home right now."

"Home?" Grace asked in surprise. "She was released from the hospital?"

"She was never at the hospital. She wasn't even in an accident. She was safe at home sleeping the whole entire time."

"I wonder if someone used that excuse just to get Daniel into the elevator."

"Seems like it."

"Did the police tell you what happened to him?"

"Someone stabbed him in the back with some fancy knife. They think he may have stopped the elevator himself by accident when he was trying to reach the call button."

"And there was no one else in the elevator when they opened the doors?"

"Not a soul."

"Do they have any idea, how…?"

He scowled. "They probably think it was a suicide." He shook his head in disbelief. "Why would someone kill Daniel? He's so boring and dull." He looked at her. "He's like you."

"Thank you."

"Mr. Letsallgetalong. Why kill him?"

"Because he knew who killed Lily."

"You sound awfully certain of that."

"I am. He told me right before he died."

Straker leaned forward. "Who did he say killed her?"

"He wouldn't say."

His scowl deepened. "That's not very helpful. What else did he say?"

Grace repeated what Daniel told her, discreetly leaving out the part about Louisa being the author of the anonymous letters.

"So, he was running around on my little girl with that magician's assistant, huh? You didn't tell the police that, did you?"

"Yes, I did."

Straker swore. "Next time, come to me first before you start tattling to the police."

"What next time? I'm hoping this is the last time. The police will have to reopen the investigation into your wife's death now, so let's let the professionals handle this. They're probably over there questioning Ilya Dragovich as we speak."

"Why him? He wasn't here today."

"You know, that fancy dagger they found in his back? Ethan told me that it looked like a dragon's head. I saw Ilya Dragovich with one just like it—"

"No good."

"But I saw him playing with it just this past Saturday."

"What kind of jewel did it have in its eyes?"

Grace thought back. "Rubies, I think. Why?"

"Lily had given Ilya a pair of dragon head daggers for his birthday this year. One had ruby eyes—Belle's birthstone—the other had sapphires—his son's. The one with the sapphire eyes went missing the night Lily died. Guess which one ended up in Daniel's back?"

Suddenly, the doors flew open. Wild-eyed, Louisa rushed into the room. "Where's Daniel?"

Immediately, Straker got out of his seat and walked over to his daughter. "Louisa, just calm down."

"Calm down? My husband has been murdered and you're telling me to calm down. I want to know what they've done with his body."

Straker wrapped an arm around his distraught daughter's shoulders. "They've taken it away."

Louisa shook her head. "I have a right to see."

Valerie came up behind Louisa. She gently steered the other woman to the leather couch.

Louisa turned panicked eyes toward her father. "The police were at the house and they were asking me all sorts of questions. They wanted to know if I knew a Tabitha Eddington."

Straker glared at Grace.

"Why would they be asking me about that woman?" Louisa asked. "I don't know her. In fact, I've never even met her. She meant nothing to me."

Straker took his daughter's hand into his and patted it gently. "What did they want to know?"

"They wanted to know if I knew about her affair with my husband."

"And, of course, you told them no," her father said.

Louisa's eyes flashed in anger. "I told them the truth."

Straker swore again. "Why? Next time the police ask you any questions, you tell them you want to speak to our lawyer."

"Why shouldn't I tell the truth?" Louisa asked. "She meant nothing to him. He told me just last night that it was over between them and that he was going to make it right again. He loved me." Her eyes filled with tears. "He was going to make everything right again. It's all Lily's fault. She's the one that introduced them."

"Did he say how he was going to make everything all right?" Grace asked.

Louisa pressed a shaking hand to her mouth. Her eyes lost their focus. "He was going to return the money," she said in a hushed voice. "Pay it all back."

"Money," Franklin said sharply, "what money?"

"It was that Tabitha," Louisa said bitterly. "She found out he was going to leave her, so she killed him. She killed my Daniel."

Thursday, December 15th

CHAPTER SEVENTEEN

GRACE LOOKED AT the somber faces sitting around the conference room. Straker had an announcement, and whatever it was, it wasn't going to be good. They all sat around the table in frightened silence, waiting for the torture to begin. All in all, it seemed like any normal Thursday.

But it wasn't a normal Thursday. Daniel was dead. Murdered. And they weren't huddled around the conference table waiting to discuss toys, or profit losses, or deadlines. This meeting was different. This was a company-wide meeting and all of Straker's employees were in attendance. The managers, the toy store personnel, the accountants, even the factory workers. Everyone was crammed into the small little room, waiting for a special announcement.

Rumors had been flying since they had found Daniel's body, but that's all they were, Grace thought as she nervously played with her pen, they were just rumors. And usually, she ignored the rumors that were passed around the water cooler. After ten years in the company she understood how things worked. She understood her boss. Straker loved rumors. In fact, he usually was the source of the rumors. He liked starting them and he liked watching as they spread like wildfire throughout the company. He did not like addressing them. And in all the years she had worked at the Straker Toy Company, she had never seen Straker address a rumor. Not once.

But today was different. Today, for the first time, he was going to address the latest rumor and that scared Grace more than anything did.

Everyone's heads turned as Straker walked into the room without his usual swagger and sat down at the end of the table. "All right, I'm not going to waste your time. I'm just going to get to it. We're broke. Everything's gone."

They all sucked in a breath.

"What does that mean?" Allen asked breathlessly.

"Mean?" Straker asked. "We're broke. We have no more money. I thought I was perfectly clear."

Everyone started talking at once. "Are we going out of business? What about our jobs? What about our pay for this month?"

Franklin held out a hand. "Thank you for your concern. I'm touched. Don't worry about me, I'll be fine."

"And us?" Grace asked.

"I have just enough to keep us solvent for another month or maybe two, so you can rest easy until then," Straker said.

Grace shook her head. "What happened?"

"My late, dearly-departed son-in-law, embezzled pretty much every dime we had," Straker said. "He was planning to run off with Tabitha Eddington—that pretty little magician's assistant that was working for Ilya Dragovich the night Lily died."

"But he's dead," Allen said quickly. "He can't do that anymore. Where's the money?"

Straker shrugged. "It's not in the bank where it belongs, so I'm guessing with her."

"You're just going to let her get away with this?" Allen asked, his voice rising with every word.

Straker looked at him in shock. Allen was usually such a good little sycophant. Never a raised voice. Never a hint of disobedience. Straker sat still for a second before finding his voice. "Yes, Allen, you know how I'm such a kind and forgiving guy. What do you want me to do? The police are out there looking for her as we speak. Hopefully, they'll find her before she spends all my money."

"Do they think Tabitha killed Daniel?" Grace asked.

"They don't know, but that's one of their theories." Straker looked at Grace. "I don't think she did it, do you?"

* * * *

"Well, that's it, I guess." Valerie sat down behind her desk. "Are you going to stay in New York?"

Grace shook her head. "No. I'll probably move back home. I don't have enough savings to survive a month here."

"Well, we're okay for a month. I'm hoping Straker can afford to keep me on after. He said he should be able to keep the toy store open and he'll still need a secretary."

"I figured you would be heading to Texas."

"No, I've changed my mind. I'm going to stick it out here. I'm not going to desert him. He's a tough old bird, but I can't leave him. Not now."

Grace drummed her fingers against the desk. "What about a business loan?"

Valerie snorted. "Four months ago, Straker gave a speech at the Better Business Bureau luncheon. The speech was entitled; *Why Bankers are Thieves.* We had received a twenty-five dollar fee on one of our statements the day before. It took me ten minutes to get it corrected and refunded to our account, but I made the mistake of mentioning it to Straker. We won't be getting a loan anytime soon."

"Wonderful. I guess Daniel was telling the truth when he said he was the glue keeping this company together." Grace looked out into the hallway. "Just what did you see in that elevator, Val?"

Valerie grimaced. "Grace, we've been through this a dozen times."

"I know, but just humor me."

"Do you know the police officer laughed at me when I told him?"

"I know," Grace said sympathetically.

"He actually laughed at me." Valerie sighed. "I was clearly hallucinating. After all, I hadn't eaten or slept well the night before."

"You must have seen something. Daniel was killed right in front of you."

"Stop saying that. It gives me the creeps," Valerie said with a shudder. "Besides, it's not true. I didn't see him die."

"Please? Can we just go over it one more time?"

Valerie gave her friend a small smile. "Okay. I was standing—"

"No, I mean, could we act it out?"

Valerie crossed her arms. "I thought you said that your detective days were over now that the police have taken over."

"They are… I'm just curious." Grace leaned forward. "You must have seen something." When Valerie shook her head, Grace quickly added, "I know. I know, but you may have seen something important without realizing it." She reached into her pocket and brought out a diagram of the office. "I made this last night," she said, handing Valerie the piece of paper. "What do you think?"

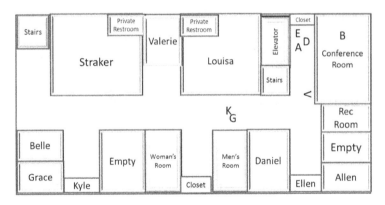

Valerie smiled. "I think you have way too much time on your hands."

"Everyone needs a hobby. Do I have everyone's positions right?"

Valerie nodded. "Looks like it."

"I just think it would help to actually go through it again."

Valerie groaned. Placing her hands on her desk, she pushed herself up. "Okay, one more time."

Smiling, Grace followed her out into the hallway and down the hall until they reached the elevator. Valerie walked over to the wall and leaned against it. "I was right here. Daniel was standing directly in front of the elevator."

Valerie paused at the sound of the elevator dinging. A few seconds later Allen and Michael walked out.

Valerie nodded at them as she continued with her narration. "The doors opened and Ethan got out first. He said hello or something to me. Allen came out next and got in Ethan's way."

"What are you two doing?" Allen asked suspiciously.

"We're recreating Daniel's death," Grace said.

"Well, I should be involved in that," Allen said.

"Why?" Grace asked.

Allen's mouth dropped open. "Because I was there. I was the first one off the elevator, so why wouldn't I be involved?"

Not feeling like arguing, Grace said, "Fine, you can be involved."

"If you're going to recreate it, then you better bet I should be involved," Allen said.

"Then get on the elevator," she directed.

Allen turned around just as the elevator doors closed. He turned back around. "Does Mr. Straker know about this?"

"No," Grace said.

Allen balled his hands on his hips. "He should."

Grace lifted her hands. "Why?"

"This is his building, so you should ask permission first. I'm going to tell him." Allen turned on his heels and dashed down the hall.

Grace and Valerie watched him run. "Amazing," Valerie said with a shake of her head.

Michael raised his hand. "Can I help?"

"Sure." Grace turned to Valerie. "Quick, let's get this over before he comes back."

Valerie leaned back against the wall. "Okay. The elevator opened—"

The elevator door dinged and Kyle and Belle walked out. They stopped short.

Kyle looked from Grace to Valerie and back again. "What's going on?"

"We're recreating Daniel's death," Michael answered.

"Oh, who's playing Ethan?" Kyle asked excitedly. "Can I?"

"I can play Daniel," Michael said eagerly.

Grace smiled at Kyle. "You can't play Ethan."

He looked at her in disappointment. "Why?"

"Because you will be playing yourself." She motioned for him to join her against the wall.

"Oh," he said disappointedly. "I'm sick of pretending to be me. I want to pretend to be someone else. Besides, you know where I was and what I was doing. You need someone to act out Daniel and Ethan's parts."

"He's right," Belle said. "It would be better if we could see exactly what everyone was doing at the time of Daniel's murder."

Reluctantly, Grace agreed. "Fine, you're Ethan."

"Good." Kyle lowered his voice a few octaves and wiped his face of all expression. "That would be acceptable."

Belle cooed. "You sound just like him."

Grace smirked. "No, he doesn't."

"Where do I stand?" Kyle asked.

Valerie pointed to the elevator. Michael recalled the elevator and held open the door. Kyle dashed forward and took his place inside the elevator.

Grace looked at Belle and nodded to the conference room. "Okay, you too, Belle."

"What?" Belle asked. "I was standing right here."

Grace shook her head. "You ran to the conference room to grab your jacket, remember?"

"Oh, that's right, I'd forgotten." Shrugging, Belle walked past Valerie and opened the conference room door. She turned back around and stood in the doorway.

They all turned to Valerie. "Okay, the elevator doors opened—"

"See, Mr. Straker," Allen and Straker came around the corner. "See, there they are."

"Why didn't someone tell me what was going on?" Straker bellowed. "Now you're going to have to start all over."

Valerie smiled at Grace and shook her head. "Fine. The elevator doors opened—"

"No," Straker said taking charge. "Start from the beginning. Where was everyone? Everyone get in your original places."

Kyle moved back out of the elevator and stood next to Grace.

"Good," Straker said. "Now—"

Allen raised his hand.

"What?" Straker asked annoyed.

Allen pointed to Grace and Kyle. "They weren't there. They were down the hall standing in front of the men's restroom, out of sight." Next, he pointed to Belle. "She wasn't standing there, either."

"Where were you, Belle?" Straker asked softly.

"I was looking for my jacket." She looked toward Grace. "Do I really have to recreate that part? I can't see anything from in there."

Grace readily agreed. "I think all we need is just a general idea of where everyone was when Daniel got on the elevator."

Straker shook his head. "No, Allen's right. We need to know exactly where everyone was at the time of Daniel's death. Thank you, Allen, good thinking."

Allen beamed.

Disappointment written over her face, Belle quietly stepped into the conference room and closed the door, as Grace reluctantly moved back out into the other hallway with Kyle. Once again, Grace could only hear what was happening.

"All right, Michael, where were you?" Straker asked.

"I was in the lab downstairs." Michael grimaced. "I changed my mind; I don't want to play Daniel. It's creepy. I'd rather play Ethan's part."

"Ethan who?" Straker barked out before realization dawned. "Oh, Grace's new boyfriend. I'm surprised he's still around. That must be a record for you, Holliday."

Valerie flashed Grace a small smile from where she was leaning against the wall.

Kyle made a disgusted noise from behind her. Leaning down, he whispered into her ear, "Michael barely knows Ethan. He's not going to get it right. He definitely won't get that *I'm better than you* sneer Ethan has. Michael's just all wrong to play him."

"Michael will do fine," Grace whispered back.

"I could do better."

"We need someone to play Daniel now." Straker walked over to stand by Valerie. Catching Kyle's eye, he shouted, "Hey, kid, what's your name?"

"Kyle."

"Not anymore. You're Daniel."

"Yes!" he said, practically skipping down the hall.

Straker looked back at Grace. "And you were all the way back there?"

She nodded.

He rolled his eyes and blew out a disgusted breath.

She resisted the urge to apologize formally. "Had I known Daniel was about to be murdered, I would have made sure to be in a prime viewing location. Unfortunately, I didn't get the memo."

"So, would I, Mr. Straker," Allen said, from his place in their little recreation, "but I would have made sure to be in the elevator with him."

Straker kept his eyes on Grace. His lips began to curve up before the gruff mask dropped over his face again. "Were you by yourself?"

"Kyle was beside me."

Straker looked into Grace's eyes. "The whole time?"

"Yes."

"Good." He walked away from the wall and out of Grace's sight. "All right. Allen and Michael get into the elevator. Good, now go ahead, Valerie."

"I was standing here against the wall and Daniel was standing directly in front of the elevator," Valerie said.

"Like this?" Kyle asked.

"No," Valerie moved out of Grace's line of sight.

Grace sighed. Quietly, she crept down the hall until she could see the elevator. Kyle was now standing directly in front of the doors, with his back to the conference room.

Valerie got back into position. "The elevator doors opened and Allen stepped out first."

"I know what I did," Allen snapped. "You don't have to narrate."

"He then tripped over his own foot," Valerie said with a smirk.

"I did not," Allen said.

Valerie crossed her arms. "You did, too."

Allen's face turned red. "I—"

"Enough!" Straker yelled. "Do exactly as Valerie says."

"Thank you." Valerie smiled at Allen. "He tripped and fell into Ethan, who was trying to walk around him."

"Then what happened?" Straker asked.

"Ethan pushed Allen back up," Valerie said. "Daniel tried to move past them, but they were both blocking the elevator doors."

Allen glared at Valerie, but played along and fell against Michael.

"Ethan pushed Allen off of him," Valerie continued.

Michael acted out the part and pushed Allen away.

"Ethan said hello or hi to me—"

"Which was it, Valerie?" Straker asked.

"I don't remember." Valerie waved her hand around. "It was something like that. Ethan tried to walk towards me, but Allen got in his way."

Allen interrupted. "I wasn't in the way. He had plenty of room to move around me." He walked up to Straker. "I wanted to speak to Daniel. I wanted to tell him about the new line of dolls I was creating."

Straker crossed his arms. "Did you?"

Allen shook his head. "I didn't get the chance."

"Then what happened?" Straker asked.

Allen moved in front of Kyle. He put his hands on Kyle's arms and moved him into position. "I said, hello, Daniel, how are you today? He said he was fine and asked me how I was doing. I said that I was doing quite well. Then he complimented me—"

"Valerie, keep going," Straker interrupted.

Valerie brought her eyes, which had rolled into the back of her head during Allen's version of events, down and continued her narration. "Daniel told Allen that he was busy or he'd talk to him later or something. Daniel was just trying to get into the elevator and leave, but Allen wouldn't listen and finally, Daniel snapped."

"He did not," Allen retorted. "He said he would discuss my ideas when he had more time to properly devote to me and give my ideas the consideration they deserved."

Michael spoke up, "Where was I? I mean Ethan."

"Ethan was standing behind both of them," Valerie said. "He tried to get out of the way and come towards me, but Allen kept blocking him."

"I did not," Allen whined. "She's got this all wrong."

Straker ignored him. "What happened then?"

"After Daniel snapped, Allen slunk off," Valerie said.

They all turned to Allen, who straightened his back. With his head held high, he walked past the elevator, muttering, "I did not slink off."

"And?" Straker prompted.

Valerie motioned for Michael to come towards her. "Ethan came to stand in front of me and Daniel stepped into the elevator."

Kyle stepped into the elevator and Michael, as Ethan, walked the few feet to stand directly in front of Valerie.

Valerie smiled. "Not that close and he was over to the side, because I could still see the elevator."

Michael moved out of the way.

"Then I waved goodbye to Daniel as the doors started to close," Valerie said.

"How was Daniel standing?" Kyle asked from his position in the elevator.

"He was facing me," Valerie replied, "with his right hand on one of the buttons."

"And?" Straker asked.

"That's it," Valerie said. "That's all I saw."

"Then what made you faint?" Kyle asked Valerie.

Everyone stared at her expectantly.

Valerie groaned. With her face flushing, she quietly said, "I saw a white mist descend from the ceiling."

"Oh, that's ridiculous," Allen said behind Grace, causing her to jump. "How come Grace's boyfriend didn't see this mist?"

"He was looking at me, not the elevator," Valerie said patiently.

"Hey, maybe it was a type of gas," Belle shouted from somewhere inside the conference room.

"But he wasn't killed by a gas, he was stabbed, Valerie," Allen said snidely.

Valerie pointed to the conference room door. "Talk to her about it. I never said it was a gas. I said it was a mist," she ground out through her teeth. "I'm telling you what I saw."

"Did Daniel react at all?" Grace asked.

"Just as it was coming down, Daniel looked up and then the doors closed." Valerie looked uncomfortable. "It looked like a hand was reaching for him."

"Was it a woman's hand or a man's hand?" Grace asked.

Valerie threw up her hands. "It wasn't real. There was no actual hand. It was this white, cloudy, misty type of thing that kind of looked like a hand. I could see right through it. I don't know what it was."

Belle opened the door and poked her head out. "Maybe Kyle is right. Maybe we do have a ghost."

Allen snorted behind her. "This is ridiculous. I want to narrate."

"How can you narrate? You had left the area by the time the doors closed," Grace said reasonably.

"And yet, I could probably still do a better job."

Grace glanced back at Valerie. "And Daniel was definitely alive when Allen walked away?"

Allen nodded his head automatically before the implication of her question finally dawned on him. "Hey, hey, what do you mean by that? Of course, he was alive. He was perfectly fine. Once your boyfriend got out of my way, I went back to my office. I had nothing to do with this."

"No one is accusing you, Allen," Straker said.

All but Grace nodded their heads in agreement. Grace looked at Valerie with a raised eyebrow.

Valerie nodded. "Yes, he was still alive when those doors closed. Something must have happened on the way down."

They all broke into little groups, discussing possible scenarios. Grace watched as Michael took hold of Belle's arm and whispered in her ear. She smiled up at him before taking his hand and leading him to the conference room.

Kyle slid past Straker and took his place next to Grace. Leaning down, he asked, "Are you sure this place isn't haunted? How do we know Valerie didn't see a ghost?"

"Actually," she said, staring at the closed conference room door, "I'm wondering if she didn't see a nice, fancy illusion."

Friday, December 16th

CHAPTER EIGHTEEN

GRACE LOOKED AROUND the conference room. There were a few less people than the last meeting. Those that could get jobs in other places did and the ones that hadn't been so lucky were sitting around the table in a sort of dreadful haze. Straker had another announcement to make. No one knew what to make of it, but decided that it couldn't possibly be good.

She leaned over to her right and whispered into Valerie's ear. "What's going on?"

"I have no idea," Valerie said with a shrug. "He just told me to get everyone together for an emergency meeting."

Everyone's heads quickly turned toward the door as it swung open. They just as quickly turned away when it was Kyle and not Straker who entered the room. He sat down on Grace's other side and handed her a bottle of water. "I'm sorry, it took me so long. Someone put a lock on the break room refrigerator."

"A lock?" Grace asked.

Smirking, Valerie nodded her head. "Allen asked for and received Straker's permission to install a lock. Our house detective," she said giving Allen a smirk, "is convinced the bottled water and the one cup of coffee cream needs protection."

Allen looked up sharply. "Someone needs to think about this company. We need to conserve our resources."

"We're not facing a drought," Grace said wryly. "We're going out of business."

All eyes turned as Straker walked into the room with his usual swagger. Belle followed him, shyly waving at Grace.

Straker seemed happy. Normally, that meant bad news for someone else, Grace thought as she sank back down into her seat.

"I have good news, people!" Straker said.

Everyone sat up straighter and looked around hopefully.

"Great news, actually." He looked at their expectant faces. He reached for Belle's hand and drew her to his side. "I've asked Belle to marry me and she said yes."

Mouths dropped. Valerie seized Grace's arm in a death grip. She turned shocked eyes to Grace, before loosening her grip and taking a deep breath. No one spoke. They all just stared at Straker in shock, their mouths slightly agape. While Grace wasn't surprised at the announcement she was surprised at her co-workers' reactions to the news.

Michael looked like he was about to be sick. He blinked heavily and averted his eyes. Allen's eye began to twitch. He reached up a finger to the corner of his eye and squeezed it shut. Valerie shook her head in shocked disbelief. Even Kyle was taking the news badly. His normally happy expression hardened as he looked at Belle. Catching Grace's eye, his features immediately changed. He suddenly smiled and nodded approvingly at the happy couple.

Louisa seemed to take the announcement the hardest. She started breathing heavily as she pressed her hand against her chest.

"Well?" Straker asked. "Where are your manners? Normally, people issue congratulations when a couple gets engaged," he lectured.

Kyle was the first to speak, quickly offering his congratulations. Grace threw her congrats in as well. Best to remain on the boss' good side. After all, there was still a chance she could work in the toyshop after this was all over, the thought, trying to inject some enthusiasm into her well wishes.

Harcourt was next. "Congratulations," he said without much feeling. "Is that all? I have some work to do." At Straker's nod, he stood up and walked to the door, mumbling, "I can't believe I came all the way up here for this."

Michael stood up; he wordlessly shook his head as he followed his supervisor out the door. Grace noticed that he shut the door a bit more forcefully than necessary.

Louisa took several deep breaths. "Congratulations? Congratulations? Are you serious? You can't be serious. This is a joke, right?"

Straker put his arm around Belle's shoulders. "I would never joke about such a thing. Belle and I are in love. I'm sure you'll come to love your new stepmother as much as I do."

"Stepmother?" she screeched. "Dear God, she's young enough to be your daughter. She's younger than me," Louisa said, angrily pointing at her chest. "This is worse than Lily. At least Lily was an adult."

Belle began twisting her hair into a knot. "I'm an adult."

Louisa's normally pretty features twisted into an angry grimace. "You—"

"Louisa, be careful what you say," her father said gruffly. "We can discuss this later."

"No, we will discuss this now," she said shrilly. "She is not going to be my stepmother. I've had to put up with these money grubbing whores you bring into our lives for the last fifteen years and each one worse than the last. I'm not putting up with this."

"Lily was not a money grubbing whore as you put it," Belle snapped, quickly jumping to Lily's defense. "She was a wonderful caring woman who loved you."

Louisa laughed harshly. "She didn't love me. She hated me just as much as I hated her. She introduced Daniel to that tramp just to spite me. If it wasn't for her, Daniel would be alive and my company wouldn't be going under."

"It's not your company yet, Louisa," Straker said softly. "I'm still in charge."

"For how long? You've managed to run our family's business into the ground. Of course, you had help. Lily's help."

Straker shook his head. "That's not true."

"Yes, it is. Lily didn't love you. She was using you. She was cheating on you with that magician. You're such a fool." Louisa wiped away the tears that were spilling over onto her cheeks. "Well, like father, like daughter. We're both fools. Still, I've wised up, but you're still making the same mistake." She looked over at Belle in disgust. "Belle's cheating on you, too, with that boy toy over there," she said, pointing at Kyle who slid down into his seat.

"Are you done?" Straker asked calmly.

Bursting into tears, Louisa fled the room. To Grace's surprise, Allen jumped up and followed her out of the office.

Straker patted Belle's arm and smiled. "Well, I think that went well."

* * * *

Grace opened the doors to the Magic Shoppe. She passed by the novelty tricks, swords, disembodied heads and various cards, and headed straight to the back offices where Michael and Harcourt designed their various devices of trickery. She wanted to speak to Michael, or at the very least Harcourt, about Daniel's death. Despite what Kyle thought, she was pretty confident the office elevator wasn't haunted, and that there was a logical explanation for what Valerie saw. And the only logical explanation she was able to come up with was that the disembodied hand that had frightened Valerie was produced by some type of trick or sleight of hand. It only made sense. Magic had been an element of the first murder, so why not the second. And with that in mind, she decided to go to the experts on trickery and sleight of hand work. With any luck they could provide her with an idea on how someone could have killed Daniel and Lily without being seen.

She knocked on the door, debating whether she should say *open sesame*. Just as she was about to say the magic words, Michael's voice came from the other side of the door. "Come in."

Grace swung open the door just as Michael threw a sheet over his work desk. His long black hair which was normally held back by a hair tie hung loosely around his shoulders, partially covering his face. He looked up at her and gave her a half-smile. "Hey, Grace. What can I do for you?"

"I was just seeing how you were. You seemed rather upset when you left the conference room today."

Michael blushed as he looked everywhere, but at her. "I don't know what you're talking about. I'm fine," he insisted, staring at a spot just to the left of Grace.

"It must have come as quite a shock to hear that Belle and Straker—"

He abruptly turned back to his desk. "I noticed that you didn't seem too surprised. Everyone else was, but you weren't surprised at all. How long have you known?"

"A while," she said.

He shook his head sadly. "I had no idea. I thought... I'm really sorry, Grace, but I have a lot of work to do." He glanced back up at her. "I really am okay," he said with a smile.

"Good, glad to hear it," she said cheerfully. "I do have another question for you though?"

His back stiffen.

Grace decided to start with something simple. "Do you know who came up with the crystal chest trick?"

He smiled, suddenly more at ease. "Yes, it was Ilya's idea."

Grace pulled up a stool and sat down. "Where did the chest come from?"

"Us. Harcourt and I created it here at the shop. Lily helped."

Grace frowned. From what she read in the news after Lily's death, Dragovich had been performing the crystal chest trick for years, but Michael had only been working for the Magic Shoppe for just a few years. "I thought that was an old trick of his?"

"It was, but he updated it about a year ago. He added several some new enhancements."

"Did he say why?"

Michael tugged on his skull and cross bone earring before shrugging. "To be new and edgy?" He gave a small grin. "Maybe some of Straker had rubbed off on Dragovich... or maybe vice versa."

Grace chuckled. "They probably got the idea from Lily."

Michael smiled brightly. "Probably. Lily hated for anything to remain stagnant. She loved to test boundaries and try new things. Some of our best designs this year came from her. She would have made a great magician. I never understood why she didn't go off on her own."

"Tell me something, do you think a magician killed Lily?"

He glanced toward the double doors leading to Harcourt's office. He dropped his voice to a whisper. "More than likely. Whoever it was would have had to know how the crystal chest trick was performed. Which tells me it had to be a magician or someone involved in the act. They also had to know she was waiting up there on the scaffolding."

"What about Daniel? Do you think a magician killed him too?"

"I don't know." He bit his lip. "Some things just can't be explained."

"Don't tell me you believe in the ghost, too?"

Michael grinned as he tucked his hair behind his ears. "No, I'm just saying that I can't tell how it was done."

Grace remained persistent. "I'm surprised. I thought for sure another magician could figure out how an illusion was performed."

"Not always." He turned back to his desk, nervously adjusting the sheet. "Take Ilya Dragovich, for instance. I've seen him perform over a dozen times and I still can't tell you how he makes himself dissolve into a mist and turn into a dozen black crows, or how he saws off his own head. I've been within a few feet when he does that and I still don't have any idea. I'd like to think that some of my illusions would baffle him, too." He smirked. "Probably not. He never seems too impressed by what I do. What does Belle think? Does she think a magician was involved?"

Grace shrugged. "I haven't talked to her about it yet." She leaned forward, balancing her elbows on her knees. "Come on, Michael, you must have an idea. Think about it. How could a magician have pulled this off?"

He looked thoughtfully at her. "The mist Valerie saw was obviously a smoke screen. While her and Daniel's attention was focused upward..." He screwed his face up. "I just don't know. I mean, the whole elevator would have to been set up and I just don't see how. The police were all over it once they found Daniel's body. They would have found whatever mechanism would have been used—if one had been used." His eyes took on a faraway look. "I guess, the killer could have set up a device and then taken it away after Daniel was murdered. Kyle thinks…"

"What?" she asked when he hesitated.

He screwed up his face. "Kyle thinks the killer could have gone through the elevator shaft. He says there's a service ladder the killer could have used to climb down to the top of the elevator."

She frowned. "How does he know that?"

Michael shrugged. "He had been in the elevator shaft that morning."

"He had?" Grace asked, surprised. "How do you know that?"

Michael started to look uncomfortable. "I overheard Belle and him talking after Daniel died," he said quickly, before looking down at the floor. "I shouldn't have said anything. Look, I don't want to get him in trouble."

"He's not in any trouble," Grace quickly reassured him. "I'm just curious as to what he was doing in the elevator shaft."

"I don't know. You should talk to him about it."

When Michael refused to say anymore, Grace decided to change the subject. "Where were you when Daniel died?"

He pointed to the desk and the thing sitting under the sheet. "I was sitting right here working on my new project."

"And Harcourt?"

He pointed over his shoulder to a pair of double doors. "He was in his office."

"How long were you two in here?"

He shrugged. "For a while." He pushed his hair back away from his face. "I was working on a disappearing sword trick and accidentally nicked myself when I heard the elevator alarm sound. I figured it was time for a break anyway and went upstairs to see what happened."

The double doors banged open and Harcourt walked out holding a pair of skulls. "What is this? Do you really think—" He stopped when he saw Grace standing there.

"What are you doing here? Is Belle with you?" He didn't bother waiting for an answer. He stalked back to his office, muttering, "Ilya Dragovich and his brood are not going to force me out." He slammed the door hard enough to shake it on its hinges.

Grace winced. "Is he always this cheerful?"

"Only on his good days."

Grace stood and walked to the double doors. She knocked on the doors, surprised when the doors opened immediately.

"Tell Straker we have a contract. This is not Dragovich's Magic Shoppe. This is Harcourt's Magic Shoppe."

"Well, the sign says Straker's Magic Shoppe," Grace pointed out, shutting the doors behind her.

"Hmm, not for long, because I'm going to buy him out." He smiled gleefully. "He's so desperate, he'll take anything."

"I don't think so," Grace said with a slight shake of her head. "This was Lily's pet project and he seemed pretty adamant that nothing change."

"So?" Harcourt walked over to a black tufted velvet couch sitting against the wall. "Haven't you heard? Lily's been replaced and sentimentality isn't going to keep his business afloat. Hard cash will. Straker will sell. You mark my words," he said, picking up his cane and pointing at her. "Mark my words."

"Duly noted."

He lowered the cane. "Why are you here? You've never knocked on my door before."

Grace hesitated. "I'm working on designing a board game for teenagers. It's going to incorporate a magician or a wizard. I haven't quite decided yet and thought you might be able to help." Not quite a lie, since a magic game had been proposed by Kyle and Belle, she thought, as she sank down into the nearest chair.

He sniffed. "You're asking the wrong person." He pointed the cane to the doors. "You want to know what the little hoodlums are interested in, go talk to the Grim Reaper out there. I'm sure he can give you some…ideas."

"Why do you call Michael the Grim Reaper?"

"Have you looked at him? Black Hair. Black Eyes. Black clothes. Black fingernails."

Grace looked at the older man in disbelief. He could have just as easily described himself. Her feelings must have been written on her face because he immediately defended his position.

"My hair and eyes are natural, but his aren't. I also didn't feel it necessary to get a dragon tattoo on my back or the grim reaper on my chest," he snarled. "I'm surprised he doesn't just throw on a shroud and walk around with a sickle. He's all show, with no talent. He thinks if he dresses all dark and foreboding, the audience won't notice how bad he is."

"That's why I want to come to you, because you are a master at your craft. You can help me with my game."

His thin lips curled into a smile. "You're not here about your game. The Straker Toy Company is going out of business. There will be no more games produced now or ever. No, I know what you're up to. Straker has everyone playing detective. Allen was just down here a few hours ago poking his nose in my designs."

Grace grimaced. "What did you tell him?"

"Nothing, I threw him out." He looked her up and down. "At least you knocked. You're wasting your time. It's perfectly obvious who killed Lily and who killed Daniel. They should be arresting him soon."

Grace raised an eyebrow. "Dragovich, again?"

He looked at her patiently. "Of course."

"What makes you think he's the killer? He wasn't here the day Daniel died."

"His spawn was." Before she could protest, he raised a hand. "Just because you didn't see him, doesn't mean he wasn't here. I'm sure you asked Death out there where I was when Daniel was being killed, didn't you?"

"Yeah."

"And what did he say?"

"You were in here."

He smiled. "I was actually down the street, getting a cup of coffee. No one pays any attention around here, especially the younger generation," he snarled. "All of you walk around with your little music boxes and your phones and your games. It's no wonder that idiot out there can find an audience. He doesn't even have to try to misdirect anyone's attention, because they're not devoting their full attention on anything, anyways. I once saw—"

Before he could continue ranting about her generation, she broke through his soliloquy. "Well, since you're paying attention and all, did *you* see Ilya here?"

"No, but like I said, that doesn't mean he wasn't. Dragovich knows what he's doing," he admitted reluctantly. "He could have easily snuck in here and set the elevator up to kill Daniel. That girl, Straker's secretary, what did she see?"

"She said she saw a white mist in the shape of a hand come from the ceiling and reaching for Daniel?"

Harcourt thumped his cane against the floor. "I knew it! It's Dragovich!"

"What makes you say that?"

"That white mist is one of his tricks; one of his older tricks. When he was just getting started, he often pretended to talk to the dead. What made him different from the rest of the conmen out there, was that he often made the dead materialize. Full body mists that could move around the room and interact with people. He even had one that distended from the ceiling as a hand reaching for the audience. It scared them to death. He was rather good at it," he said grudgingly. "That was before he became a sellout."

"Hmm. Did the dead then up and stab people in the back?"

"No, of course not." He leaned against his cane, with his lips pursed together. "That hand that came from the top of the elevator was simply misdirection. He waited until the elevator doors closed, then he popped open the service hatch, hopped down, and killed Daniel. He stopped the elevator between floors and then climbed back out the way he came. Or he had one of his kids do it." He shook his head, suddenly changing his mind. "No, what am I saying? He wouldn't leave something so serious up to them. Neither of them are too competent. The girl maybe, but the boy is definitely crazy. He spent some time in a mental institution, you know. Dragovich hushed it up, of course. No," he said emphatically, "Dragovich wouldn't leave it up to his children. He did it himself."

"But why use the mist at all? He could have just waited until the doors closed and then hopped down. He didn't need the smoke screen or to make it look like a hand."

He merely shrugged. "He's a magician and we magicians tend to be theatrical." He snapped his fingers and the lights went out. When they came back on a few seconds later, Harcourt was gone. Grace looked around the empty office. She didn't even hear him leave.

"Go to Dragovich," his disembodied voice said from above her head. "See if he could do anything remotely like this."

CHAPTER NINETEEN

GRACE WALKED INTO Belle's office. Kyle was perched on the metal stool in front of her drafting board, doodling a picture of a lantern jawed detective. Belle was standing next to him, tying one of Grace's scarfs around her neck.

Hearing the door open, Kyle swiveled around on the stool. "Hey, where did you disappear to? We've been looking for you everywhere."

"Why? Has something happened?"

Belle untied the scarf from around her neck and instead tied it around her hair. "No, I just wanted to invite you to my engagement party. I thought we all could go someplace to celebrate tomorrow night. Wouldn't that be fun?"

"Who's going?" Grace asked.

Belle said, "Me, Franklin, Louisa—"

At the mention of Louisa's name, Grace snapped her fingers. "I completely forgot that I've got this thing to go to."

Belle weaved her arm through Grace's and dragged her inside the room. "Oh, it will be fun. Louisa was just surprised, the poor thing. I know how I would feel if Papa brought home someone younger than me. I'd be a little upset, too." She let go of Grace's arm and flopped down in the nearest chair. "Once I got to know me, and realized what a wonderful person I was, then I'd be happy as can be."

Kyle laughed. "You'd be ready to kill and you know it. You had better prepare yourself. Don't let Louisa sit next to you and make sure all the knives have been removed from the table. You might also want to hire a food taster."

"As soon as she gets to know me, she will love me," Belle declared. "How could she not? I'm lovable."

Grace walked over to the drafting board. "I'd listen to Kyle. A food taster might be a good idea." She looked over his shoulder. Smiling she said, "Penelope looks like she's been in the ring one too many times. I like the scar going down her face."

Using his pen, he pointed at the drawing. "This is Marshal Grant Senet."

Amused, she picked up the drawing. "You've changed the name again?"

"He should be on the cover. See his steely-eyed determination. No one messes with him. You put him on the box and they will be flying off the shelves."

"What shelves?" Grace sighed. "We're just biding our time until the business closes. Have you applied anywhere?"

Belle spoke up from behind them. "Franklin says not to worry, because our jobs are secure."

"How?" Grace asked skeptically.

Belle pulled the scarf off her head and began braiding her long blonde hair "I don't know. He says he'll figure it out. If all else fails, I'll ask my father for a loan. That could be his wedding present to me."

Grace dropped the sketch back on the table. "Would your father be able to come up with that much money?" she asked, thinking back to that check Lily wrote him in July.

Belle nodded. "Absolutely. Papa has plenty of money. More than he knows what to do with." She shook her head disgustedly. "I don't know why he doesn't spend any of it. What good is it just sitting in a bank? He just keeps saying that he's saving it for my future." She unbraided her hair. "I'm more interested in my present, than my future."

"You say that today—" Grace started before being interrupted by Kyle.

"I agree with you, Belle. How do we know if you even have a future? You might as well spend it now, while you're alive, since you could be gone tomorrow."

Belle stopped playing with her hair long enough to glare at Kyle. "I don't like this topic of conversation."

"You're the one who started it," he pointed out testily, before turning to Grace. "Where have you been, anyway?"

"I was downstairs talking to Michael and Harcourt."

"Why?" Belle and Kyle asked in unison.

"I wanted to see what they thought about Daniel's death." They looked at her expectantly. Deciding it was best not to accuse Belle's father while she was in the room, Grace gave a short version of her talk with Harcourt, leaving out Ilya's name. "Harcourt thinks the killer was hiding on the top of the elevator, waiting for Daniel. I figure the only way the killer could have gotten on top of the elevator without being seen was to go through the attic elevator doors."

"That's what the police think," Kyle said. He looked up at their questioning faces. "I asked them when they were poking around up there," he explained. "They think that when Daniel got on the elevator, the killer opened the service hatch, dropped down, and stabbed Daniel in the back and then climbed back up through the attic door."

"And the cops just told you that?" Grace asked doubtfully.

He gave her a wide smile. "Sure, people seem to like me. They find me very charming."

Looking at his handsome face, Grace easily believed it. He was practically angelic.

"I also heard one of them say that it looked like someone had tampered with the elevator hatch," Kyle said.

Grace smiled. "That doesn't mean much. The elevator malfunctioned four months ago. Poor Louisa was trapped in there for over an hour. Oh, she was furious. Just screaming and crying for the whole time. We could hear her all the way over here. Allen, our resident hero, attempted a rescue. He went up to the attic and opened the elevator doors—he must have done something to the elevator, because it hasn't gone to the attic since—he then climbed down through the hatch and promptly broke his ankle. I won ten dollars in the office pool."

Kyle chuckled. "Very impressive."

"Not really," Grace said with a smile. "Half the office bet he'd break his ankle. Anyway, they had to wait for the technicians to rescue them both." Grace looked at Kyle closely. "You were running around the attic the day Daniel died. Did you see anything suspicious?"

He looked at her curiously. "Other than the fact someone's been living in the attic?"

She nodded.

"Not really."

Grace narrowed her eyes. "What about with the elevator? Did you take a look at the elevator?"

Kyle cocked his head to the side, as a big grin spread across his face. He turned and looked at Belle. "I told you Michael was eavesdropping on us the other day."

Belle sighed. "I'm sure he wasn't doing it intentionally."

Still grinning, Kyle looked up at Grace. "I thought whoever it was might have been hiding up there, so I took a look."

"And?"

"There was no one there. Just a ton of spiders," he said with a shrug. "It was really too dark to see anything, so I just closed the doors and moved the boxes and toys back where I had found them." He paused. His features twisted into a grimace. "Nah, I think the cops are wrong. I don't think the killer went down the shaft."

"What do you mean? You suspected that's how Daniel was killed too," Belle said sharply.

"Yeah, but that was before Harcourt suggested the idea to Grace."

"What difference does that make?" Grace asked.

Kyle smirked. "I think Harcourt killed Lily and then Daniel. If he did, he certainly wouldn't tell you how he did it. He must have killed Daniel another way."

"Why would he kill Lily?" Grace asked. "They were friends."

"No, they weren't," Belle said. "They hated each other."

"But, I thought they used to work together. When she was setting up the Magic Shoppe, she recommended Harcourt. In fact, it was her idea to bring him aboard."

Belle shook her head. "She wanted Papa but he refused, so she went to Sidney Harcourt instead."

"If she didn't like him, then why would she have hired him?" Grace asked.

"Harcourt is well known in the magic community," Belle said. "He has a lot of connections. Next to Papa, he's one of the best stage magicians out there. On top of that, his family had owned and operated several magic shops throughout Europe for several generations. Lily figured that they could set aside their differences and work together as they had when she was his assistant, but it didn't quite work out that way. Harcourt fought with her on every little thing. She complained that he still treated her as his assistant instead of his boss. She even got so mad that she went to Franklin and tried to have Harcourt fired."

"So, why is he still here?" Grace asked.

"Franklin told her no," Belle said. "There was no one else of Harcourt's caliber willing to take over and the Magic Shoppe was doing so well and bringing in so much money that he didn't want to mess with it."

"Lily must have loved that," Grace said sarcastically.

Belle nodded. "She was furious. That's why Michael is here. When Franklin said no, Lily brought in Michael. She thought if she could get Michael trained, then eventually she could fire Harcourt and Michael could take over."

"Well, that explains why Harcourt hates Michael," Grace said.

"It also gives Harcourt the perfect motive for killing Lily," Kyle said. "He was probably hoping that Franklin would give him her position when she died."

Belle twisted the scarf into a knot. "It would have been easy for him to set the elevator up. He certainly has access to it."

"Could he have created the white mist?" Grace asked.

"Absolutely," Belle said quickly.

"How?"

Belle shrugged. Looking down at her lap, she said, "There are ways to pull that off." Belle lost in thought, looked up at the ceiling. "Harcourt probably took everything with him when he climbed back out of the elevator."

"If it was him. He's not our only resident magician," Grace pointed out.

"It wasn't me." Belle sat up straighter. "I was in the conference room the whole time. I had to get my jacket, remember?"

"Yeah, about that," Grace said, crossing her arms. "What exactly happened to your jacket?"

"What do you mean?" Belle asked.

"Well, for one, you were in there an awfully long time, and for another, when you came out you didn't have it with you."

"I... It wasn't there," Belle said with a frown.

"What took you so long?" Grace asked.

"I called Franklin. I wanted to see how Louisa was doing." Belle looked from Grace to Kyle. "I promise, I had nothing to do with this."

Kyle spoke up in Belle's defense. "The conference room is across from the elevator, so she couldn't have stabbed him in the back from there; not without Valerie seeing her."

"Yeah, Valerie was standing right by the door." Belle's voice began to rise. "She would have seen me."

Grace held up her hands. "Relax, I wasn't referring to you, anyway; I was talking about Michael."

"Oh," Belle sank back down into her chair, "but it couldn't be Michael. He doesn't have a motive for killing Lily. Besides, he's just starting out, so I doubt he could have pulled off such a complicated illusion."

"Yeah, I heard he's not very good," Kyle said.

Belle glared at Kyle "He's new and still learning. I'm sure he'll be a great magician someday."

Kyle didn't contradict her. "That just leaves Harcourt then."

Grace looked out the window. Rain was streaming down the glass. "Well, there's also Tabitha. Has anyone found her yet?"

Belle shook her head and sighed. "I haven't heard from her in weeks and I am beginning to worry about her. I called her mother this morning and left a message. I just hope she calls me back."

"She's probably lying low," Kyle said. "The police are looking for her now that they've reopened Lily's death."

Belle shook her head. "Tabitha wouldn't kill anyone. She's really a sweet girl. I bet she's scared to death." Belle stood up and picked up Grace's raincoat. Tying the scarf around her hair, she said that she was going to go outside and check her phone messages.

"Try the closet near the elevator," Kyle said. "You can usually get good reception in there."

Belle opened the door. "No, thank you. You've scared me to death with all of your ghost talk. The last thing I want to do is sit in a dark closet trying to check my voice mail. Besides, you have to stand on that box and point the phone toward the corner. I mean, honestly, between that and the elevator of death, it's getting scary working here." Belle closed the door after her.

Kyle rubbed his hands together. He smiled at Grace. "Well, what's next on the agenda, Marshal Grant?"

"I'm Marshal Grant?"

He nodded.

Grace lifted up his drawing of the lantern faced Marshal Grant. "I don't think that's quite a compliment."

Kyle laughed and took back his drawing. "No, that's not you." He shuffled some papers around. Pulling out another drawing, he proudly handed it to her. "This is you."

Grace looked at the drawing of a beautiful red haired detective in a trench coat and hat. She had to admit Kyle had a lot of talent. "I think it's great. Now, this belongs on the cover." They laid the two drawings side by side. For the next few minutes, they argued over the various merits of each, before finally deciding to go with Penelope.

"It doesn't matter," Grace said with a sigh. "This game is never going to see the light of day."

Kyle laid the drawings on the table. "Don't be so certain. Belle believes he'll be able to get financing and Straker *has* scheduled another design meeting tomorrow."

"I feel like one of the musicians on the Titanic—Just playing along until the ship goes down." Grace sighed. "How's Belle coming on her design?"

He shrugged. "I don't know. I don't think she's been working on it much. That reminds me, I want to show you something." He stepped out of the office.

Grace walked over to the wall next to Belle's bookcase. Like her father's dressing room, Belle had covered the wall with pictures, most of her and her father performing. She smiled at one of a young tuxedoed Belle on stage holding a small white rabbit and standing next to her obviously proud papa.

Kyle returned less than a minute later, holding a baseball cap and a handkerchief in one hand and a lighter in another. "I've been doing some research on magic—"

"Why do you have a lighter?" she asked worriedly as HR safety videos replayed in her mind.

"It's part of the trick or illusion—"

"Could you do it without the lighter?"

"Well, yes, but it's not nearly as much fun."

Grace made a grab for the lighter, just as Valerie knocked on the door and let herself in. "Hey, Belle?" Seeing Kyle and Grace, she said, "Oh, I need to talk to Belle. Have you two seen her?"

"Yeah, she ran downstairs," Grace said. "She'll be back soon. What's up?"

"I wasn't able to get a reservation at the restaurant she wanted to go to—" Valerie paused as Belle walked back into the office.

"That's okay," Belle said. "We can have the party at Franklin's place." She flashed her phone at Grace. "I finally got a call from Tabitha. I'm meeting her at five o'clock at that Italian restaurant." Unbuttoning her coat, Belle turned to Valerie. "We'll have the party at Franklin's. I'll let him know. Is he still in his office?"

Valerie shook her head. "He's having lunch at the deli across the street."

Groaning, Belle began buttoning her coat. "I wish he had told me and we could have had lunch together."

"He couldn't find you," Valerie said. "He said to let you know if I ran into you."

"I hope he hasn't finished, yet," Belle said, walking out the door again.

"Lunch sounds good," Kyle said, "I'm starving."

"Why don't you go to the deli, too," Grace said. She reached into her pocket and pulled out a twenty. "You can bring something back for me when you're done," she said handing him the money.

"The usual?" he asked, already reaching for the door.

She nodded.

He glanced at Valerie who placed her order as well.

As soon as the door closed, Valerie said, "Ethan called me again. He wanted to talk to you but couldn't reach you. He says that he called your direct line and that someone hung up on him. You need to speak to Kyle."

"How do you know that it was Kyle who hung up on him. Belle hangs around in my office all the time. To tell you the truth, I have the feeling that she doesn't particularly care for Ethan, either. I think she's *accidentally* erased a couple of phone messages that he's left for me at home."

"Ah." Valerie raised her eyebrows, but didn't say anything else. "Anyway, Ethan wants to meet you in a few minutes for lunch. He said he'd come by and pick you up. He has some news."

"Did he say what?"

"No, but I got the impression it was about our little mystery here."

"I hope he has good news, because I'm stumped."

Valerie sighed. "Well, you know who my first suspect is."

"Still Belle?"

"Mm hmm. I told you she wanted Straker, and you just laughed."

"I just don't get it," Grace said. "Why would a pretty, successful twenty-seven year old woman want the spawn of—"

"Straker has a lot to offer."

"Money?" Grace guessed.

"Well, no, not anymore."

"Lively conversation?"

Valerie made a face. "Of course not."

"His love and devotion?"

"Probably not."

"Sex?"

Valerie smirked. "No, that I think she's getting elsewhere."

"From who? Michael?"

"Michael?" Valerie asked in surprise. "No, not him. She treats him more like a kid brother than a lover."

"Then who?"

"You haven't guessed already?"

Grace shook her head.

"Love has blossomed under your very eyes and you've missed it. Well, maybe not love. Lust would be a far more accurate description."

"Kyle?" Grace asked a little more loudly than she intended. "You still think there's something between them? They just met last week." She smiled. "Oh, you're way off."

"You should have seen them yesterday in the break room. The looks they were exchanging when they thought no one was watching them." Valerie fanned her face. "Intense."

"She just announced her engagement. Surely, they're not that stupid. I mean, right under Straker's nose?"

"I'm telling you, it's Lily all over again. I showed you those checks to Dragovich. She wasn't even trying to hide her affair."

"But she couldn't have killed Lily. She was standing right next to me when Lily fell. Don't forget, Straker received that text message no more than a minute before Lily died and I didn't see Belle texting anyone." Grace shook her head. "That's the problem with Lily's death—the timing is all wrong. Someone we know had to have been up there with Lily. They grabbed her phone and texted that suicide message to Straker—while she sat there, not complaining—then they strangled her—again without any sort of struggle from Lily—in full view of Dragovich—then the killer pushed her off the scaffolding at the precise moment that she was supposed to come down—again with Dragovich down there watching—then dropped the phone for the police to find and they did all this while simultaneously sitting in the audience watching the show. Or, in Belle and Tabitha's case, when we were all backstage."

"Yeah, but—"

"You didn't see Belle's face when we stepped out on that stage and saw Lily hanging there. She was as shocked as I was. I just can't believe she had anything to do with Lily's death."

"She's a performer, so I'm sure she's a good little actress when she needs to be." Before Grace could protest, she held up a hand and said, "She must have had help."

"But why would anyone help Belle kill Lily if her ultimate goal was to marry Straker? What would be in it for her accomplice?"

Valerie shrugged. "I don't know. I just don't think we can trust her—"

They're heads whipped toward the door and the sound of someone screaming.

Valerie closed her mouth. They both looked to the door and back at each other, unsure of what they heard.

At the sound of another scream, Grace threw open the door and ran out into the hall. People were milling around, trying to determine where the screaming came from.

Another scream echoed through the hallway.

"It sounds like it's coming from downstairs," Valerie said.

Grace dashed down the hallway next to Straker's office and threw open the door to the stairwell. She looked over the railing.

Michael was down on the next level bending over Belle's body.

CHAPTER TWENTY

GRACE AND VALERIE rushed down the stairs. Grace pushed Michael away from Belle's body and reached for her wrist while Valerie lifted the edge of the blue velvet hood that partially obscured Belle's face.

Grace breathed a sigh of relief when Belle moaned softly and opened her eyes.

"What happened to her?" Michael asked coolly.

Grace looked up and saw Michael standing against the wall. His hands were behind his back and he was looking down at them dispassionately.

Valerie, who was kneeling on the other side of Belle's body, looked up at him angrily. "Instead of standing there, why don't you do something useful and call for an ambulance."

"Why?" Michael asked. "She's dead. They can't help her."

Grace and Valerie exchanged worried glances. Belle was struggling to sit up, but they kept a firm grip on her shoulders. Valerie leaned over and whispered for her to be still.

"Michael," Grace said slowly, "she's not dead. She's still moving. Go call for an ambulance."

He shook his head, as he slowly slid down the wall. He wrapped his arms around his knees. "No, there's no point, she's gone now."

Grace looked up. Allen stood on the upper landing, watching. "Is she all right?"

"She needs an ambulance."

Allen nodded before turning around and rushing out into the hallway.

Softly speaking in Russian, Belle reached out a hand and gripped Michael's ankle.

Finally realizing that she was still alive, he curled up into a ball next to her and softly stroked her hair.

* * * *

"Belle, would you stop fidgeting?" Grace asked exasperated.

"I'm tired of lying here. I want to go home."

Grace thumbed through the magazine lying on her lap. "You can't go until they release you."

"Has anyone gotten hold of my father, yet?"

"Not yet, but don't worry, Valerie said she'll keep trying until she reaches him."

Belle threw up her hands before folding her arms across her chest. "This is ridiculous. I'm fine."

"Yes, I know. It's a veritable miracle." Grace looked up from the magazine to the woman lying in the hospital bed. Other than the setting, she looked the picture of perfect health with bright eyes, rosy cheeks and not one broken bone or sprain. "You're very lucky."

Belle nodded solemnly. "As soon as I get out, I'm going straight to the nearest church. I thought I was a goner."

"What happened?"

Belle shrugged and then winced. "I don't know. I couldn't find Franklin at the deli, so I came back to the office and I was grabbed as I was climbing up the stairs."

"Did you see who it was?"

"No, I heard someone come behind me, but I thought it was Kyle."

Grace looked up from her magazine. "Why?"

"I had just seen him at the deli. He was gathering up everyone's lunch when I left, so I just assumed it was him coming up the stairs behind me."

"Are you sure it wasn't?"

"Positive." Belle shook her head quickly, only to wince. She reached a hand behind her neck and groaned. "Kyle wouldn't hurt me. Like I said, I just assumed it was him. Anyway, all of a sudden, that hood was thrown over my head and someone tried to push me down the stairs. So, I reached out and grabbed hold of the bannister. And then when whoever it was couldn't push me down, they tried choking me. I pushed them off me and I think I fell down the stairs, but I don't think I fell far. I was already pretty close to the third floor landing anyway. I must have blacked out for a few seconds. The next thing I remember is hearing Michael's voice." Belle looked around as the emergency staff milled around them. "I hate hospitals."

Grace dropped the magazine on the table next to her chair and picked up another one. "It shouldn't be much longer."

"Where's Michael?"

"He's out in the waiting room with Valerie."

Belle chewed her lower lip. "Can you go check on him?"

Grace smiled. "You're the one who was hurt. Besides, I think the police will be checking on him."

Belle shook her head. "Did you see him attack me?"

"No."

"Then you don't know for certain that he was the one who tried to kill me."

"He was kneeling over you."

"I know, but he... Please, just make sure he's okay."

Nodding, Grace laid the magazine down and walked out of the emergency room and back toward the waiting room. Before she could open the door to the waiting room, she could hear shouts and the sound of things crashing about.

She warily opened the door. The waiting room was a mess. Chairs were scattered across the floor, and in the center of the room was Michael lying on his back, holding a hand to his jaw while medical personnel kneeled over him, shining a light into his eyes.

On the other side of the room was Ilya Dragovich, his arms pinned to his sides by several large men. His fists were clenched and he was breathing hard, but he didn't seem to be struggling.

Cautiously, a couple of the men stepped away from him. Once they did, she caught a glimpse of Ethan who had his arms wrapped around the magician's waist.

She looked around the rest of the room. Everyone was breathing hard and stood restlessly around the edges of the room. The only one who didn't look tense was Straker, who was sitting against the wall, his feet propped up on an overturned chair. He looked back from the magician to Michael on the floor, a small grin on his face. The only thing missing was a drink and a bucket of popcorn. The grin quickly fell from his face when he realized the show was over. Glancing at his watch, his perpetual scowl returned.

Dragovich looked behind him and snarled something causing Ethan to loosen his hold.

The men surrounding Dragovich took a few more steps away from him. Their bodies were still clenched and ready to rush him if he made a move towards the young man on the floor.

Dragovich took a step toward the emergency room doors but was intercepted by a couple of police officers who had just arrived.

Once he and Michael had been removed, Grace walked over to Ethan, who quickly enveloped her into a bear hug.

Looking over Ethan's shoulders, she saw Straker sneak through the emergency room doors. Pulling back, she asked, "How did you know I was here?"

"I saw the ambulances out in front of your building and rushed out. Allen told me what had happened."

Valerie stood next to him. "Good thing you came, too." She pointed to the center of the room. "We almost had another murder."

"What did you tell Dragovich?" Grace asked.

Valerie shook her head. "Nothing. I never spoke to him. He just suddenly appeared out of nowhere and the moment he saw Michael, he attacked."

Grace glanced at her watch. Five-thirty. "Valerie, can you stay with Belle. I'm going by that Italian restaurant. Maybe Tabitha is still there."

Valerie shook her head. "Don't bother; she's not. I called the restaurant and asked the bartender if anyone was there that fit her description. He was supposed to call if she showed up." She held up her phone. "So far, nothing."

Ethan looked at them curiously. "What about Tabitha?"

Grace filled him in on the message Belle received before she was attacked. "She might be late, but I'm going to run by there anyway."

"I wouldn't count on it," Ethan said.

Grace and Valerie looked at him in surprise.

"That's what I wanted to tell you tonight. Tabitha's dead and has been for several days."

"How do you know that?" Valerie asked.

"One of my friends at the police station told me that a body of an unidentified woman washed up on the shore. They couldn't make an identification, but from the description, it sounded a lot like Tabitha."

Valerie shook her head. "But didn't Belle say that Tabitha left her a voice message wanting to meet tonight?"

"Yeah, but she could have been lying." Ethan picked up a chair off the floor. He slowly sat down. "Let's think about our suspects. Who knew Lily was going to be there that night?"

"It seems everyone knew she was there, but me," Grace said. "Dragovich, Belle and Tabitha knew, of course. Allen admitted he knew she had been staying at Dragovich's for a week before her performance, but he didn't say how he knew. Harcourt and Louisa knew. Although, Harcourt swears he didn't know when or in what act she would reappear in. Michael overheard them talking about it which means he knew."

Ethan shook his head. "I think we can eliminate Allen and Louisa. We're obviously looking for a magician. It had to be Dragovich, Belle, Tabitha, Michael, or Harcourt."

"Or a combination of them," Valerie said.

Ethan held up his hand. "That just leaves us with five suspects—"

"Six," Grace corrected him. She smiled at their obvious confusion. Before they could start listing the suspects and counting on their fingers, she said, "There's also Aleksis Dragovich."

"Who?" they asked in unison.

"Belle's brother. I think he might be in New York, somewhere."

"What makes you think that?" Ethan asked.

"Just something Harcourt said about Ilya Dragovich's brood forcing him out."

Valerie sighed. "Then he could be helping his sister. They could have set up this little performance this afternoon to draw suspicion away from her."

Ethan's smiled broadened. "That's it. That explains it," he said happily. "Her brother must have been the one who actually committed the murder."

"His father would have seen him," Grace said.

"So? Maybe they were all in on it together," Ethan said. "They all conspired to kill Lily."

Grace paced in front of them "What's their motive? That's what I don't get. Why would they kill Lily? And Daniel? The one person with the really good motive for doing them both in is Louisa, but I doubt she would have known how to set up these illusions."

"Which brings us back to the killer being a magician or someone affiliated with them." Valerie shook her head. "We know Dragovich and Lily were having an affair, so what if something went wrong? They fought and Dragovich decided to kill her. He sets it up so she does this grand entrance—"

"On his own stage and in front of over a hundred people?" Grace asked. "Not exactly a shrewd marketing plan."

"But it gives him a perfect alibi," Ethan said. "He was on stage when it happened. Do you know how hard it would be to convince a jury that he committed the murder in front of some of the city's leading citizens? His defense attorney would bring them in one by one to testify that they saw him standing on the stage when she died."

"But why would either of his kids help him?" Grace asked playing devil's advocate.

Ethan shrugged. "They might have had their own reasons for hating her."

"Or…" Valerie said slowly, "they might not have had a choice."

Ethan looked at her curiously. "What do you mean?"

"Remember that hypnotism act he put on?" Valerie asked. "He had Allen completely under his control."

Grace smiled. "It almost makes me wish Dragovich had come to work for us."

Ignoring her, Valerie continued, "What if he brainwashed his kids? What if he had them under his control?"

Grace shook her head. "Eh, I don't think so. From what Lily and Belle were saying in his dressing room, it didn't sound like he had any control over Aleksis. Frankly, I don't think he has much control over Belle, either. I just don't think Lily was killed over some lover's quarrel."

Ethan smiled gently at Valerie. "It was a good thought, though."

Valerie shrugged her shoulders. "I still think it's Belle. I mean, why has she suddenly glommed onto Straker?"

Ethan ran his hand over his face, covering a yawn. "Maybe she is in love with the man."

Grace looked at him in pity. "No. No way."

"It's possible," Ethan said. "He is handsome for an older guy, right. Weirder things have happened."

Valerie nodded. "He's got a point, Grace. Straker has managed to have five women fall in love with him during his lifetime. I even…"

"What?" Grace asked when she didn't continue.

Valerie shrugged. "He can be charming when he wants to be."

"Since when?" Grace asked.

Her friend stifled a yawn. "You've never spent any time with him alone, but I have. He's different one on one. He's very nice, sweet even." She looked off to the side. "It's just upsetting. Belle's taking advantage of him. He just lost Lily. I mean, she may have been a horrible wife, but he did love her. Now, here's Belle wiggling her way in, when he's at his lowest. I just don't understand how she could move in so fast."

Grace smiled. "Straker's never alone for long, you know that."

Valerie stifled another yawn.

Ethan stood up. "There's a cafeteria here, isn't there? Let's go get some coffee. It will be my treat."

Ethan took Grace's hand and smiled down at her as they walked to the small cafeteria in the hospital. "What would you like to drink?" he asked when they reached the cafeteria counter.

Grace looked at the menu for a second before asking him to order a cup of hot chocolate for her.

He looked over at Valerie who sank down into the nearest chair and laid her head on her arms. "Coffee, please."

Grace sat down across from her friend, as Ethan walked to the counter. Emotionally exhausted, they sat in silence until Ethan came back carrying their drinks on a tray.

"A hot chocolate for you," he said, placing a cup in front of Grace and another in front of Valerie, "and coffee for you."

"Thanks." Grace cautiously took a sip. Pleasantly surprised, she took another sip. "I agree with Valerie. I don't think Belle is marrying Straker for love. I don't know why she is marrying Straker, but I'm pretty sure it isn't for love."

"I married for love, look at how well that turned out," Valerie said, took a sip and grimaced. "Next, I would like to marry for money."

Grace laughed. "You had your chance with Straker when he was rolling in the money."

Valerie made a face. "He's never been that rich."

Ethan took a sip of his drink before placing it on the table and pushing it away. "You could have been Mrs. Straker and you turned him down?"

"Yes, I did and I don't want to talk about it," Valerie said.

Grace was more than happy to fill him in. "It was a couple of months before he met Lily. He said he was madly in love with her, even following her around. Telling her how she was his right hand and how much he depended on her."

Valerie pushed her drink aside. "Yeah, that didn't last long."

"So, what happened?" Ethan asked.

Grace made a sad face. "Broke his heart in two."

"I was still married, at the time, happily married," Valerie said.

Grace rolled her eyes. "That's not what you were saying at the time."

"Well, I wasn't completely unhappy, not enough to break my vows. This was before I discovered my ex wanted to change careers."

"What did he want to do?" Ethan asked.

"He went from a mild mannered delivery driver to a getaway driver overnight," Valerie said in disgust.

"Lost your chance to be a lady of leisure," Grace said.

Valerie snorted. "Franklin has never been rich. I keep the books, remember? That viper daughter of his treats the company's account as her personal piggy bank. Franklin Straker has been bled dry. I always hold my breath when checking the accounts on Friday afternoon, wondering if we're still going to be in business Monday. Now, I don't have to bother."

Closing his eyes, Ethan rubbed a hand over his face. Softly shaking his head, he looked at Grace. "What happens when Straker finally shuts down the company? Do you two have anything else lined up?"

Grace shook her head. "According to Belle, we'll all be able to keep our jobs."

Valerie shook her head. "Trust me, there's not enough money for us all to stay on. She's lying to you, or Straker's lying to her."

Ethan's eyes lit up. "You two could work at my firm. I remember one of the partners saying something about hiring a few new secretaries or paralegals. Have you ever done any paralegal work?"

They shook their heads.

"You'd have to get a certificate, but I think we could work something out until then."

"I should be okay," Valerie said. "Straker has enough to keep the toy store open for a while. He'll still need a personal secretary." Valerie smiled. "But I think that would be a wonderful idea for Grace. You two could see each other all the time then and you'd still be close to the toy store. We could still have lunch together."

Ethan leaned in closer to Grace. "She's right. It's a great idea. I'd like to be able to see you more often."

Giving a small laugh, Grace shook her head. "No. I have one rule and that is to stay away from office relationships. What if something went wrong?"

Ethan smiled at her. "Nothing will go wrong, I promise."

"I'll be fine," Grace said, with more confidence than she felt at the moment. "Besides, I'm not giving up on Straker just yet. We just need a miracle. If we could find the money Daniel took, then we could stay in business."

"Tabitha ran off with it," Valerie said. "It's long gone now."

"Not necessarily," Grace said. "If the cops are right and Tabitha is dead, then whoever killed her might have the money. That may be what all of this is about. Maybe the killer was after the money Daniel had stolen."

"But why kill Lily?" Valerie asked.

Grace shrugged. "Daniel and Lily were supposedly close. She introduced Tabitha to him, just to get back at Louisa, so maybe she knew something she shouldn't and had to be killed to keep her quiet. If we could find out when Daniel took the money and how, maybe that would help us figure this all out." She looked over at Ethan and smiled. "Do you have plans for this weekend?"

He smiled back, before leaning forward. "No. What would you like to do?"

"I'd like your help in searching our office building."

Ethan dropped his head and laughed. "Oh, I just remembered I've got this…thing to go to."

"Too late. I know you're free," she teased.

"What do you hope to find, Grace?" Valerie asked.

Grace shrugged. "I don't know, but I definitely want to check out the attic and maybe look at our accounts."

"The police have already done that," Valerie said looking from Ethan to Grace.

"It couldn't hurt to take a second look," Ethan said.

Valerie grimaced before reluctantly nodding. "Okay, count me in, but you're going to need Straker's okay, you know?"

"I know." Grace pulled out her phone and dialed Straker's office phone, intent on leaving a message. Hopefully, he would check his messages sometime during the weekend, she thought as she glanced at her watch. Her eyes widened in surprise when he answered the phone. She had assumed he'd still be with Belle in the ER. Recovering from her surprise, she outlined what she wanted to do. He agreed with the understanding that he would join them in their search.

Dropping her phone back into her purse, she smiled. "It's all set, but he wants to do the search Monday night."

"Okay, it's probably best that he tags along. It avoids any legal entanglements." Ethan raised his arm and laid it behind her shoulders. "So, where's your puppy?"

With a half-smile, Grace looked at him curiously. "I don't have a puppy. My apartment won't let me have pets."

She caught Valerie's smile as she raised her cup to her lips before grimacing and placing it back on the table again.

"You know," Ethan said, "that big Labrador that's been following you around lately."

Sudden realization dawned on her. "Kyle is not a Labrador."

"No," Valerie quickly agreed. "I was thinking German Shepard. You know, this is the first time since Daniel died that he hasn't been hovering around somewhere."

"That's not true," Grace protested.

"Yes, it is," Valerie said. "He's always around now. I thought it was because of Belle, but I'm not quite so sure anymore."

Ethan looked around the cafeteria. "Where is he, anyway?"

"I don't know. I haven't seen him since he ran off to get lunch." Grace reached into her purse and pulled out her phone. No messages. Suddenly worried, she was just about to call his cell phone when her own phone rang.

Belle was on the other end, asking if she could drive her home.

* * * *

Grace handed Belle a glass of water and her pills. "You should have stayed at the hospital," she scolded.

"I hate hospitals," Belle complained. She scowled at the pills Grace thrust into her hand. "There was no reason for me to stay."

"That's not what the doctor said." She pointed to the pills and the water. "She wants you to take your medicine."

"Oh, what does she know? I can't stay at the hospital. I have to prepare for my engagement party."

"You are in no shape to go to a party tomorrow night. Why don't you cancel it? You can have a party next Saturday."

"Next Saturday is Christmas Eve. No one's going to want to come and you're heading to Hawaii." Belle stubbornly shook her head. "No, it has to be this weekend. I want you to be there, Grace."

Grace sighed. "How about Sunday? We'll get someone from the office to decorate. We'll have a combination Christmas and engagement party Sunday night."

"Sunday?" Belle asked doubtfully. "At the office?"

"If you insist on having it this weekend, at least it'll give you an extra day to rest. We'll bring food in—"

"I don't know. I was really looking forward to having it tomorrow night. I'm much better now that I'm home. Besides, you and Abry are here to take care of me," she said sweetly, picking up the bunny and cuddling it next to her chest. She tilted her head, considering. "Actually, you know, it's not a bad idea having it at the office. Franklin would probably prefer having it there. We have to have a Christmas Party anyway." Decided, she nodded her head. "Okay, Sunday it is. Who usually handles the decorations for the office?"

"We take turns. Straker will assign someone to take care of it."

Belle smiled. "You're right, Sunday will be perfect."

"Wonderful," Grace said sarcastically, "take your medicine."

Belle sighed heavily before swallowing the pills and taking a gulp of water.

Satisfied, Grace turned to the closet. Picking up a quilt, she laid it over Belle's legs and tucked the ends under the bed.

Belle kicked out her legs. "I can't move."

"Good," Grace said under her breath.

"What?"

"I said, goodnight."

"But I'm bored. I don't want to go to sleep."

"You don't have to sleep. You just have to rest." Grace turned on the television and handed the remote to her bedridden roommate. "I'll check on you a little later. Promise."

Grace quickly opened the bedroom door and shut it behind her before Belle could think of another excuse to keep her in the room or send her on another errand. She had spent the last hour running back and forth from the living room to Belle's bedroom, collecting books, fingernail polish, an assortment of snack food and anything else Belle could think of and she was worn out.

She stood at the door, waiting for Belle's call. When it didn't come, she gratefully sank down into the armchair, nearest the door.

She just wanted to rest, but her mind kept mulling over Daniel's death. Something was there that she was missing. If Belle wasn't faking her injuries, then who attacked her and why would the killer want to kill Belle? Grace glanced at her raincoat lying over her dining room chair.

Belle was wearing Grace's clothes when she was attacked. What if it wasn't Belle the killer was after? Grace shook her head. No, she and Belle didn't look anything alike. Sure, they were the same height and they had the same build, but... Grace twisted a tendril of her red hair around her finger. Belle had a scarf wrapped around her head when she had left. If the killer was in a hurry, he or she might have confused Belle for Grace. The killer could have seen her go into the stairway and just assumed it was Grace.

Suddenly, the phone rang. She ran over to the desk and looking at the caller id saw that it said UNLISTED. Taking a deep steadying breath, she picked up the phone and raised it to her ear. "Missed you," was all the voice said before hanging up.

Sunday, December 18th

CHAPTER TWENTY-ONE

"AH, I SEE Kyle was put in charge of decorations," Grace said as she shielded her eyes with one hand. Over the weekend, the toy store had been transformed into a Christmas wonderland, or what a Christmas wonderland would look like if it were set on the sun. There were more Christmas lights in the store than at Rockefeller Center, Grace thought in amusement. She blinked rapidly, trying to adjust to the light. Once the spots were no longer obstructing her vision, she shrugged out of her white, wool coat, walked to the large Christmas tree in front of the entrance and dropped the brightly decorated present at the foot of the tree.

"I think it's wonderful," Belle shouted over the sound of *Hark! The Herald Angels Sing* blaring over the loudspeaker. "It's like being in Santa's workshop." Belle carefully lifted a bright pink bear out of the tree. "It must be nice doing this every single year."

Eyes now adjusted to the lights, Grace scanned the store. "This is actually the first time we've ever had the party in the toy store. We usually just set up something on the fourth floor."

"Well, I'm glad Kyle was put in charge this year," Belle said as she carefully placed the bear back into the tree.

She had to admit it was rather nice. The lights, toys, garland, and fake snow dusted throughout, did create a rather festive atmosphere. She noticed that even her normally recalcitrant co-workers seemed to be getting into the spirit. Granted there were seventy percent less than in former years, but those present seemed to be enjoying themselves. No one was looking at their watch or edging toward the door. In fact, a few people actually were smiling—or grimacing, she thought, shielding her eyes once again; so difficult to tell.

She took a step forward, just missing the toy train running through the store. She lifted her black Italian leather high heel in time to avoid a horrific train derailment. Luckily, the little toy train, with its fashion doll passengers, safely continued on its way.

"There you are, darling." Straker walked past Grace and kissed Belle on the cheek. "Are you ready for tonight?"

"Absolutely," she said brightly.

"Are you sure?"

Belle's smile faltered. "Yes, Franklin, I'm sure." Catching Grace's eye, Belle plastered a smile on her face. "I was just telling Grace how magnificent everything looks."

"Why? She didn't have anything to do with it." He turned to Grace. "Where's your report?"

"Merry Christmas to you too, sir."

Belle stood on her tiptoes, her head arched at an angle as she scanned the room. A small frown furrowed her brow. "Is everyone here?"

Straker nodded. "You two were the last hold outs."

Belle took a deep breath and wiped her hands on her red knit sweater dress. Grace looked at her curiously. The blonde was obviously nervous about something. "I guess it's time to tell everyone."

Straker shook his head. "Not yet." He jerked his head toward the Magic Shoppe. "Let's talk first."

Grace watched them walk away, wondering what they were up to. Straker unlocked the glass doors leading to the shop. Placing a hand on Belle's back, he escorted her past the door and into the other room. They stopped in front of the door, their heads bent together, taking surreptitious glances through the glass as they spoke.

Valerie walked past the doors. Spying Grace out of the corner of her eye, she turned and strode toward her friend, easily hopping over the toy train barreling down the tracks in front of her foot. Grace felt her eyebrows rise. Valerie, decked out in a low-cut blue cocktail dress, cut four inches above the knee, came rushing forward. Quite a difference from her usual Christmas Party attire, which for the last ten years consisted of a Christmas sweater and jeans. And here Grace was afraid her low cut white, satin dress would be too risqué, but next to Valerie, she was positively conservative. She schooled her features to hide her surprise.

Valerie gave Grace a quick hug. "Look at you. You look absolutely beautiful."

Grace quickly returned the compliment. "What happened to the Christmas sweaters? That was an annual tradition."

"Time for a change," she said with a smile. "I just wanted to look nice. I figured I needed to compete with you and Belle tonight."

Smiling, Grace shook her head. "Oh no. What gives? Where did you get that dress and who is it for?"

Valerie adopted an innocent expression. "This old thing. I wear this around the house every evening."

Grace laughed.

"There's someone I want to impress tonight," Valerie admitted with a slight shrug.

"Here?" Grace asked in surprise. "Who?"

"Oh no. I don't want to jinx it." Valerie looked around. "Where's your date?"

"Ethan's at a meeting, but he'll be here soon." Grace shifted her clutch and coat to her other arm. "How long have you been here?"

"Just thirty minutes." She motioned for Grace to follow her. "You haven't missed much. Everyone's been waiting for Belle to arrive. Straker's been an absolute bear tonight. I've spent the last thirty minutes keeping him from biting everyone's heads off." She led Grace to a small bistro table in the corner of the store. "I'm glad she's finally here."

"Where did these come from?" Grace asked, indicating the six little tables arranged around the store. She waved at Bourget and Ellen sitting at the table to their left.

Valerie shrugged. "Kyle said he got a deal, whatever that means."

"Speaking of Kyle, where is he?"

"Last I saw him, he was chatting with Jackie and a few of the other girls from the store."

Grace's smiled. "Jackie's here?" At her friends nod, she said, "Good."

"I didn't know you two were friends."

"We're not. She just thinks I'm sleeping with Straker. I'm hoping tonight's party will convince her otherwise." Grace looked over her shoulder, a smile lighting up her face. "Why's Santa here?"

"What's a Christmas party without Santa," Kyle said, sidling up to the table, looking incredibly handsome in a black tux. He handed Grace and Valerie a cup of punch.

"Oh my, look at you!" Grace said laughing. "You look absolutely—" Grace bit her tongue before she said something that could end up being the basis of a future sexual harassment suit. She doubted Ethan would appreciate the work. She dropped the smile and toned down her voice. "You look very put together tonight."

He grinned. "I don't think that's what you were going to say." Suggestively leering at her, he mimicked her tone of voice. "You look very put together, too."

Suddenly uncomfortable, Grace cleared her throat and took a step back. Desperately seeking a way to change the subject, she pointed toward Santa picking up the presents lying around the tree. "Where did you find him?"

Sensing her sudden change in attitude, Kyle added a few more inches of distance between them. "That's Michael. He volunteered."

"Really?" Grace asked in surprise. "I would never have guessed." Gone was the young, slight man with the foreboding tattoos, ink black hair and black clothes. In his place was jolly ol' Saint Nick.

Valerie nodded. "Straker donated some toys to the children's hospital and Michael volunteered to deliver them."

Kyle drummed his fingers on the table. "And that's a job usually reserved for Santa. Hence the Santa suit." He motioned for Michael to join them.

Michael waddled up to their table, carrying a green velvet bag. "Ho ho ho!"

Valerie looked past Grace's shoulder. "Here comes the boss. I hope you have your report ready, because he's complained about nothing else since he arrived."

"Valerie, there you are." Straker pushed his way up to the table. "Where have you been?"

"Right here, waiting for you, sir," Valerie said with a small smile.

Straker nodded approvingly. "Good. Have you seen Harcourt?"

"He's in his office."

"Not anymore, I just checked." Straker shook his head. "I need to talk to him."

Belle bit her lip. "It can wait," she said tensely.

"Is everything okay, Belle?" Michael asked.

Straker screwed up his face. "Of course it is. Why wouldn't it be?"

Belle smiled. "Just a little nervous. Tonight's a big night for us," she said, taking Straker's hand into hers.

Michael nodded. He looked at Valerie's cup of punch sitting on the table. "I'm thirsty. I think I'll go get a cup of eggnog."

Belle tucked an errant strand of hair behind her ear. "Let's go ahead and get started, Franklin."

Straker turned to Belle. "I thought you wanted Harcourt here?"

Belle craned her neck to the side. "There he is. He just got off the elevator."

Belle sighed heavily. "I guess we're ready. Kyle, can you turn off the music for a second."

Nodding, Kyle turned around and headed for Bourget's office, earning a glare from the store manager.

Straker inclined his head. "Go ahead, Belle. I'll watch from over here."

"Oh no." Belle pulled on Straker's arm. "You have to say something. This is your party," she whispered. "Remember what we discussed?"

Straker looked ready to refuse. In the end, he reluctantly allowed himself to be led to the center of the room.

Turning around, he glared at his employees, until they, one by one, clustered around. Grace felt Michael brush up against her as he leaned against the table. "All right, listen up. It's the holiday season and I guess I'm supposed to say something inspirational to get this party started, so here goes. We're broke. Don't destroy what's left of our inventory. Merry Christmas and Happy Holidays."

A smattering of clapping could be heard through the store as Straker walked back to his table and stood next to a black clad Louisa, complete with mourning veil.

Still standing in the center of the room, Belle smiled brightly. "I want to personally thank everyone for coming out tonight to celebrate the season and to celebrate mine and Franklin's engagement."

Out of the corner of her eye, Grace watched as Michael crushed the paper cup in his hand.

"I can't tell you how much it means to us that you are all here. I have some good news to share. As you know, Franklin and I are engaged, but what you don't know is that we are planning on marrying Christmas Day, here in the store."

Michael bent his head down. Carefully placing both hands on the table, he pushed himself away from the table and quietly walked towards the main entrance and out the doors. Grace swung her attention back to Belle.

"Everyone here is invited, of course," Belle said with a slight frown, as she stared at the front doors. She plastered another big smile on her face and returned her attention to the others gathered around her. "Now, I know you all are worried about the coming year, but I assure you that Franklin and I will do everything possible to keep the Straker Toy Company running for another hundred years. Let's not worry about the future. Let's just enjoy tonight—"

"Oh, yes!" Louisa chuckled. "By all means, let's enjoy tonight. Daniel's been dead for less than a week now, but we shouldn't let that stop us from enjoying ourselves."

"Louisa, we talked about this," her father said softly.

"I was agreeing with her." Lifting her cup into the air, Louisa smiled. "It's time to celebrate, so turn on the music and let's dance." She grabbed Allen by the hand and led him to the center of the room.

With a tight smile, Belle shrugged and stepped out of the way, joining Straker at the table.

Louisa pointed at Kyle. "Kirk, or whatever your name is, hurry up, because I want to dance."

Shrugging, Kyle, stood up and walked toward Bourget's office. A few seconds later, the Christmas music began blaring through the speakers once again.

* * * *

"Congratulations on your new promotion," Jackie said sweetly. "I'm sure you worked so hard for it," which was said not so sweetly.

Grace smirked. "Thank you, I did. Perhaps, you've seen some of my designs."

"Yes, I have. They're very…cute," said in that same condescendingly sweet tone of voice, which was setting Grace's teeth on edge. "I understand Mr. Straker absolutely loved them."

"Yes, he did. So did a lot of other people," Grace ground out through her teeth. Be nice, you need her to cooperate, she told herself for the third time since she started this conversation with Jackie. "By the way, I've been meaning to offer my condolences on your loss. I understand you and Daniel were rather close."

The smirk fell from Jackie's face. "At one time."

"Did he happen to confide—"

"Do you mean, did he tell me who killed Lily?"

Taken aback by the other woman's frank question, she said, "Yes," a bit suspiciously.

"Don't look so surprised," Jackie said, taking a deep breath and arching her back as Kyle passed. Her long bleach blonde hair slipped off her shoulders and fell down her back. Licking her lips, she gave him a suggestive smile. She dropped the pose when he turned a corner and disappeared. "Everyone knows that Straker's issued orders to be on the hunt for any clues to Lily's death. You're not the only one after the reward."

Grace sighed. "I'm just curious—Wait, what reward?"

"Well, I'll tell you what I told Allen. Daniel didn't tell me anything."

Grace held up her hand. "That's too bad, but let's not get off-topic. What reward are you talking about?" As far as she knew, Straker was just going to give the employee who figures it out a pat on the back. She didn't recall him mentioning anything about a reward. She turned her head and glared at her boss' back.

"All he said was that if anything should happen to him that I was to check his computer. He had everything saved in a file named Expense Report 5J."

"Did you?"

Jackie made a face. "How am I going to get in his computer? I told the police what he said and they searched his computer. They didn't find any file though."

"How do you know that?"

Jackie shrugged one slim shoulder. "I want that reward as much as you. So, I talked to the detective in charge. He said that the file didn't exist. That's not that surprising. Louisa probably wiped it clean before they got to it."

Unbeknownst to either woman, Louisa was standing only a few feet away. She whirled around and confronted Jackie. "I didn't destroy anything. Who is starting these rumors? Why would anyone think I would do anything to prevent my husband's murderer from being brought to justice?"

Jackie, without missing a beat, immediately turned to Grace. "Yeah, Grace, why are you starting these rumors?"

* * * *

"Louisa, are you okay?" Grace asked, knocking on the bathroom door.

Louisa came out of the stall, sniffling and dabbing her eyes with tissue. She pushed her mourning veil away from her face. "I'm sorry, Grace. I shouldn't have lost my temper like that. That woman…"

"Louisa, I didn't start any rumors—"

"I know you didn't. I learned a long time ago not to believe a word that Jackie says. She and my husband were—" Louisa swallowed hard as tears sprang to her eyes.

"If you knew she was fooling around with Daniel, why didn't you fire her?" Grace asked.

Louisa laughed bitterly. "She's the daughter of a good friend of my father."

"So?"

"A very rich friend of my father."

"Oh."

Leaning against the sink, her back to the mirror, Louisa covered her face with her hand as she wept. "I don't understand how any of this happened. I just can't believe Daniel's dead."

"I'm so sorry, Louisa," she said giving the other woman a hug.

Louisa closed her eyes. "I loved him, I really did. Despite it all, I did love him. I just wish he had loved me," she said softly as she pulled back and faced the mirror. "I don't understand what he saw in these other women. I work out. I take care of myself." Her face crumbled. "Or at least I used to. I didn't always used to be like this. When we first married things were so good. Then he started cheating and I just fell apart." She glanced at Grace. "I'm sorry, for the way that I've been acting. I know that I've been a terror to you all for a while now." She wiped the tears off her face and stiffened her spine. "But that's going to change."

"Louisa, not to change the subject, but why did you drag me backstage during the magic show?"

Louisa leaned toward the mirror. With her pinky finger she wiped off the trail of mascara that had made its way down the side of her eye. "I saw Daniel walk back there with that girl, Tabitha Eddington. I tried following them myself, but I got scared. I don't know why. I just didn't want to go back there by myself, so I dragged you along with me. I'm sorry, Grace. I know that I shouldn't have done that, but I wasn't thinking clearly that night."

Grace nodded. "Where did you go after you left me by the stage door?"

"A few seconds after I left you, I ran into that magician. You know that tall good-looking one with the black eyes. He threw me out. I'm sorry, I was just so angry, I forgot all about you."

"Only a few seconds?"

Louisa turned back to the mirror. She made a face at her reflection. She opened her clutch and reached for her lipstick. "You can ask Dragovich if you don't believe me." She glanced at Grace. "I know what you're thinking. I didn't kill Lily or my husband. I hated her, but I knew she was only a temporary nuisance. Daddy never stays with anyone for too long."

"Then why did you send those letters to him?"

Louisa frowned. "What letters?"

"The letters he received from a *concerned friend*."

"I don't know what you are talking about. I didn't send any letters to daddy."

"Okay," Grace said, "do you know anything about the message Daniel supposedly left on his computer?"

Louisa shook her head. "He didn't confide in me," she said softly.

"Did he have a personal laptop—"

"The police took that, too. They even took Valerie's computer for a couple of days."

"Valerie's? Why?"

"Valerie and Dad caught Daniel using her computer a few days before he died. He told them that his wasn't working and he just wanted to type up a report. They took hers just in case, but they didn't find anything."

* * * *

"Poor Jackie," Kyle said, shaking his head. "I finally got her to stop crying. Why did Louisa go off like that?"

Grace shrugged. "It's a mystery."

Smiling, Kyle leaned against the half shelf of action figures. "You look very pretty tonight."

Blushing, she shook her head. "Kyle... I'm your supervisor—
"

"Not right now," he said leaning closer. "We're not working right now."

She placed a hand on his chest. "There are rules."

He grinned. "You are absolutely correct. People should abide by the rules."

"Yes," she said, suspicious at his sudden change in attitude.

"If more people followed the rules, then there would be fewer problems in the world."

"That's right."

Placing his hands at her elbows, he leaned in closer. "So, we're agreed. You should always follow the rules, no matter what."

His handsome face was only inches away. Grace felt her heart begin to thud in her chest. She recognized a trap when she saw one, but wasn't quite sure how he was going to spring it. "Kyle—"

"Right? You agree that we should follow the rules?"

"Yes," she said slowly as a silly grin began to spread across her face.

He leaned in closer. She leaned back and smiled. "Where are you going with this?"

He looked up at the sprig of mistletoe above their heads.

She laughed. "Kyle—"

"It's a rule," he protested. "I didn't create this rule. It's such a hassle, but a rule is a rule, and we must obey the rules."

"Funny, you didn't think so when you filled out your time sheet last week."

"I'm reformed."

She placed her other hand on his chest. Patting his chest, she gently pushed him away. "Nice try, but Straker has a rule about fraternization."

Sighing, he stepped back and shoved his hands in his pockets. "For or against?"

"Against. At least, for his employees."

"Fine, then let the bad luck be on your head." He leaned back against the shelf. "Where's Ethan? I'm surprised he's not here."

"He's working."

"All work and no play—"

"He'll be here soon. Probably any minute," she said walking toward the entrance. "Where's Valerie? Do you see her?"

Kyle pointed toward the Christmas tree. Valerie was standing with Harcourt, who was performing a magic trick. She laughed as he pulled a rose from her ear. Taking the rose out of his hand, she playfully hit him across the chest. She was just about to say something when she saw Grace. Smiling, she waved goodbye to Harcourt and dashed over to stand next to Grace and Kyle.

"What was that all about?" Grace asked with a smile.

"What?" Valerie asked innocently.

Grace's mouth fell open. When Valerie said she wanted to look nice for someone, she would never have guessed it was for Sidney Harcourt. She raised her eyebrow.

Valerie looked back at Harcourt and waved. "It's not what you think. He was just showing me a magic trick. What did you find out from Louisa?"

Grace glanced over at Kyle who was standing a few feet away chatting with one of the toy store employees. She dropped her voice to a whisper. "Daniel left a note in case he died."

Valerie gasped. "He did? Where is it?"

Grace shrugged. "It was supposed to be hidden under an expense reports file, but they didn't find anything."

"That's why they took my computer," Valerie said in a rush. "I'm so stupid. Of course, Grace, I forgot to tell you about Daniel using my computer one day. I didn't think anything about it, but now—"

"What are you two talking about?" Kyle asked as he rejoined them.

Grace shook her head. "It's not important, just another dead end. Do you two know anything about a reward?"

* * * *

"I'm so sorry, I'm late," Ethan said, kissing Grace softly. He smiled at Valerie before sitting down next to Grace. He laid his arm across the back of her chair and loosened his tie. "I didn't expect my meeting to last this long."

Smiling, Grace asked, "How did it go?"

"Good, I think my client may actually be innocent. I love that. It's a nice change of pace from my usual clients." He looked around the store. "So, what did I miss?"

Grace shrugged. "Not much, other than Belle and Franklin are getting married on Christmas Day here in the store—"

Ethan's hazel eyes widened. "You're kidding? Already?"

"Straker's never been one for waiting," Valerie said.

"I guess not," Ethan said, chuckling. "Anything else?"

"Daniel left a note," Valerie said, "but no one can find it."

Grace looked over her shoulder. Lowering her voice to a whisper, she asked, "Are we still on for tomorrow night?"

"Yeah, I'll meet you two over here after work," Ethan said.

Valerie snorted. "You still want to search the building? I doubt there's anything here."

"Kyle's was convinced that someone was hiding upstairs," Grace said softly. "Maybe we can find something the police missed."

Valerie laughed. "I thought he was convinced it was a ghost."

"He's keeping an open mind," Grace said with a smile. "I think we should check out the attic and then go through Daniel's office. Who knows, maybe Jackie was wrong. What if it wasn't a computer file he was talking about? Maybe he wrote out a message and hid it somewhere. After that, I want to look at the books. Maybe we can figure out when Daniel took that money."

"The police have already done that," Valerie countered. "In fact, they've been all through the building, so I don't know what you hope to find."

Grace shushed Valerie, when she noticed Allen nonchalantly walking past their table. He stopped in front of the fire exit map hanging on the wall behind them. Strangely fascinated by the informational drawing, he devoted all his energy into studying it, while simultaneously leaning back toward their little group, attempting to be the picture of innocence. She waited until he stole a glance over his shoulder, before smiling and waving at him, until he walked away in a huff.

"Do you think he heard us?" Ethan asked.

Grace shook her head. "I don't think so, but let's talk about something else. We don't want to take a chance on someone finding out what we're planning." Changing the subject, she said, "Let's see, what else did we do tonight? Oh, we just did Secret Santa." Grace pulled out a set of toy pistols, from a Straker Toy Company paper bag. "Allen was my Secret Santa."

Ethan picked up the toy guns. "Why would he..." His handsome face darkened. "Do you think this could be a threat?"

Grace and Valerie laughed at his serious expression and shook their heads.

"No, but think about it." He picked up the pistols and looked at it in disgust. "Why would he give a set of toy pistols to a grown woman?"

"Trust me, Ethan," Grace said. "It's not a threat."

Valerie smiled. "It's just a joke."

"Don't be silly, Val. Allen doesn't have a sense of humor." Grace turned back to Ethan. "Allen was a bit appalled at my Halloween costume and its lack of Straker Toy accessories."

Ethan shook his head. "If you say so." Smiling, he looked over at Valerie. "What about you?"

"Oh, I got lucky. My Secret Santa was Kyle."

Grace tried not to laugh, but failed.

Valerie pulled out the hula dancing Santa that had been sitting on Kyle's desk since he redecorated.

Grace smiled. "I actually like that thing. I play with it every day."

"Well, you can come visit it in my office whenever you want," Valerie said, placing it back in its box.

"So, how did Dragovich take the announcement?" Ethan asked.

"Ilya Dragovich?" Grace asked. "I don't know. He wasn't here tonight."

"Isn't Dragovich still in jail?" Valerie asked.

Kyle came up behind her. Pulling a stool from a nearby table, he squeezed in between Grace and Valerie. "Jail? The magician? Why would he be in jail?"

Scooting over to make room, Valerie answered him, "For assaulting Michael at the hospital."

Ethan ran his hand through his black hair, causing one long piece to fall across his forehead. "You should have seen them at the jail. I've never seen a more nervous group of people in my life."

"You were at the jail?" Grace asked, resisting the urge to push his hair back off his forehead.

"That's where I was meeting my client today." Ethan shuddered. "It was spooky. They let me go back into the holding cell to talk to my client and he was in a cell with a bunch of other men. Dragovich was on one side, staring down a group of five or six men who were all huddled together on the other side, just frozen. Even the cops were nervous. That man is truly scary. My client said he'd never been more freaked out about someone in his life."

Kyle rolled his eyes. "You're not buying all this hocus pocus stuff that Dragovich puts out, are you? He's just a man."

"I know that," Ethan snapped. "Aren't you the one running around talking about ghosts in the attic?"

Shaking his head decisively, Kyle said, "That's completely different."

"You weren't there. Those guys were still as statutes. I think he had them hypnotized. Even the cops were a little spooked." Ethan gave a little involuntary shudder.

Valerie began tapping on the table. "Speaking of Dragovich, take a look at his daughter over there," she said pointing to the elevator.

They all turned their heads to see Belle and Michael in what appeared to be an argument. Belle looked as if she was begging. She wiped a hand across her face.

"Who's in the Santa costume?" Ethan asked.

"Michael Talon," Grace whispered.

They watched as Michael spun away from Belle and stormed out of the store.

Monday, December 19th
12:00 a.m.

CHAPTER TWENTY-TWO

"HEY, WAIT UP!"

Grace and Valerie turned in time to see Belle run down the hallway towards them.

When Belle reached their side, she paused a second to catch her breath. "Are you leaving already?" she asked breathlessly.

"I'm exhausted," Grace said, buttoning her coat.

Valerie nodded her head. "We still have to get up early to go to work in the morning."

"Ethan offered to drive us home," Grace said. "Do you want to come with us?"

"Well…" Belle looked over her shoulder.

"The doctor told you to take it easy for the next few days," Grace said, suspiciously sounding like her mother.

Belle looked at her watch and sighed in disappointment. "I guess the party's over anyway. Hang on a second, while I grab my coat and purse out of my office."

Valerie lifted her wrist. Checking the time, she groaned. "I can't believe I'm here at this time of night."

"It wasn't as bad as last year. At least, no one's threatening to burn the toys this time."

Valerie looked past Grace's shoulder. Dropping her voice to a whisper, she said, "Don't you think it's kind of strange that she's not going home with Straker tonight? This is their engagement party."

"Maybe she's old-fashioned."

Valerie made a face. "I don't think so. She spent more time worrying over Michael tonight than spending it with Straker."

Grace had to agree with Valerie. Belle didn't exactly act like a woman celebrating her engagement with the man she loved. She seemed more like a woman enduring a root canal.

"Have you seen them together?" Valerie whispered.

"Who? Belle and Michael?"

Valerie shook her head. "No, her and Straker."

"No, not really."

"Does she talk about him at all?" Valerie's expression darkened. "I mean, what does she say about him? Grace, I don't think she loves him at all, so why is she marrying him?"

"I don't know, Val. I don't know why anyone would marry Straker. Maybe she—"

"Shh." Valerie grabbed Grace's arm. "Here she comes."

Belle closed the door to her office and walked over to where they were standing. "Okay, I'm ready. Do you think Ethan could stop—" Belle stopped speaking. Her face lit up, as she waved her hand. "Michael."

Michael, still dressed as Kris Kringle, was at the opposite end of the hall, leaning up against the wall.

Belle's face fell, when he didn't return her wave. "He must still be upset," she said in a whisper. "I'll be right back."

Michael pushed himself off the wall and started walking toward them.

Something was wrong. Grace wasn't quite sure what, but she suddenly felt sick, as a chill ran down her spine.

Belle must have sensed the danger as well. She abruptly stopped walking and took a couple of steps back.

Grace reached out a hand towards Belle. "I don't think that's Santa."

No sooner had the words left her mouth than Santa rushed toward them. Belle screamed and Grace grabbed her arm with one hand, and then pushed Valerie toward Val's office with the other. Once inside, she turned around and locked the door behind her. Only seconds later, Santa began pounding on the door.

Running around the desk in the center of the room, Grace reached for the phone. She dropped the receiver back in the cradle. "The line's dead."

Grace ran her hand through her hair in frustration. Whoever was on the other side of the door had stepped up their assault. She watched as the doors began to shake.

"What is going on?" Valerie said in confusion. "Why is Michael acting like this?"

Belle shook her head. "That's not Michael."

"He's wearing the Santa suit," Valerie said.

"I don't care," Belle snapped, "that's not Michael."

Grace ran forward and braced herself against the shaking door. "Whatever. Would you two help me, please?" She hooked the nearest chair with her foot and brought it closer. With Valerie's help, she slid the chair under the doorknob.

The door jamb splintered.

"This isn't going to hold him." Grace ran to the other side of Valerie's desk and began pushing it toward the door, when the assault on the door suddenly stopped.

Belle pointed at the double doors to Straker's office. "What about Franklin's private entrance? We could sneak down the back stairs."

"I'm not leaving this office," Valerie said. She grabbed the end of the desk and helped Grace push it toward the doors. "We're safe in here. We'll just barricade ourselves in until help arrives."

Once the desk was in place, they stared at the double doors. Grace leaned forward. "I don't hear anything."

"Do you think he left?" Belle asked trembling.

Grace climbed on the desk and leaned her ear against the door. "Valerie, is the door to Straker's private entrance locked?"

She got her answer when Belle let out a blood-curdling scream. Grace jumped off the desk and ran toward Straker's office door. Santa was standing in the doorway across the room. Grace watched with dread as he closed and locked the door behind him. He calmly walked toward them, as the three women backed away. Reaching the double doors, he extended a white gloved hand towards the light switch and flipped it off, plunging them into darkness.

Grace suddenly felt Belle grab her wrist and pull her toward the double doors of Louisa's office at the same time she heard Belle say, "Hurry, Val."

They stumbled toward the door, quickly shutting it and locking it behind them. Grace and Belle wasted no time in moving Louisa's sofa in front of the door. "Val, do you have your cell phone?" Grace said. "See if you can get a signal."

"We can't get a signal anywhere in this building," Belle complained. "He's not banging on the doors. Maybe he gave up."

"Val?" Grace felt her heart skip a beat. "Valerie?" She reached for the light switch on the wall. Valerie wasn't in the room.

Grace and Belle looked toward the doors. They both reached for the sofa at the same time and began dragging it away from the door. Grace fumbled with the lock, before finally opening the door. Valerie was lying on the floor. Santa was kneeling over her, his hands wrapped around her throat. Without thinking, Grace jumped on his back. He easily knocked her off and reached for Valerie's throat again. Belle came at him from the other side. She picked up the computer off the desk and dropped it on his head. He shook his head, dazed for a moment, before grabbing Belle's ankle and flipping her to the floor.

Grace, meanwhile, reached under Valerie's arms and began pulling her toward Louisa's office. Santa reached up and touched the back of his head before grabbing Valerie's ankles, pulling her back towards himself. Slightly dazed, Belle jumped to her feet, looking around frantically for a weapon. Seizing the phone off the desk, she lifted it up and hit their attacker on the head. He fell over with a groan.

With Belle's help, Grace was able to pull Valerie into Louisa's office. They quickly barricaded the door again. To Grace's relief, Valerie was trying to get to her feet.

Grace pushed her back down. "Don't try to move." She looked over at Belle, who was leaning over the sofa, her ear pressed to the door. Grace could hear the sound of glass breaking. "What's he doing?"

Belle shook her head. "I don't know. It sounds like he's destroying the room."

By the time Grace reached the door, there was silence. Grace and Belle traded worried glances, wondering what he was planning next.

To their surprise, there was a tentative knock on the door, followed by the sound of Kyle's voice calling their names.

Belle blew out her breath and smiled. She hopped off the couch. "Hurry, help me move the sofa."

Valerie sat up, gingerly touching her throat. She shook her head, wincing with the effort. Voice hoarse, she said, "No, don't."

"It's okay." Belle pulled at the edge of the sofa. "It's just Kyle."

Valerie started to argue again, but stopped suddenly and grimaced in pain.

Grace, still leaning against the door, sighed softly, "Val, it's okay, I can hear Ethan on the other side of the door."

Within seconds, the door was open. Ethan rushed forward and took Grace into his arms, while Kyle and Belle helped Valerie to the couch.

"Are you okay?" Ethan whispered into her ear.

Grace nodded as she quickly filled him in on what happened.

He leaned back. Concerned, he ran his hand over her hair.

"We need to call an ambulance," Belle said, pushing Valerie back into a reclining position.

Valerie pushed back. Sitting up, she insisted that she was fine.

"No, you're not." Belle leaned forward and pushed Valerie's hair out of the way. "It's already starting to bruise."

Valerie lifted a hand to her neck. "I'll survive. Santa's a bit more militant this year about the whole naughty or nice thing," she said with a grimace. "I just don't understand why Michael would do this? He was always so nice and friendly. Painfully shy but—"

"No!" Belle said quickly. "It wasn't Michael."

Ethan came to stand in front of Valerie. He leaned forward and inspected her throat. "Why did he attack you?"

"I don't know. I think we have a lunatic running around. First Lily, then Daniel, then Belle." She turned to look at Belle. "He must have been after you and I just got in the way."

Out of the corner of her eye, Grace noticed Kyle slipping out of the room. She walked to the door and watched him as he looked around Valerie's office. Standing in the doorway, she said, "I don't think he was after Belle."

Belle agreed. "I think he was after Grace. She's the one that keeps getting those weird phone calls."

"She may be right, Grace," Ethan said, frowning.

"No. He wasn't after me." Grace watched as Kyle disappeared into Straker's office. She turned back to the others. "He was after you, Valerie. Every time Belle or I pulled him off of you, he went straight back for you."

"But that's ridiculous," Valerie said. "Why would he be after me?"

"You must have done something to attract his attention," Ethan pointed out. "I saw you talking to Michael tonight. What were you two talking about?"

Valerie closed her eyes and shook her head. "Nothing that he would kill me for. We were just chatting."

"About what?" Grace asked.

"I was trying to cheer him up. He seemed rather depressed." Valerie opened her eyes and bit her lip. She looked over at Belle uncertainly. "I spoke to him about Daniel's death."

All eyes turned to Valerie.

"That can't be it though," Valerie said. "I mean, I didn't say anything that I hadn't already said before."

Ethan sat down next to her. "You must have said something. Why else would he suddenly want to kill you?"

Unable to keep quiet any longer Belle snapped. "Michael didn't try to kill her. It wasn't Michael."

"What if it was, Belle?" Kyle asked behind Grace, causing her to jump. She turned to look at him, surprised that she hadn't heard him approach.

"It wasn't," Belle repeated angrily. "He's gentle. He's sensitive. He would never do something like this. Besides, I saw the guy in the Santa suit and it wasn't Michael."

"How do you know?" Ethan asked. "Did you see his face?"

"I could tell immediately that it wasn't him," Belle said.

"No, that's not true," Valerie said. "You called his name and waived at him."

"Yeah, because of the costume, but once I got a good look at him, I realized it wasn't Michael." Belle pointed at Grace. "Ask Grace. She knew it wasn't him."

"I don't know," Grace said. "I couldn't tell who it was. I just could tell something was wrong."

"He was the only one wearing a Santa costume tonight," Ethan pointed out.

Kyle brushed past Grace, carrying a red bundle. "Which he ditched in the stairwell."

Ethan shook his head angrily. "What are you doing? That's evidence, you know. You should have left it where you found it."

"You think the cops can get fingerprints off of crushed velvet?" Kyle asked sarcastically.

"You've contaminated it," Ethan said harshly. "It has your DNA on it now."

"It was lying on the hallway floor," Kyle snapped. "I work here. I'm sure I've left traces of my DNA all around this building. We all have. Just relax," he said with a sneer. "I just moved it so the psycho couldn't come back and take it away." He knelt down and laid the costume on the floor. Grace noticed a spot of red running down the back of his neck. She reached forward and delicately touched the back of his head, eliciting a small groan. "You're hurt."

"He hit me in the back of the head when I came through the door. We ended up struggling for a bit before he ran off." Reaching back, he grabbed her hand. Running a thumb across the back of her hand, he tilted his head up and smiled. "It's okay. Just a scratch."

She felt Ethan move closer. Pulling her hand away, she said, "We need to find a phone and call for an ambulance."

"I don't need an ambulance," Kyle and Valerie said in unison.

Ethan reached around and placed a hand at her waist. "Well, we still need to call the police. They'll want to question Michael—"

"About what?" Michael asked. "What's going on in here?"

They turned to find Michael standing in the doorway, still in costume, with a bemused expression on his face.

Belle quickly walked to his side, drawing Michael away from the doorway and out of the room.

Kyle rose to his feet, swaying slightly.

"Are you okay?" Grace asked worried.

"Fine," he said, carefully touching the back of his head.

Valerie started coughing uncontrollably. Grace walked over to where she was sitting. Valerie looked up at her through watering eyes.

"I'll go get you a bottle of water," Grace said.

Kyle reached out and touched her arm. "I'll go. I want to check and see what Michael's doing out there anyway."

Grace smiled gratefully. "Thanks, Kyle," she said, toward his retreating back. "It's a good thing Kyle showed up when he did and chased the guy away."

Ethan walked through Valerie's office, through the double doors to Straker's office, and across the room towards Straker's private entrance. "Yeah, he's quite the hero," he said sarcastically.

Curious, Grace followed him into the room.

Bending down, he examined the lock and then the frame. "You said your attacker locked this door before shutting off the lights?"

She nodded.

Ethan stood up. "Does Kyle have a key to this office?"

"No."

"Are you sure?"

"Positive," Valerie said hoarsely from behind them. She stumbled to a chair in front of Straker's desk. "There are only two keys. Straker has one and I have the other."

Turning to Grace, he asked, "You're absolutely sure the killer locked the door?"

"Absolutely."

"Then how did Kyle get in? The door to the outer hallway is still barricaded from the inside. The only way in is through this door here and it isn't damaged, so he didn't break in."

Grace stood up and walked to the door. Ethan was right. There was no damage to the door.

Kyle walked in. He kneeled down next to Valerie and handed her a bottle of water.

Valerie opened the bottle and winced when the water hit her throat.

Grace winced with her. "Don't worry. The ambulance will be here soon."

"I don't need an ambulance," Valerie croaked out. "I just want to go home and go to bed."

"I think I should stay with you tonight," Grace said.

"Oh, don't be silly," Valerie said.

"No, she's right, Valerie," Ethan said. "If you are being targeted, you would be safer if you had company."

Kyle snorted. "I don't know about that. Grace and Belle were with her tonight and that didn't stop the guy from attacking her."

Ethan looked down at the other man still kneeling next to Valerie. "I know that," he snapped. "That's why I was about to suggest that I would stay with both of them." He turned to Grace. "In fact, you both should stay with me at my apartment."

"I can't really leave Belle by herself at our apartment. She's a target, too." Grace looked at Valerie. "Would you like to stay with us? There's safety in numbers."

Valerie smiled. "Sure."

"I can stay with you, too," Kyle offered.

"I don't think that's necessary," Ethan replied testily.

Kyle stood up. "I wasn't asking you."

"Kyle," Grace touched his sleeve, "how did you get in?"

Kyle frowned. "What?"

"How did you get into the office tonight?" she repeated.

Shrugging, Kyle pointed to the door. "I walked through Straker's side door."

"But it was locked," Ethan said.

Kyle shook his head. "No, it wasn't. It was wide open."

* * * *

Grace came out of a deep slumber. The phone next to her bed was ringing. She buried her head into her pillow, as she reached for the phone. Bringing it to her ear, she muttered a sleepy hello.

Her mysterious caller was back. She was about to hang up the phone when she heard a deep gravelly voice say, "How are you feeling, Gracie? I hope I didn't scare you last night. I wouldn't want to do that, not at least until you and that idiot boyfriend of yours has a chance to search your office building for something that doesn't exist. That should be good for a laugh. See you soon," before laughing and hanging up.

Suddenly wide-awake, Grace sat up in bed, her heart thudding against her chest. She reached for the knife lying on her nightstand. Breathing heavily, she laid back down, clutching the knife to her chest. She closed her eyes and tried to relax. She was safe. She was home in her own bed with her friends camped out a few feet away. He couldn't hurt her. At least not at the moment. She felt herself relax and start to drift off.

Creak.

Her eyes flew open. She looked toward her door, which was just closing.

Worried, Grace threw back the covers, tiptoed to the door, and opened it a crack.

Ethan was sound asleep on the floor next to her bedroom, snoring softly. Kyle was camped out in one of the armchairs, wide-awake. He turned off his phone and tossed it on top of his tuxedo jacket lying on the floor.

She opened the door wider and peeked around the corner. Valerie was slouched over the dining room table. Her head lying on her folded arms. Grace felt a pang of guilt. She had offered taking the sofa last night, but Valerie refused, saying she was too nervous to sleep and the sofa would be perfectly comfortable.

Opening the door the rest of the way, she quietly entered the living room.

Ethan jerked awake. He looked at everyone for a second before closing his eyes and lying back down.

Kyle rubbed a hand over his face, before looking at his watch. "Who called you at this ungodly hour?"

"It's seven-thirty," Grace explained patiently.

Kyle laid his head back. "Exactly."

Stifling a yawn, Grace said, "It's time to get up."

Valerie lifted her head and turned red-rimmed eyes toward Grace. "You're not going to work today are you?"

Grace nodded her head. "I'm not staying here." The last thing she wanted was to stay in her apartment by herself. At least she would be surrounded by people at the office. Not that it's any safer there. Besides, she wanted to talk to Straker.

Something in her voice must have caught Kyle's attention. His eyes flew open and focused in on her. "Who called?"

"A concerned citizen. He wanted to know how I was feeling."

"What did he sound like?" Valerie asked at the same time Kyle asked, "Did you recognize his voice?"

Grace shook her head. "No. I think they were using some type of voice changer. The voice didn't sound real."

Belle stumbled out of her bedroom, yawning. She glanced at the grandfather clock against the wall and groaned. "I promised Papa I would meet him for breakfast today." She took one look at the group in the living room and then at the only bathroom in the apartment, before rushing towards the bathroom door.

"Straker texted me a few minutes ago," Valerie mumbled from the dining room, her head once again lying on her folded arms. "He wants to see you as soon as you get to work."

Grace smiled. "Good. I want to see him too."

* * * *

Without waiting for an answer to her knock, Grace barged into Straker's office.

Straker pointedly looked over at the grandfather clock sitting in the corner of the room. Its hands showed the time as eight-thirty. "Apparently, it's a holiday and no one told me. Perhaps you would like to sleep in a little longer."

"I don't even start work until nine o'clock."

"I'm not surprised."

"No, I mean, I'm not supposed to be… You know, never mind, I want to talk to you. I've had about enou—"

Straker tossed a gold dragon pendant on the desk between them. "The police just released this."

"Lily's pendant."

He looked at her in surprise. "Yes. How did you know that was Lily's?"

"She showed it to me before she died." She picked it up and ran a thumb over its emerald eye. "They found it on her body?"

He shook his head. "Daniel's."

"Really?" she asked, interested despite herself. She quickly shook herself. This isn't what she was here for. She set the pendant back down on the desk. "Someone tried to kill us last night."

"Yes, I know. Good!"

Grace's mouth dropped open. "How is that good?"

"It means you're making Lily's killer nervous. You must be onto something. I knew I made the right decision hiring you."

Normally, Grace would be happy with his last statement, but she was still a bit thrown by the first. "I'm not exactly happy about making Lily's killer so nervous he feels that he has to kill me."

"Nonsense, you should be proud of yourself. You have already gotten further than those overpriced fancy detectives I hired. No one tried to kill them," he complained. "From now on, I want a report every hour, and make it as detailed as possible."

"Can I sleep or would you like me to stay up just so I can write up this report for you?"

"Bifurcated sleeping is what you need. That's how our ancestors slept, and that's how I sleep. If it's good enough for us, it's good enough for you. Now get back out there. Hopefully, he'll try again soon and we'll be able to catch him."

"Before or after he kills me?"

"Well, I would prefer before. I have ten years invested in you."

"Speaking of investment, I want a raise."

"You just got one, when you got that fancy new title."

"It was only a half a percent raise."

"We're in a recession. Besides, I don't know if you were paying attention at our last conference meeting, but we're going under."

"Dig deep. I want hazardous duty pay."

Straker shook his head.

"If you want me to continue, you need to pay me more."

"Fine," he said with a sigh. "I'll put a little more in your next paycheck. Happy?"

"No, actually, I'm not. And a little more? Try a lot more."

"It will be a substantial raise, don't you worry. You just continue what you're doing. You lasso that cotton-pickin rustler or whatever you would call him."

"My lasso's at the cleaners. About searching the office tonight—"

"No good. I have to meet with my lawyer tonight. Besides, Valerie needs the rest," he said gruffly. "We'll do it this Saturday."

Grace balked. "On Christmas Eve? I'm leaving for Hawaii."

"Didn't you just take a vacation during Thanksgiving?"

"Yes, I did, and after last night, I think I deserve another one."

"Hmm," he said tilting his head back. "Do you already have your plane ticket?"

Grace reluctantly told the truth. "I meant to buy it but little things like death threats and assaults, keep distracting me."

"Good. You can fly out Christmas morning then." When she looked ready to object, he added, "Of course, I don't actually need you here to conduct the search. I'm sure Allen would be happy to take your place."

Grace snapped her mouth shut. "Fine," she snapped, "I'll be here, but I want you to pay for my plane ticket."

His mouth fell open. "Do you know how much a plane ticket to Hawaii on Christmas costs?"

"No, but if you want you can tell me after you make the reservations."

"Lily was right. I'm far too good to my employees," he grumbled. "You'll get your ticket. You just keep asking questions and file your reports. I want to know everything you know, and when you know it."

Grace nodded. Turning to the door, she abruptly stopped and turned back around. "Did you tell anyone about our plans to search the building?"

"Yes, in between board meetings and possible merger discussions, I got together with all my best girlfriends and discussed your night life. Are these the types of questions they taught you to ask in those criminal justice classes that you took?"

Grace sighed. "Again, it was one class and I got a C-minus."

"I should have hired the kid who got the A," Straker grumbled.

Thursday, December 22nd

CHAPTER TWENTY-THREE

"THAT'S WHEN THE guy threw the ventriloquist dummy at me. I swear, the thing got up and ran from the room. Then I turned to my buddy, and told him that I didn't care how the elephant got into the room, we had to get it out of there before my mom found it," Kyle said.

Grace smiled from her office door. "I don't believe these stories you tell."

He crossed his hand over his heart. "Would I lie to you?"

"Yes," she said amused, "I believe you would."

"Well, that's only the beginning. Once we—" The phone ringing interrupted him. He lifted the receiver, and held it up to his ear. Grimacing, he opened up the drawer and laid it inside. "We ended up taking the elephant, monkey and—"

"Kyle, I hate to interrupt, but we really need to discuss your phone etiquette."

"It's our silent caller again. Have you changed your home phone number yet?"

Grace rubbed her eyes, tiredly. "Yes, I had a couple of days of quiet, but he found my new number, somehow. He woke me up at five o'clock this morning. He's added to his repertoire. He's now giving me this creepy laugh."

"Did you call the police?"

She nodded. "They told me to change the number again."

A shadow crossed his face. He nodded toward the outer hallway. "Your boyfriend is here."

"Ethan? What's he doing here?" Grace set her coffee cup down on Kyle's desk and walked out to the outer hall.

Kyle was right. Ethan and two others were standing in front of Straker's office door. Straker was shaking their hands and he looked pleased.

She felt Kyle stand behind her. "I've never seen Straker smile like that before."

"I know," she said suspiciously. "I wonder who died."

Ethan caught her eye. He broke with his group and walked over to her, grinning from ear to ear.

She felt, more than saw, Kyle walk away.

Ethan looked around before leaning down and giving her a brief kiss.

"Who are those people talking to Straker?" Grace asked.

He glanced back to the group. Straker was slapping one on the back and laughing. "Colleagues. The man shaking your boss' hand is a partner at my firm."

"What's going on?"

Ethan smiled. "I can't say. I'm actually not involved in it. I just found out about it today and asked if I could tag along."

"Found out about what?"

He grinned. "You were asking for a miracle the other day, weren't you?"

"Yeah," she said trying not to get her hopes up.

"Well, your prayers have just been answered."

"Meaning?"

"I can't say just yet, but I have excellent news." He gently ran his hands up and down her arms, biting his lip as he smiled. His smile must have been infectious, because Grace felt herself starting to smile with him. She thought he had never looked more handsome.

Ethan leaned down and kissed her again. "Let's meet for lunch." He looked over his shoulder. Straker and the other suits were heading for the elevators. "I better go," he said reluctantly before leaning down and kissing her once again.

She smiled as he walked away. Turning back to her office, she ran into Kyle.

"Valerie just called. Conference room. Five minutes," he said in clipped tones.

* * * *

Grace sat in her usual position. Kyle and Belle sat on either side of her. Those, who hadn't jumped ship, were haunting their usual spots, except for Allen. Allen had moved into Daniel's position.

Apparently, in more ways than one, she thought, as she saw Louisa take Allen's hand in hers, gripping it tightly.

They turned their heads as the conference door opened and Straker stalked in with Valerie on his heels.

Valerie was the one who captured Grace's attention. She was beaming.

Everyone must have noticed, because suddenly her co-workers were coming back to life. Even Harcourt opened his eyes and leaned forward in interest.

Straker sat down at the head of the table and smiled at the room. "Well, I have good news. Excellent news, and I wanted to share it with all my employees." He paused, looking at each person in the room intently.

Everyone looked at each other and a few began to smile in relief, but no one said a thing.

Satisfied that he had everyone's attention, he took a deep breath and let it out slowly. "My only brother, Preston Straker, who I've hated for over thirty years, died last night."

Everyone leaned back in their chairs. One by one, the hopeful smiles that had begun to emerge began to fall away. One of the girls from the toy store began to cry.

"No. No. Don't cry." He held up his hand. "It's good news."

They looked at him expectantly, wondering how Preston Straker's death could possibly translate to good news.

"He was a horrible man," Straker said. "A monster. He once tried to run over me. Good riddance, I say."

Ellen stood up suddenly, her entire body trembling. "I can't take it anymore. I have worked here for—"

Valerie stepped forward and held up her hand. Her smile must have stopped Ellen, because she suddenly snapped her mouth shut and sat down. Valerie placed her hand on Straker's shoulder. "Tell them the good news."

"I just did," Straker said.

She gripped his shoulder tighter.

"All right. All right. We're solvent. Preston left me a substantial amount of money."

* * * *

Grace felt like dancing. Strange how someone else inheriting a large fortune should make her so happy, but she was.

She opened her door. Feeling more relieved than she had in days, she picked up her designs out of the trash and smoothed out the edges. Momentarily forgetting that a murderer was still out there and targeting her, she threw herself into her work. She hadn't even realized Kyle had walked into her office, until she bumped into him when she took a step back from her design table.

Smiling, she handed him a sheet of blank pages.

To her surprise, Kyle took the pages and quickly laid them on the table. Turning around, he shut the door a touch too forcefully, causing the door to slam.

He crossed his arms and stood in front of her.

"What's wrong, Kyle?"

"Did you know that Ethan was representing Straker's brother?"

"He wasn't. One of the partners at the firm he works for represented him."

"That's kind of convenient, isn't it?"

"He said he just found out about it this morning."

"Did it occur to you that he might be involved in Lily's death? Did it occur to you that he might be lying to you?"

"Don't be insulting." Grace sat on the stool next to the design table. "If he is, he's not the only one," she said quietly.

"What does that mean?"

She swiveled around on the stool to face him. "How did you get into Straker's office the night Valerie was attacked?"

"I told you that the door was unlocked."

"No, it wasn't. Our friendly neighborhood Santa locked it himself. I watched him do it."

He shook his head. "Maybe after you all locked yourselves in Louisa's office, he unlocked it and hid. Did you think of that?"

Grace tilted her head, considering. "I wonder if he would have had enough time. Just out of curiosity, how did you get that bottle of water the other day?"

He looked at her in confusion.

"Allen put a lock on the refrigerator. He's the only one with a key and the only other person I've seen whose been able to pick the lock was Belle, but you never seem to have a problem with getting into the refrigerator. Why is that?"

"It's a cheap lock," Kyle said with a smirk. "Your boyfriend got up to Straker's office awfully quick the other night. Ethan arrived only a few minutes after I had chased Santa away."

"Ethan was driving us home and he came upstairs to check on us. What were you doing up there?"

He didn't answer.

"Besides, give me one reason why Ethan would kill Lily. He didn't know her and he wouldn't have been at the Dragon's Lair if I hadn't invited him."

"But his firm represents—"

"So, what?" she snapped. "He has no motive."

He dropped his head to his chest and sighed.

"Come on, Kyle. You're so certain he did it, then give me a motive. Think."

He shook his head, running his hand over his eyes. "I'm sorry, Ms. Holliday, I'm just tired. You're right, he doesn't have a motive," he admitted reluctantly.

"Right." Angrily, she swiveled back around and faced the table.

His hands appeared on the table on either side of hers. As he whispered in her ear, she felt him brush against her back. "Of course, that means that I don't have a motive. I don't know these people, either. I wasn't even at the Dragon's Lair the night Lily died, so why are you suddenly so suspicious of me?"

* * * *

"All right." Valerie dug through her filing cabinet and pulled out a folder. "Here it is."

She walked to the desk and opened the folder. Grace was sitting in the chair in front of Valerie's desk. She leaned back in the chair and nervously looked out at the hall. Standing up, she leaned over the desk to take a better look.

"Kyle started working downstairs in the toy shop on November second," Valerie said.

"Three days after Lily died, so what was he doing before that?"

Valerie lifted up the page and turned the folder around. "This is interesting. He was working as a paralegal."

"Really? What firm?"

"The Law Office of Felix Hutchinson. His website is WeSueYouRetire.com."

"I've never heard of him."

"Neither have I. You should ask Ethan, maybe he knows him."

"Anything else?"

Valerie shook her head, as she handed the folder back to Grace. "It's just your typical basic employment information. What do you hope to find?"

"I don't know," she said, flipping through the application information. "Look at this. All of it is so generic that it could apply to anyone."

Valerie chuckled. "I have a full drawer of generic background information on everyone who works here. Yours is just as generic as his."

Grace flipped the folder back around. "We ask for emergency contact information, don't we?"

Valerie took the file from her and flipped to the last page. "Here it is. Ah…look at this." She pointed to the contact information. "Felix Hutchinson. Cousin."

"He was working for his cousin. I wonder why he left. What about a background check?"

"What about it? There isn't one and before you ask, Straker's not going to authorize it. It costs too much money."

"So what? He has plenty money now."

"Yes, and he's bound and determined to keep all of it. I just asked him for a new stapler and he told me to use scotch tape."

Grace took the folder back and began flipping through it, only stopping when she came to Kyle's thirty-day performance evaluation Henry Bourget had filled out.

Valerie looked over Grace's shoulder. "Oh nice: Should be considered a walking disaster area… dangerous, approach with caution."

Valerie smirked. "This is my favorite: Widely considered a Doomsday machine."

Grace shook her head. "Kyle's got four references down here." She handed the file back to Valerie. "Can you take the first two and I'll take the last?"

Taking the file, Valerie let out a small groan. She walked over to the copier and made a copy of the reference sheet before handing it to Grace.

"When you're done, call me," Grace said, walking out the door and to her office.

Kyle wasn't at his desk or in her office. Just as well, she thought, closing and locking the door. No chance of him overhearing. She walked to her desk and sat down.

Ten minutes later, she hung up her phone and laid her head on her desk.

The phone rang. She looked at it in trepidation. Leaning over she looked at the number on the screen, relieved to see that the call was coming from Valerie's office.

"Well, what did his references say?" Valerie asked.

Grace sighed. "Never heard of him. Did you have any luck?"

"The second one never heard of him either, but Felix Hutchinson remembered him, eventually."

"Eventually?"

"Yeah, when I first asked him if Kyle Drake had ever worked for him, he said he didn't know any Kyle Drake. I was just about to hang up when he suddenly remembered his, apparently, entirely forgettable cousin and paralegal who worked for him over a year and who just quit a couple of months ago. Once he remembered, he wouldn't shut up about him. According to Felix, Kyle's an excellent worker and he was so sorry to let him go. He provided a glowing recommendation before asking how often the Straker Toy Company has been sued and who is currently handling our legal representation."

"Did you ask why he had trouble remembering Kyle?"

"Felix said that he thought I was asking about someone else. He heard me. He just didn't recognize the name. So, what do you think?"

"I don't think Kyle Drake is his real name."

"Well, I don't know about that. To tell you the truth, ol' Felix sounded a bit crazy."

* * * *

Grace rubbed her eyes. She was getting tired of staring at the computer screen. For the last couple of hours, she had stayed locked in her office, scouring the internet. She had tried every search string she could think of and had been on every website devoted to Ilya Dragovich—even the ones that just mentioned him in passing—and had come up with very little on his only son. There were some mentions of him of course, but nothing of any importance. His name came up on several European websites, but her German was rusty and her knowledge of French had somehow evaporated since high school. She didn't spend much time on them since they didn't include photos anyway, which is what she was really after. She sighed. She had no problem finding pictures of the other Dragovich's. There were thousands of Ilya, a few of Juliet, a few more of Belle, but absolutely none of Aleksis.

And after fruitlessly searching for over an hour, she had changed her search to Kyle Drake, hoping to find some mention of him, but still came up empty-handed. There was nothing there. Not a mention. Not even a social profile.

She leaned back in her chair and stretched her hands above her head. That alone wasn't that suspicious, she thought, giving him the benefit of the doubt. She preferred to live off the grid as much as possible herself. No one needed to know what she was doing every hour of the day.

She groaned, remembering Straker's latest order. She quickly typed up an email message which said, *I know nothing more than I did an hour ago*, and hit send. It wasn't exactly the truth. She had her suspicions, but she wasn't just ready to share them with Straker just yet.

After all, she could be wrong. She could be very wrong about Kyle.

She picked up the phone and called the magic shop.

* * * *

"I'll have the ravioli." Grace handed the menu back to the waitress. "Thank you."

"Pretty exciting day, wasn't it?" Ethan grinned at her.

Grace nodded. "Very."

"I couldn't believe it when my buddy, Ray, told me this morning who he represented and what was happening. I wanted to call you right then and give you the good news, but I couldn't until Ray met with your boss."

"How did Preston Straker die, or can you not say?"

He waved a hand. "No, that's a matter of public record now. Cancer."

Grace breathed a sigh of relief. "So, he wasn't murdered."

Ethan laughed. "Listen to you. I think you need to take a vacation and relax. Not every death is the result of a murder."

"The ones I've known about in the last month and a half have been," she said. She jumped at the feel of her phone vibrating in her pocket. Reluctantly, she pulled it out. No name. She lifted the phone to her ear. Silence. Her anonymous caller had found her new cell phone number. She closed her eyes tiredly. She was getting tired of this game.

Her feelings must have registered on her face. "Who is it?" Ethan asked harshly.

"Just my secret admirer."

Ethan grabbed the phone out of her hand. "Listen to me, psycho, if I find out—" He handed the phone back to her. A muscle in his jaw, jumped. "He hung up."

She shook her head. "Was your detective able to find the information I asked for?"

"Grace…" He took a deep breath. "Grace, I think you should go home."

She picked up her iced tea and took a drink, before nervously setting it down on the table. "It's the middle of the day."

"No, I mean back to Colorado." He laid his hand on her arm, his eyes pleading with her. "It's too dangerous for you here. I'm worried about you."

"As soon as we figure who is behind all of this, then I'll be safe."

He shook his head. "I don't want you to leave, but I don't want you to get hurt. I can continue to investigate. I'll keep you informed every step of the way."

"I'm not leaving." Grace looked over his shoulder. "When we're done, let's go back to my office and go over the information you've compiled." She waved at the black cloud that just walked through the door.

"What's Michael doing here?" Ethan asked.

"Oh, I'm sorry, Ethan. I've been so preoccupied, I forgot to tell you that I invited him to lunch with us."

Michael walked up to the table and sat down in the booth next to Grace.

"You want something to eat?" Ethan asked politely.

Michael shook his head. "No, like I told Grace, I can't really stay long." He turned towards Grace. "Why did you want to meet me?"

"I just wanted to ask you a few questions."

Smiling shyly, Michael took a bread stick out of the basket on the table. Snapping it in half, he dipped one end in the olive oil next to the basket. "Sure, you can ask me anything. I'm an open book."

"How long have you known Belle?" Grace asked.

"A long time." He shrugged. "Since we were kids."

"How did you meet?" Ethan asked.

"At a magician's conference in Paris."

"Have you always wanted to be a magician?" Grace asked.

Michael nodded. "Since I was little. I love it. I've wanted nothing else."

Grace smiled at his enthusiasm. "How did you meet Lily?"

"Same place. I had seen Dragovich and his show a dozen times growing up. It's all I talked about as a kid. My dad hated it, but Mom would always find a way to take us every year to one of his shows."

"She took you all the way to Europe for a magic convention?" Ethan asked with a raised eyebrow.

"My family was living in Sweden at the time. Anyway, I met Lily when I was thirteen and she was great. She talked to me for a long time and gave me a lot of encouragement. Besides my mom, she was the only person to pay any real attention to me. And after my mom…left, Lily became like another mother to me." His smile faded. "My dad got really angry."

Grace glanced down at his hands, which were now gripping the edge of the table. "Did you meet Belle that night?"

Lost in thought, Michael stared at the table. He shook his head. "No…it was the next year. Why are you asking me all of these questions about Belle?"

Ethan's eyes fell to Michael's hands. He instinctively moved closer to Grace. "We're just trying to figure out who pushed her down the stairs the other day."

"Good." He lifted one hand and picked out another breadstick. Snapping it in half, he said, "I want to know who tried to kill her, too." He looked up at Grace, as his eyes began to water. "It wasn't me. I love Belle. I would never hurt her. When I saw her lying there… I thought she was dead."

"I know. You kept saying that," Grace said.

"I…don't handle death well or blood for that matter," he said sheepishly.

Ethan threw Grace a disbelieving look. "Why did Dragovich try to kill you at the hospital?" he asked.

Michael shrugged. "Since I was the first one to find Belle, I think he just assumed that I was the one who attacked her." He looked down at his black clothes. "I know how I look. I know what people think, but to be perfectly honest, I don't really like this look." He pointed to his clothing. Dropping his voice to a whisper, he leaned forward conspiratorially. "This isn't me. It's all for show. I've built a certain reputation, based around this look and I can't seem to break free from it. The tattoos aren't even real. No one, but Belle knows that. No one else understands."

"What about Lily?" Ethan asked.

"Yeah, Lily understood, too," Michael said with a sigh. "I miss her. She was big help to me."

"How?" Grace asked.

He smiled. "She hated Harcourt. She wanted me to take over. I could have done it, too. Harcourt's rarely around, because he's too busy showing off at the local bars for the ladies. I've been running the Magic Shoppe for the last year with very little input from him, but that wasn't the only reason." He glanced at Grace. Reluctantly, he added, "She was helping me with Belle."

"What was she doing?" Grace asked.

"Belle doesn't think of me romantically. I'm just her friend. Her weird friend, who her father absolutely hates. Lily said she would talk to Belle and her father about me. She thought that we would be good together, but I don't think she ever got the chance to talk to them."

Ethan leaned forward. "It must make you angry to see Belle with Straker. I'd be pretty angry if the girl I loved hooked up with my friend's husband only a month after she died."

Michael nodded his head before suddenly looking up. "Hey, wait…it's not like that. I'm not angry. I'm just disappointed." He pushed back his long hair. "Look, I've got to go."

Grace laid her hand on his arm. "Wait. Do you know Aleksis Dragovich?"

"Yeah," he said hesitantly.

"Have you seen him lately?" she asked.

He shrugged. "Maybe."

"At the office?"

"Look," he said, sliding out of the booth, "Harcourt is going to be furious if I don't get back to work. I'm sorry, Grace, I've got to go."

CHAPTER TWENTY-FOUR

ETHAN SPREAD OUT the files on the conference room table. "It wasn't easy, but I did a little digging and came up with a small biography on all of our suspects. I have to admit this was kind of fun."

Grace sat down in her usual spot. "Let's start with Straker."

Ethan shook his head. "I don't know why you're interested in him. Out of all of them, I think he is one of our least likely suspects."

Grace shrugged. "I don't consider him a suspect, but everything seems to revolve around him."

"Okay." Ethan took out a legal pad and flipped through it. Clearing his voice, he read from the page. "Franklin Straker was born in 1961 to Arthur and Adele Straker. Arthur and Adele were a part of the jet set back then. Very wealthy. They had two sons, Preston and then a few years later, Franklin. Arthur ran a rather successful ad agency and intended to leave the company to both his sons, but father and son had a falling out when Franklin married a burlesque dancer named Louisa Scarlatti. They eloped at eighteen years of age."

Ethan handed Franklin Straker's file to Grace.

"Franklin's father hit the roof," he said continuing his narration. "He disinherited Franklin then and there. He left the entire Straker fortune, of which there was a considerable bit, to the older boy, Preston. When Louisa Straker was born a year later, it seemed that Arthur started to have a change of heart. According to some witnesses, he talked about changing his will and leaving half of the fortune to Franklin again. Unfortunately, the day before the will was to be changed, he suffered a major heart attack and died. Franklin went to his brother for his half of the inheritance and Preston said tough."

"Well, that explains why we had never heard of Preston Straker." Valerie picked up a folder and flipped through it.

Ethan nodded his head. "They despised each other. They haven't spoken one word to one another since that day."

"If they hated each other, why did Preston leave Franklin all of his money?" Grace asked.

"From what my co-worker says, Preston was a horrible man who drove away everyone from his life. All his wives, children, friends—well, he didn't have any friends—left him years ago. He was a miserable old man."

"He could have given the money to charity," Grace said.

Ethan shook his head. "This man hated everyone and everything. He'd make Ebenezer Scrooge proud."

"But why leave it to the brother that he despised?" Grace asked.

"Maybe there was some familial loyalty left in his cold dead heart." Ethan shrugged. "Who knows. In the end, he decided to let Franklin have it all."

"Was Straker surprised that he inherited?" Grace asked.

Ethan nodded. "Absolutely. You should have seen his face when Joe read the will. I don't think he ever expected to get his hands on the family fortune again."

"I don't understand something," Valerie said. "If Arthur died before changing his will, how did Franklin get control of the toy company?"

"Franklin inherited the toy company from his Uncle Harold Straker, Arthur's older brother. Arthur had sold his interest in the company to his brother after their parents died long ago. Harold hated the way Arthur and Preston had treated Franklin, and since he didn't have a wife or children, he left the toy company to his nephew when he died in the mid-80s."

"And Franklin then proceeded to run it into the ground," Valerie said.

"Well, to be honest, it hasn't done well since the 1950s. Some years were better than others," Ethan said.

"What else did you find out?" Grace asked.

"Ten years after Franklin inherited the toy company, his wife died of cancer. Six months later, Franklin married Hannah Adams, his secretary. According to the rumor mill it was not a happy marriage."

"Isn't she the one Louisa said she hated?" Grace asked.

Ethan nodded. "I'm not surprised. The first thing Hannah did was ship Louisa to a boarding school in Europe. Up until then, the kid had everything she ever wanted. She was able to do as she pleased. Then Hannah stepped in and started issuing orders and the first one was that Louisa had to go. So, off she went."

"How long did their marriage last?" Grace asked.

"Less than five years. Turns out Hannah had a peanut allergy. One Christmas she ate something that contained peanuts and died. Franklin sued the bakery. He eventually won a judgment against them, which came in just in time. The Straker Toy Company was about to go under. The sudden influx of cash saved it for another decade."

"Who was next?" Valerie asked.

"Courtney," Ethan and Grace said in unison.

"Courtney Harris," Ethan continued his narration. "Louisa's roommate in college. She brought Courtney home to meet her daddy one day and romance blossomed. Franklin and Courtney lasted just under two years."

"Louisa helped that one go away," Grace said. "She apparently let her father know Courtney was fooling around with her fitness instructor."

Ethan picked up another file. He took out a copy of a newspaper article. "The old boy didn't marry for a few years after that. His next wife was Ashley Powers in 2003. The marriage didn't last long. Just a year. After the divorce, she ended up marrying a preacher and moving to Maine."

"Louisa said she liked her." Grace picked up their engagement announcement. "I don't remember her at all."

"Well, you were just an intern," Valerie said, taking the article from her. "I barely remember her myself. I was working as Daniel's secretary at the time. She only worked here for a few months before she and Straker married. After that, I barely saw her."

"Is that when you moved up as Straker's secretary?" Ethan asked.

Valerie nodded.

"Then we have Lily, whom he married two years ago." Ethan picked up a folder marked, Lily Davenport Straker, and handed it to Grace.

"Yeah, they met at the Dragon's Lair on his forty-eighth birthday," Valerie said. "They married just a month later. What were you able to find out about Lily?"

Ethan picked up a legal pad and began reading. "Lily Davenport. Born in Charleston, South Carolina. Father is a lawyer; mother a society maven. Left South Carolina to tour with Ilya Dragovich at eighteen years of age. Stayed with him on and off for over fifteen years. Been married five times. First to her childhood sweetheart. Divorced three years later. Accusations of infidelity. Then she married a writer, who she divorced five years later. She then married an actor, ten years her junior. They stayed married the longest; seven years. Then a college student that lasted only two years. Her husbands tended to be younger artist types. She eventually broke type and married Straker."

"What about Ilya Dragovich?" Grace picked up a file with the magician's name scrawled across the top. She leafed through the pictures and copies of newspaper articles.

"Let's see," Ethan flipped through his legal pad. "Ilya Stefanvich Dragovich is the youngest son of Colonel Stefan Dragovich and Katja Antonova. He is the youngest of ten children. Except for his father and siblings, the Dragovich family has always been involved with magic in one form or another for centuries. Ilya took after his grandfather and began performing at a very young age."

"How did he meet Juliet?" Grace asked.

"I'm getting there. I'm getting there. Be patient," he said with a smile. Clearing his voice dramatically, he resumed his narration.

"At eighteen, he defected to the west. He first settled in South Carolina where he met Juliet Anna Love, the middle child of Andrew Michael Love and Lucille Isabelle Love. The Loves are an old and well-known family from the south. They objected to her falling in love with a commie, but despite her family's objections, Juliet and Ilya married and had two children. First born was Anya Isabel Ilyinichna Dragovich and then three years later came Aleksis Mikhail Ilyich Dragovich. They both take after their mother in looks; both blonde and blue-eyed. Apparently, the family lived happily until Juliet's death twelve years ago and that's when everything fell apart."

Grace handed the file to Valerie. "South Carolina? Isn't that where Lily was from?"

Ethan nodded. "Lily was Juliet's best friend growing up. Juliet met Ilya and ran off with him one night. Then a year later, Lily followed them to Europe and joined their magic tour. The rest is history, as they say."

"Did you find out if Ilya and Lily were having an affair?" Grace reached across the table, her fingers grazing one manila folder.

Ethan picked the folders up and set them on the other side of the table out of her reach. "Patience," he said with a smile. "My source says not during the marriage. In fact, there were no rumors of infidelity, not even a hint. The Love's weren't too happy when Juliet eloped with Ilya, but they all agreed that he absolutely adored his wife. He was pretty devastated by her death. My detective couldn't find anyone who believed that Ilya and Lily were having an affair, at least not while Juliet was alive. Nevertheless, the Love's told my detective that they believed Lily was secretly in love with Dragovich and that was the reason she followed them to Europe and joined their show. The Love family did not like Lily. They believed that Lily took advantage of Juliet's death. According to Juliet's sister, Lily moved in on Ilya rather quickly after Juliet's accident. She tried to claim that it was just so she could help Ilya take care of the children, but Juliet's family didn't buy it."

"Help with the children?" Valerie scoffed. "I don't buy it either. Belle's twenty-seven now, so wouldn't they have been teenagers when their mother died?"

"Belle was in her late teens when Juliet died and her brother was about fifteen. After the death, the family, including Lily, relocated to their home in Charleston. Ilya apparently locked himself up after Juliet's death. He wouldn't talk to anyone. In fact, he didn't come out of it until his son started acting up and getting into trouble. Aleksis did not take his mother's death well. He was even sent to a mental institution for a small period of time. There's a rumor that Ilya blamed Lily for it and that's why they had a falling out."

"That's interesting." Discreetly reading off his legal pad, Grace asked, "What happened?"

Smiling, Ethan lifted the pad up and held it to his chest. "I don't know, because those records were sealed. After Aleksis' stay was completed, Lily moved out the very next week."

Eyeing the stack of folders just within reach, Grace asked, "What about Belle?"

"She apparently handled it better than her younger brother did," Ethan said. "The detective didn't find out very much other than she graduated from the University of South Carolina with a 3.2 and a BA in child psychology and education, and after graduation, she joined Ilya's show full time. She's becoming a rather well respected magician in her own right. She's had a few serious boyfriends, who were usually older. Of course not as old as Straker. Nothing that shocking actually."

"And Aleksis?" Grace asked.

Ethan sighed. "Aleksis is another story. After his stay in the state loony bin…"

Grace made a face.

"He followed his father and sister on the magic tour express. By all accounts, he's something of a prodigy; a very gifted student. He's fluent in six languages: English, Russian, Korean, French, German, and Spanish. At first, it appeared he was going to follow in his father's footsteps, but it didn't happen."

Valerie dropped Ilya Dragovich's file on top of the others. "He's not a magician?"

"The kid apparently didn't have any talent for it, which is surprising, considering how smart he is. He spent some time at Oxford and then transferred to Harvard. His grades were stellar, despite spending very little time in class. He did get into some trouble during his senior year when he made the vice dean of academic affairs' car disappear."

"Let me guess," Grace said, "he didn't make it reappear."

Ethan shook his head. "No, it reappeared, just not in the same form as when it disappeared. Anyways, Ilya went ballistic. It was actually Lily that smoothed things over with Harvard. Dragovich was so angry, he even refused to let Aleksis perform with him and ordered him to find another type of career."

"That seems rather harsh for one prank," Grace said.

"Yeah," Valerie said, "most fathers want their sons to follow in their footsteps."

Ethan grimaced. "I think it was more of the straw that broke the camel's back."

Impatient, Grace leaned across the table, grabbed several folders out of the pile on the table, and began leafing through them. "Any pictures of Aleksis?"

"Hang on, I'm getting to that." Ethan grabbed the folders and set them back down on the table. Exasperated, he shuffled his papers around, purposely drawing out the silence. Once he felt that enough time had passed, he started back up. "Apparently, there was an incident. Actually, there were a couple of them. Once when he was fifteen, Aleksis almost killed Belle while conducting some sort of magic trick."

Grace lifted her head up sharply. "How?"

Ethan shrugged. "I have no idea. My detective didn't have much time to do a really thorough search. He heard that Belle almost lost her head."

Valerie gasped. "The scar on her neck."

"No wonder Dragovich doesn't want him performing," Grace said.

Ethan picked up another folder and thumbed through it. "There was also an incident in Spain. The boy ran away and tried to perform his own death defying escape trick." Ethan handed them a picture of a tank and what appeared a young man floating inside. "His father found out and arrived just in time to break open the container and perform mouth to mouth respiration." Grace peered closer at the image. Unfortunately, the boy's features were obscured.

"Then there was the time in Kiev." Ethan handed them another photo. This time depicting a man with his hands tied behind his back, a hood over his head and a noose over his neck. Grace noticed the blue hood was of the same type that the killer had thrown over Belle's head the day before. "Someone in the audience had to save him that time."

Grace laid the photo down on the table. "Sounds like he has a death wish."

"Then there was another incident in Paris, but details are very sketchy," Ethan said. "Ilya apparently paid the owners of the theater off."

"For what?" Grace asked.

"Fire damage. No deaths, but—"

Valerie interrupted, "Where is he now?"

"No one knows. Aleksis was jailed for arson in Mexico a few months ago. They dropped the arson charges, but then charged him with three counts of escape. He escaped two weeks before Lily's death."

"Really?" Grace asked. "Belle acted like he was still in jail when she told Lily about his charges the night she died. What about the pictures?"

"My detective said they weren't easy to find. It's like the kid went out of his way not to be photographed."

Valerie sighed. "Is there a description of him?"

Ethan nodded. "Twenty-five; blond; blue eyed; no noticeable scars or tattoos; six foot one; athletic build."

Grace shook her head. "So far it sounds like our Kyle."

"I thought so, too," Ethan smiled ruefully. "I really hoped it was, but..." He tossed a picture onto the table. "This is his most recent mug shot. It was taken when he was arrested for arson in Mexico."

"This is Aleksis?" Grace asked in surprise. She held the photo out and grimaced at the grimy young man sneering at the camera. Reaching over, she grabbed the Dragovich file and laid the picture next to one of Ilya Dragovich and one of Belle Dragovich. "Wow, are we sure he wasn't adopted?"

She passed the photo to Valerie. "Of the two, Belle certainly got the looks," Valerie said.

"What about Michael Talon, did you find anything out about him?" Grace picked up Aleksis' photo again and grimaced. Definitely not Kyle. She should have felt relieved, but she wasn't.

"My detective couldn't find anything out about him," Ethan said.

Valerie shrugged. "Maybe Michael Talon is his stage name."

"It's possible," Ethan admitted.

"Anything about Kyle?" Grace asked, thumbing through the folders.

Ethan shook his head. "Not much on Kyle, either." He reached in a folder and pulled out a newspaper article. "He worked as an actor a few years ago." Ethan handed her a newspaper review of an off-Broadway play. "For some reason, the director and cast tried to kill him on stage. The reviewer said it was the best part of the play. After that, he got a job with Felix Hutchinson."

"Do you know him?" Grace asked, handing the article to Valerie.

Ethan shook his head. "Not really. I heard he's being investigated by the state bar, but here's the really interesting part," he said, taking out three traffic tickets out of Lily's file, "three years ago he represented Lily two times for just a speeding and a parking ticket. Then two years ago, he represented her for another speeding ticket."

Valerie whistled. "What do you know, Kyle knew Lily. Funny, he never mentioned that."

"Two years ago Kyle was busy trying to keep his cast mates from killing him," Grace said with a smile. "He didn't start working with Felix until last year."

"Still, it is rather strange," Ethan said. "Do you know how many attorneys are in this city alone and it turns out Kyle's cousin represented Lily Straker?"

"It's rather suspicious," Valerie said.

"Who else do we have?" Grace asked looking through the folders.

Valerie held up Allen's folder. "What deep dark secrets have you uncovered about everyone's favorite co-worker?"

"He has a massive amount of complaints," Ethan said.

Valerie laid the folder back down on top of the table. "That's not surprising, he's a whiner."

"No, not from him, the complaints were from his neighbors and members of various toy forums on the internet. He's known as the *Forum Sheriff* on a few forums for his penchant for policing the boards and attacking anyone who disagrees with him. He's also gotten into trouble for attacking competitor reviews while using a false name. He's been exposed, but he just changes his name and picks back up where he left off. He's been thrown off this one forum three times. The last time was for a scathing review of another participant's review of the Straker Interstellar Space Doll series."

"My dolls?" Grace asked. "Why? What did they say?"

"They hated it and Allen came in, guns blazing," Ethan said.

"He defended my dolls?" Grace asked in surprise.

"He defends anything your company produces. He seems to be rather obsessed with his job. Did you two know that he has a tattoo of the first Straker toy ever produced on his back?" He handed a picture of the tattoo to Grace. *Straker Toy Co.* was written above a tattoo of Marty the Martian.

Grace and Valerie's eyes widened.

"How did you get this?" Valerie asked.

"That's his forum picture," Ethan said.

Grace grimaced. "Well, he's nothing if not loyal."

"And that's why Straker puts up with him," Valerie said. "Daniel tried to have him fired a few years ago, but Straker and Louisa said no. As long as Straker is in business, Allen will have a job. Straker has his faults, but he's loyal to those that are loyal to him and Allen is very loyal to this company. Allen's job, I'm sorry to say, is secure."

"So, who's left?" Grace asked.

"Louisa and Daniel," Ethan said. "I didn't really learn anything that we don't already know. They were unhappily married for the last five years until his death. No one quite knows why they married. They had nothing in common. She likes to drink and gamble, and he liked to chase anything in a skirt. That's about it."

"Anything new about Tabitha?"

Ethan shook his head. "No, my buddy on the police force is almost certain it was her body that washed up on shore. No one has seen or heard from her since Lily's death."

"I saw her right before Daniel died," Grace admitted.

"Has Belle had any more calls from her?" Valerie asked.

"No, at least not that I know of," Grace said, picking up another file. "What about Harcourt?"

"Um, Harcourt," Ethan flipped through his legal pad. "All I found on Harcourt were just the usual press clippings, but nothing too scandalous."

Taking back the photo of Aleksis, Valerie turned it at an angle. "Maybe he got reconstructive surgery. He looks a little like Kyle."

Grace shook her head. "There's not enough plastic surgery in the world to turn that man into Kyle Drake. At least not in two weeks."

"Disappointed?" Ethan grinned. Picking his briefcase off the floor, he laid it onto the table next to the folders. "Don't worry, this doesn't mean Aleksis isn't out there causing mayhem and destruction."

* * * *

"That's not him," Grace said emphatically. She pushed the rubber tree leaf down an inch to get a better view.

"There's some resemblance," Valerie insisted.

"No way."

"The hair and eye color is the same."

Grace held up Aleksis Dragovich's picture. "His eyes are too far apart and the cheekbones are all wrong." She looked back at Kyle where he was sitting at his desk drawing, completely oblivious to their inspection.

"Hey, my Aunt Harriet went in for a nose job last year," Valerie said. "She went in looking like Boris Karloff and came out looking like Grace Kelly. And that was just a nose job."

Grace shook her head and looked down at the picture in her hand. She looked back up at Kyle's handsome profile and back down at the picture. "No way. There's no way. This man looks like he's been run over by a train and thrown from a cliff."

Kyle looked up suddenly.

They jumped back.

Valerie grabbed the picture. Walking over to Grace's desk, she laid it down. "We need a picture of Kyle and Michael. Put them side by side and see which one best resembles Aleksis."

Grace joined her at the desk. "Michael can't be Aleksis."

"Why not?" Valerie said.

"Michael was at the theater the night Belle and Lily were talking about Aleksis being in jail."

"Oh… still, we need Kyle's picture. Just go over there and ask him if you can take his picture."

"He'll get suspicious."

"Tell him it's for the office bulletin board. We'll snap pictures of everyone, so it won't look so obvious."

"Okay. Do you have a camera?" Grace asked.

A cell phone appeared over her shoulder. "Here you go," Kyle said. "You can take my picture with my phone."

* * * *

Grace stared at the ceiling. Voices. She was definitely hearing voices and as far as she knew, the only other person in her apartment was Belle. Ethan and Kyle had wanted to stay and watch over them again, but she had said no. She refused to live in fear. They weren't happy, but they grudgingly left. It seemed like a good idea at the time, but that was three hours ago, and now she was lying in bed, wide-awake and jumping at every little sound.

Raising her head off the pillow, she cocked her head to the side. Belle was definitely talking to someone in Russian. She couldn't understand what was being said, but it was definitely Belle speaking.

She picked up the butcher's knife lying next to her bed and slid out from underneath the covers. As quietly as possible, she crept out into the living room.

Belle's light was on. Thinking her roommate was up and talking on the phone, Grace lifted her hand to knock when she heard a deep voice from the other side of the door.

Kyle's voice.

She glanced down at the doorknob, which was just starting to turn.

Quickly, Grace slipped back into her room, and shut her door a little harder than she intended. She winced at the sound and turned the lock. Hopefully, they hadn't heard her, she thought.

Just then the doorknob jiggled. Breathlessly, she watched as someone tried to open her bedroom door. When the door wouldn't open, they rapped lightly on the door. A few seconds later, Belle's voice softly called out her name.

Grace debated whether she should open the door. It's not as if the cheap door would hold Kyle back if he wanted in. She wasn't even sure it could hold Belle back if she wanted in. Taking a deep breath, Grace held the knife behind her back and opened the door.

Belle was standing on the other side. "Is everything okay?"

Grace nodded, gripping the doorknob tightly in her hand. "Sure, I was just sleeping. Is everything all right?"

"Yeah." Belle looked over her shoulder nervously. "I just thought I heard a noise."

"You know, so did I." Grace opened the door wider and took a step out. "Maybe we should search the apartment, just to make sure no one's hiding."

Belle quickly shook her head. "No, it's okay. I already did and everything is fine. There's no one else here." She glanced back to her room. "Well, I'm just going to go back to sleep. Goodnight, Grace."

"Night night, Belle." Grace backed into her room. She laid the knife on the small dresser next to the door. Walking to the side of the dresser, she pushed it forward until it blocked the door.

Friday, December 23rd

CHAPTER TWENTY-FIVE

GRACE LOOKED UP from her book and noticed Belle standing in the doorway.

"Hey Grace, Kyle said that you wanted to see me."

The first thing Grace noticed was the golden dragon pendant with a sparkling pink eye, fastened to *Grace's*, or rather Grace's sister's, pink and white tweed jacket. "That's pretty," she said, pointing to the pendant. "I thought Lily's was one of a kind."

"Oh, it is." Belle reached up and touched the dragon lying against her chest. "Hers had a green emerald and mine has a pink ruby. It looks great with your jacket."

"Yes, and my shirt, too."

"And your skirt," she said, doing a little twirl in the center of the room. "What did you want to see me about?"

"I need your expert opinion."

"Really? About what?"

"I've been thinking about creating an educational board game. Something involving history or science and I figured you could help me come up with something that parents and grandparents would snap up in a heartbeat, but wouldn't scar a teenager for life." Grace closed the book she was reading and handed it to Belle. "I want something that they would be willing to play with, but would also teach them. I was reading about—"

Belle looked at her curiously. "Why would I be an expert?"

"You're the one with the BA in child psychology and education."

Belle wagged her finger in front of Grace. In a singsong voice, she said, "You've been checking up on me, haven't you?"

"Just a bit," she hedged.

Belle laughed. "Just like a real detective. I'm impressed." She sat down, crossed her legs at the ankle and leaned back. "So, what did you find out? What deep dark secrets have you unearthed about my family?"

Grace related most of the basic information she had learned the day before. After all, there seemed no point in hiding what they had learned. Belle, of all people, would already know her family's vital statistics and if Grace was lucky, she would open up and reveal more. She began with Belle's history and as she anticipated, Belle happily stopped her periodically to elaborate on some of the more mundane instances as they popped up.

When Grace finished retelling what they had discovered about Ilya, Belle blurted out, "What about my Papa? Any more about him?" The sudden gleam in Belle's eyes worried Grace. "Specifically during the summer of 1988?"

"Um, no."

Disappointment clouded Belle's face.

"Why?"

Belle shrugged. "No reason. Just curious," she said as she glanced toward the door.

Grace worried that Belle was losing interest and quickly moved on to Aleksis. Belle's demeanor changed abruptly. She stopped interrupting with family anecdotes and sat quietly in her seat.

When Grace came to the end of her report, Belle swiftly stood up and walked to the bookcase. Scanning the titles on the wall, she blithely reported, "Most of your information's correct, except for one thing." Belle pulled out a book on toy design and began leafing through it. "The only reason my brother was ever in that mental institution was because he tried to break into it in order to show Papa he could do it." Putting down the book, Belle crossed to the design table. "Only problem was that once he was there, they decided it wouldn't hurt to keep him for a few days. For some reason, Papa gave his permission. He was released three days later.

Perfectly sane. We know because Papa insisted that they run a battery of tests on him."

"Belle!" Ilya Dragovich stood in the doorway and glared at his daughter.

Belle snapped her mouth shut and looked contritely from Grace to her father.

"I'd like to speak to you in your office," the elder Dragovich said in clipped tones.

Belle waved bye and followed her father out into the hallway.

Curious, Grace stood up and walked out into the hallway, just as Belle was shutting her office door.

She was about to turn around and go back to her book when she heard her name.

Despite her normally good manners, Grace snuck up to the door. She looked both ways, relieved to find herself alone. She briefly wondered where Kyle was as she stuck her ear to the door. She couldn't understand a word Belle and her father were saying, but every few seconds, she could hear her name being mentioned. Thinking that if she got lower to the floor she could hear better, she bent down.

She felt something brush against her arm and turned her head to see Kyle kneeling next to her.

Whispering, he asked, "What are we doing?"

"Shh, Belle's father just dragged her in there and they're talking about me."

She leaned her head against the door. She could just make out a few words. "How's your Russian coming along?" she asked, trying to keep her voice neutral. When she didn't receive an answer, she leaned back and looked over her shoulder.

Kyle was gone.

The door suddenly swung open. Off balance, she fell to the floor at Ilya Dragovich's feet.

He looked down at her with an amused expression.

"I, uh, dropped my earring," she muttered, her face flushing with embarrassment.

He reached out his hand and helped her to her feet. "I wouldn't worry too much about it, considering they're both still in your ears."

Should have gone with lost contacts instead, she thought, still embarrassed by the whole situation. "I should go back to my office."

He smiled. "I was leaving anyway. Have a nice day."

She watched as he sauntered out to the main hallway and turned the corner. She turned back to Belle, "I'm so sorry."

"It's all right." Belle twisted a long blonde strand around her finger. She motioned for Grace to follow her inside her office. "Grace, he wants me to go with him."

"Where?"

"Germany. He's booked a tour through Europe again and he wants me to go too." She shook her head, sadly. "I don't want to go."

"Don't you have to stay? You're marrying the boss."

Belle crossed her arms. "Papa says that if I go through with the wedding, he won't come." She looked sadly at the floor. "I'm not leaving. I don't care what he says."

"It might be safer for you if you go." Grace frowned. "Belle, I'm worried for you. I think the killer wants to kill you."

Belle shook her head. "Why would anyone want to kill me? I think whoever attacked me on the stairwell made a mistake. I think they were after you." She looked down at her outfit. "You probably haven't noticed, but I've been dressing like you for a while now."

"Really? No, I hadn't noticed at all." Grace said, trying to keep the sarcasm out of her voice.

Belle nodded sincerely. "You should be the one to leave. I think you're making the killer nervous. You've been asking a lot of questions."

"So, has Allen."

Belle snorted. "Get real," she said, "no one's worried about Allen. But you... Franklin's been talking about opening another store somewhere out west. I could talk to him..."

Grace shook her head. "No. No one's chasing me out of here." With an incline of her head, she motioned to her office.

"Come on, let's go back to work. I've got some new ideas for the characters we're going to use for the mystery game."

She led Belle back into her office. Opening up her desk drawer, she laid out a group of pictures on the desk.

Belle placed her hands down on the desk. "What's all this?"

"Pictures of the characters." Grace spread each picture out.

"But I thought we were going to draw the characters."

"I've decided against that. We're going to go with models." Grace picked up the first picture and handed it to Belle.

Belle made a face. "Ugh, who's he supposed to be?"

"That's our victim."

"Is he supposed to look like a Nazi war criminal? I thought the victim was supposed to be a doctor." Belle grimaced as she handed the photo back. She glanced at the rest of the pictures on the table. Picking up one of a handsome middle-aged man with black hair, slightly graying at the temples, she cooed, "I like this one. He looks distinguished, just like a doctor."

She pointed to the photo in Grace's hands. "That one could be our murderer."

"Haven't you heard the old saying never to judge a book by the cover?"

Belle shrugged. "Oh, by the way, Tabitha left me another message."

"Really, what did she have to say?"

"I don't know, she was whispering. I couldn't really understand what she was saying. Hopefully, she'll call me again soon."

"If you hear from her, let me know. I don't think you should meet her by yourself."

"Don't worry, I won't be alone." Belle glanced at her watch and then groaned. "I was supposed to meet Franklin downstairs ten minutes ago. See you later," she said as she walked out of the room.

Grace looked down at the picture in her hand. She laid Aleksis Dragovich's picture down on top of the other headshots. Gathering the pictures, she placed them in her drawer and locked her desk.

* * * *

"A dollar?" Grace asked in disbelief. "Unbelievable. That's my raise?"

Kyle fanned out a deck of cards in front of Valerie. "Don't look at it as one dollar. Think of it as an extra dollar every month."

"Consider yourself lucky." Valerie took a card out of the pack. "I talked him up from fifty cents."

Grace pushed a strand of her red-gold hair out of her face. "He's crazy if he considers that substantial."

"Grace, I've worked for Straker for ten years now," Valerie said. "Trust me, for him, that is incredibly substantial."

Kyle took a card from the deck. Turning it around, he asked, "Is your card the Queen of Diamond?"

"No, but close," Valerie said. "It was a diamond."

Grace paced the floor of the break room. "Where is Straker?"

"Is it the two of diamonds?" Kyle asked hopefully.

"He's in his office." Valerie looked over at Kyle. "You're getting better. It was a three of diamond."

Grace walked out of the break room and stalked into Straker's office. He was sitting at his desk. Without looking up he asked, "Where's your report?"

"I don't have one."

"I thought we agreed that you would send in a report every hour."

She thrust her check in front of his face. "This is not a substantial raise."

"You're not happy?"

"No, I'm not. I've worked here—"

Straker held out his hand. "Spare me the speech. I'm sorry. You're absolutely right."

"No, you need to listen—" His last words finally registered in her mind. She sat down with a thump. She had never heard Straker apologize before. "Go on."

"Tell you what, I'll make a deal with you. If you figure out who killed my wife and can bring me solid evidence of their guilt, I'll give you a choice."

She looked at him suspiciously. "What sort of choice?"

"You can choose between either ten thousand dollars, or complete creative control on your next design. I'll give you a few days to think—"

"I'll take the ten thousand."

"Why don't you mull my proposal over—"

"No need. Ten thousand will be fine."

Straker's scowled. "Are you sure you wouldn't want to think it over."

"Nope." Grace shook her head. "Ten thousand."

* * * *

Grace found Kyle and Valerie still sitting where she had left them. Kyle was dividing the deck of cards in two. Belle was standing at the refrigerator, holding up a plastic container to the light. The lock Allen installed laid on the counter next to her.

"You're smiling," Valerie said in awe. "No one has ever left Straker's office smiling."

She sat down at the table. "He apologized."

Valerie's eyebrows inched up higher on her head. "Are you sure?"

Grace nodded as she explained the deal Straker made with her.

"I'm very impressed, Ms. Holliday." Kyle fanned the cards out. "Very mercenary of you."

"And you took the money?" Valerie asked in disbelief. "I'm shocked. I thought you would have gone with creative control."

"Uh uh," Grace said. "Once I have that ten thousand in my hand, he can't take it away. The creative control would only have lasted as long as it takes for Straker to form the word no."

Belle stopped staring at the container and brought it over to the table. "Would one of you all taste this?"

"What is it?" Valerie asked.

"It's beef stroganoff."

"That's left over from last night, isn't it?" Grace asked. "I brought a container of it from home, too. It tasted fine to me."

"What's wrong with it?" Kyle asked.

"There shouldn't be anything wrong with it." Belle screwed up her face. "It just tastes funny."

Kyle took her fork and speared a noodle. He popped it into his mouth. "It tastes all right to me."

"Why don't you throw it out, Belle?" Grace asked, suddenly worried. "Call and have something delivered."

Kyle stood up. "I can go get you something, if you like."

"No." Belle rubbed her stomach. "Actually, I'm not that hungry. I think I'm just going to go home."

Grace turned around in her chair. "Maybe you should go to the doctor."

Belle smiled from the door. "It's just a little tummy ache. I'll see you later tonight."

Valerie watched her walk out the door. "I like her outfit."

"Thank you. So do I," Grace said wryly.

Kyle stood up and walked to the sink carrying his lunch container. While he washed out his dish, Grace and Valerie talked about the upcoming weekend.

"Are you going out with Ethan tonight?" Valerie asked, standing up and walking to the sink.

Grace nodded. She was about to answer when Valerie blurted out, "Hey, what's this?" Valerie asked as she bent down and picked something off the floor. She held out her hand to Kyle. "Did you drop this?"

He dried his hands before taking the object from Valerie and walking back to the table. "No, that's not mine. Pretty, though." He held it up for Grace to see.

Grace looked at the golden pendant in his hand. "That's Belle's. It must have fallen off."

Valerie reached out and touched it, turning it over in Kyle's hand. "It looks like the clasp is broken."

Kyle turned it back around. "No, it's all right," he said, attempting to pin it to his tie.

Grace laughed. "That's too big to be a tie pin."

He turned his tie over. "My fingers are too large. I can't close it."

Grace stood up. She moved his hands out of the way and closed the pendant's clasp. Turning the tie back around, she laid her hand against his chest. To her surprise, he reached out and ran his hands down her arms.

Suddenly warm, she took a step back. "If you hurry, you might be able to catch Belle and give it back to her."

"She's probably long gone now. I'll hang on to it until tomorrow morning." Kyle stepped around her and gathered up the cards. "I'm going to go back to my desk. I thought of an idea for the mystery game and I want to test it out."

"Oh, what is it?" Grace asked.

He opened the break room door and smiled. "I want it to be a surprise. Don't worry, I'll tell you when I have it worked out."

As soon as the door shut behind him, Valerie leaned over and whispered, "That sounded ominous."

"He's been working hard on the game, so I'm sure it's completely innocent."

"I don't think Belle's sudden sickness is too innocent," Valerie said conspiratorially.

Grace looked at Valerie wondering if they were thinking the same thing.

"She seems to have put on a few pounds. I wonder if she's pregnant, and if she is, who's the father?"

Grace shrugged noncommittally. Recalling Lily's odd illnesses after eating at the toy company, Grace suspected a far more sinister reason for Belle's sudden sickness.

Valerie looked out the window. "It looks like there's going to be another storm tonight and they're predicting snow in the morning. I hope you don't get snowed in and miss your flight, Sunday."

"Me either. Can you come with me tonight?"

Valerie looked at her in surprise. "You want me to go on your date with you?"

Grace shook her head. "It's not a date. It's work. Ethan said he's discovered some new information."

CHAPTER TWENTY-SIX

GRACE OPENED BELLE'S closet where Belle had secreted away most of Grace's clothes. One by one, she moved aside the dresses, until she came across her black cashmere sweater. Tearing off her jacket and shirt, she slipped the sweater over her head. She then dug through the clothes in Belle's dresser until she came across her black denim jeans. Next, she went on the hunt for a pair of tennis shoes. She was just slipping them on her feet when her doorbell rang.

Quickly tying her hair into a ponytail at the base of her neck, Grace reached for the front door and let Ethan inside.

She glanced at the clock. "You're early," she said, as he reached out and hugged her.

"I couldn't wait to see you." He looked past her head. "Is Belle here?"

"No, and I have no idea where she is," she said worriedly.

"Good."

"Why do you say that?"

Ethan stepped back and looked into her eyes. "I don't think you should stay here with Belle anymore." He placed his briefcase on the dining room table. "I've discovered something important. I think Belle and Michael Talon killed Lily and Daniel. They're after Straker's millions."

Grace shook her head. "Straker didn't have any millions until after his brother died. How could they have known Straker would inherit? He and Preston were estranged."

Ethan pulled out a dining room chair and sat down. "Because Lily knew. I just found out that she had been secretly meeting with Straker's brother before she died. About seven months ago, Lily discovered that Preston was dying and sought him out, ostensibly to reunite the two brothers before Preston died. Lily somehow convinced him that Franklin was sorry for all he had done. It was only after her contact that he changed the will leaving the majority of his estate to his brother."

"So, you think she told Belle?"

He nodded. "I know she did. A paralegal from my office just told me that Lily and Belle were both present when Preston contacted him about changing his will. Belle knew this money was coming. Didn't she keep telling you not to worry and that your job was safe? Of course, it was safe. She knew that Preston was dying and that Franklin was going to inherit a small fortune."

"That explains why she moved in on him so quickly after her godmother died," Valerie said from the doorway.

Ethan spun around. "What are you doing here?"

"Grace invited me." Valerie shook her head. "I knew it. I told you Belle was up to no good."

Grace shook her head. "Belle doesn't exactly strike me as that mercenary. Her father sells out shows worldwide. I'm sure she could have whatever she wanted. Why would she want Straker's money?"

"Independence? I think she wants to get away from her father," Valerie said. "I heard her complaining about it while we were in the break room today."

"Revenge too," Ethan pointed out. "She might have blamed Lily for her mother's death. If it weren't for Lily twisting her ankle, she would have been on that beam that day, not Juliet. Then you factor in how Lily moved in on Ilya right after their mother's death. I bet Belle has hated Lily for a while now."

"But why wait all this time to kill her?" Grace asked. "It's been ten years since her mother's accident."

"It might have been festering inside her for a while now. Let's not forget, Lily has actually been away from the family for some time. Belle only had to put up with her every so often, but I think she was worried that their affair had started back up. That affair devastated her family. Her little brother ended up having to be put away because of it. I bet it wasn't until Franklin's birthday bash that Belle realized her father and Lily had become romantically involved again. She probably saw Lily's dragon pendant and underwear on the floor and realized that they had rekindled their affair."

"Rekindled?" Valerie snorted in derision. "Please, they probably never stopped having an affair."

"She must have blackmailed Tabitha into helping," Ethan said.

Grace started to feel sick as everything began falling into place. But how did he kill her while sitting in the audience? she thought as her mind raced. "Just how does Michael fit into this?"

"She's using him," Ethan leaned forward excitedly. "I called a couple of friends in Paris and I got hold of the police department there. I started asking questions about Lily's stalker who apparently committed suicide. They told me that the young man didn't die, instead he was transferred to a hospital for evaluation."

"What was his name?" Grace asked.

"They wouldn't tell me, since he was a juvenile at the time," Ethan said, "but I found out the hospital he was taken to. So, I called them."

Valerie dropped her purse onto the table. "What did they say?"

"Well, they wouldn't give me his name either, but I asked them if his name was Michael Talon."

"And?" Grace asked.

"They stumbled around a bit, before repeating they couldn't confirm or deny," Ethan said. "They hesitated, just enough to make me think I was right. I think he was obsessed with Lily and I'm betting that not only has he transferred his obsession from Lily to Belle, but that Belle has manipulated those feelings and used him to kill Lily, as well."

"He was missing quite a lot during Dragovich's performance," Valerie said.

"But he was present when Lily fell from the scaffolding," Grace pointed out. "And let's not forget, Belle was standing right next to me when Lily died. How could either one of them killed

Lily? That's the problem. We still don't know how the killer was able to kill Lily without being seen, or even how the killer got to Daniel in the elevator, and until we know, we can't really say with any certainty who it was that killed them."

"It has to be Belle," Ethan said. "No one else fits."

Valerie sighed heavily. "What about Aleksis Dragovich? He could be our killer. After all, he would have the same motive as Belle."

Ethan shrugged, "I'm sure he's involved somehow, but until he shows his ugly face, there's nothing we can do about it." He looked at his watch. "I've got to go."

"Go?" Grace asked in surprise. "You just got here."

"I know, but I have an important client meeting. We're going to court in the morning and my client's panicking and wants to meet with me tonight." He stood up, and kissed her. "I'll call you tomorrow. Promise me you won't stay here tonight with Belle."

"I'll be fine," she assured him.

Valerie spoke up. "Why don't you stay with me?"

Resolute, Grace shook her head. "I'm not afraid of Belle. She's not going to hurt me. It would look too suspicious if I suddenly died in my apartment with her just in the next room."

They looked at her doubtfully.

"I'll be fine," Grace said. "I promise."

Valerie admitted defeat. Turning to Ethan, she asked, "Do you want to split a cab?"

He looked back at Grace. "Please, lock your door tonight. Don't let her anywhere near you and if anything happens call me."

Grace handed him his briefcase. "Ethan, please don't worry. I'll be fine."

Ethan gave her a small smile before reluctantly turning away and walking to the elevator.

"Ethan, I'll meet you downstairs," Valerie said. She closed the door and sat down at the dining room table. With tears in her eyes, she said, "Grace, go back to Colorado, please."

Grace patted her friend's shoulder. "I'm going to be fine, Val. Everything's going to be all right," she said with more confidence than she felt.

"Promise me, Grace," Valerie said, "promise me that you'll be extra careful. If Ethan is right, you could be living with a murderer."

"I'll be careful, Val." She crossed her heart. "I promise. I'm just going to turn in early. If anything happens, I'll give you a call."

* * * *

"You should sue. You really shouldn't put up with a hostile working environment," Felix Hutchinson said with a thick southern drawl.

"Yes, I know, Mr. Hutchinson. You keep saying that." Grace moved the phone to her other ear. "I just want to know more about your cousin, Kyle."

"We should set up a client consultation. It's perfectly free, so it won't cost you anything. Now, I understand your boss recently came into some money."

"And just how do you know that? Have you spoken to Kyle lately?"

Felix laughed. "Ma'am, everyone round these parts knows that."

"You're not from around here, are you?"

"I've been licensed to practice in this great state for over five years."

"You sound like you're from the south."

"Yes, ma'am. South Carolina, born and raised."

"What brought you to New York?"

"I have family in these parts, but here I am yacking your head off. You're probably bored hearing about me, so let's go back to you and your substantial troubles. How much do you get paid?"

Grace reluctantly told him.

"Highway robbery. Tell me, does Straker treat all his employees as badly as he treats you?"

Grace shrugged. "Well, he treats all of us about the same."

Felix clucked his tongue. "How horrible. You shouldn't let him get away with that. Why, he's endangering your life by just having you there. Elevators that spontaneously stab people in the back. A lady being thrown down the stairs. A Santa Claus that goes crazy and attacks young women. It sounds like a veritable death trap," he said, making it sound like the greatest thing he had ever heard. "How do you all survive? Maybe I could meet with you and your co-workers all at once, before anyone else meets their unfortunate end."

"Uh, no, let's get back to Aleksis. When was the last time you spoke to him?"

There was silence on the other end and then a chuckle. "I'm sorry, ma'am, I don't know any Alex, or what did you say?"

"Aleksis."

"No. No, I can't seem to recall any Aleeksy," he said, seriously mangling the name. "Is that right? Or did you say Alec or was it Alice?"

"Uh huh. Tell you what, Mr. Hutchinson, you tell your cousin that I want to meet both of you tomorrow morning in your office. I'll give you that client consultation you're dying to have," she said, before hanging up the phone.

She jumped at the sound of the phone ringing. She lifted the phone to her ear.

Her anonymous caller was back and laughing at her again. She was just about to hang up when she heard, "You're going to die tonight."

She slammed the phone down. Picking the phone back up, she scrolled through the previous calls until she found Ilya Dragovich's number and pressed send.

* * * *

Ilya Dragovich leaned against the wall. "This is a waste of time."

"Humor me," she pleaded.

Sighing heavily, he pushed himself off the wall and motioned to the ladder. "Go ahead."

A sudden feeling of dread came over her. What if she was wrong? "No, after you."

Chuckling, he reached for the ladder. "If you insist." He swiftly climbed the ladder up to the landing, with Grace following close behind. "I can't tell if you're really brave or really stupid."

Grace couldn't agree more.

When they finally reached the scaffolding, he walked to the end and leaned against the railing, his arms crossed and completely at ease.

Grace felt slightly nauseous.

"Well, we're here, so what was so important that we couldn't discuss this in my office in the morning?" Dragovich asked.

"I don't think I have 'til morning."

He looked at her strangely, but didn't say anything.

"Lily was murdered," Grace said. "Somehow, someone got up here and pushed her over the railing."

He shook his head. "I would have seen them."

"Could they have worn dark clothing?"

He laughed. "No," he said, pointing up. "There's a light right above our head. If someone were up here with Lily, I would have seen them. There was no one up here with her." He paused, before adding, "I saw her jump, Ms. Holliday."

"How? Did she climb over the railing?"

Dragovich reached around and unlatched the railing, pushing it to the side. "This was open." He pointed to his feet. "Lily was sitting here with her feet dangling off the edge."

"But—"

He shook his head. "No one, but my staff and I knew that she would be up here. And like I said before none of us had a reason to kill her."

"More people knew than you think."

"Even if you are right, they wouldn't know when or where she was going to appear. How could they have known she would have been up here?"

"I think her killer had help. Someone who could not only tell him where Lily would be, but how your illusion worked."

"Why would any of my people do that? I pay them very well."

"I don't know. Maybe they were duped into helping Lily's killer. Maybe they were frightened and felt they had no choice.

Maybe they trusted the wrong person and didn't realize what the killer had planned."

"Even if all of that was true, I would have seen them," he said, pointing to the stage below.

"You couldn't have been watching the whole time."

"No, but when the chest rose to the ceiling, I was. Lily was sitting right here, waiting. I didn't see anyone up here with her."

"You said she was sitting. Did she normally sit here waiting for her cue to jump?"

"No," he admitted slowly. "Usually, she stood."

Grace tilted her head as a sudden thought occurred to her. "What if she was already dead?"

"But the killer would have had to text the suicide note to Straker, push her dead body off, drop the phone down on the scaffolding and climb down the stairs all without being seen by me."

"Think," Grace said. "You're the master trickster. How could someone have done all those things, without being seen and while being somewhere else in the theater? There must be a way."

He sighed. Turning to the side, he leaned out over the railing. His brow furrowed in thought. "It would be too risky and I'd need an accomplice." His lips quirked up. "I'm assuming you're not talking about me, but someone in the audience, right?"

She nodded her head.

He walked back over to the landing and looked down at the stairs. "I couldn't kill her up here because the magician on the stage would have seen me. I would have had to kill her downstairs and bring her up."

"In her dressing room?"

"No, that is too risky. I would have been caught." He grimaced slightly. "The ladder would have made it difficult. If I knew she would be coming up here… I would have hidden. But where?" He paused as he drummed his fingers against the railing. He suddenly pointed to the black magician's box on the lower landing. "There. I would have jumped out when I heard her coming up the stairs. I'd strangle her there on the landing. It's the safest place, because it's completely hidden from downstairs."

"She'd fight," Grace pointed out.

He folded his arms across his chest. "It wouldn't matter. With the audience and the music playing, no one would have seen or heard a thing."

"What then?"

"I'd carry her up the stairs, but... I would have been seen." He rubbed a hand along his jaw. "There's still the problem of the magician down on the stage."

Grace closed her eyes in disappointment. She looked around the small scaffolding. Lily was definitely murdered. The killer found a way; they just needed to think.

The magician suddenly laughed. "It's so obvious." He passed a hand over his eyes, smiling. "I don't know why I didn't think of it. If I were the killer, I'd wait for intermission. No one's on the stage, so no one would be looking this way." He walked back to the end of the scaffolding. Reaching over, he pulled a hook from a box attached to the middle railing and pulled a pulley towards him. "The chest would have already been in place up here. If I had someone who showed me or told me how it worked, then I could have set her body here," he said, pointing to the railing. "Tied the silk around her neck." He furrowed his brow, as he looked back between the railing and the pulleys. "I could set it up, so that when the chest... when the chest comes up, the silks retract, and it pushes her off the railing."

"So, the killer could have been somewhere else when she finally fell."

He nodded. "It could work, but he'd be taking a big risk that she would fall at the right time and not earlier."

"Our killer takes a lot of big risks," Grace said. "He seems to strike whenever opportunity presents itself. What about the text message? How could he have pulled that off?"

He stood silently for a moment, considering. "That would have been easy. I could have stayed on the landing. Once she fell and had been cut down, I could have snuck back up and dropped the phone where the police found it. Everyone's attention would have been on Lily at that point."

"But what if you had to be somewhere else? What if you wanted a solid alibi?"

"I'd need an accomplice. Someone who could run up here and drop the phone. It would have to be someone I trusted or someone who was in on it."

"Or someone who was too afraid to say no." Grace smiled at the magician. "Thank you for your help." She turned to go back down stairs but paused and looked back at Dragovich. "Just out of curiosity, that fifty thousand—it wasn't for you, was it?"

The magician shook his head. With his hands gripping the railing, he dropped his head to his chest. "Do you happen to know where my children are?"

"Sorry, I don't." Grace turned around and ran back to the landing. "But when I find them, you'll be the first to know."

Saturday, December 23rd
12:00am

CHAPTER TWENTY-SEVEN

GRACE WALKED OUT of the elevator. She had to hurry, because time was running out. She was pretty sure she knew who killed Lily and how, but Daniel's death confused her.

She looked at her watch. Hopefully, Valerie would show up soon. She was certain that Valerie saw something the day Daniel was killed. She might not know what it was, but she must have seen something that could help her prove that the same person who killed Lily killed Daniel, as well. She just needed Valerie to re-enact the scene one more time. Perhaps, it would trigger some type of memory.

Remembering what happened the last time she was on the fourth floor at night, she held up her pepper spray as she entered her office. Quickly turning, she flipped on the lights and breathed a sigh of relief when she saw the room was empty. She automatically shrugged off her coat and hung it up on the coat rack next to the door and then shoved the umbrella into the umbrella stand next to the coat rack.

She glanced out the side window, just as thunder rumbled and a lightning bolt lit up the night sky. Rain was coming down hard.

Turning around, she walked the rest of the way into her office but stopped as the hairs on the back of her neck stood up. Someone was in the room with her. She couldn't see them, but she was positive she wasn't alone. She began to back out when her eye caught a purple tipped finger poking out from underneath her desk. Thinking it was Belle, she called out her name.

Grace heard a heavy sigh and the sound of someone moving under the desk. To her surprise, it wasn't Belle that emerged from beneath the desk, but Tabitha Eddington; a very tired, very dirty and older looking Tabitha. She looked absolutely awful. Her hair was a mess, her clothes were filthy and hung from her body, and her eye makeup was smeared across her cheeks as though she had been crying recently.

Grace threw her purse on the floor next to her desk. "Where have you been?"

Tabitha came around from the desk. "Please don't be mad. I didn't know where else to go." She raked a ragged hand through her blonde hair. "He's going to kill me, I just know it."

Grace took the hysterical woman by the shoulders and led her to the chair. "Just calm down, you're safe now. Let's call the police."

Tabitha jumped up. "No! No police. I can't go to jail. I just can't."

"What are you doing here? I figured you were half way around the world by now." Or dead and buried, she thought, but decided not to say.

"Around the world?" Tabitha walked over to the credenza and grabbed a handful of tissue. Blowing her nose loudly, she walked over to the chair and sat down, too weary to stand any longer. "How could I possibly go anywhere? I have no money. I've been too afraid to go back to my apartment. I have nowhere to go. At least I'm somewhat safe here."

"Were you the one hiding in the attic?"

Tabitha nodded. "Daniel hid me there from the killer. It was the only place that we thought I would be safe, but *he* figured out where I was, so I ran. I ran down the stairs and I just kept running, but I ran out of places to run to."

"Who figured out where you were?" Grace asked. She had a good idea who it was but wanted confirmation just the same.

Tabitha wiped her eyes. "I can't tell you."

Grace sighed. "Where did you go after you left here?"

"I ran to a little fleabag hotel a few blocks from here. I hid out there until my money ran out."

Grace leaned against her desk and crossed her arms. "I thought you and Daniel emptied out Straker's account. That should have left you more than enough money to take a little trip. Or did you come back here to steal some more?"

"It wasn't like that. We didn't empty anyone's account," she said bitterly. "Daniel only took out forty thousand. He called it his severance pay. Straker owed him much more than that, but Daniel said that he would only take out a little, just enough to get us started somewhere else."

"Then where did the rest of Straker's money go to?"

Tabitha hung her head. "I have no idea. I don't have it. Daniel put most of the money he stole back. He gave me a couple of thousand, but I only have a little of it left."

"What exactly happened, Tabitha?"

Tabitha took a deep breath. "Daniel took the money out on a Friday afternoon and we made plans to make a run for it Saturday morning before anyone could find out and stop us. But that night, he had second thoughts. He told me that he still loved Louisa. He said, that he couldn't go through with it. He was going to return the money on Monday morning before anyone discovered it was missing."

"What happened?"

"We got caught." Tabitha started to cry. "Saturday morning, Daniel received a phone call from a man who said that he knew what Daniel had done. Then everything started to snowball. I swear I didn't know Lily was going to die."

"Who contacted Daniel? Who knew that he had stolen the money?"

"Trust me, you don't want to know. I know and I'm going to die because of it."

"How could someone have discovered the embezzlement that fast?" Grace asked, more to herself than to Tabitha. "Did you tell anyone what you and Daniel had planned?"

Tabitha shook her head. "Not a soul."

"What about Daniel? Do you know if he told anyone?"

Tabitha shrugged. "He might have told Louisa. I'm not sure."

"You must know Tabitha."

"I don't. I swear."

"But you know who killed Lily? Who is it?"

Tabitha wordlessly shook her head.

Grace pressed the scared woman for details, but Tabitha refused to give up the name of her tormentor. "Were you the one I heard crying backstage the night Lily died?" Grace guessed.

Tabitha nodded her head furiously. "Yes. He knew Daniel and I had been having an affair, and he knew about the money Daniel took. He threatened to tell the police about the embezzlement. He said that if we wanted him to keep quiet then we were going to have to do things for him?"

"What sort of things?"

Tabitha sniffled. "He wanted to know how Ilya performed his illusions. He wanted the secret to the crystal chest." Tabitha began to cry. "I didn't know that he was planning to kill Lily. I wouldn't have told him if I had known."

"What else?"

"I thought that once I told him how it worked, he would leave us alone, but then he suddenly showed up at the Dragon Lair a few days before Lily died and demanded that I *show* him exactly how it worked, as well. I thought it was over after that. I thought he would leave us alone, but then I saw him at Franklin Straker's birthday party…" She pressed a shaking hand to her cheek. "He slapped me and told me he would kill me if I didn't do exactly what he said. I was scared to death. He told me to steal Lily's phone and give it to him. So, I did. Then when he gave a signal I was supposed to take it back, run up stairs and lay it down on the scaffolding."

"Is that why you were crying that night?"

Tabitha nodded. "I had no idea what was going on. I was just so scared. I didn't know he was going to kill Lily and then once Lily was dead, he threatened to kill us if we said anything."

"Why didn't you go to the police?"

"We would have been arrested. I helped…" Her voice started to crack. "I would have been considered an accessory. He said that no one would believe us and that they would say Daniel and I killed her together. I wanted to run away, but Daniel wouldn't leave. Daniel was so angry. He hated being told what to do."

"Do you know why Lily died?"

Tabitha shook her head. "No, but Danny said he knew. He said it had something to do with Mr. Straker's brother. Danny came up with a plan." She sniffled. "A very stupid plan. He said he was going to turn the tables on Lily's killer."

"How?"

Tabitha shrugged. "I told Danny that I wanted no part of it. I knew he was going to kill us, so I hid."

Grace looked at the woman thoughtfully. "Why would he kill you?" She asked more to herself than to Tabitha. "I mean, didn't he need you for the rest of his plan to work?"

Tabitha stopped crying and looked up at Grace in confusion. "What are you talking about?"

"The plan to steal Straker's inheritance. I would have thought he could have still used you."

"I haven't mentioned his name, but you know who I've been talking about, don't you?"

Grace nodded. "It wouldn't hurt if you could confirm it for me."

Tabitha took a deep breath. Just then, a loud thunderclap rattled the building, causing both women to jump.

"Did you hear that?" Tabitha slowly stood. She looked at the office door warily.

"It's just thunder."

"No," Tabitha said softly, "someone's out there."

"It's probably my friend." Grace started for the door before stopping. Deciding safety before valor was in order, she walked back to her desk. Turning the phone around, she called Valerie's cell phone. Better to know for certain that it was Val in the building than just to assume. Val picked up on the third ring.

"Where are you?"

"I'm in a taxi and we're just pulling up to the building. Is everything all right?"

"Yeah, why?" Grace asked.

"You sound worried?"

"We just heard a noise. I guess my nerves are a bit on edge."

"We?"

Grace glanced back at Tabitha. "I'll explain when you get here."

"Okay, I'm just opening the door. Oh no…"

Whatever Valerie was saying was covered by static when she entered the building.

"Are you okay?" Grace repeated for the third time before she got an answer between static bursts.

"Yeah…dropped…umbrella…drenched," Valerie said in between static bursts before the line went dead.

Grace placed the phone back into the receiver. "It's all right. Valerie will be here in a second." Grace turned around to discover she was speaking to an empty room.

* * * *

Grace paced anxiously down the hallway. Twenty minutes had passed without any sign of either Tabitha or Valerie.

She opened the door to the stairwell and dashed up the stairs to the next floor. She had searched all four floors of the building, top to bottom and was now searching them once again. Just as she was about to search the workroom, she stopped and looked up at the ceiling. She could hear someone walking in the hallway directly above her.

She raced to the stairwell, climbed back up to her office floor, and entered an empty hallway. She was about to start calling Valerie's name at the top of her lungs when she heard the telltale click clacks of high heels walking across the hardwood floors. The sound of a door swinging shut came next. Following the sound, Grace ran down the hall and opened her office door.

She blew out a relieved gust of air. Valerie was standing at her desk, holding the phone up to her ear. She turned just as Grace shut the door.

"Where have you been?" they asked in unison.

Valerie placed the phone back in its cradle. "I thought we were going to meet in your office."

Grace quickly filled her in on her conversation with Tabitha.

"Tabitha has been hiding out here?" Valerie asked. "I guess Kyle was right. I figured he was just making all that stuff up about a squatter living in the attic. Where is she now?"

"By the time I hung up with you, Tabitha was gone. I chased her down the hall, but lost her. Then I couldn't find you."

Valerie smiled. "I was worried and went looking for you. Did Tabitha tell you who killed Lily and Daniel?"

"No, she was too afraid to tell me."

"Perfect. That's just great. You know what's going to happen now, don't you?"

Grace shook her head.

"We're going to be tripping over her body any second. That's what's going to happen."

"Don't be so morbid," Grace said. "No one knows she's here."

"What was she doing here?"

"I don't know. When I found her, she was hiding underneath my desk."

Thunder boomed overhead as the lights began to flicker.

They stood still, waiting to see if the lights were going to give out or not, but the lights held.

"Well, what was so urgent that I had to come here at this time of night?" Valerie asked.

Grace walked over to her desk, bent over and checked underneath. Just in case. "I want to go over Daniel's death again."

Valerie groaned. "Not again."

"Yes," she said quietly. Rising, she brought up a bright blue sequined backpack and laid it on the desk. "There were too many distractions before. Too many people wanted to get involved. Here, it's just you and me... and well, Tabitha."

"Are you sure she's still here?"

Nodding, Grace passed the bag to Valerie. "She left this."

"She's not the only one here, by the way."

Grace waited for Valerie to explain.

"You really need to start locking this door, Grace. I found Allen snooping around in here a few minutes ago. He was hiding behind your desk."

"What is it with people hiding under my desk tonight?" Groaning, Grace walked to her desk and began searching through each drawer. "Is he gone?"

Valerie nodded. "I followed him to the elevator. It stopped on the first floor, so I'm hoping he's left, but who knows."

"Unbelievable," she said, angrily slamming the last drawer shut.

"What's wrong? What did he do?"

"The files are gone." She began pacing the office.

"Your designs?"

"No, all of our research: the pictures, the notes Ethan took. Everything."

"Sorry, Grace, when I found him, I just threw him out. I guess I should have strip searched him, too." Valerie grimaced. "No, actually, I love you, but my loyalty just doesn't extend that far, sorry."

"I don't blame you."

"We'll tell Straker in the morning. Allen can't get away with this."

"Straker would just say he was showing initiative. No, it's okay. We didn't have much anyway. Still, I would have liked to have kept that picture of Aleksis Dragovich."

"Why? Were you going to pin it up on the wall?"

Grace walked to the window. She could barely see the street. "I wish this rain would let up."

"Grace, you know something. What is it?"

"I don't know. I'm just not sure, Val. I don't want to accuse someone without having all of the facts." Grace motioned to follow her out to the hall. "I also don't want to influence you in any way."

Walking towards the elevator, Valerie asked, "Why didn't you call Ethan? He was here when Daniel died, too."

"But you were the one standing in front of the elevator looking at Daniel when he died."

"But I didn't see anything."

"Yes," Grace insisted, "you did, remember? You said you saw a white mist."

Valerie leaned against the wall. "I don't know what I saw, Grace."

"Let's just go through it once again. Tell me everything."

Sighing, Valerie described everything she saw. When she got to the part of the white mist, Grace held up her hand and tilted her head.

"What's wrong?" Valerie asked.

"Did you just hear something?"

"No, nothing," Valerie said.

"Must be my imagination." Grace shook her head. "Let's bring up the elevator." She reached out to press the up button. Before her finger could make contact, the elevator began to rise on its own. "Maybe it's Tabitha or Allen. I hope it's Allen," she growled, envisioning all the horrible things she would like to do to that backstabbing low-life snake.

"It's probably Ethan," Valerie said.

"Why? I didn't call him."

"When I couldn't find you, I got worried and called him for help. He said he would be right over."

"How did he get in?"

"I hid my office key outside and told him where to find it."

The elevator doors opened. Startled, Ethan jumped back a little. "What are you two doing huddled around the elevator?"

"Waiting for you," Valerie said.

Shaking his head, he smiled at Valerie, before hugging Grace. "I see you found her."

"You're all wet," Grace mumbled into his shoulder.

"The storm's directly overhead. It doesn't look like it's going to get any better," he said.

"Wonderful," Valerie said. "Let's get this over with."

Ethan looked at them both in confusion. "Will one of you tell me what's going on?"

Valerie quickly filled him in on Grace's plan.

"Now?" He laughed. "We're going to be here tomorrow night."

Grace took his arm. "I know, it's just that Straker was going to be here and I was afraid it would turn into a three-ring circus. I figured Valerie would be able to concentrate better if we were alone with no distractions."

"If you two wanted to do this alone, you picked the wrong night," he said with a smile.

"What do you mean?" Grace asked.

"I saw Kyle and Belle sneak in downstairs. Here's your key by the way," he said, handing the key to Valerie.

"Kyle and Belle, too?" Grace asked, exasperated. "What in the world goes on here at night? Is this one of New York's nightly hot spots?"

"I think we should call the police," Ethan said.

"What for?" Grace asked. "The police can't arrest them for trespassing. They both work here and she's the boss' fiancé. She even has a key to the door."

Ethan frowned. "But—"

"Ah, don't worry," Grace said, smiling up at his handsome face. "They probably broke in so they could play with the toys."

Valerie smiled. "Sorry, Grace, maybe we should do this tomorrow night, when it is less crowded. At least Tabitha won't be skulking around."

"Tabitha's here too?" Ethan asked. "Are you sure? The cops I spoke to thought—"

Grace shook her head. "No, it's definitely her. I doubt she's still here though. She disappeared thirty minutes ago."

"Do you think Kyle and Belle know that she's here?" Ethan asked.

"I don't know," Grace said.

A thunderclap, loud enough to rattle the windows and cause the building to shudder, sounded above their heads.

They looked up as the lights flickered before going out, and plunging them into darkness. A shiver ran up Grace's spine.

Ethan swore. "I hate this building."

Grace nodded. There was just enough light from outside to see Valerie turn around and walk down the hall. "Where are you going, Val?"

"Stay here," Valerie said. "I'll get the flashlights."

Ethan looked down at Grace. Smiling, he pulled her into his arms, as he lightly kissed her on the lips. "It's too bad we're not in my apartment right now."

"Why?"

"My apartment has a fireplace. We could be curled up in front of it right now." He kissed her deeper, only letting go when the sound of Valerie's high heels could be heard coming down the hallway.

Valerie rounded the corner, carrying three flashlights, her coat and umbrella. "We'll have to take the stairs."

Grace sighed disappointedly. "All right, I'll just go back and get my purse."

Ethan shook the rain from his thick hair. "I still think we should call the police. They're looking for Tabitha and she doesn't work here. And I don't care if she's the boss' fiancé, I think they'll be interested in knowing that she and Kyle were roaming around here tonight, too."

Grace pointed out that they were also roaming around.

Valerie slipped her coat on. "Come on, Grace, we'll walk with you."

Ethan leaned against the wall next to the elevator. "I'll wait here. I think I would like to have a little talk with Ms. Dragovich."

"Oh no, you don't," Grace said, grabbing a hold of his hand. "Knowing the way my luck is going, we'll come back and find you gone."

He cupped her cheek. "Trust me, Grace, I'm not going anywhere."

Grace smiled. "To be perfectly honest, I'm kind of nervous, so I'd feel better if you came with us."

Valerie quickly agreed. "We should all stick together. That way no one will get hurt."

"She's right," Grace said, feeling more and more nervous with each passing second. All she wanted was to get out of the building and to safety. Knowing Kyle and Belle were running around somewhere did not fill her with any hope that was going to happen. Then there was Allen to consider. He might still be in the building somewhere, lurking. "Remember, there's safety in numbers. We'll go get my purse and then go to the police. I think you're right. They should know that Tabitha was here, and that Kyle and Belle were running around. They might not be able to do anything about it, but they should know just the same."

Ethan sighed, but reluctantly followed them back to Grace's office.

"Let's meet here tomorrow morning." Grace opened the door to her office. Picking up her coat and umbrella, she handed them off to Valerie. She walked toward her desk. She glanced over her shoulder and said, "All I need is my purse and we'll be set."

She took a step around the desk and let out a little scream when she tripped and fell to the floor. Ethan and Valerie ran forward.

"Are you hurt?" Ethan asked. He started to reach for her hand, but stopped suddenly. He shined his flashlight down on the floor next to Grace.

Valerie gasped.

"Is that...?" Ethan asked.

"Tabitha," Grace answered, her heart thudding against her chest. She reached over and felt for Tabitha's pulse. A few seconds later, she let go of the other woman's wrist. Sitting back on her heels, she said, "She's dead."

"What?" Valerie asked in a panic. "Are you sure?"

Ethan grabbed Valerie's arm. "Quick, Val, call the police."

Grace leaned over Tabitha's body. One side of her face was bloody and Grace's phone lay in pieces by her side. "Positive, she's dead. Someone hit her over the head with my desk phone."

Ethan's worried voice finally reached her. "Grace, are you all right?"

Nodding, Grace shakily stood. Ethan took her into his arms. Running his hands first over her arms, he gently reached out and cupped her face. "You're okay? Nothing broken?"

"No, I'm fine, but we need to call the police." Grace pulled away. Bending down, she retrieved the flashlight from the floor, and noticed Belle's golden pendant lying in Tabitha's hand. The pink sapphire sparkled when Grace shined the flashlight over the dragon's eye. Somehow, she had a feeling that was going to show up again.

Ethan grabbed her arm. "Don't touch it, its evidence. Look, you and Valerie stay here and lock the door," he said, pulling out a gun.

Grace's eyes went wide. "Where did you get that?"

"Grace, since I've met you, people have been dying around you. I thought we should have some protection. Whoever killed Tabitha might still be here. You two stay in here and don't make a sound. I'm going to go downstairs and wait for the police." Ethan gently grabbed the back of her head. Pulling her closer, he kissed her passionately. "Stay here, I'll be right back."

Before she could stop him, Ethan ran out the door, just as Valerie ran back in. Grace watched as he ran down the hallway. She would have dashed after him, but was stopped by Valerie, who pushed her back in the room. Quickly pulling the door shut, she locked it and faced Grace.

"We need to go after him, Valerie."

"I'm not going anywhere." Valerie shivered as thunder shook the building again. "I'm going to wait right here until the police arrive."

"Did you call them?" Grace asked.

Valerie nodded. "We just have to sit tight until then."

Grace rushed past Valerie, unlocked the door, and ran out in the hall with Valerie calling her name. Grace didn't listen. She tiptoed out into the hallway, with Valerie right behind her, looking both ways, her ears straining to hear. If she could get to the staircase maybe... She froze. The private entrance to Straker's office began to open.

Heart beating fast, Grace pivoted around and dashed down the hallway. She could take the stairway next to the elevator, she thought, running as fast as she could. She threw open the stairway door and looked behind her. Valerie was gone.

CHAPTER TWENTY-EIGHT

GRACE CLIMBED THE steps to the attic, and reached for the door, praying that it was unlocked. Thankfully, the knob turned easily in her hand. She winced as the door's hinges squeaked loudly in the silence. Holding her breath, she waited for the sound of running footsteps. When none came, she carefully stepped through the doorway.

Reaching into her coat pocket, she took out the mini flashlight attached to her key ring and shined it into the interior of the attic. She cocked her head to the side. Except for the thunder overhead, the attic was silent.

Carefully making her way through the maze of toys and broken furniture, she tried to make as little noise as possible. She walked past the elevator and stifled a scream. In front of her was a human sized shape under a sheet. It has to be that creepy harlequin, she thought, nervously. Counting to ten, Grace pulled the sheet off, happy to see the harlequin's glass eyes staring back at her. Letting out her breath, she closed her eyes in relief. She was just about to recover the harlequin when she heard a noise to her left.

The sheet slipped from her fingers. It was just a whisper, completely unintelligible, but it was enough.

She shut off the pen light. Far in the back of the attic, to the left, she could see a soft glow. Slipping off her shoes, she tiptoed toward the glow, only using her pen light when necessary. Their whispers became louder as she neared. Turning a corner, she found them huddled around a set of tools. A small kerosene lamp lay between them.

"Grace!" Kyle said in surprise while Belle let out a startled little squeal.

Grace put her finger to her lips. "Shh," she whispered. "What are you two doing here at this time of night?" she asked as quietly as she could.

"Searching for the ghost," Kyle whispered back.

Grace threw him a withering look.

"Would I lie to you?" Kyle asked.

"I don't know, would you, Aleksis?" Grace motioned for them both to stand. Once Kyle was up, she reached into his coat pocket.

Belle pointed to Grace. "I told you she'd figure it out."

"Shh," Grace said once again.

Kyle shook his head. "Kyle, please, no one calls me Aleksis," he said, as she reached into his other pocket. "What are you doing?"

"Saving your life," she whispered, pulling out his cell phone. "Now, be quiet."

Belle and Kyle exchanged looks as Grace held the phone up, not too terribly surprised to find that there was no signal.

Kyle pointed to the elevator. "If you stand near the elevator, you can usually get a signal."

Grace put her finger to her mouth before motioning for them to follow her.

The elevator was only a few feet away. She looked down at the phone, hoping that it would pick up a signal soon.

Still nothing.

She took a step back and bumped into the harlequin standing next to the elevator. Irritated, she glanced over her shoulder at the sheet-covered head behind her before glancing back down at the phone.

"What is going on?" Belle whispered.

"We need to call for the police and an ambulance," Grace said. "Tabitha's unconscious and Ethan's running around downstairs with a gun. We need—" She felt the blood drain from her face. She glanced behind her as the sheet fell to the floor, revealing Ethan's smiling face.

Grace felt Kyle pull her back against him, as Belle let out a scream.

Pointing his gun at Grace's chest, Ethan laughed. "I'm surprised, Grace, and impressed. So, Tabitha's still alive? I guess I didn't hit her hard enough." He clucked his tongue. "Should have checked her pulse myself. I just figured I had you wrapped around my finger. What made you suspect me?"

"See," Kyle said to Belle, "I told you it was him." He turned back to Ethan. "The only thing I couldn't figure out is how you were planning on stealing Straker's inheritance. You don't really seem to be Straker's type."

All their heads turned at the sound of the attic door opening. They could just make out Valerie making her way down the aisle.

Kyle and Belle shouted her name, screaming at her to run.

"Don't bother," Grace said harshly. "She's with him."

Valerie stood next to Ethan. Wrapping her hand around his bicep, she said, "I'm so sorry, Grace. How did you guess?"

"The lights, Valerie. The lights were off when you made the phone call to the cops. If the power's off, then how did you make the call?"

Ethan glared at Valerie. "You should have thought of that."

Kyle inched forward. A warning glance from Ethan stopped him in his tracks. "How is she involved?"

"I think, initially, the plan was for Valerie to seduce Straker," Grace answered. "They were hoping Straker would divorce Lily, marry Val, and then I guess die shortly thereafter, leaving Val a very rich widow. I'm sure they assumed it was going to be easy. After all, he had shown an interest in Valerie in the past and Straker isn't exactly known for his loyalty to his wives. What they didn't count on was Straker being in love this time. Despite those hateful letters they sent, nothing could convince him that Lily was unfaithful and nothing could convince him to be unfaithful to her. So, since they couldn't break up Straker and Lily, they decided to kill her."

Valerie shook her head. "I didn't want Lily dead. I just wanted her to divorce Straker and leave. I never wanted her to die."

"That's not what you told me," Ethan said in amusement.

Valerie's jaw tightened. She glared at Ethan before turning back to Grace. "I swear, I didn't know anyone was going to die."

"Val," Grace said, "he tried to kill her before she left for Europe. According to Straker, he tried several times. How could you have not known this is what he intended all along?"

"I thought she was just being dramatic," Valerie said. "Ethan swore he had nothing to do with her accident."

"Well, obviously, he was lying to you," Grace said.

Valerie looked up to Ethan who was still smirking at Grace. "Yes. I'm more than aware of that now, but I wanted to believe he was telling the truth. It wasn't until he told me that he planned to kill Lily during the magic show that I realized how dangerous he was. I cut off all ties with him after that. That's why he wasn't at the Dragon's Lair with me."

Grace nodded. "And that's when I so conveniently ran into him at the park near my apartment."

Ethan shrugged. "I needed an invitation. You were so easy, Grace."

"Why didn't you say anything to me, Val?" Grace asked.

"I wanted to, but I was so frustrated and angry with Lily," Valerie said. "I ran into Ethan during intermission and he convinced me that he had changed his mind. I had no idea that he was going to kill her. He convinced me that he had changed his mind and that we were going to go back to our original plan and try to convince Straker that Lily was cheating. He showed me Lily's pendant and underwear. He said he was going to plant them under the couch in Dragovich's dressing room and that once the show was over and we were in the back celebrating his birthday, I was supposed to drag them out from underneath the couch and show them to Straker. I swear, I had no idea he was going to kill Lily."

Grace wanted to believe her.

"But once Lily was dead, I didn't have much choice, but to go along with him." Valerie smiled sadly. "I'm sorry, Grace. I never wanted any of this to happen and I didn't want you involved. I've been trying to protect you."

"Really?" Grace asked in disbelief. "You two were tag-teaming me on the phone calls, weren't you? I'm betting you were the one who tore up my designs, Val."

Valerie bit her lip. "We were hoping we could scare you away. We were afraid that you would eventually figure things out. But trust me, you were never in any danger."

Ethan rolled his eyes.

"Never," Valerie said. "I told him that I wouldn't allow you to be hurt. We just wanted you to give up and leave."

"I'm curious, Grace," Ethan said. "Where did I go wrong?"

"Why do you want to know?" Grace asked. "Do you want to correct your mistake for the next time you try something like this?"

"What next time?" Ethan asked. "There's not going to be a next time."

Valerie nodded her head. "That's right. With Franklin's inheritance we won't ever need money again."

Ethan grabbed Valerie around the waist and pulled her next to his side. "I bet you started to suspect me when I attacked you three. You somehow knew it was me, didn't you?"

"Why did you do that?" Grace asked.

"I didn't really want to, but your friend here," Ethan said, nodding toward Valerie, "screwed up at the hospital. She just had to start talking about how she checks the books on Friday and then you started yacking about searching the office and looking over the accounts. I was afraid you'd eventually find out about the forty thousand Daniel stole before Lily died and then wonder why Valerie didn't say anything to anyone about it."

"I didn't know about the forty thousand until I spoke to Tabitha," Grace said. "But you were right, as soon as she said it, I started wondering how the killer could have found out about the money and why Valerie didn't notice."

Belle frowned. "So, you two put on that performance in Valerie's office the night of the Christmas Party to throw suspicion off of her?"

"And to throw it onto Michael." Ethan glanced at Kyle. "But when Kyle picked the lock to Straker's door and walked in on me, I decided he would do just as well. We also thought that if Valerie was attacked, it might dredge up some protective feeling in Straker." He smiled. "It worked too. Straker's been very attentive lately. Personally driving her home, making sure she's safe before leaving. He even offered to let her stay with him. Right now, we're playing hard to get, but I don't think it'll be much longer now."

"No," Valerie said coldly, "not much longer."

"So, come on, Grace, what was it?" Ethan asked. "Where did I go wrong? When did you start to suspect me."

Grace sighed. "I didn't really suspect you till just recently. But there were all these little things that bothered me about you. For instance, you disappeared after Lily's death, but showed up suddenly when I started telling people—when I told Valerie," she amended sadly, "that I thought Lily had been murdered."

Ethan smiled and kissed Valerie on the cheek. She turned away from his kiss.

"Then it turned out that you knew Louisa," Grace said. "She claimed that you had made a pass at her. Of course, Louisa wasn't exactly credible, but I still thought it was very strange." She paused and looked at him curiously. "Were you trying to seduce her? Go after the Straker fortune by romancing his daughter, perhaps?"

Ethan smiled. "Guilty as charged, but she wouldn't have anything to do with me. So, Val and I decided to target Straker instead. We figured he would have been the easier mark. He did have a fondness for his secretaries. What else made you suspicious?"

"There was the way we met. Out in the park, next to my apartment, but it turned out that you lived several blocks away and belong to that nice fancy gym that—as you said—you practically live in. Also, you were always showing up, eager to help me with the investigation. In fact, that's all you ever wanted to talk about."

"If you had so many doubts about me, why did you let me hang around?" Ethan asked.

Grace sighed. "I liked you and I wasn't certain that you were involved. I kept wanting to give you a chance. Plus, there was the problem of motive. As far as I could tell, you didn't have one. What could you have to gain by killing Lily? You didn't even know her. But then you told me that your firm, out of all the firms in New

York, just happened to represented Preston Straker." She shook her head. "I found it very coincidental that your firm just happened to represent Franklin Straker's brother."

Ethan smiled. "*I* represented Preston. I'm afraid, I lied about that too. Jay was just tagging along the day I came to Straker to give him the good news."

Grace nodded. "That's when I realized the motive for Lily's death had to have been about the inheritance. The letters from the concerned friend, the attempts on Lily's life—they were all designed to get her out of the way. I became further convinced after the target shifted to Belle—right after Franklin announced his engagement to her." She shook her head. "Well, all of a sudden you had a motive. Money. I just had one problem—well, two actually. One, I just couldn't figure out how you managed to kill Lily while sitting in the audience, and two, I couldn't wrap my brain around how you killed Daniel with Valerie standing there watching you. I trusted her so much that I just couldn't see how you managed to kill, not one, but two people in front of others without anyone seeing you."

"I thought for sure you were starting to suspect Kyle," Valerie said.

"I did at one point," Grace admitted. "When it started to become clear that Kyle was Aleksis Dragovich…" She glared at Kyle who simply shrugged his shoulders. "I had to admit he was looking more and more like the guilty party. But it wasn't until we were at my apartment a few hours ago and Ethan mentioned the pendant and the underwear in Dragovich's dressing room that I knew for certain that he was the killer." She looked at Ethan. "How could you have known about Lily's pendant or her underwear lying on the floor of Ilya's dressing room? You couldn't, unless you had been there."

"You were busy that night," Kyle said, "running around backstage, fighting with Tabitha, and planting evidence in my father's dressing room."

"Once I knew for certain that it was you," Grace said, "I went to Ilya Dragovich. I couldn't accuse you without knowing how you killed Lily without being seen by him. Luckily, Ilya figured it out for

me. That was very clever. Risky but clever. And once we figured
that out, I only had Daniel's death to work out. But once I realized
Valerie was involved, it all became clear. There wasn't anything
special or clever about Daniel's death. You simply stabbed him
while Valerie stood there and watched." She looked at Valerie.
"The fainting and carrying on about a mist falling from the ceiling
was a nice touch. I'm guessing it was designed to make me think
the killer was Dragovich."

Valerie looked sick. "I didn't know he was going to kill
Daniel."

Ethan laughed. "You knew."

"I didn't know you were going to do it right there in front of
me," Valerie snapped back. "I did faint. That wasn't an act."

"The only thing I don't understand is why you two emptied
the bank account out after Daniel died," Grace said. "If you were
intending on Valerie marrying Straker, why bankrupt the
company?"

Ethan shrugged. "Why not? We knew Daniel would be
blamed for it. Besides, we were also hoping it would drive you and
the others away. We left just enough so the toy store could
continue to operate and Val would have a job. I also thought for
sure that if the money was gone, Belle would leave, but no such
luck." Ethan leveled the gun at her. "Well, Grace, it has been fun."

Thinking fast, Grace blurted out, "I was a bit confused why
you insisted I be part of the crystal chest act."

"It didn't have to be you. I just wanted to make sure it wasn't
Valerie." He glared down at Val. "She backed out at the last
moment and threatened to tell everyone. I couldn't take the chance
that she wouldn't panic and say something stupid or warn
Dragovich, so I tried to get Tabitha to take you instead. Stupid girl.
She saw me waving at her and still went to Val. I'm betting Lily told
her to do it. Everyone knew Val had a fear of enclosed spaces.
Luckily, Straker spoke up when he did. Now, you two," he said,
gesturing at Kyle and Grace, "move."

Grace lifted her hands. "Wait, just one more question. Why
did you destroy the dolls in Allen's office?"

Ethan and Valerie exchanged confused glances. Ethan gave a low chuckle. "What?"

"Allen told me that someone broke into his office and destroyed my dolls," Grace said.

Kyle made a noise in his throat and all eyes turned to him. He looked sheepishly at Grace. "It was an accident. I was searching his office and accidentally knocked against his bookcase."

"Why didn't you say anything?" Grace asked.

Kyle shrugged. "I told Straker, but he said not to worry about it."

Ethan aimed the gun at Kyle's chest. "Time to say bye-bye, you two."

"Do you really expect to get away with this?" Belle asked. "You can't kill us all. The police are going to figure it out."

"And you can forget about trying to pin this on our father, because no one's going to believe that he killed either one of us," Kyle said, gesturing between him and Belle.

"Well," Belle said, "definitely, not me."

"That's right," Kyle agreed, "they'll never believe it."

"Oh, I'm not going to try to frame Dragovich again. I thought about it, but I decided it would make more sense to frame you, Belle." Ethan turned the gun on Belle. "So, you see, I'm not going to kill all of you, just you, *after* I caught you killing them. The police will believe it. Especially after they find your dragon pendant in Tabitha's hand."

"How did you get a hold of my pendant?" Belle asked.

"I found it in the hallway," Valerie said. "It must have fallen off Kyle's tie."

Belle turned to her brother. "What was it doing on your tie?"

"Who cares?" Ethan snapped. "I'll also let the cops know that I found you here with three dead bodies. You tried to kill me and I shot you in self-defense." He inclined his head towards Valerie. "Grace's best friend will back me up, won't you, sweetheart?"

Valerie looked down at the floor.

"Won't you, sweetheart?" he asked a little more forcefully.

"We don't have to kill them," Valerie said softly.

Ethan rolled his eyes. "Valerie, we already talked about this."

"I bet Belle and Kyle will keep their mouths shut if we cut them in on the deal," Valerie said.

Kyle and Belle both began talking over each other in their haste to agree.

"Absolutely," Kyle said.

Belle nodded her head. "Not a word."

"You can count on us," Kyle added.

"Shut up!" Ethan snapped.

Valerie persisted. "We'll lock Grace up in our apartment. Once Belle is married to Straker, she can get access to his account, then we'll move the money over to a Swiss bank account just as we discussed."

"Why don't you two just embezzle the money now?" Grace asked. "It worked so well a few weeks ago."

"Because Daniel's not around to blame," Ethan said. "I'd rather not sully my reputation just yet or have the police after me. If Valerie took the money, the police would eventually find her. No, it would be much safer if she inherits it after poor Franklin's eventual accident. Then she and I will be wealthy beyond our wildest imagination."

"That's right," Valerie said. "We'll have more money than we'll know what to do with. We can split it four ways. We wouldn't even notice half of its gone."

Ethan looked down at his partner in crime. "Are you crazy? I'm not splitting anything."

"Really," Kyle said, pointing to Belle, "we're brother and sister, so I don't mind sharing my share with her."

Belle quickly agreed with her brother.

"Shut up!" Ethan said.

"And what happens to me, while you two are enjoying your ill-gotten gains?" Grace asked.

"You won't tell, Grace. We'll share the money with you too," Valerie said.

Ethan laughed bitterly. "You are such a stupid—" He swallowed whatever he was going to say and roughly pushed her away from him. "Go stand with them."

Valerie wheeled around. "You need me, remember? You can't get to Straker's money without me."

Grace felt Kyle wrap his fingers around her arm. Out of the corner of her eye, she noticed Belle take a side step away from her.

Ethan was so focused on Valerie that he didn't notice. "There are a million of women just like you," he spat out. "I can find someone else. Someone Straker would prefer. Or maybe now that that lush of a daughter of his is a widow, she'll be more agreeable. Go stand with them!" he barked, pushing her in front of Grace.

"Then you'll just kill off father and daughter." Valerie's voice began to rise. "You don't think that would look a bit suspicious, sweetie, especially with all that's been going on around here? You can't do this without me. I've got news for you, lover, if anything happens to me, a letter is going to be mailed to the district attorney's office, along with the file Daniel kept on his computer. I didn't destroy it like I told you I did. I just switched his computer out for another one, so the police wouldn't find it when they searched his hard drive. I don't think you're going to like what either one say."

"Shut up," he shouted, turning the gun on Valerie. "I don't need you."

Grace watched out of the side of her eye as Belle inched closer to the elevator. Kyle gripped her arm tighter, as he and his sister exchanged a look. Hands trembling, Belle reached for the side of the elevator.

Suddenly, Ethan swung his gun around. Pointing it at Belle, he snarled, "Where do you think you're going?"

Grace felt her heart drop. Whatever escape Belle had planned was obviously not going to work. Belle dropped her hand and shrugged. She caught her brother's eye, a small smile playing around her lips.

There was a rumbling sound as the elevator rose. Ethan looked at Valerie in confusion. "I thought you said the elevator wouldn't come up to the attic."

Valerie shook her head. "It's not supposed to. The power's off, so it shouldn't be moving at all."

They watched intently as the doors slowly opened. Ethan trained his gun on the interior. His gaze fell to the elevator floor. He took a surprised step back as Valerie screamed.

Lily was sitting on the floor of the elevator, smiling up at them. Ethan fired his gun, but Lily didn't move—didn't even flinch.

While Ethan was distractedly shooting at the figure in the elevator, Kyle rushed the other man before he had a chance to swing the gun around. The fight only last a second. Ethan was caught off balance by Kyle's attack and fell into the elevator. To Grace's surprise, he fell through Lily and disappeared underneath the floor of the elevator.

"How?" she asked pointing to the elevator.

"Now you see him, now you don't," Kyle said with a smile.

EPILOGUE

"HOW'S TABITHA?" GRACE asked as she lounged on her sofa with a cold washcloth pressed to her eyes.

Belle laid the phone back into its cradle. "She's awake and talking to the police right now. She's going to be fine."

"Good," Kyle said from somewhere nearby. "What about Ethan?"

"Two broken legs," Belle called out from the vicinity of her bedroom.

"Good thing the elevator was just on the next floor." Grace lifted the edge of the washcloth. Kyle was leaning back in the armchair with his feet propped up on the coffee table. Abry was curled up on his lap, a happy grin spreading across his face. "I still don't understand how you two pulled it off."

He shook his head. "A magician never reveals his secrets."

"A holograph?"

She watched as the grin fell from his face. "It's not fun if you try to guess."

"What was your plan, exactly?"

"We were going to lure Ethan up to the attic and force a confession." He screwed up his face. "We weren't ready yet. He actually wasn't supposed to fall through the floor. We were going to set up a nice little cage for him."

"How long have you known that Ethan was the killer?" Grace asked.

"All along."

Outraged, she sat up and glared at him. "You knowingly let me date a murderer."

He shook his head. "I didn't really know until Tabitha called us from your office. Until then, I just suspected him."

"Why?"

He shrugged. "He had shifty eyes." When she continued to glare at him, he said defensively, "You suspected him too and you didn't say anything to us. Besides, I was watching out for you."

Slightly mollified, she laid back down.

He gently petted the bunny's ears. "I just wished we had more time."

"Why? It worked." Grace laid the washcloth back over her eyes before lifting the corner back up again. "How did you get the elevator working without the power?"

"It wasn't." His eyes went wide as he wiggled his fingers at her. "It was just an illusion. We set up a small generator to run the hologram and open the doors. While Belle was distracting Ethan, I was reaching for the remote control lying on one of the boxes."

Grace dropped the washcloth and faced the window. The rain from the night before had turned to snow and was now blanketing the city. She smiled at the winter wonderland outside her window.

Belle walked out of her bedroom, dragging a suitcase. "Are you sure I can keep this?" Belle asked, holding up a green sleeveless sundress.

"Merry Christmas." Grace patted her velvet couch. "Or better yet, consider it an early wedding present."

Kyle, crossed his arms, and shook his head disapprovingly. "He going to be furious. You know, he doesn't like Michael."

"That's just because Papa doesn't know him. Once he gets to know Michael, he'll love him as much as I do."

Kyle rolled his eyes.

"Well, surely, he'll be happier having Michael as a son-in-law than Straker," Grace pointed out.

"Oh, Papa never believed I was really going to marry Franklin," Belle said. "He knew it was just a trick to lure out Lily's killer."

"How did you two know that the killer was after anyone who was with Straker?" Grace asked.

"We didn't really," Kyle admitted. "It just seemed strange how determined they were to either kill Lily or try to break up her marriage. And we knew that Preston was going to die soon and leave Franklin a small fortune. We just figured someone wanted Lily out of the way, so they could inherit instead."

"We thought it was Louisa with Daniel's help, at first," Belle said as she walked back through the living room. "Then we thought it was Harcourt. He was the only one with the expertise to pull off the spectral illusion with the hand reaching from the elevator ceiling."

"But we couldn't figure out how he hoped to get his hands on Straker's money," Kyle said. "And we were certain it involved the money."

Grace chuckled. "You know, you could have just waited to see who Straker married next. Valerie was apparently trying her best to seduce him."

"She would have had a lot of competition." Kyle shook his head. "Do you know how many women are after Straker?"

Belle smiled. "I went out with him one night before I started work at the company; women were flocking to him in droves. You should have seen them after Lily died. Women were even hitting on him at the funeral home."

"Jackie made a pass at him too," Kyle said.

Grace's mouth fell open. "You've got to be kidding."

"Franklin is very charming," Belle said simply.

"When?" Grace asked in shock.

Belle didn't answer, instead, she said, "In the end, we decided to force the killer's hand. We figured that if I got engaged to Franklin, the killer would have to strike again."

Horrified, Grace turned to Kyle. "So, you used your sister for bait?"

"It wasn't my idea," Kyle said a tad bit defensively. "Straker and Belle came up with the idea. I was just as surprised as everyone else was when they announced their engagement. But she was going to go through with it, whether I wanted her to or not. I told her it was a bad idea."

"No, it wasn't. It worked. Besides, like I told Kyle, we had no choice," Belle said. "We knew the killer had tried to frame our father in case the cops didn't buy that Lily committed suicide. Not only that, but Lily was our friend and we loved her. We couldn't let her killer get away with it. Anyway, the day Straker announced his engagement and I was attacked on the staircase, we knew we were on the right track. Although, I was rather concerned that it was you they were after. You kept getting those phone calls and it was common knowledge that you were going to be the next Mrs. Straker."

Outraged, Grace sat up. "What? How? Wh—I—no, just no! Ugh."

"Jackie seemed convinced," Kyle said with a shrug.

Grace laid back down and covered her eyes. She lifted the washcloth off again and asked, "Have you and Michael set the date, Belle?"

Belle shook her head. "It won't be until after we return from Europe. We're doing a six-month tour overseas. I've convinced Papa to let Michael perform with us. You know, give them a chance to get to know each other."

"Before or after you break the news of your engagement to the old man?" Kyle asked.

"I'm going to tell him soon," Belle said. "I'm just waiting for the best time."

Kyle made a noise in his throat. His sister threw him a dirty look as she walked back into her bedroom. He looked at Grace and smiled. "They could have a double wedding with Allen and Louisa."

Grace groaned. "Don't remind me. I've been sick all morning. I can't believe he let us know by email. It's got to be a joke."

"Oh, I think it'll be nice having Allen as a boss," Kyle said teasingly. "Just think of all of the changes that are coming. Straker retiring in four months, Allen and Louisa getting married, Allen's sudden promotion—"

"I'm going to have to find a new job." Grace looked over at Kyle. "What about you? Are you going to join your dad's show too?"

Kyle laughed bitterly. "Sure, if I want to sit quietly in the audience and not make a sound." He looked at her shyly. "I kind of like working here with you. Franklin said I could stay if it was okay with you?"

Grace smiled. "It's only four months until Straker retires, after that, we'll be lucky if we don't get demoted to the toy store. Speaking of the toy store, I'm going to have a little talk with Jackie."

"I think there's been enough ugliness around here, don't you?" Kyle asked.

"By the way, Ethan received a mug shot of Aleksis Dragovich. Whose mug shot—"

"Oh, that was my cellmate; nice guy, well, for a convicted murderer. I figured Ethan would eventually start trying to check me out, so I talked one of the guards into sending in his photo instead of mine if anyone called."

"How did you manage that?"

Kyle shrugged. "I have a way with people."

"Good," she said hopefully. "Maybe you can convince Allen not to fire us on the spot four months from now."

"Don't worry, I think Allen likes me. By the time I'm through, we'll be running the toy company."

The End

Book two in the Grace Holliday Cozy Mystery Series is now available

Deadly Reunion

When Grace Holliday received her high school reunion invitation promising a killer reunion, she didn't think they meant literally.

Grace Holliday has come back home to Rabbit Falls, Colorado. Regrettably, not as successful or as wealthy as she had intended, when she left her small town ten years before. Fired from her job, evicted, and having to move back in with her parents was not how she pictured her life turning out, and the last thing she wants is to attend her ten-year high school reunion.

Unfortunately, her twin sister has other ideas. Determined to settle an old score, Hope drags Grace back to their old school, intent on humiliating her rival. Despite the best efforts of the planning committee, things quickly go from bad to deadly and before the night is through, one of Grace's classmates will be murdered.

All Grace wants to do is put the horrible night behind her, go home, and scour the want ads. Unfortunately, the only job available is the only one she doesn't want: figuring out who killed the Reunion Queen.

CARROLL COUNTY
MAR 2021
PUBLIC LIBRARY

CPSIA information can be obtained
at www.ICGtesting.com
Printed in the USA
LVHW111707090321
680995LV00002B/198

9 781475 067453